THE
INTERDICTIONIST

By

John Edward Collins

Library and Archives Canada Cataloguing in Publication
Colins, John Edward, author
The Interdictionist / John Edward Collins

Issued in print and electronic formats.

ISBN: 978-1-998501-59-5 (hardcover)
ISBN: 978-1-998501-51-9 (paperback)
ISBN: 978-1-998501-52-6 (ebook)

Cover Design: Axel Peralta
Interior Design: Richa Bargotra

Warpath Press
Toronto, Ontario, Canada
www.warpathpress.com

To Mary Ann, my soulmate and muse

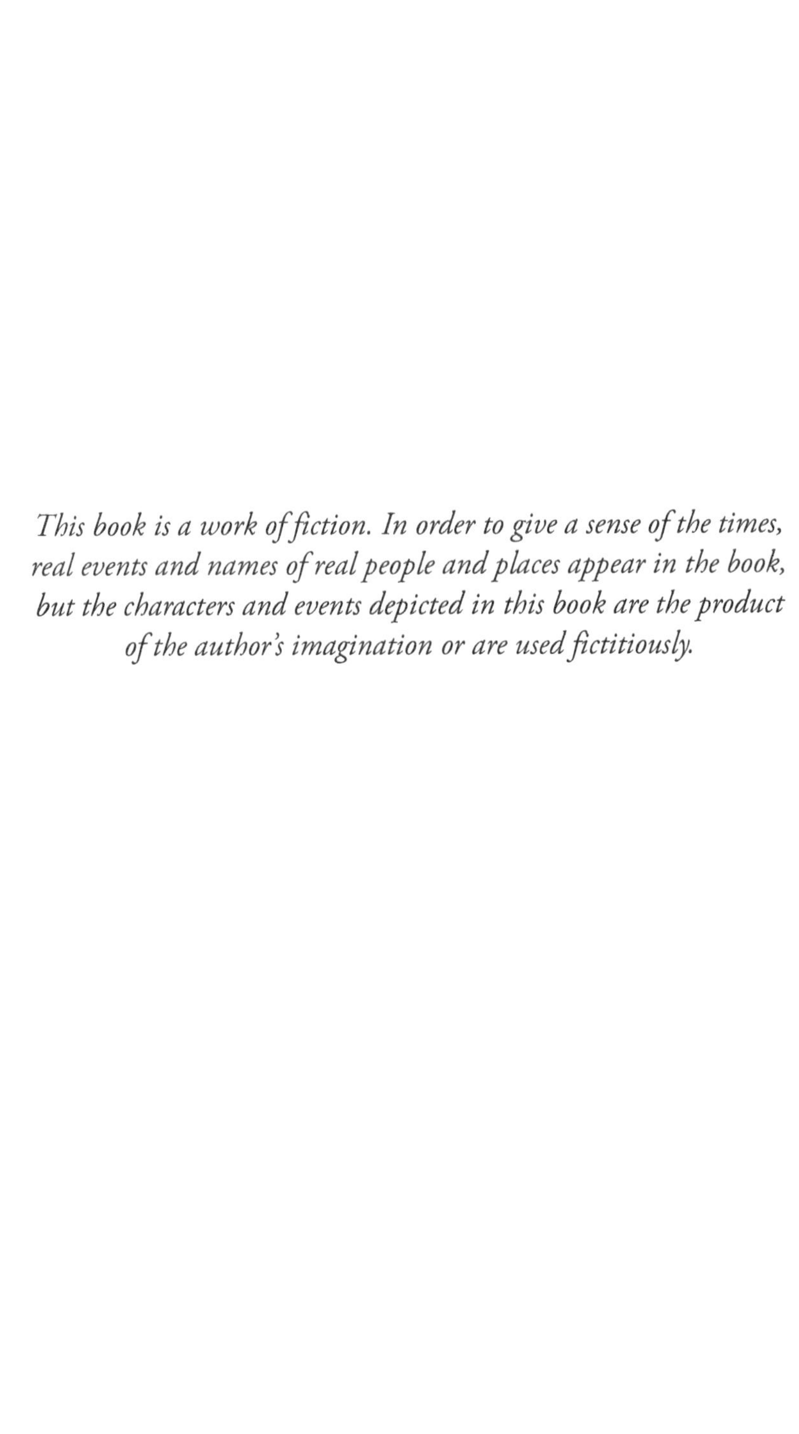

This book is a work of fiction. In order to give a sense of the times, real events and names of real people and places appear in the book, but the characters and events depicted in this book are the product of the author's imagination or are used fictitiously.

PROLOGUE

The Dilemma

0800 Hours, 3 January 1969 Hurlburt Field, Florida

Jake Crowley took a seat in an empty row and stashed his gear against the chair in front of him. He surveyed the briefing room for possibly the last time. The hall consisted of a wood framed structure with a cheap texture T1-11 siding, a steel roof, and no insulation or sheetrock on the interior. Brown metal folding chairs sat in rows on the cement floor facing a lectern on a dais. The Department of Defense had not gotten the memo concerning creature comforts. As far as they were concerned, air conditioning was invented to keep expensive machines like computers running at top efficiency. Soldiers could live without it and the discomfort was one reason why they were paid for their service. Fluorescent shop lights glared overhead and large industrial fans on stands blew the scent of musty sweat across the room. A brightly painted Special Operations Command insignia hung on the front of the podium, with military flags and the Stars and Stripes lining the back of the dais.

I can smell the fresh paint. The hall has that 'If it doesn't move, paint it' look about it. Even the rocks bordering the flower bed at the entrance have a clean coat of white paint, thought Crowley.

He had just completed combat controller tech school and hoped this meeting would shed some light on his assignment. He kept his fingers crossed for a permanent assignment at the Special Operations Headquarters right here in Hurlburt Field, but an interview yesterday raised some doubts. Crowley felt a tap on his shoulder, and he looked up to see his buddy, Tom Newman, pass around him and take the adjacent seat. The airman first-class stripes sewn to their sleeves labeled them as neophytes in a room full of veterans.

Where are all our classmates? We're the only two tech school graduates at this meeting, noted Crowley as he looked around.

An aide turned off the noisy fans, signaling the meeting was about to start. Crowley noticed perspiration stains forming on the combat fatigues of the other attendees.

Are they sweating over news of a new assignment too, or just hot from the sudden lack of ventilation, thought Crowley.

He glanced over at Newman, looking around and taking it all in.

Newman could be the poster boy for a Special Forces recruitment drive with his tall, rugged good looks, mused Crowley.

Crowley's own well chiseled features and light brown hair were complemented by the physique built for speed and endurance. Weighing one hundred and forty pounds and rising to a height of five foot nine inches, he could run all day stalking prey. Like the leopard, he knew he wasn't the biggest cat on the Kalahari and therefore maintained caution. Training so far included stalking, but not killing—the thought of which kept him up at night. Tech school had been as exciting as the recruiter promised. The next step, On-the-Job-Training, or OJT as they called it, involved supervised training during actual operations. During this phase, the thrill-a-minute experience might include killing enemy combatants while a supervisor grades his efficiency.

As Crowley scanned the room, heads turned and nodded. He returned their glances with steel-blue eyes shining like beacons. His performance under stress and ceaseless perseverance during training had earned him a fair bit of clout. Men in Special Forces units bonded quickly to help each other survive the physical and mental trials they endured.

He glanced over at Newman again and then looked down at his own loose-fitting camouflage uniform hiding his well-defined torso.

Jesus! When we train, Tom gives the impression I brought along my big brother for protection.

When Captain Worthington arrived, First Sergeant Stevens called attention, and the attendees rose as the intelligence officer made his way to the podium. He climbed the steps, said "At ease," and waited for everyone to take a seat before he began his briefing.

"Men, I scheduled this session to conduct the final review before the deployment to Honduras. I will begin with a summary of the mission rationale and objectives for those of you newly assigned."

The officer glanced over at Crowley and Newman before continuing, "Since this is a joint special operation, a review of the specific roles of the Army, Navy, and Air Force will follow the mission summary."

The intelligence officer began his history lesson on the situation in Honduras and El Salvador. Newman turned to Crowley with upturned palms and a quizzical look. Crowley pulled a slip of paper out of his breast pocket and double-checked his appointments for today. *Yup, right place and time.*

He shook his head in disbelief and signaled the same upturned palms back to Newman.

Worthington completed the mission summary and turned the page in his looseleaf book. "OK, now for the mission assignments. I will start with air operations. Airmen Crowley and Newman—Please stand up."

They stood with trepidation.

Worthington addressed the attendees, "Airman Crowley will control air operations for the mission and Airman Newman is his back up."

The shock felt like a sucker punch to his gut. Crowley felt the stares and heard the murmurs grow louder as he raised a hand.

"Sir, permission to speak freely!" shouted Crowley over the din.

"Quiet down men! Airman Crowley, do you have a question?" replied Worthington.

"Yes, sir. I expected to receive my OJT assignment orders at this meeting, not the lead combat controller position on an air operation. How am I expected to lead a special air operation before OJT certification?" stated Crowley.

Worthington replied, "You have just completed field training with the Tactical Air Command units assigned to this mission, making you the best-qualified combat controller available."

Navy SEAL Lieutenant Blackstone stood up to object. "Sir, why hasn't headquarters assigned certified combat controllers to the mission? After all, we volunteered our own air operations master chiefs."

"The TAC commander, General Hunt, interviewed these combat controllers and approved their assignment," replied Major Worthington.

Crowley felt the heat of blood rushing to his neck as he now realized what the interview yesterday really meant. Blackstone shook his head in disbelief and sat back down.

Worthington said, "Crowley and Newman, please take a seat and we will move on to the Navy SEAL team assignments."

Crowley spotted the Navy Sea, Air, And Land team shake their heads and then turned to see the shock on Newman's. He sat still and waited for a break in the meeting.

"What the hell is going on? Did you see this coming?" asked Crowley.

Newman replied, "I should be asking you that, since they put you in charge. I have felt out of step since that interview yesterday. The first sergeant told me to report to this meeting for assignment information. I thought I would get my orders for relocation to my OJT base."

"Yeah, me too. The first sergeant told me the same story, and I assumed it would be my permanent assignment. I've had it with all these temporary training assignments," said Crowley.

"We are supposed to be certified by master sergeants on OJT missions before we go it alone. Instead, I'm taking this chopper ride as your backup, with no senior airmen to advise us," said Newman.

"Preaching to the choir," responded Crowley.

After the briefing ended, they grabbed their gear and walked out of the hall into a warm Florida Panhandle sun. Newman, a local boy with a keen eye for snakes in the grass, both literally and figuratively, took the lead as they stepped into tall sawgrass.

I wonder why Newman didn't see this assignment coming, thought Crowley.

Newman turned toward Crowley and said, "Follow me. There have been reports of copperheads in the area, and they can be very aggressive."

Crowley grunted as he thought about how inhospitable Florida could be with snakes, spiders, alligators, bugs and other creatures working their way out of the swamps for a visit. No wonder the Air Force built a special operations base here. It provided the perfect training environment for some of the challenging places special operations wind up in.

The grass reached over their heads and cut at their uniforms and hands, making Crowley itchy as he walked three paces behind Newman. Crowley could smell the stench of a rotting carcass somewhere close by. Newman heard something and pointed his machete at a vibrating sound as he guided Crowley around the viper.

"I won't kill a copperhead except in self-defense. They keep down the rodents," whispered Newman.

Crowley cringed, *Yeah, another denizen of the swamps as big as cats.*

They pushed their way through the tall grass, and Crowley heard a vibrating sound behind him. He turned around to see a copperhead coiled in the path he had made. Its colorful, wedge-shaped head stared at him, and for a moment, he stood mesmerized. The serpent lunged at his leg and Crowley swatted it away with the broadside of his machete.

Like Newman said, no sense killing the rat eaters.

Once they made their way around the meeting hall, they found the grass mowed along the tarmac, making their trek easier. The pair started shouting at each other to be heard over the noise from the flight line. They lined up along the edge of a landing strip and put down their gear. Crowley looked back to make sure snakes had not followed them out of the tall grass. His attention focused back on the airfield, where he looked out at the heat shimmering up from the runway, turning the control tower in the distance into a mirage.

If I hadn't volunteered for additional training to become a combat controller, I could be a happily married air traffic controller in that tower over there, he thought. *I volunteered for the added adventure and now I'm paying the price.*

"I see now how my focus on a permanent assignment kept me from realizing General Hunt referred to a specific mission during the interview yesterday," shouted Newman.

Crowley frowned, "Yeah, now that I think about it, the TAC commander seemed pissed about my junior rank and lack of combat experience. I remember saying to myself, 'Doesn't the general know we're talking about my OJT assignment?'"

"He must have gotten his ass in a sling by committing combat controllers before he checked availability. I heard it through the grapevine that the Navy wanted their own air ops guys," Newman said.

Crowley nodded and kicked some dirt along the edge of the tarmac with his boot. They both plugged their ears with their fingers as an A-10 Wart Hog taxied right in front of them with its turbojet engines screaming. Their freshly starched combat fatigues were becoming damp from the humidity and dirty from the dust blown about by the passing aircraft.

"Tactical Air Command blocked their request and Blackstone just confirmed that in the meeting. I heard General Hunt has a hard-on for the SEALs because they botched an air rescue for one of his pilot buddies," shouted Crowley.

Newman stopped talking as a C-130 Hercules cargo plane taxied by and then raised both his hands in a mock surrender to his frustrations.

"How come Hunt gets to decide our assignments instead of our own commander?"

"General Hunt's TAC owns all the aircraft assigned to this operation." shouted Crowley.

"He made a big impression flying here in his F4 Phantom to interview us," replied Newman.

Another A-10 Warthog taxied by interrupting Newman.

"Meanwhile, I heard his adjutant beat the bushes at Special Operations Headquarters, trying to flush out senior-level controllers," added Newman.

"I didn't get any reports of them chewing anybody out for the staffing shortage. Did you?" asked Crowley.

Newman shook his finger at Crowley. "Man, you don't raise your voice at guys with notches on their guns! Being a general means he's smarter than that. Or he's supposed to be, at least. Why do you think they picked us for this operation, anyway?"

"I guess 'cause we are the best of the rest," Crowley replied.

"Isn't there some regulation about minimum experience required before they can assign us to something this big?" asked Newman.

"Yeah, you have to be eighteen."

"You're not taking this seriously."

"Shit man! Why should I take this seriously? General Hunt complained to our commander about my lack of combat experience right in front of me. Major Young just flat out told him to take it or leave it," said Crowley.

"How come the SEALs seem to like us now?" asked Newman.

"I told them having you and me direct the Air Force bombers meant they would not have to take it in the ass during live fire training," said Crowley.

"Did they believe you?" replied Newman.

"I drove the point home when I asked the SEALs if they knew 'friendly fire' was a misnomer. They got the message," said Crowley.

"Why no support from Blackstone during the briefing?" asked Newman.

"I believe Blackstone preached the party line in the meeting to disguise trying to help us out. He is the one who told me Hunt had it in for the SEALs," replied Crowley.

Crowley paused while an F-4G Wild Weasel thundered overhead, gaining altitude. It was a perfect day for flying, and it seemed like all the pilots on base had jockeyed to get their flight time in. It suddenly grew quiet on the flight line and the conversation deepened.

"This Honduras operation throws a wrench into my plans. I was waiting on orders for my first permanent assignment and now I gotta call my fiancé back and tell her to postpone our wedding… again."

Newman grinned. "If it was me, the delay would feel more like a reprieve."

Newman picked up on Crowley's stiffening posture and threatening glance.

"Relax Crowley! Didn't you get the memo about this being the age of Aquarius? You know—free love and all that. Why do you so intent on getting married?"

"You don't know her, or you would understand. We have been making plans to get married ever since I enlisted, and the Air Force keeps screwing up our plans with more temporary assignments," said Crowley.

"Having a fiancé creates a tie that binds. I kept things casual with my live-in girlfriend, which enables me to go with the flow of military life. A more serious relationship means too much extra baggage for me."

"She is not the type to have a live-in relationship. You don't know what I went through to win her over. The way things are going, I am afraid I am going to lose her. I have a recurring nightmare about trying to schedule our wedding and suddenly, a bell starts ringing, indicating my time just ran out. I usually wake up to find my alarm clock ringing."

Newman, not relating to Crowley's concern, decides to change the subject.

"What did you think about Major Worthington's briefing this morning?"

"Sounds like some greedy plantation owners caused a peasant uprising by allowing illegal migrants to work for them," replied Crowley.

"So how did we get sucked into all this?" asked Newman.

"The plantation owners played into the hands of Cuban subversives in Honduras, and now it's our job to stop the spread of communism," replied Crowley.

"So, how come the *federales* couldn't handle it?"

"The Salvadorian migrants now make up over twenty percent of the population in Honduras. The problem stretched their national security force too thin to be effective," said Crowley.

"You still haven't explained why we are involved."

"When the *federales* in Honduras failed to police the situation, the American plantation owners complained to Washington for help in solving a problem they created," responded Crowley.

Newman palmed his forehead in frustration. "Worthington said in the briefing that the newspapers called them terrorists after they took up arms and threatened the plantations with violence."

"One man's terrorist is another's freedom fighter. It all boils down to the choice of a label to emphasize one's perspective or agenda," Crowley opined.

"They are threating American lives and interests. That's what matters," retorted Newman.

Crowley turned away from the flight-line and glared at Newman.

"Diplomacy and humanitarian aid flew out the window and instead, a call took place to fly in the cavalry," replied Crowley.

"But American interests are at stake." insisted Newman.

"What ever happened to 'love thy neighbor?'" retorted Crowley.

"Why in the hell did they pick you to lead this air operation?"

"I am still trying to figure that out. In the meantime, I need to know if push comes to shove, do you have my back? After all, neither of us has ever killed an enemy combatant," said Crowley.

"I got your back. The question is, do you have mine? You don't seem to be committed to the mission."

"What I know is recent newspaper reports have confirmed attacks against Americans in Honduras. I believe this all happened because of a lack of charity. Somehow, we will do our part in sorting out the refugees from the terrorists."

"Sure, Jake. But since you seem to have all the answers, explain to me just one more thing. Why did the intelligence officer talk about trying to hunt gorillas and pheasants down in Central America? Does he think the mission is a wild-game safari?"

Crowley smiled. "Worthington was describing how to flush out guerillas wearing peasant clothing, since they can blend into their surroundings and hide in plain sight."

"I must have misheard him," said Newman.

"You didn't get it all wrong. Hunting peasants is our new national sport. It started with the pajama-clad Viet Cong and now it's open season for the Central American variety," said Crowley.

Newman bowed toward Crowley. "Man, oh man, now you got my head spinning over this. Should I kiss your ring or turn you in as a communist sympathizer?" questioned Newman.

Crowley played along and held out his ring finger. Newman stood back up in surprise and laughed.

"I don't want to burst your bubble, but we are being put in a no-win situation. If we follow our training and kill everything that moves, the press will label us warmongers who annihilated innocent freedom fighters. If we don't follow military doctrine, the mission might fail, and the Air Force will charge us with dereliction of duty," said Crowley.

They stood there all sweaty and dirty, as if field training had already been completed. Their faces looked like they had painted on camouflage grease. A familiar chopping noise interrupted their conversation. Instinctively, they held onto their hats as a gigantic helicopter landed in front of them, kicking up more dust. Crowley spotted Lieutenant Blackstone, sitting at the side door hatch, waving them over for another training exercise. Crowley and Newman saluted the SEAL officer, picked up their gear, and hustled over to the waiting aircraft.

As they ran, Newman shouted, "I guess it comes with the territory! Damned if we do and court-martialed if we don't."

Crowley replied, "Don't get your hopes up about just getting court-martialed! We don't know if we got what it takes to complete this mission alive."

1

Zero Hour Honduras

0030 Hours Central, 6 January 1969

Rapped in a cocoon of combat gear, Crowley found it hard to stay perched on his seat and impossible to rest. He had the feeling he had dozed off but wasn't sure. How could he have slept when, every time he leaned back, the radio pack pinched him in the ribs? Enveloped by a satchel of explosives strapped to his chest, a web gun belt strung with ammo pouches covering his midsection, and a ground-to-air FM radio backpack behind him, the burden felt like it would pull him over at any minute. Two holsters protruded on his hips, grenades dangled below the ammo belt, and his M16 hung off his left shoulder. They needed the plastic explosive when it was time to clear the landing zone for the second insertion team. The ground-to-air radio would serve as his lifeline to tactical air support and air traffic control of landing operations. He would use the belt of ammunition to defend the landing zone if necessary. Crowley and Newman each carried eighty pounds of equipment into battle.

He thought about the adage, *Never let them see you sweat.*

Well, in jungle warfare training, he learned everybody sweats like racehorses. His concern right now was controlling his urge to puke.

He consoled himself. *It is a syndrome caused by a lack of control. The pilot said flying a chopper did not affect his stomach but put him in the backseat of a car on a hilly, winding road and he would become motion sick. I never felt it when skydiving, surfing, snorkeling, motorcycle riding, or drag racing, which kind of proves the pilot's theory. That experience made me think I was immune. This helicopter nausea is going to be my cross to bear.*

Crowley tried to take his mind off his nausea by daydreaming about the recruiter's spiel back at Keesler AFB during his air traffic controller schooling. *Airman Crowley, this additional training the Air Force is offering, will transform you into a military Renaissance man with the physical ability of an Olympic athlete, the technical knowledge of an air traffic controller, and the fighting know-how of an elite commando. A combat controller uses your air traffic controller expertise to lead the vanguard of Special Operations. Where else can you get paid to jump out of planes, swim out of submarines, and fast rope down from helicopters?*

The aircraft cabin smelled of puke and sweat. Not being able to see outside from his seat, he felt like he was inside the guts of a leviathan as it swam through a violent storm. The cabin walls looked like the insides of a giant rib cage. He pictured himself as Jonah, trapped in the belly of a whale with his only hope of being spit up on shore. His seat shook him like a martini as he held off nausea with shallow breaths to not puke in front of a team of Navy SEALs.

Crowley tried to sit back, and the radio pack pinched his ribs again. He muttered. "God, how I hate helicopter rides!"

He had endured short hops in training, but the "never give up" mantra of special forces training got him through it. Suddenly, a strong, swaying motion shook him off his seat. A loose-fitting safety belt stopped his downward slide as it caught under his satchel of explosives.

"What the hell?" yelled Crowley.

A badger stared back at him.

"Tom!" Crowley roared. "What the fuck are you doing?"

The badger's shit-eating grin shined through the camouflage grease. "I saw you fall and came over to check on you. You have been taking this ride well up until now. I wondered if you would get sick."

Crowley smelled something, looked around, and nodded in agreement.

Newman grinned as his teammate sniffed. "Man, the stench of puke has everyone else on edge, while you, dude, even dozed during the noise of the mid-air refueling! How do you stay calm like that?"

"I needed my beauty sleep," said Crowley.

"I bet you did, pretty boy. Who conned you into believing camouflage grease is makeup?" replied Newman.

"Your momma told me she uses it all the time."

"Yeah right. You don't even know my mother. Anyway, I couldn't sleep a wink while you were getting your nap time. My mind just kept going over the mission briefing back at Eglin. I started barfing to get the turbulence out of my system."

Crowley cringed as Newman handed him a barf bag and shouted over the engine noise. "Try puking. Misery loves company."

He struggled to his seat, threw the paper pack on the floor, and complained, "The swaying is getting worse," as he felt his body swing and surge up and down as he sat.

His buddy held up another bag. "Hold on to it this time. I don't want you barfing all over me."

It's comforting to know everyone else is air-sick too. It appears both sweating and puking are acceptable behaviors during combat operations, thought Crowley.

He grunted to himself over Newman's comment, "Misery loves company!"

Looking around in the dim light, he saw the SEAL team sitting on chairs like his, with their seat backs bolted to the walls, facing each other. Cargo padding covered the structural ribs of the fuselage, giving the cabin an organic feel, reminding him of the animal he imagined riding inside a few minutes ago. He stared down its stinking gullet using the dim cabin light and confirmed it was an illusion.

Newman repeated his concerns about their lack of certification training.

"Tom, just deal with it. Somehow, we make up for no OJT with increased effort and attention to detail. I get it about your concerns. It's like we are a high-wire act, and they snatched away the safety net too soon."

Crowley recalled boarding the chopper three hours earlier in Panama. They were now the tip of the spear—a special operation ordered into the jungles of Central America. In an hour, he will be directing air operations from a makeshift LZ.

The pilots used the moonlight to find their navigation points. Strong sea breezes continued to buffet the fuselage, causing the chopper to shake and roll from side to side.

Crowley thought, *I recall catching a few zees en route to the objective. As our technical instructor preached, 'Training and preparation are key to success'.*

The pilot and copilot picked their way along the coast by moonlight as the aircraft's turboshafts created the din in the cargo bay. Designated as the model HH-53B, the giant aircraft carried the vanguard of the force ordered in to protect American citizens in Honduras.

Newman crossed over to the seat next to Crowley and spoke into his ear, "Have you given the mission anymore thought? Are guerrillas still refugees in your mind?"

"The dilemma is figuring out who the bad guys are. It is the same situation our buddies are facing in Vietnam. It goes back to the American Revolution," replied Crowley.

Newman raised his hands and asked, "Why bring up ancient history?"

"A rebel's wife might come from a loyalist family, and he winds up sleeping with the enemy. Battle lines are a nicety not found in modern warfare," lectured Crowley.

"Man, you've always got some cockamamy rationale. Why do you New Yorkers seem to look for every angle?" Newman asked.

"I was born in Texas, lived in West Germany and grew up all over the West. Now I call Long Island home. Guess that just gives me a wider perspective than most."

Newman hung his head down and made a disappointed nod as he moved back to his seat across the aisle. Crowley knew his buddy wanted a black-and-white explanation of their situation to make him feel planted and ready, whereas he believed they were dealing with shades of gray. Recalling the Uniform Code of Military Justice training he attended at Lackland Air Force Base, Crowley knew they had to be wary of their situation. The part where the class discussed war crimes came to mind. He learned that following illegal orders was no excuse. His technical instructor summed up what constitutes a war crime for his class.

"It's kind of like any other abomination you may encounter in life. You'll know what it is when you see it, and it's your responsibility to call it out for what it is."

The chopper, nicknamed the Super Jolly Green Giant, gained altitude as it headed onto the mainland. The moniker accurately depicted the size and color of the aircraft, but not its demeanor. Designed to fly up to thirty-eight troops into combat, the huge helicopter carried two General Electric GAU-2B/A miniguns mounted in the forward hatches protecting its flanks. A third minigun on the rear ramp door completed the ensemble. Similar in function to the old Gatling gun, the rotating barrels of the miniguns fire rifle-sized bullets at high speed. Larger models of the design accommodate cannon-caliber projectiles. 1,200 pounds of titanium armor on the fuselage provided some crew and passenger protection during flights.

Air Force Captain Jeff Mason and his copilot, Lieutenant Ben Segal, ignored the bumpy ride, as they scanned the terrain looking for the infiltration zone. The platoon sat spread out on the seats lining both sides of the cabin. The clamor from the turbine engine and six rotor blades made normal conversion impossible. They perched in small groups and yelled in each other's ears.

"Let's check the radios again!" shouted Crowley.

"In this goddamn dim light, I can hardly see you in that camouflage gear. The black tiger stripes overlaying the bands of brown and green make you blend into the padding on the walls. You look like a pair of eyes floating in a sea of shit," commented Newman.

"I have blue eyes, and you have brown eyes. That's how the SEALS will identify us," replied Crowley.

The combat controller's blue and silver patches sewn on their pockets were the only non-camouflaged badges on their battle fatigues. They covered them over with brown tape for this nighttime operation. Regulations required camouflaged versions of his chevrons sewn on the sleeves.

Why sew on insignia you can't see? wondered Crowley.

Then he remembered the sign by the toilet handles in the barracks reminding them to flush. The Air Force labeled everything. The camouflaged uniform made the embedded controllers appear to blend into the SEAL platoon. It was the specialized training that distinguished them.

The airmen had met at Navy schools in Coronado, California, and Little Creek, Virginia. They qualified for Basic Underwater Demolition/SEAL, or BUD/S for short, because their branch of service did not operate their own school for underwater operations certification. The pair collaborated as swim buddies to watch out for each other's safety. A platoon comprised sixteen men. The embedded combat controllers stood in for the usual air operations master chief positions to facilitate the joint operation.

A dome light flashed red in the cavernous cargo bay, warning the final approach to the mission's jump-off point.

Airman Crowley scanned the cabin and thought, *Man, the platoon looks so calm as they go about their business. Cool exteriors mask what was happening inside their heads. The SEALs are focusing on their assigned tasks, scanning checklists burned into their memories, and trying to visualize a successful outcome. A few of the squid trained with me for my sea operations certification. I know they endured the same intense training.*

Crowley grew up as a military brat and the constant relocation helped him learn to adapt to new situations. It seemed natural for him to form up with different units and personalities.

The combat controllers stood up for the final buddy check of their identical equipment. Their size, however, was not the same and Newman towered over him, causing the SEALs to joke about Mr. Air Force bringing along his own bodyguard. Each man faced backward and forward, as his peer checked clips and straps on the radio, ammo, and demolition packs. A signal test of the-PRC-77 FM ground-to-air gear set off some beeps, followed by the clicks and snaps of the M16 assault rifles and Colt 0.45 automatic sidearms. Satisfied with their preparation, the airmen each took a station at one of the side-hatch windows while they hovered low over the brush of a pine barren next to the abandoned airport. Crowley's mass seemed to expand with the communications case hung on his back, satchel charges in a knapsack strapped to his chest, and the weapons slung around the sides of his body. The eighty-pound load he carried made the jump a challenge.

The Air Force loadmaster worked the controls to open the ramp in the aircraft's tail. A crew member manned the third minigun position as the ramp door came down. The gunner fired from the cargo bay and the other positions joined in. As the chopper stopped its forward motion and hovered, the gun crew continued throwing down a withering rate of strafing fire. The miniguns sounded like sheets of linen being torn as four-thousand rounds per minute spent enough tracer bullets to light up the airport compound not far away.

Thousands of 7.62 mm caliber NATO rounds erupted from each weapon, cutting down the vegetation, and clearing the area of any surprise attackers during the jump-off. The miniguns turned quiet except for the whirl of the revolving barrels as they spun to a halt. The flashing red status light on the cargo bay ceiling lit solid green.

A knot formed in his stomach as Crowley looked out from his station and spotted the ground just below. Jumping with this load was like shooting craps. The injury rate was too high to train for it. He knew that was one reason they assigned two airmen to the mission. A signal came from the crew chief, allowing Crowley and Newman to advance to the cargo exit as the chopper hovered low to avoid any land mines. They were cheaper to replace than the helicopter.

The loadmaster yelled, "Go! Go! Go!"

The combat controllers ran out onto the greasy ramp and jumped. The heavy packs and rotor blast drove them to the ground. Crowley landed first, did a side roll to break the fall, raised the Armalite night vision scope on his rifle to his eye, and started counting. *I count Fourteen SEALs beneath the hovering chopper like a hen with her brooding chicks.* Suddenly, his air sickness was gone.

SEAL Team O-3, Lieutenant Harry Blackstone, hand signaled, and they headed for the mission objective while the helicopter ascended high enough to strafe the area designated Sector A. Crowley could see the rear cargo ramp door closing as it passed overhead. The miniguns began hitting the buildings in the compound as the platoon approached the area through the pine barrens. Crowley could make out the crumbling facades of the white buildings with tile roofs. Dark Figures of combatants were scurrying between buildings as the helicopter passed over them. Taking in the scene, Crowley recalled what his technical instructor said during a training mission, *"War is where you find out how well you deal with chaos."*

When they arrived at the perimeter of the airport, Crowley radioed the helicopter. "Greenman-One, this is Talon. Advance to Sector B for a strafing run. We are at Sector A."

"This is Greenman-One, Sector B strafing directive acknowledged."

Once the pilot, Captain Mason, replied, Crowley signaled to the SEAL officer the all-clear, and the chopper tilted forward in the dark sky to fly over to the next target area.

Crowley looked up as the huge aircraft ascended into the darkness and mused, "There goes the mother ship! No turning back now."

2

Secure the LZ

0100 Hours Central, 6 January 1969 North Coast of Honduras

Jose Garcia awoke to a hail of machine-gun fire racking the building in which he slept. He found himself covered with glass and dust as more rounds poured in through the shattered windows and ricocheted off the plaster walls. As luck would have it, the builders placed the window openings up high, and thick concrete blocks designed to help keep out the humid climate protected him. The guerrilla leader rolled off the side of his cot onto his hands and knees as he shook off the debris from his off-white farming togs and dark hair. He slipped on his sandals and grabbed an AK-47 assault rifle and a RadioShack walkie-talkie next to his bed. His men scrambled to their feet while shaking the dust and glass from their clothes. The guerillas had volunteered and only received the food Garcia scrounged for them from the council as pay. They followed his commands with respect and appreciated the rations Garcia provided.

Garcia yelled, "Andale, Andale!" as he felt his way to the door. He peered out and saw the tracer fire hit one of the other structures.

In Spanish, he called out, "*Amigos*, find your rifles and follow me!"

They ran to a control tower to use the vantage point to determine what was happening. As Garcia's party approached, they spotted figures in camouflage uniforms and gas masks in front of the building.

Garcia whispered, "Take cover!" as he dove into some brush while his team followed his lead.

The leader peered between bushes to see *hombres* with strange uniforms and weapons smash the glass door with their gun butts. A few minutes later, the strangers re-emerged and called on their radio as they headed for the next building.

"These men are foreign. It looks like we have yet another enemy to fight," whispered Garcia.

"*Jefe*, why do they object to our people growing a little food to eat?" said Jorge, Garcia's second in command.

"The world is selfish, my brother. We must fight just to have a place to eat and sleep," said Garcia.

"Si, vigilantes ran my family out of the country after the war," said Jorge.

"Now we are being forced to survive like our hunter-gatherer ancestors," said Garcia.

"So, what do you want us to do about this new enemy?" asked Jorge.

"Let's show them how good we hunt," declared Garcia.

He led his men up the stairs to the control room. When he peered in, a sea breeze blew through the shattered windows, scattering refuse into the air. The guerrilla leader saw the movement and raised his AK-47 to fire. He realized it was just junk floating around in the moonlight.

"*El cabron*, that giant helicopter made me jumpy. Get in the room and take cover!"

The guerillas took defensive positions. Garcia squatted behind the bottom ledge of a control tower window and observed a foreign aircraft flying with its nose down, strafing the buildings one by one. The aircraft's emblem was not Honduran. Although he was a foreigner himself from El Salvador, he did not consider himself such when surrounded by his comrades. The migrant council elected him the head of security.

Garcia pulled his portable radio out of his pants pocket and put it to his ear. "Cortez, quick, get on the call!"

Manuel Cortez was sitting next to a workbench in the motor pool garage north of the airstrip, holding his rifle in his lap, waiting. He picked up his walkie-talkie and answered Garcia.

"*Jefe*, this is Manuel. What are your orders?"

"Drive your trucks and men into the jungle before that helicopter comes your way."

The guerrilla leader could hear a truck engine fire up in the background as Cortez acknowledged his order. Again, he scanned the compound from his high vantage point, but he could not see any Honduran police in the area.

0115 Hours Central, Abandoned Airport in Northern Honduras

Crowley keyed his mike and said, "This is Talon calling Viper One. Do you read, over?"

The lead Sky Raiders pilot, Major Ben Grossman, flipped on his microphone and responded, "This is Viper One. I read you loud and clear, Talon."

As the SEALs paired up and entered the buildings of the airport compound, the mission plan called for an aerial bombardment of the nearby motor pool by Air Force tactical fighter bombers circling the objective.

"Viper One, your target is Sector Echo. Do you read me?"

"Talon, Roger that, Sector Echo."

"Viper One, your UTM grid coordinates are Easting 522264, Northing 1744424.2 zone 15P. Please confirm,"

Grossman found the location on a map card in his cockpit. Seeing they matched the codeword, he replied, "Talon, Viper one confirms Sector Echo coordinates."

"Roger that, Viper One. Good hunting!"

In a few minutes, the distinctive drone of the 18-cylinder rotary engines on the Douglas A-1 Sky Raiders grew louder as they approached the north end of the airport. Manuel Cortez couldn't identify it.

The motor pool commander yelled. "Where is that noise coming from? It sounds like airplanes. Let's get moving!"

As he sat waiting for his men while warming up the hard starting engine of an old olive-green Land Cruiser, four guerillas jumped into the back seats, and he put the truck in gear. He heard a whistle and looked up.

Crowley viewed the scene with his night vision binoculars as the prop-driven Sky Raiders made the bombing run appear to be in slow motion as bombs exploded on the target.

He turned to his buddy and said, "Bright burning buildings and smoking overturned vehicles are visible. Looks like either the bombs got them all or they died of fright from all that noise the Sky Raiders generated."

Newman grunted in reply. The bombing served a dual purpose by creating a diversion, while also eliminating a potential response from those forces around the motor pool once the landing operation started.

Crowley called out. "Tom, you monitor the progress of the SEALs with your radio, and I will coordinate the strafing runs with Greenman-One."

Small-arms fire erupted as the SEALs dispersed in teams of two to clear the buildings one sector at a time. Meanwhile, Greenman-One strafed the next sector to soften it up for the SEALs. The assault proceeded using a classic house to house search for enemy combatants.

Lieutenant Harry Blackstone's voice came on the tactical ground frequency of Newman's radio. "Sector Delta clear."

'Sector Delta clear' indicated the initial objective was secure. The combat controllers deployed to the center of the compound and tied their C4 explosive satchel charges around the base of palm trees in the large central courtyard to prep a landing zone referred to as the LZ.

Newman waved a hand signal and called, "Fire in the hole!"

He waited till the word passed down the line before setting off the explosives. Splinters scattered everywhere from the blasts and coconuts bounced off the buildings and landed among the rest of the debris on the sandy floor of the courtyard. With the smell of cordite and C4 in the air, Crowley got on his FM radio to call in another helicopter with two additional SEAL platoons. As the second chopper descended from the dark sky onto the LZ, he couldn't help recalling his personal nickname of "Dragonfly" for the aircraft.

Crowley mused, "Yeah, that should be its moniker, not Super Jolly Green Giant."

The SEALs jumped off onto the courtyard and established an initial defensive perimeter around the main landing strip, with teams of four men each. Shots rang out from the trees surrounding the runway.

Blackstone signaled and called out, "Commence fire!"

The Stoner 63B MK23 machine guns erupted, generating crossfire in the location of the enemy muzzle flashes. The jungle went quiet, and the American snipers and spotters continued scanning their area of operations, known as the AO, for activity with their night vision scopes and binoculars.

Shots exchanged for a while and gradually the AO grew calm again. Crowley directed his assigned SEAL squad as they set up landing beacons in the prescribed recognition pattern. They placed the lights and returned to their respective fire teams. Their duty was to hold the perimeter until relieved by the airborne ranger battalion.

Meanwhile, Garcia observed the sporadic gunshots from the vantage point of the control tower, but he could not spot any Honduran police in the vicinity. As he scanned the area below him with the aid of the moonlight, two military figures appeared in camouflage uniforms holding scoped M16 assault rifles as they approached the tower. The guerrilla leader concluded from the weapons that they must be American troops, which explained the strange giant helicopter.

He wondered aloud. "Why are we being attacked by gringos?"

Jorge spoke up, "*Jefe*, the Spanish conquered this land. Maybe the Americans think it is their turn now."

Garcia and his men did not know they were squatting on *gringo* plantations while threatening American citizens with their militia. From its inception, the U.S. military's primary purpose encompassed protecting trading interests from the Halls of Montezuma to the Shores of Tripoli.

Garcia spotted figures and called out, "Felix and Jorge, kill the *gringos*!"

The SEALs finished deploying the beacons returned to their fire teams. Crowley and Newman maneuvered over to the control tower entrance and started humping it up the stairs with their heavy ground-to-air FM radios to set up command and control for landing the armored battalion. Although it had been the SEAL'S job to clear the tower, they still followed urban warfare procedures. After reaching around corners and spraying bullets in short bursts, they waited for the return fire before moving up. On the third level, they encountered a fusillade from above.

Newman shouted, "Shit! Who the hell cleared this building?"

They could hear AK-47 rifles in the dark stairwell. The pair took turns sighting around the corner at different heights while picking off the riflemen above, using their night vision scopes. They found themselves at a distinct disadvantage. The enemy held the high ground.

Crowley called, "Attacking is a suicide mission. Stay behind cover and pick them off."

The firefight continued even though the gunmen dropped like flies up on the landing above from the accuracy of the combat controllers' night vision scopes.

They realized the hostiles were getting reinforcements. Crowley looked at his watch. They were running out of time to set up the command-and-control position. He signaled to his comrade to lob a fragment grenade up while he provided covering fire. It clattered on the floor above as they pulled back and plugged their ears. The detonation tore off the railing above, and they charged up the stairs with their Colt sidearms drawn and scanned for movement. Finding none, Newman covered his buddy as he stepped over the blood streaming from the corpses. As he advanced, Crowley noticed the off-white hand-sewn peasant clothing and sandals of the guerillas.

He thought, *they look ill equipped; yet those AK-47 assault rifles were their equalizers. Reminds me of my technical instructor's stories about firefights with black pajama-clad Viet Cong.*

When they reached the top floor, Crowley tried the heavy steel door and found it locked.

Newman banged on the door with his fist and yelled, "Surrender now with your hands up!"

He did not get a reply, so he wedged a brick of C4 in the door handle and retreated to the stairwell. The explosion blew the metal door into the room as dust and debris filled the stairwell. They entered, crouched low, and both scanned their field of vision back-to-back with their Colt automatics in two-handed grips and their rifles hung by web slings over their shoulders. Crowley drew another pistol from its holster and held the guns in front of him.

The smoke cleared quickly as a breeze passed through the blown-out windows. They saw figures moving, and a shot rang out, missing Newman by inches as it ricocheted off the cinderblock wall. The bullet tore off a sharp piece of cement, which hit Newman on the cheek, drawing blood. They returned fire, taking out the man in the corner. The two airmen squatted down behind a high counter. They pulled the pins on fragmentation grenades, counted for four seconds, and lobbed them over to the other side of the room.

The blasts blew out any remaining glass in the control tower's windows. The controllers stood up and took out three more guerillas with their Colts. Garcia pushed away the bodies of his fallen comrades as he popped up like a jack-in-the-box.

The guerilla leader appeared with a machete and an AK-47. As he raised his brush-cutter, Crowley dropped a Colt on the counter, grabbed his rifle low, and used the web sling to pivot the weapon up to block the blade with the plastic stock. He heard a thud, pulled his M16 off his shoulder, and swung the barrel end around, hitting Garcia in the face. Stunned by the blow, the guerrilla stepped back slightly and tried to raise his gun with one hand. The weight of the assault rifle caused him to pull on the trigger and he fired off a full clip. One bullet hit Newman's left arm and blood spurted out down his sleeve.

Crowley lurched to the side with the heavy radio on his back as the guerrilla's rifle sawed the counter between them in half. Garcia, now incensed at having missed the American, started swinging his machete at him as the airman blocked the blows with his rifle butt and then a piece of the tabletop.

As they parried, Crowley called out, "Drop your weapon or I will shoot!"

Garcia continued to swing his blade like a sword as the airman jumped out of the way and triggered his second pistol, putting a round into the guerrilla's chest. The shot propelled Garcia's body against a wall. A second shot hit Garcia on the forehead as he slid down to the floor. The former peasant leader landed propped up against the white stucco, clutching the machete and the AK-47. Crowley leaned over the counter and pointed his Colt down at his adversary. He couldn't help staring at the hole in the man's head. A tie-dyed tee shirt pattern from two red splatters decorated the wall behind the corpse. The shock of killing at point-blank range overwhelmed Crowley. He turned away from the blood-stained, lifeless torso and grimaced as he consoled himself.

He thought, *God damn it! No refugees here.*

Still operating on survival instinct, Crowley returned to being one with the moment. He used the Colt's gunsight to scan the room for more targets.

Newman yelled, "I'm hit!"

He was on the floor with blood flowing from his shoulder.

"Put a compress on it from your ditty bag while I make sure we're secure!"

The wounded controller groaned, "Where did these guerillas come from?"

"They must have snuck in after the SEALs cleared the building. That's why we followed protocol and came up the stairs with our weapons on automatic. Let me see that wound of yours."

He cut off Newman's sleeve with his ka-bar knife and pulled a clean bandage and medicine out of a pouch on his gun belt.

As he poured on an antiseptic, he spoke to Newman, hoping to take his mind off the burning sensation.

"You can't predict what will happen on the battlefield. The best-laid plans go to shit once the bullets fly."

"Ow, that burns!"

"Tom, hold on. Let me wipe off some blood and bandage it tight to stop the bleeding."

"Jake, do you recall that campsite we established with the Force Recon Marines?"

"Yeah, what about it?" asked Crowley. "The gunnery sergeant toasted us at the campfire. 'To kill or to be killed. That is the question.'"

"I know what you mean. They just did not give us a chance to let them surrender."

"Those peasant clothes the guerillas were wearing! It reminded me of a scene from The Magnificent Seven we watched back on base. Which part did we play?" asked Newman.

"Eli Wallach and his gang, from the looks of it."

"Oh, I thought you were going to say Steve McQueen and Yul Brynner."

"They shot the bad guys and protected the peasants. We shot the bad guys, and they were the peasants."

"What are you saying? Do you think we killed the wrong people?"

Crowley wrapped a tourniquet around Newman's upper arm. "No, they were the bad guys. It's unfortunate they didn't surrender. I wanted to hear their side of the story."

3

The Main Assault

0130 Hours Central, 6 January 1969

All the complications getting into position made the past half hour feel like five minutes. Crowley dragged a dead guerrilla away to make way for their radios up front. Next, he went over to his comrade, lifted him up, and wrapped his uninjured arm around his neck to lift him. Newman groaned and then held on as they moved to the front of the control tower. He sat his buddy down, brought over his equipment, and positioned it close to him.

The smell of death in the humid air made Crowley queasy as he wiped the sweat off his brow with his sleeve and took the pack off his back to switch on the FM receiver. He noticed the main control tower window had a ledge in front of it. He carried his radio over, sat down, and overheard Newman using his good arm to call the SEAL O-3 on a tactical frequency to ask for medics with stretchers.

Once Crowley's set warmed up, he keyed his mike and said, "This is Talon calling Blue Goose One, do you copy?"

The lead C-130 Hercules aircraft in the formation replied to the call. "This is Blue Goose One. Do we have clearance to land?"

Crowley surveyed the area from the control tower windows with night vision binoculars to find the beacons in position and the defensive perimeter established.

"This is Talon, Sir, you are clear to begin your approach. I will provide visual instructions on this frequency as your aircraft approaches. The beacon lights are in place, and we are ready to guide you in."

Crowley reviewed the operational strategy in his mind. It called for two C-130 cargo transports landing side-by-side per wave. One transported thirty airborne rangers, an Armored Cavalry Assault Vehicle, and the ACAV's operating crew. The second carried two more ACAVs and their crews. This cargo configuration optimized unloading and deployment efficiency per wave.

The South Vietnamese Army christened the ACAV as the "Green Dragon," because of its ability to slither through the jungle while roaring noise and belching smoke from its diesel engine. The vehicle's armaments completed the fiery image its namesake portrayed. It looked like a high-sided tank with treads on each side. Weapons arrayed on the top of ACAV supported the current mission.

Crowley recalled reading about the Green Dragon starting life as a battle taxi designed to ferry troops through harm's way while protecting them from enemy small-arms fire. The vehicle's thick lightweight military-grade alloy armor, along with its powerful V6 aluminum block diesel engine, made the personnel carrier suitable for airborne deployment. The South Vietnamese modified the vehicle with shielding around the armament and top turrets after suffering high crew casualties during close-in support of troop advances. These changes transformed the battle taxi into an assault vehicle worthy of its nickname. The American Army adopted the modifications in 1965 after witnessing its successful use by the South Vietnamese forces as they punched through the jungle and overran Viet Cong encampments. This mission specified .50 caliber M2 machine guns and 107 mm mortar racks as Green Dragon weaponry, with the strategy being to overrun the guerilla camps surrounding the LZ.

"Tom, remember to count twenty-four waves to land and deploy the battalion and their equipment."

Newman spotted the heat signature of the aircraft as they approached using his night vision binoculars. "The cargo planes have their lights off to evade enemy sniper fire. Their images are faint at this distance. They are getting brighter as they get nearer."

Crowley talked the pilots down, giving them Newman's visual approach information over his ground-to-air FM radio set.

"Blue Goose One and Two, your landing gear is down, and your glide path is on target. You are good to go."

Both cargo transports landed side by side. As they neared the end of the runway, Blue Goose Two caught its right-side wheels in a sinkhole, which forced the C-130 to turn clockwise. As the plane rotated, the turboprops on its left wing collided with the other aircraft. Tom Newman witnessed the spectacle in infrared, as the turboprops cut through Blue Goose One's wing like a buzz saw.

Newman reported, "Jake, Blue Goose Two just shredded the left wing of Blue Goose One. Now it is burying its nose in the fuselage of the other aircraft!"

"No fires so far. The rubber fuel cells in the damaged wing are not leaking," shouted Newman as he stayed glued to his binoculars.

Crowley replied, "Tom, Blue Goose One was carrying the third Green Dragon and the thirty Airborne Rangers assigned to all three vehicles!"

"When the planes collided, the pilots of Blue Goose Two must have gotten pinned to their seats by controls and structural supports in the cockpit based on how crushed the nose of the plane looks. I hope they're okay," said Newman.

Inside the C-130, bodies flew from left to right as Blue Goose Two pushed into the fuselage where the troop transport seating was located. While Newman watched this crash unfold, he called out to let his partner know what was happening blow-by-blow.

"The planes have stopped all movement and the cargo doors on both Hercules transports are opening now!"

Over the radio came a call, "Mayday! Mayday! This is Blue Goose One calling ground control."

"This is Talon at ground control. Give me your status."

"Talon, this is the Blue Goose One Loadmaster. We have ten injured rangers. The medics on board are already working on them. Their injuries are serious, and they need to be evacuated."

"Talon, this is the Blue Goose Two Loadmaster. We're cutting away the wreckage to free our pilots."

The controllers needed an emergency plan with no time out in Special Operations. A light bulb in Crowley's mind lit as he recalled a lecture on armored cavalry tactics, and he called over to his buddy.

"Tom, the Green Dragons double as a field ambulance. Let's get them deployed!"

Crowley switched to the tactical frequency on his radio and picked up the mike.

"Talon to Blue Goose Two Loadmaster, do you copy?"

"Copy that, Talon. This is Blue Goose Two Loadmaster."

"Unload your vehicles from your Hercules and use them to tow the planes apart and off to the taxiways on both sides of the landing strip. Then we will deploy the Green Dragons as ambulances. Make it quick! We have more C-130s bearing down on us!"

The Green Dragon crews mounted up and emerged from the plane, speeding down the loading ramp. After their exit, the loadmasters raised ramps for protection against snipers. Internal winches spit out cables as the vehicle gunners tied them off on the tails of each plane. The gunners signaled their drivers when the tie-offs were complete, and the tracks dug in as the Green Dragons fought to pull the C-130s apart and disengage them from the wreckage.

Newman watched through his night vision binoculars as the armored vehicles did their job of separating the cargo planes. Suddenly, small-arms reports erupted as bullets ricocheted off the cargo planes and assault vehicles.

"Enemy fire coming in from the far side of the airfield. Two SEAL spotters have gone down. They are staying down and may have caught a round," reported Newman.

Crowley checked his map and made a broadcast to the A1-Skyraider fighter-bombers orbiting overhead.

"Viper One, this is Talon. I have coordinates for a fire suppression run on the edge of the jungle."

Major Grossman received the call sign and responded, "Talon, this is Viper One, ready to receive the coordinates."

"Viper One, Sector Tango at UTM Easting 522264, Northing 1744424.2 zone 16P, please confirm."

The Skyraider pilot found them on a map card in his cockpit. Seeing the location matched Crowley's area codeword, he replied. "Talon, Sector Tango confirmed."

"Roger that, Viper One. Good hunting!"

Before Crowley completed the request, the SEAL teams opened fire, aiming at the perimeter of the jungle with their machine guns.

The lead pilot radioed his wingmen. "Viper Two, I will take the drop since my 200-pound munitions are clear from the racks."

"Roger that Viper One."

Grossman had already used his M82 fragmentation ordnance on the guerilla motor pool and this made clearance on the rack to allow him to use his 500 LB incendiary bombs on this hostile fire suppression request. From his time in Southeast Asia, he knew napalm was the most effective option for a jungle area. The Skyraider pilot made the corresponding weapons selection from his bomb racks using a knob on his dashboard and headed into the coordinates Talon had given him.

In a few minutes, Crowley could hear the drone of Major Grossman's A1-Skyraider overhead as it dove in low to make his drop and then gunned its engine to start his ascent. Bright flares appeared to shoot from the front of the bombs. The casings struck the ground, split open, and sprayed the jelly fuel on the white-hot phosphorus-propelled grenades. *Boom! Boom!* The area erupted into a wall of ivory flame while the Skyraider struggled to gain altitude and avoid the onslaught of the massive fireball.

Crowley felt a heat wave coming through the broken windows of the air traffic control tower, followed by the stench of gasoline. He held his breath and sensed he heard screams coming from the jungle.

He dismissed the thought. *It must be the sound of the blast playing tricks on me.*

"Jake, the SEAL teams are pumping their fists and cheering like they are watching fireworks. You made their day by eliminating those snipers."

The drop area grew dark and quiet as the Skyraider ascended out of sight. Once the cargo plane wreckage came apart, the gunner-commander of Green Dragon Bravo unhitched the tow cable and rolled it up on the internal winch.

He called over to Green Dragon Alpha. "Let's hook up the nose gear!"

The assault vehicles swung around to the front of the aircraft. Next, the gunners tied the cables to each plane. The two worked to minimize the exposure of their crews to guerrilla snipers. Green Dragon Alpha toiled away, trying to free Blue Goose Two from the sink hole. The damaged landing gear acted like a hook, stopping the extrication. The Green Dragon Alpha driver gunned the diesel engine and dragged the plane along, leaving a small ditch in the tarmac from the broken landing gear. Meanwhile, the combat controllers sweated it out, knowing more C-130s were bearing down on the LZ.

"Blue Goose Three and Four, this is Talon. The first landing formation crashed on the runway. Circle your wave to buy time for the clean-up."

"This is Blue Goose Three. Roger that. We are orbiting back to the rear of the formation."

These air traffic control instructions kept the momentum going by bringing up the next pair of cargo planes, which would soon be in a better position to begin their landing approach.

"Blue Goose One and Two Loadmasters, this is Talon. I have bought you some time to medevac the wounded. Don't waste any of it. Blue Goose Five and Six are bearing down on us.'

"Roger that on Evac. We are on it."

The pair of Green Dragons on the field drove around to the rear cargo doors of the sidelined aircraft and discharged rangers with stretchers to medevac the wounded.

Meanwhile, Newman turned on his flashlight and placed his map on the floor of the control tower as he looked for a rendezvous point.

When a suitable position was located, he picked up his radio mike and called the choppers orbiting the area. "Green Men, this is Hawkeye. I have coordinates for an EVAC, acknowledge!"

"Hawkeye, this is Greenman One. We are ready to receive EVAC instructions."

Newman read off the location from his map and the chopper pilots each repeated them back for confirmation. He switched to the tactical frequency and called the rendezvous point to the Green Dragon drivers.

Twenty rangers came running out from Blue Goose One as the loading ramp swung down. They grabbed stretchers from the Green Dragons and loaded the ten wounded soldiers into the vehicles. Four troops ran to the other cargo transport to get the pilots. The flight crew had pried them out while waiting for the stretcher-bearers.

As the armored vehicles took off, ranger medics jumped in and closed the doors. They continued attending to the injured as they traveled off to meet the helicopters in a designated rendezvous.

The third Green Dragon remained in Blue Goose One. The loadmaster positioned the vehicle on the loading ramp and the crew members drove it down. Once on the ground, the rear armored doors of the assault vehicle opened, and ten rangers mounted up inside and buttoned up as they drove away to deploy with the perimeter guard. The Green Dragon circled back for the rest of the rangers.

"Talon calling Blue Goose Five and Six. Alter your flight for a staggered landing. You must stop before you reach the crashed C130s to avoid runway obstacles. Do you copy?"

"Copy that, Talon!"

This new formation gave room to maneuver in case the heavy Hercules cargo planes ran into any more issues. Seventy-two Green Dragons were unloaded, each with ten mounted soldiers and an ACAV crew comprising a driver and a gunner-commander.

A Ranger medic arrived to treat Newman with a painkiller and redressed the wound while he continued to direct air traffic. The medics then put the dead guerillas in body bags and hauled them out on stretchers. By 0800 hours central time, the airfield was secure, and the battalion was setting up command headquarters around the control tower. Communications from Panama reported the injured rangers were doing well in the hospital thanks to Crowley's quick thinking.

The local federal police arrived in their jeeps and deployed behind the Green Dragon squads to apprehend the insurgents. The vehicles broke through the jungle around the airfield to flush them out. Federales in jeeps brought up the rear. All they found were surviving refugee families hiding in the woods and fields.

Crowley recalled a class about fighting guerilla tactics. *They blend into the woodwork because they wear indigenous clothing and can easily hide their small arms in the jungle.*

A ranger captain arrived in the control tower and slapped Crowley on the back. "Congratulations, airman, you wiped out all the guerillas with that incendiary drop you called in. That order saved our brigade from a lot of casualties. I am sure of that!"

"Well, credit the Skyraider pilot, Major Grossman, for that. He decided to use napalm," replied Crowley.

"I credit you for the decision to call in air support. Of course, collateral damage is always a given with napalm," said the captain.

"Sir, you mean someone complained about the jungle fire?" asked Crowley.

"No, no. The stupid insurgents had their families with them to help. It appears family members spotted targets from what we can see from the remains," said the captain.

Crowley replied, "The bomber pilot made the decision on which ordinance to use. He should get all the credit."

"Don't sweat it, airman. It wasn't your fault," replied the captain.

He did not know what to say. Tears welled up as he turned away and radioed an approaching cargo plane. Crowley thought, '*Damned if we do and court-martialed if we don't*'. *Newman might be right. Will the carnage from this intervention in Honduras be damned in the news media, or will Vietnam continue to suck all the oxygen from the room?*

The captain sensed that Crowley was upset over his revelation and changed his tone. "Soldier, sending a ranger battalion on a peacekeeping mission is like ordering someone to make tea with a blow torch. No matter how hard you try, something is going to get burned. No pun intended. You made sure it wasn't us. I thank you for that."

As they flew in and out, Air Force flight crews heard about the actions performed by the two inexperienced airmen and climbed up the tower, bringing rations, and congratulations for their handling of the landing crash.

A colonel and his entourage came up and met with Crowley and Newman.

The officer said, "We believe you boys saved our bacon at the start of the air operations. Because of your decisive action, the mission was a success. Reports show the injured soldiers are doing well in Panama. My hat is off to you both!"

Following the colonel's lead, everybody rose to their feet and shook hands to congratulate the combat controllers. As the pair thanked the officers, Crowley recalled a warning his father told him about the military: "No good deed goes unpunished." The dilemma of the napalm drop kept haunting him. He tried to console himself with the knowledge it was the pilot's decision to use napalm. It didn't help. A headache had been hovering over him during the operation, but he fought it off by keeping focused. It hit him in a torrent. At that point, a revelation struck him like a lightning bolt.

Were those screams from women and children I heard coming from the napalm blast?

4

I Say a Little Prayer

Anna Maria Bertolini sat at her dressing table applying make-up. The mirror reflected large almond-shaped green eyes accentuated by arched eyebrows, a well-proportioned nose, full lips, and a flawless olive complexion. Her coifed brunette hair style framed a face that could model for a statue of Athena, and her flowing white nightgown completed a classic image of beauty. Those green eyes projected intelligence and a tendency not to suffer fools gladly. At the bank where she worked, customers commented that she looked like Sophia Loren. Her reply never varied: "Sophia comes from the same town in Italy as my mother's family," leaving them guessing.

As she finished her makeup, the hit song "I Say a Little Prayer" by Dionne Warwick played on the morning AM radio show. She sang along and dressed in a navy-blue suit jacket and miniskirt. Saddle brown go-go boots, matching leather belt, and a white silk blouse completed the ensemble.

The lyrics reminded her of Jake. Not that she needed reminding. He told her on their telephone call last week he would be away on a mission and couldn't say anything else.

What does 'away on a mission' mean and when will it happen? Until now, Jake described only training exercises and even they sounded dangerous, she thought.

The horrors of Vietnam came to mind. She had prayed at mass for his safety and a permanent assignment, so they could start their wedding plans. The engagement ring wasn't much consolation for all this waiting and worrying.

Despite all the uncertainty, she had to admit that her heart fluttered whenever her fiancé came to mind. But the pressure was growing. After all, she was twenty-two and her high school friends were already married. Whenever she visited them, she had to endure the endless commentary about how her "clock was ticking" and she "better get moving." With him away and everybody involved in family stuff, she was lonely. Baby showers were becoming a downer for her.

She walked down the stairs into the kitchen to eat breakfast before heading to her office. Her mother was at the stove cooking a batch of pancakes as she looked up and greeted her daughter.

"Anna Maria! Why do you look so sad in that beautiful suit? You should be happy to buy such nice clothes at your age. When we lived in our old neighborhood in Brooklyn, a lot of the women continued to wear the same black dress every week to church, even though they were way past the mourning period for their dead relatives. They could not afford to do otherwise."

"Yes, Mamma. I am worried about Jake. He is no longer performing training exercises. On our last telephone call, he told me he was going on a mission, and he could not give me any details. That made me worry even more!"

"Anna Maria - I know how you feel. Your papa fought the Japs during the war. It was 'Loose lips sink ships' and all that back then. At least you can interact on the telephone and understand how he feels. We only had censored letters delivered months after being sent."

"Yeah, mamma, but I want to be with him, not just talk to him! He seems so depressed because military service is keeping him from opening his own bicycle shop."

"Business is important to men. Try to be more understanding."

Anna Maria picked at her pancakes and pondered. Life was hard being engaged to Jake. They had met two years ago at a wedding while he was still attending a local university on a full academic scholarship. She remembered just how much he complained about college being a waste of time.

She recalled a trying conversation she got in the middle of at his parent's home when they first started dating.

"Dad, I learned all there is to know about managing a business. I got my first job when I was fourteen."

"Staying in school and graduating will increase your prospects."

"You think wearing a suit and tie means you are successful? I'm not cut out for that. The owners at the bike shop each pull down seventy-five thousand dollars a year in their blue-collar work uniforms. When did you ever hear about any fancy executives living in Garden City making that much money?"

She could understand both sides of the argument. From her future father-in-law's perspective, she knew education mattered. The training courses she attended at work resulted in her promotion to the financial services department. Jake had to deal with boring classes where the professors would tell rather than show. Anna Maria knew from her own experience that learning by doing things was better.

She recalled how Jake later turned to her and whispered, "If it wasn't for the draft, I would already own my shop, and we could get married and buy a house. Instead, I live hand to mouth in college, memorizing and testing like I was back in high school. My old man thinks he missed out by not having a degree."

Their engagement must have gotten the evil eye. The first thing to happen after she accepted his ring was the university gave Jake an academic dismissal because of his poor grades and pulled the scholarship. With the draft hanging over his head, he found it impossible to start his own business. Then his letter from Uncle Sam came in the mail.

Having read President Eisenhower's farewell address for a political science class paper, Jake had done further research on the topic and found out that Eisenhower was referring to World War II and how the 'Arsenal for Democracy' had turned into a defense industry driven by a guaranteed profit motive. He believed America should defend itself against direct attacks and stop the spread of communism by demonstrating the superiority of democratic capitalism instead of using proxy wars. The NASA Apollo Program had already proved this superiority, and he believed America should continue to hammer away at building economic superiority while maintaining superior military deterrence. For this reason, he protested the Vietnam War while in college.

With the draft board breathing down his neck, he enlisted in the Air Force, promising her they would get married as soon as he received a permanent assignment. The whole situation didn't sit well with her, but after she discussed it with her parents, she reconsidered. The way her father regarded him, she knew Jake was a man's man. Her dad greeted previous boyfriends with an expression on his face communicating "look at what the cat dragged in".

She recalled him saying, "Your fiancé has talent. At work, they all called him a real mensch after meeting him.

After breakfast, she slipped into her winter coat and walked to the garage. Outside her parent's cape cod home, she looked down the street at similar houses as far as the eye could see. They now lived in a modern housing development in Bayshore, a suburb on Long Island. Their new neighborhood of single-family homes displayed well-kept lawns bordered by new sidewalks and well-paved roads.

At least our new neighborhood is safe and quiet. We even have a yard with a barbeque, thought Anna Maria.

Once in the driver's seat of her shiny white 1967 Malibu two-door coupe, her spirits picked up a bit. She backed out of the driveway and headed to the bank via the Southern State Parkway. As she cruised down the tree-lined highway, her thoughts turned again to Jake and frustration welled up inside her as she realized she didn't even know when the mission would take place. She hummed the words again to "I Say a Little Prayer", determined to keep him in her thoughts and prayers until he returned from the mission.

As she approached the Nassau County line, the traffic picked up as usual and the disk jockey on her favorite radio station announced a traffic accident just before the Meadowbrook Parkway interchange.

Oh, great! The accident happened just before my exit. I don't see an ambulance. That is a good sign, thought Anna Maria.

She had been lucky so far this winter. They hadn't had a white Christmas or New Year. The traffic got crazy when it snowed on Long Island. As she drove closer to the scene of the accident, the traffic got slower and slower. Her mind wandered to her mother's comments about life back in Brooklyn. They lived in the Bensonhurst neighborhood of south Brooklyn, close to Coney Island and Sheepshead Bay.

I recall the apartment on 81st Street as if it was yesterday. They were all red brick duplex row homes with large high stoops, front patios defined by wrought iron fences, and ornate white doors trimmed with white ram's head molding, thought Anna Maria.

She recalled that life was difficult in Brooklyn. What the politicians called 'the great melting pot' consisted of ethnic neighborhoods where everyone knew the bounds and stayed in their enclave to avoid confrontation. Sometimes gangs from other neighborhoods would come through and try to rob the older people on the streets doing their shopping and errands. The wise guys who hung out in the pool hall chased the gangs out of the area. They did not do this out of the kindness of their heart. The mafia justified their collection of tribute from the businesses in the neighborhood as protection money. Some shop owners accused the mafia of arranging gang attacks to justify increases in their protection money.

Despite all the pasta she ate, Anna Maria grew up thin and looking young for her age. It was not until her late teens that she developed into the swan everyone admired today. The wise guys made wolf whistles when she walked by, but otherwise acted as gentlemen. It was the gangs from the other neighborhoods that made it dangerous for Anna Maria to go to school. Public school and work were the only places where the ethnic groups had to mingle. Many Romeo and Juliet stories developed from that mingling along with many a fight.

So, her two brothers taught her how to defend herself. In their back yard, they nailed a wooden panel to the fence, drew the outline of a male figure on it, and taught her how to throw and fight with a switch blade knife. Since she was a girl, they taught her how to kick an attacker or smash him in the head with a heavy metal framed pocketbook she carried, then run like hell. All her defensive training was based on fight and flight tactics. She learned to be aware of her surroundings and not take her safety for granted.

Oh, here is the exit for Garden City. I made it on time, after all, thought Anna Maria.

Anna Maria focused on the car wreck as she passed the accident and took the exit to Meadowbrook Parkway. Once she was heading north, the traffic cleared, and she reached Stewart Avenue, a main drag. As she approached Garden City, the upscale colonial homes came into view. Professionals desiring an affluent lifestyle called this town home. Stores like Lord and Taylor and Abraham and Straus lined the commercial streets, catering to the residents. When she arrived at the Garden City Savings and Loan office, she pulled into a parking space in the employee parking area. As she passed through the lobby, the branch manager waved to her from his glass walled office. She waved back as she strode past, looking like a runway model. The branch manager noticed how she drew in the customers and made sure she got the biggest Christmas bonus in her department, and he took it upon himself to perform her annual review instead of leaving it up to her supervisor.

Her father was in the fashion business, and it showed. She dressed to kill with her petite frame and impressive looks, causing a good deal of jealousy among the other women at her workplace who called her "a clothes horse" behind her back. Anna Maria made her way to the customer service platform and took her place at her desk, where she provided financial services to the firm's affluent customers. She was very popular with the bank's business clients. They asked for her by name and would sit and wait their turn. Today was no different. A young man in a dark gray three-piece-suit stood up, straightened his tie, and walked over to Anna Maria's desk.

She told him to take a seat and said, "I am Anna Maria Bertolini. How can I be of service?"

"My name is Jack Bradshaw. I am new in town, and it was told you are the lady to see about opening a new savings account. All my friends at work recommended you."

"Well, I am glad to hear you were recommended because of our bank's excellent service."

"Oh yes. They can't wait to see you again. I can understand why now that I have met you."

"That is kind of you to say. We have a regular savings account with a passbook or a certificate of deposit account. The regular savings account is used to accumulate savings, and the CD is used to maximize interest on a fixed deposit over a specified period."

"Like I said, I am new in town and just started my job. The passbook savings account sounds right for me," said Bradshaw.

As she typed up a form for the account, Bradshaw looked around and then bent towards her, trying to be as discrete as possible when he spoke.

"I was wondering if you would like to meet me for dinner one day this week at the Garden City Bowl. I am trying to make friends since I arrived, and I hear they have a great band and food at the jazz club."

"That sound very nice, however I am engaged to be married and the bank frowns on bonded employees like me socializing with the customers."

"Does your fiancé live here in Garden City? Maybe we can double date sometime,"

"He is in the Air Force assigned to Hurlburt Field in Florida."

"Isn't that the headquarters for Special Operations? My brother is in the Marines and told me about that place."

"Yes, he is a combat controller. Do you know what that means?"

"They call them the tip of the spear. First in and last out. They don't get any tougher than those guys. He must have some interesting stories to tell. I would like to meet him when he comes home."

"Jake is on his first mission, and he could not tell me anything. I'm waiting for it to be over so that we can book our wedding."

Her eyes welled up as she pulled the form from the typewriter and handed it to Bradshaw for his signature. Bradshaw saw the tears and knew he, like his friends before him, had failed to win her over.

"I'm sorry. I did not intend to upset you. Don't worry about your fiancé. My brother told me combat controllers get the best training in the Air Force. They are trained to succeed against all odds. He will get you to the church on time."

Bradshaw smiled and signed the form. Anna Maria wiped her eyes and smiled back as she took the form and escorted him to a teller. The teller stamped a passbook with his account number and filled in his ID information.

"Thank you, Mr. Bradshaw, for opening an account at Garden City Savings and Loan. We look forward to serving you in the future."

"I look forward to meeting you again and hearing about your wedding plans," said Bradshaw.

He turned and made his way out of the building, not sure if he had made a new friend. Anna Maria went back to her desk to find her phone ringing. She breathed deeply and picked up the receiver. It was Jake!

5

Back on Base

2300 Hours Central, 5 January 1969. North Coast of Honduras

The combat controllers walked up the loading ramp of the C-130 Hercules troop transport.

Newman said, "We are leaving the Caribbean the same way we arrived, with all our equipment strapped to our bodies. At least the load is lighter because of the ammo, rations, and satchel charges we expended."

The walkway was greasy from the cargo skids, which made the climb harder.

The loadmaster stopped them at the entrance. "Take a seat and put your gear in the back."

Newman turned toward Crowley as they found their seats. "The operation really gained speed once the airborne rangers determined most of the armed guerillas died from the napalm drop you directed at the sniper fire."

Crowley cringed. He was sick of hearing about how effective the bombing was. "I thought we were on a policing mission. The first thing we do is kill all the suspects with napalm."

"But Jake, that was standard operating procedure to protect the SEALs and landing craft. You didn't hear me objecting to your bombing run call, did you?"

What made it worse for him was mock thanks for "hosting the cookout." Then, without warning, the operation's brass flew in air traffic controllers, who relieved Crowley and Newman and passed along orders to report to Headquarters at Hurlburt Field as soon as possible. The pair walked up to the passenger seating area, where they found their SEAL team already there, playing cards and trying to get a transistor radio to work.

Before they could sit down, one of the SEALs pointed at Jake's M16. "What happened to your rifle? Putting notches in your gun is against regulations. The armorer will be very upset with you!"

Crowley looked down at the gashes in the plastic stock and stared at the SEAL "That's the souvenir your friend Jose Garcia gave me with his machete. You remember Jose, don't you? You let him and his friends up the control tower to throw us a little surprise party when we arrived."

"We cleared the entire area, so the flyboys didn't have to get your uniforms dirty," replied the SEAL, nodding to his buddies.

"Yeah, and you did such a good job that you missed the leader of the insurrection and his merry band of pranksters. We had to do your job for you and kill them all. Jose got his at point blank range," said Crowley.

The SEAL smirked as he responded to Crowley's criticism. "What are you complaining about? Figuratively speaking, you've both earned notches on your pistols. Welcome to the club. I guess that's why they say, 'Never bring a knife to a gunfight.'"

Crowley gave him the finger, and the squid jumped up as Newman came between them and handed his buddy a canteen. The sailor looked at the airmen. Then he raised his hand and smacked his forehead.

"What am I thinking? I should thank you both! We are going home early because you threw that barbeque, leaving us with no more guerillas to fight!" said the SEAL.

"Yeah, and we combat controllers are going to have to change our motto to 'If you want it done right, do it yourself.'" replied Crowley.

A transistor radio found an English-speaking station and the hit "Fortunate Son" by Creedence Clearwater Revival came on the air. The music cut the tension, and all the commandos joined in.

Newman shouted over the din, "Hey Jake, like the song, nobody in this unit was rich enough to buy their way out of serving their country."

Crowley sat down next to his buddy. "I think Fogerty was missing something when he wrote the lyrics."

"What's your point?"

He moved closer and whispered in his buddy's ear. "The song infers men avoiding the draft are the bad guys. I believe the military-industrial complex is the real villain. Special interests want us here fighting the commies to use up the equipment they sell to the armed forces. If we die in the process, so what?"

"The communists are taking over the world," replied Newman.

"Tom, I think that left to their own devices, the commies will collapse and grind to a halt because of the philosophy's inefficient economic model. I learned about that in economics class, but our elected officials ignored that lesson to serve their own personal interests."

Newman asked, "How do legislators benefit from your military-industrial complex?"

"It is a win-win proposition. Constituents get a job at the local defense factory, so they are happy to pay taxes to support their government's war effort. The profiting industries donate to the reelection campaigns of politicians who back their agenda. The conflicts grow larger, so everyone in the military gets promoted and on it goes. It's a vicious circle. Kennedy wanted to withdraw from Vietnam. You know what happened to him. I believe Eisenhower was right."

"He didn't stop any wars. He led a war," declared Newman.

Crowley answered, "In his presidential farewell address to the American people, he said 'Beware of the military-industrial-complex.' Who knows better than that president what the Pentagon and Congress are up to?"

"Jake, I think you are making more of this than it is."

"I have two more years to serve because private enterprise supplies our armies with guaranteed profit contracts. Take the profit out of the equation and see how many wars we have to fight," said Crowley.

They celebrated for a couple of hours and then "Guinevere" by Crosby, Stills, Nash, and Young played on the radio. The lyrics reminded Crowley of his emerald-eyed fiancé. Sometimes she surprised him with a stare of anticipation, as if she was checking out her prey. He missed her beauty and excitement and couldn't wait to return home to be with her. Their current frustration came to mind about getting a permanent assignment so she could start the wedding plans. Exhaustion hit him from all the fighting and drinking, so he sat down on some cargo padding and nodded off.

When Crowley awoke, the cargo plane touched down at Hurlburt Field after a direct three-and-a-half-hour flight. He caught an Air Force shuttle bus back to his unit, where he checked in his gear at one of the Special Operations armories. As he turned over his weapons to the armorer on duty, the action in the control tower flashed in his memory. He handed the pistols over, wondering how such a simple weapon could cause so much carnage and chaos. The best made battle plans always failed to come to fruition. He headed for his dormitory to get some sleep.

It was almost noon when Crowley awoke from a nightmare. Glimpses of the operation flashed in his mind as he arose and stretched. Images of blood, bodies on stairs, machine-gun fire cutting through wood, screams, and the stare of a peasant with a hole in his head came to haunt him as he headed for the bathroom. He felt hungover, but a cold shower helped to clear away the cobwebs. He shaved and put on stove pipe jeans, a polo shirt, wellington boots, and a motocross jacket. His taste remained blue collar in keeping with his short haircut. He didn't have to report for duty until the next day. Once outside in the bright sunlight, he found he needed his sunglasses because the Florida sun, combined with a slight hangover, was giving him a headache.

He walked over to the phone booth by the sidewalk and dialed his fiancé's work number. It was Tuesday and she should be on her lunch break.

She picked up on the first ring. "Garden City Savings and Loan, Anna Maria Bertolini speaking."

It was like listening to an Italian movie star speak English. Very sexy! Crowley leaned on the door of the phone booth. "Ciao *Bella!* How I miss you more every time I hear your voice. Somehow, they ordered me to return early from the mission with my buddy Newman, and I have today off."

"Oh, Jake, I was waiting for your call. I was so worried about you. I attended mass twice on Sunday. Are you okay?"

"I'm fine. We did well for our first mission. You will probably read about it in the papers," said Crowley.

"In the newspapers! Are you talking about Vietnam?" said Anna Maria.

"No darling. We were in Central America helping put down an insurrection. It's all over now so I can talk about it," said Crowley.

"I'll have to call my parents and let them know you are OK. We were all so worried about you," replied Anna Maria.

"Well, I miss them, too. Let your mamma know I keep recalling her Sunday dinners back on Long Island. *Spiedini alla Siciliana* is to die for, and your father's barbeque chicken is the best," said Crowley.

"I'll let them know. You're sure you are alright? I wish I could see you!"

"I am fine. Our job is directing the air operations. You know—air traffic control stuff. I didn't get injured. My buddy Newman just got grazed by a bullet. Nothing serious. I'm going to have lunch with him later today in Panama City."

"How did Tom get shot, if all you were doing is air traffic controller duties?" asked Anna Maria.

"We had to capture the control tower to set up the LZ. Some Salvadorian guerillas were in the tower. One thing led to another, and we had to fight our way in," said Crowley.

"How can you take Tom's gunshot wound so casually? It makes me think you are hiding something," said Anna Maria.

"OK—We had to kill the guerillas. They would not surrender. Newman and I are upset over what happened. It wasn't our fault. They shot first and would not surrender. That is why we are going to lunch today to talk it over," said Crowley.

Anna Maria knew there was more to the story than what he was telling her. She knew he was upset over the experience, and she would let it go for now. After all, she didn't tell him everything. If he knew how often she got hit on by her rich male business clients, he might get jealous and show up at the bank. That would not be good for business.

"You're sure you are not injured? You don't sound OK."

"Well, If I was injured, I wouldn't be reporting tomorrow for my permanent assignment, would I?" assured Crowley.

"I guess so. Call me tonight. I want to hear how your lunch with Newman went," said Anna Maria.

"OK, I will call you. I'm not sure if they'll assign me to headquarters, though. They seem to be short-handed everywhere with war in Vietnam raging on. The people in the town are friendly. I think you would like it here. How are you doing, babe?"

"Work is going well. I am learning how to review financial statements and make business loans. Once I complete the training, I am eligible for a promotion. Of course, that's not as exciting as dodging bullets on your job, but I like the work. I don't know what kind of job I will get in Panama City if that is where we wind up," said Anna Maria.

"Once I have orders in hand, I can check with personnel on job opportunities. They have information services for dependents."

"Oh, that's great. I'll be called a dependent once we get married. I have a customer coming over to my desk. Call me at work after you talk to someone in personnel. Leave a message if you must."

Crowley realized from Anna Maria's comment and tone that he was becoming out of touch with her life back on Long Island. He needed to get his orders and their wedding plans back on track.

"I will. Love you, babe!"

"Love you too, darling. Talk soon."

Crowley looked around. "The Commando is right where I left it parked, under the tarp."

With a practiced set of moves, he peeled off the motorcycle cover, rolled it up, and tied it to the back of the seat. Next, he swung his leg over the bike and kick started it into life as he sat down and rode away. He was off to meet Tom Newman for lunch in Panama City.

He thought, *I want to send Anna Maria flowers if the assignment is good news. If not, well, let's not dwell on that just yet.*

The wind in his face cleared his head, and he noticed how quiet the area was. When he arrived downtown, he parked his bike in the business district near Tom's car and started walking down a street lined with shops when it hit him. Twelve hours earlier he had been "let slip" like one of "the dogs of war" in Shakespeare's Julius Caesar. Next thing he knew, they plucked him out of "a rumble in the jungle" and flew him to "Pleasant Valley Sunday."

He was passing what appeared to be a giant Trailways bus with shiny chrome trim parked along the sidewalk when he realized from a sign it was the diner he was looking for. As he climbed some cement stairs to the front entrance, he spotted his buddy through a picture window, sitting in the back of the restaurant. His buddy's head was three or four inches above everyone else, and the bandages caught his eye.

Crowley sat down in the booth opposite Newman and picked up the menu. "So, how's your shoulder? You look wrapped up pretty good."

"The doc told me since I am not an officer, I want big stitches to leave a large scar on my arm to impress the ladies. I replied, 'Whatever floats your boat!' It's still sore when I move it and a constant reminder that we were fighting guerillas, not the refugees you were worried about."

"That reminds me, Tom. Did you hear any screams when the napalm dropped?"

"What are you talking about?"

"When I called in the bombardment to suppress the sniper fire coming from the jungle."

"I was distracted by my gunshot wound, if you recall. Besides, you went by the book using an effective response to the threat. I didn't question it then, nor do I now."

"Look, Tom, I'm feeling guilty because America should have offered charity instead of guns blazing. Put yourself in their sandals. They were on tenuous ground trying to scratch out a living by growing food to eat. Why, even the few armed guerillas we captured said they fought for rations—their only pay. We forced them into a primeval situation—kill or starve."

Newman laughed. "I'm glad our country doesn't treat us like that."

Crowley replied, "Yeah, right. Last time I checked, my income was seventy-five dollars a month less than federal minimum wage."

"We have benefits, too," Newman reminded Crowley.

"Oh, so living in a barracks and eating mess hall food is a benefit? We sacrifice rather than serve in the military. The pay is abysmal, the housing is substandard, and when you think it can't get any worse, they send you to a war zone."

"Well, the Republicans are in now. Maybe things will change."

"They forced my father out into the reserves during the Eisenhower administration. No matter who is in, if a defense bill has money to pay for new civilian jobs building bombs, they are all over it to keep their voters happy. Bring up legislation to increase soldier or veteran benefits and you would think they were talking about a dole for people who don't deserve it."

"Like I said, my arm is all right, but you are giving me a headache with all this political talk. I thought this lunch would help us decompress."

Newman nodded at the crowd passing outside the diner. "Folks seem focused on the good life, oblivious to the multiple wars going on."

"Yep. My town shunned or ignored my buddies when they returned from serving in Vietnam. They couldn't understand how people acted like the war did not exist," replied Crowley.

"Hey man, Americans watch TV and see the raw footage on the evening news and still they don't get it. Do they think they are watching a John Wayne movie?" questioned Newman.

Crowley considered Newman's observation for a moment and replied, "What I find missing in America is a shared sense of sacrifice."

"How do you come to that conclusion?" asked Newman.

"Well Tom, we missed out on the Civil War and World War Two. After Pearl Harbor, nobody had to clarify what we were fighting for and during the insurrection, they had President Lincoln to explain everything."

"I think you're onto something, Jake. What impact Vietnam and the other surrogate conflicts have on Americans is the misguided notion that the soldiers serving their country are causing the problem."

"Tom, we are being thrown into insurgencies, where it is hard to distinguish friend from foe. Then we are told to use our training in overwhelming force tactics to perform what are called policing actions. So, we catch the usual suspects and light them up with napalm."

"Jake! Don't let that napalm drop get you down. It was a standard procedure, but it threw me for a loop too when they brought up collateral damage."

"Do you recall when I told you I took part in some protests while I was in college?"

Newman nodded. "Why do you keep bringing up school? You complained about not learning anything there."

Crowley smiled. "I got worked up about the war. I wrote a paper about how Vietnam fought for their autonomy over a thousand years. They fought the Chinese and then the French and now it's us. Why would they give up now?"

"Have you noticed everybody we serve with comes from the wrong side of town? That song we sang by Creedence Clearwater Revival is no lie."

"Tom, I don't know what category you can put me in. The Republicans funnel my taxes to the rich. Democrats dole it out to the poor. I guess I am the monkey in the middle."

“Hey, just find a way out of these interdictions against peasant guerillas. With no battle lines or uniforms, they stash their weapons, pick up a shovel, and blend in. The brass says we got them all, but I doubt it. I’m sure the Salvadorians are already back at it,” said Newman.

Crowley noticed the other diners looking at them as Newman spoke.

He stood up and said, “I bet you all think we are talking about somebody else. Well, we are not. It’s you!”

Suddenly, the crowd turned to their meals and their own conversations.

Tom observed, “Folks have learned to cancel out what they don’t want to hear or see from flipping channels on TV. Man, they all switched you off. You’re canceled!”

The server came over to their table and they ordered lunch. When she left to fill their order, they changed topics to the women in their lives.

6

The Widow Maker

0800 Hours, 3 January 1969 Soviet Air Defense Forces PVO Headquarters, Moscow

The PVO Strany commander stood at his large ornate French provincial desk with his adjutant by his side as they pored over papers and diagrams spread out before them. The PVO Strany Command provided all the air defense capabilities for the motherland.

The general turned to his adjutant with a serious look. "Major, today I must do my deal with the Devil. I couldn't sleep last night. When I closed my eyes, a hairy, foul-smelling demon with a goat's head and barbed tail materialized to do my bidding. He startled me into waking up each time he appeared. Is this an omen?"

The adjutant replied, "Are you pulling my leg again, sir?"

"No, this project is a demon keeping me up at night with fitful dreams! Failure is not an option."

"Rest assured, Comrade General. I received a message this morning from the First Directorate informing me they were sending Gurkin to help. My liaison said you and he were comrades during the Great Patriotic War."

"That creature? Those beady eyes and black mustache of the Russian are no lie. He bragged to me about his idyllic childhood spent tearing the wings off butterflies to watch them die."

Abramovich chuckled. "Well, I tried to get the GRU to help, but this effort may require wet work. Not our military intelligence organization's brand of espionage. Based on your description, he sounds like the perfect man for the task."

The PVO Strany Commander heard a forceful knock, followed by a loud creak as an aide opened the massive double doors of his office.

"General Petrenko, your visitor is on his way up."

"Don't just stand there. Usher him to my office the second he arrives!"

The aide turned on his heels and hurried out to find the KGB general.

Petrenko dismissed Major Abramovich and walked over to a decorative wall mirror to check his appearance.

He scowled as he thought, *I dressed this morning in my best tunic with the Hero of the Soviet Union pinned to my chest. Why then is this Gurkin fellow making me so nervous?*

The PVO Strany officer's dress uniform with its gold braid and sky-blue cloth complemented his hair and eyes. Petrenko's light features were not unusual for a man of Ukrainian descent. His thick blond hair, with not a hint of gray, belied his age. He grew up in Kamianets-Podilskyi, a city founded by Viking traders near the Black Sea. The commander continued to study the latest reports on the airworthiness of the new fighter interceptor while waiting for his KGB liaison to arrive.

General Vladimir Gurkin arrived at 0900 hours in his dark blue dress uniform with gold braid and the shoulder boards of a KGB general. His dark features and black mustache gave him a sinister look in keeping with his calling. Before he could sit down in the waiting room, Petrenko's aide rushed over and escorted him to his commander's office.

The PVO Strany General shook hands with his KGB guest and turned to his assistant. "Please bring out the silver samovar tea service and place it on the side table."

Petrenko thought, *What do I have in common with this knuckle-dragger? Maybe I can recall some people we both knew during the war.*

As the trip down memory lane progressed, familiarity grew, and they started using each other's patronymic names.

"Well, Vladimir Nikolayevich, do you know what happened to our old friend Boris Romanoff? He disappeared from our regiment after the Berlin bombing mission, and I never saw him again."

"He died during the war."

"How did you learn of his death?"

"I was the regimental political officer if you recall. It was my job to find and apprehend him. They executed him for desertion of duty."

The aide, outfitted in spotless dress blues, came over and lit the warming pot at the base of the samovar. He stood up, bowed, and left the room, walking backward and closing the high double doors behind him. Petrenko noted the aide's body language, and it reminded him not to turn his back on Gurkin.

He sighed, poured tea, and said, "I invited you here today to discuss the future deployment of the MiG-25 fighter. This aircraft will be our primary defense against the Valkyrie supersonic bomber the Americans have under development."

"How were you able to produce this capability ahead of the American threat?"

Petrenko took a sip of the strong tea and replied, "The Mikoyan Gurevich Design Bureau paired two turbine engines powerful enough to propel a rocket and, as an afterthought, they added wings."

"*Da*, Alexander Mikhailovich, I have read reports of brute force being employed to test this aircraft as well. Isn't this the plane pilots have dubbed 'The Widow Maker?'"

Petrenko slammed down his cup of tea and thought, *The arrogance of this man who made his rank in the rear echelon from shooting deserters and dissidents!*

Gurkin added, "I learned it would fall out of the sky like a brick. I remember this epithet because our sources confirmed the Americans call their F100 Super Sabre by the same name, but in English, of course."

Petrenko's light skin color turned red, and he felt hot under his collar as he tried to calm himself.

Petrenko replied, "Well, Comrade General, have you ever confronted someone or something trying to kill you?"

"I did my share of killing during the Great Patriotic War."

"Yes, I heard about that. The veterans on this project faced down the cannons of the German Me-109 fighters head-on. Now they defy the danger of flying experimental aircraft."

"Comrade, I am only relaying to you what your own men have named it."

The pilot general bit his lip and replied to Gurkin's insulting remarks. "It is true, the experimental version had stabilization problems while at top speed, and those issues had to be resolved with incremental aerodynamic changes to the fuselage."

"Oh, the accidents were only during experimentation. That explains it," Gurkin demurred.

"The production version cruises at Mach 3. It required a lot of trial-and-error testing to reach this speed," added Petrenko.

"What do you mean by trial-and-error testing?" asked Gurkin.

"For example, two massive Tumansky R-15B-300 afterburning turbojets power the jet to 3,467 kilometers per hour at high altitude. We reached 3,952 KMPH during a test flight; however, the turbines overheated. The pilot had to eject while trying to land the plane."

"The performance is remarkable, comrade. What is the size of the aircraft?" said Gurkin.

"The fuselage is large, and we dedicated every nook and cranny to fuel tanks, given the thirst of the turbine engines. We packed the powerful avionics into its nose, resulting in the interceptor weighing 40,000 kilograms loaded. It stands over seven meters high with a wingspan of fifteen meters and a length of over twenty-two meters. Like a giant rocket, its major strength is traveling in a straight trajectory to its target, but its capabilities include a surveillance and bombing role as well."

"Sounds like the Swiss Army knife I always wanted as a child. What is the mission statement?" asked Gurkin.

"The MiG-25's mission is strategic bomber intercept and air reconnaissance. If you want to research what the allies have on this plane, the NATO code names for fighters begin with an F, so the Mikoyan Gurevich 25 became codename FOXBAT."

"*Da*, Alexander Mikhailovich, I know about this naming assignment. Our sources in NATO say from the limited information they have available, the MiG-25 must be a maneuverable fighter because of the large surface areas of its wings."

"That may be what they believe, but it is only an illusion created by the need to provide enough lift for the extra heavy fuselage of nickel steel alloy," replied Petrenko.

"Intelligence reports indicate the wing design caused so much concern that the U.S. delayed the F-15 project to improve its maneuverability. With all the angst going on over the MiG-25, an agent reported to me that a NATO general quipped the code name should have been Bat Out of Hell instead of FOXBAT," reported Gurkin.

Petrenko laughed, not catching the slight concerning the bat's origin. "That man is right! Our interceptor should give the Valkyrie crews much concern when their aircraft comes online. In addition, it is being developed to provide high-speed nuclear bomb delivery capability to counter their B58 Hustler!"

Petrenko changed his voice to a conspiratorial tone. "Vladimir, the PVO Strany commander, Marshal Pavel Batitsky, ordered the MiG-25 into service in the Warsaw Pact without NATO's knowledge. I have chosen the *Deutsche Demokratische Republik* for the first deployment, because of their loyalty to the world communist movement.

"*Da*, the Polish and Czech governments provide low levels of cooperation. Meanwhile, the DDR in East Germany has been very supportive of our common goals," replied Gurkin.

"Our experience with the West has made us believe it is easier to get forgiveness than permission. This is where you come in," said Petrenko.

Gurkin chuckled and said, "Tell me more about your strategy. It sounds like the beginnings of a new philosophy!"

Petrenko thought about how to best describe to Gurkin the existential threat posed by the American strategic bomber. The breakthrough technology of its delta wing allowed the aircraft to surf its own shock wave for increased lift and speed. Leaked intelligence on the fantastic performance envelope of the experimental airplane was sending shock waves through the entire Soviet air defense forces. Paranoia, resulting from the leaks, was keeping his staff up at night, toiling on their fighter-interceptor response.

"The Goriki factory is manufacturing enough production models to equip a full regiment in six months. Once we have the fighters built, we have another half year to train the pilots and manufacture spare parts before we send them to the forward area."

"That sounds like a very ambitious plan," replied Gurkin.

"It is, and I need to deploy the MiG25s to East Germany without NATO being able to track and detect the operation," said Petrenko.

"Why all the secrecy? Won't American reconnaissance aircraft discover the fighter planes, anyway, sitting on the ground once you deliver them?" asked Gurkin.

"We must surprise the American reconnaissance aircraft with our MiG-25 interceptors to shoot them down. Large bomb-hardened hangers are being built to hide the fighters when they are not airborne. To win this shell game, we are relying on you to figure out what NATO knows regarding our air defense forces and how best to sneak this new jet into position."

Petrenko believed the KGB must use their counter-intelligence apparatus to verify the effectiveness of Western spying.

"Comrade, this deployment of the MiG-25 is of top priority given its importance as both a strategic and tactical weapon against the West," said Petrenko.

Gurkin said, "Yes, and don't underestimate the psychological impact of shooting down their spy planes. The KGB has issued a bounty notice to our agents as an incentive to kidnap American National Security Agency personnel in Berlin."

"Are you telling me you have the information I need?"

"Not yet, I am afraid."

"Does that mean that you have changed your methods and success is imminent?"

"The abduction attempts, along with some failed 'Honey Trap' operations, have resulted in the NSA ordering their military operatives into civilian attire and cover assignments while on duty in West Berlin."

"So, who am I dealing with here? Are your people a bunch of clowns?"

Gurkin responded. "Don't forget that illegal agents risk their lives every day in the field. This move out of uniform made it impossible to identify the American spies in the NATO sector, which is the ideal place to abduct them with secret tunnels to nearby East Berlin."

The KGB general added, "Alexander, the U.S. Air Force Security Service airmen stationed in the West German BRD still wear their uniforms, including their distinctive unit insignia on their battle dress. They are the NSA operatives to whom I was referring."

"Then go grab them before they hide as well!"

"I have to delve further and get back to you."

"How quickly?"

"This problem will require a trip to meet with my Stasi contacts. I'm not sure they have the resources needed. We must engage their agents as our proxy to mask our involvement and leverage off their assets already deployed in the West. Give me two weeks."

The game was on and Petrenko needed to keep the pressure on General Gurkin to help figure out how to sneak a flight of seven-meter-high aircraft under NATO's nose.

7

A New Religion

0200 Hours Eastern, 3 January 1969 Fort Meade, Maryland

Bart Sedgwick and his staff burned the midnight oil trying to get a software fix installed before the quality assurance team arrived for their regular shift at 8 AM.

Sedgwick called out, "Okay, Jesse, start the stream of test data, and let's find out how the patch holds up."

"Bart, the program is working! We are displaying four times as many plots as before and no errors."

"Okay, keep on increasing the volume to test for a crash like they got at the field site."

He took a break and walked to his office to check for messages. Dressed in a white lab coat with a buttoned-down short-sleeved oxford shirt, tan khaki slacks, and penny loafers, Sedgwick arrived at his cubicle and sat down at his desk. He pulled a pen from the pocket protector and made notes on the latest maintenance reports for the first RUBICON prototype system. His lab coat served as his surplice and protected the rest of his vestments when he needed to get his hands dirty by opening a computer cabinet to troubleshoot a hardware glitch. His garb designated him as one of the high priests of the catacombs under the NSA building.

Surrounded by gleaming, flashing, and humming monoliths, he offered them a sacrifice of long hours of coding and held vigils to test the prognostications they emanated.

The RUBICON system was his baby. He had nursed it through development and now his responsibilities included proving the system could report foreign intelligence events from the field in real time. To accomplish this feat, Sedgwick supervised the installation in West Germany of his codename RUBICON prototype system and subsequent training of the surveillance and warning center airmen assigned to his project. He insisted the airmen assigned to the project have their titles changed to 'data system analyst' to differentiate them from the old school 'traffic analyst' moniker.

After the on-site training sessions were completed, Sedgwick returned to Fort Meade to learn that the field prototype suffered a disk drive failure, which required a technician to fly with replacement parts to Frankfurt-Main to perform the repair. Then a software crash occurred. The field personnel produced a memory dump on magnetic tape, which they couriered to his office. Once the dump arrived, Sedgwick's team of engineers evaluated a printout of the dump to determine the root cause of the crash. Intercept data from the time of the glitch accompanied the dump, so the engineers at Fort Meade could simulate input activity to duplicate the problem. The computer scientists were now using the intercepted data to test the software patch.

Sedgwick's alarm buzzed, reminding him to make an overseas call. He hit the button on the clock and dialed the number.

"Greenspan speaking."

"Hello, Master Sergeant Greenspan. How is RUBICON holding up?"

"Well, sir, as you know, we suffered a hardware failure recently and lost some intercept data, but everything seems to work now."

Sedgwick thought, *The hardware fix and the software bug patch are the least of my worries. Getting Greenspan and his men to be effective intelligence analysts is the major problem.*

"So, where do we stand?"

"My analysts are focusing on enemy broadcast station identification and tracking data collection. We are measuring their productivity based on how many radars they have identified and how much of the identified station tracking they forward to you at NSA via magnetic tape for further analysis."

Sedgwick thought, *Our RUBICON development team appreciated receiving target codeword SWAMP tracking data, which they used to run high volume tests on his lab system, but the whole point of the project is to have the analysis done in the field in real-time.*

He replied, "I know broadcast station identification is one item on the test protocol, and it is good to hear it is being accomplished. What are the next steps?"

"We are reverse engineering the Soviet Air Defense Forces order of battle by using the identified radar station locations and signal traffic patterns."

Sedgwick considered the reply. *Now we are getting somewhere. This type of information is invaluable in times of war to locate and destroy the enemy's air defense organization, opening the air routes needed by our bombers. The field analysts are still not using the system's ability to identify threats before they turn into attacks. Why are they dragging their feet?*

"So, when will you report tracking information to your surveillance and warning center?"

"The air order of battle needs more work. We are concerned about having the operation fail while we report real-time activity."

That confirmed the problem. Nobody liked change and, to top it off, the analysts in the field lacked confidence in RUBICON. He recalled the day the system booted up in the S&W center in West Germany. He felt like the Star Trek character, Captain Kirk, flying the shuttlecraft into a cave full of troglodytes. The initial hurdle was communication. He talked digitally, and the troglodytes conversed in analog. At first, they stayed away and appeared preoccupied with their manual operation.

After a while, they could not resist their analytical nature, and the airmen started pointing and comparing the manual and new automated processing methods. They began using RUBICON to increase their efficiency in sending identified tracking data to the NSA, but no real-time reporting from the intercept site occurred. Sedgwick wrote letters encouraging the field unit to act on what they intercepted and if they made mistakes, that's okay because they are testing a prototype system. His encouragement fell on deaf ears.

"Thank you for your report, Master Sergeant. I will let you know as soon as we have the software patch ready for you." Then he reached out to hang up the phone.

Sedgwick looked up from his frustrating conversation to see a young woman in a Class A Air Force uniform drop off a Teletype message in his in-basket.

She said, "I think this is the news you've been waiting for."

The WAF jogged away to resume her monitoring of high-priority communications traffic before Sedgwick could reply.

Sedgwick jumped up and called out after her. "Thanks! I owe you one!"

He reached over to his inbox and pulled out the Teletype message. The message header showed it was from Special Operations Command and the addressee was to him. This got his full attention as he sat back in his swivel chair and read the body of the letter.

We have considered your request for temporary assignment of one of our combat controllers to the U.S. Air Force Security Service Command. A journeyman candidate has been located who we believe meets your specifications. He has completed his Level 5 training and passed all reviews of performance and required tests. Hs records show he exceeded your qualifications for Air Force entrance exam scores. He is presently leading his first special operation and, barring injuries, we expect to make him available in a week or less. The nominee we have available is an E-3 with two years of service.

He is the only qualified combat controller available. Our staffing is tight and the demand for our specialists keeps growing.

If you want to pass on this offer, please contact us so that we can put him back on the pending operations duty roster.

Sedgwick sat up in his chair and thought it over. "That Air Force air traffic controller led me down this rabbit hole. After his briefing on new computerized tracking displays, I told him the problems I encountered getting RUBICON operational.

He recalled the air traffic controller's reply. "Mr. Sedgwick, what you need is a combat controller to get the project in gear. They have a get the job done attitude!"

Sedgwick pursued the idea all the way to Special Operations, and they had just given him a take-it-or-leave-it offer. He asked for a candidate with at least an E-6 rank and a minimum of six years' service to provide feedback to the development team, based on multiple years of combat experience. What he was being offered was a green airman with only one mission under his belt and the caveat "barring any injuries."

He threw up his hands and said, "Man! How dangerous is this combat controller job, anyway? If I am getting a version of John Wayne, maybe it would be better to get a trained but inexperienced airman not set in his ways."

Sedgwick mulled over the problem. "Well, an airman with two years' service means I have enough time left in his current enlistment to send him to the Air Force signals intelligence school for instruction before I put him in the field. Passing that training program successfully will confirm his fitness for the analytical job. The instructors could speed things up by cutting short his Phase I studies because most of it overlaps with his combat controller education involving communications procedures, air traffic control regulations, and practices."

He accepted the candidate and jotted a note to speak to the commandant of the Air Force Security Service School. He made notes to request a tutor to cover only the Phase I lessons needed to get him up to speed, given his previous training. Phase II encompassed the TOP SECRET heavy lifting covering crypto analysis, reporting criteria and methods used to determine enemy command hierarchy. For that instruction, the RUBICON chief wanted the airman to attend only the classes required to be effective in performing the field trials for his project. He typed a letter to Special Operations accepting the candidate conditional on the airman, volunteering to take the additional instruction at the NSA signals intelligence school conducted by the Air Force. Sedgwick pulled the message out of his typewriter and handed it over to the comm center for transmission. Then he dashed off a letter to his liaison at the technical school, outlining the specific instruction requirements and asking for resources to achieve the course of study in six to eight months instead of the usual full year.

A smile came to Sedgwick's face. "I wonder how the codebreakers in Germany will react to a combat controller in their midst! Maybe he can get them to believe in RUBICON."

8

What Did I Do to Deserve This?

When Crowley arrived at headquarters, Chief Master Sergeant Stevens informed him that the commander wanted to see him right away. Orders usually trickled down the chain of command. What was so important that military protocol was being bypassed?

He entered the major's office, came to attention, and saluted. "Airman First Class Crowley reporting as ordered!"

Young replied, "At ease and take a seat. I want to congratulate you on the success of the Honduras mission. The way you handled the cargo plane crash reflected your initiative and drive. Your staggered landing idea is now standard procedure. The officers involved reported good things about you and Newman. Is there any feedback you want to give me on what transpired?"

He knew Young was a flight officer. "Sir, the pilots were very cooperative."

The commander laughed. "Airman, your decorum will allow you to go far in this man's Air Force."

Young's demeanor turned serious. "Do you have any issues you want to discuss?"

This question caught him off guard. He responded with a look of surprise and said, "No, sir, not that I know of, other than my lack of a permanent assignment. Why do you ask?"

Young, who was sitting on his desk, reached back to his blotter, picked up a message, and handed it over.

"Colonel Franklin requests your presence ASAP. "

He read the note. No details.

"Sir, the last time I dealt with the Office of Special Investigation was when I got my secret clearance for this job. I haven't heard from them since."

"Well, Airman, they want you right away. Let me know if you need my assistance."

The combat controller saluted, turned, and marched through the administration area and out the front door of the unit's command center. He remembered the OSI building was a Quonset hut at the north end of the field in the middle of nowhere. As he walked in that direction, he wondered what this all meant. They performed his background check before the start of his sixteen months training. He concluded the reason for this meeting was a higher clearance required for his next assignment. After fifteen minutes, he saw his destination off in the distance.

"The Air Force labels everything with either a sign or a stencil, yet this building only has a number painted on the arch above the door," he noted.

Crowley entered the hut and approached a civilian secretary seated at her desk in front of an inner hall. He noticed the doorway behind her was dark as he made eye contact.

"Major Young ordered me to report here immediately. Here is the request."

"Please take a seat in the waiting area and I will check."

She took the message from him and walked into the back office.

"Airman Crowley is here to see you."

The colonel looked up from a pile of papers on his desk. "Angie, give me a few minutes to go over his file again. I'll buzz you when I'm ready."

The officer wore civilian clothes, but the lifer haircut gave him away as career Air Force.

Franklin thought, *It's not every day that the OSI gets a request to clear a Special Forces operative for assignment to the intelligence community. Something big must be up. I better handle this one myself.*

The secretary emerged from the dark office. "He will let me know when he is ready for you."

Franklin opened the candidate's file and started scanning his notes. There he found his notes on the derivation of the surname Crowley. It was of either English or Gaelic origins and could have meant "son of the warrior" or "woods of crows."

He reminded himself, "Those birds are raptors and mate for life, indicating loyalty. The soldier is a volunteer and a descendant of a World War Two veteran."

This was a hobby of Franklin's. It helped him remember the candidates, and often, the derivation suited the soldiers he investigated.

Next in the file, he flipped through Crowley's current security clearance, which included just about his entire life history. He was born on June 17th, 1947, in Brook General Hospital, Fort Sam Houston, Texas. He is the son of a decorated World War II vet named Jacob Cowley, Sr. His father led a combat intelligence squad during The Battle of the Bulge. This unit was part of the U.S. Army Signal Corps and comprised German-speaking soldiers who infiltrated behind enemy lines and located command posts with their radio equipment. Patton converted them into MPs ordered to advance in jeeps with the spearhead forces to direct traffic and guard captured prisoners with the benefit of their language skills.

To disrupt the rapid advancement of Patton's Third Army, Lt. Colonel Skorzeny's dreaded SS commandos infiltrated behind the lines posing as American military police. This plan, called "Operation Greif," included disrupting allied troop movements by changing road signs and misdirecting convoys. The hysteria that ensued caused Eisenhower to be locked up in his headquarters for his own security. The spies all affected accents they learned while visiting relatives in the U.S.

Warrant Officer Crowley picked up on this when his team encountered another group of MPs at a crossroads. Sensing something was not right, he tricked them into speaking German by switching to that language while he was asking them what unit they were with. A firefight ensued, with both sides sporting automatic weapons. He got the drop on them and his men shot all the spies as they tried to escape. Germans getting caught in U.S. uniforms incurred a hanging as spies. The warrant officer used this proven technique to kill or capture five more SS commando units. He received a battlefield commission by order of General Omar Bradley and an assignment to lead Patton's personal bodyguard. Patton enjoyed having this type of soldier around him. "Mustang" officers like Crowley had a bravado that was infectious. He retired as a major after commanding Strategic Air Command atom bomb security at several bases in the Midwest.

Colonel Franklin mused, "Apparently, Special Operations work runs in the family. This kind of tradition is not uncommon. I went overboard on the background check, but the father's military history reads like a novel! What fascinated me is the son is following in his father's footsteps without even knowing it."

Next, he scanned the file of the "son of the warrior."

"This kid is a real scrapper. His record includes arrests for street racing and fights on beaches over surfing territory. Special Operations people love this stuff in a recruit's background. It shows the candidate has daring and aggressive tendencies. The service, recruiting him, wanted a quieter type of airman, one who did not bring any attention to himself."

Franklin snorted, "You can't have your cake and eat it too."

The colonel noted that Jake Crowley's entrance test scores were all 95s, which was the highest possible for electronic, mechanical, math, and general categories. That meant his skills were higher than the standard tests covered. Crowley got into the air traffic controller school at Keesler AFB, where he volunteered for the Special Operations command.

Franklin read on. "His ratings from his military training are outstanding. His entrance exams show he has what it takes to be a cryptologist. If he passes the interview, I'll order a top-secret background check with the signals intelligence code word designation to confirm there are no skeletons in the airman's closet."

Franklin buzzed his secretary on the intercom. "Angie, I'm ready to see him."

As Crowley entered the dark office, he could make out a man in civilian clothes seated with a bright light shining behind his head. This made it difficult to distinguish the colonel's features, and he thought it seemed dramatic for an investigation agency that did routine background checks. He walked up to the desk and saluted. The colonel returned the salute and ordered him to take a seat.

"A high-level authority at the NSA requested raising your security clearance level for a top secret codeword assignment. Your aptitude tests have shown you possess a required skill set and your combat controller qualifications also contributed to your selection. As soon as we complete your background investigation, you can be read into the program on a need-to-know basis. They plan to reassign you as detached service to the NSA. Of course, you should know by now that the NSA stands for 'No Such Agency.' You are not to confirm nor deny your involvement. You will use a cover story to mask your actions. If anyone asks, reply that you must go through more background checks. It's no lie and doesn't give away anything. Are you following all this, soldier?"

"No sir. I was expecting this meeting to discuss my first permanent assignment as a combat controller. Instead, I am hearing about more training and temporary duty," replied Crowley.

"Like I said, your current security status prevents me from giving you further information. Let's get that behind us."

"Yes, sir."

Franklin could tell by his curt replies that the NSA job did not impress Crowley. He tried to put the airman on the defensive to elicit his cooperation.

"By the way, your last background investigation turned up arrests for speeding, fist fights, and being involved in altercations at war protests. The agency takes a dim view on candidates with arrest records."

This got his Irish up. He replied, "Sir, that was all fun and no harm to anyone. Same goes for the demonstrations I took part in at college. They were peaceful and only the cops became disorderly. As you know, I didn't ask for TOP-SECRET clearance and what smells like a desk job. I would rather start a permanent assignment in the specialty they trained me for."

The reply knocked Franklin's head back a little, but he remained perfectly composed and replied, "OSI rarely digs into dismissed arrest records, but if you do not cooperate on this interview, you could lose your clearance, making you ineligible for future special ops. They could always use more people serving up grub in the mess hall or greasing aircraft engines."

Franklin saw his comment had gotten Crowley's attention, and he picked up some papers as he continued, "I'll level with you. I can see they dropped the charges, or else we would not be having this interview. But as far as a desk job, the command you are being considered for operates a plethora of dangerous operations. By the end of this, though, you might wish you were at a desk. So, want to get started?"

Crowley smirked and they went on with the interview. Once it was completed, he thought of one last question. "Sir, how does this affect my standing as a combat controller?"

"When you complete this mission, you will have a choice of assignments in your primary specialty."

I've heard that promise before, Crowley thought.

He stood and saluted the officer before walking out of the office into the bright sunlight of the warm Florida morning. As he headed back to the headquarters building, questions kept popping into his head.

"I'm still in the dark about the NSA. Maybe I should go to the public library and check it out. This TOP-SECRET business will not help me explain things to Anna Maria. She might get the impression I am stalling. I need something positive to tell her."

His Norton 750 Commando started up on the first kick and he was off to Panama City. The motorcycle rode like the Grand Prix Road racing bike they based it on. He arrived at the library and got a parking spot right by the main entrance. Crowley walked over to the card catalog and began looking for the National Security Agency. Finding nothing, he headed over to the reference desk. There he saw a man in his forties, also with a short haircut. He hesitated for a minute, thinking about whether the librarian might be in the military, working a side job, or retired.

He thought, *Man, this is like asking for condoms at the drugstore.*

"Excuse me, sir. I am searching for information on the National Security Agency."

The man stared at him for an uncomfortably long time. Then he grabbed a piece of paper and wrote something down and handed it as he glanced up.

The librarian said, "An article in the New York Times a while back about the National Security Agency caught my eye. I did some research in the government documents area of the reference room and found that official manual. Check it out. It may answer your questions."

Crowley took the note and thanked the librarian as he turned around and walked to the reference room as nonchalantly as possible. He soon located the government publications arranged by date of issue.

Slowly working his way down the aisle, he found what he wanted.

"There it is, the United States Government Organization Manual dated 1955."

He opened the soft cover manual to the index and found the page for the National Security Agency.

Crowley mused, "The organization's description is very vague. It mentions a mandate to secure communications from foreign spying, to improve U.S. signals technology, and to support special intelligence operations."

Crowley considered what he read. Why did this agency want him? He felt the job was unrelated to his Air Force training. Feeling paranoid, He decided not to borrow the book. He didn't want to leave a record. He put the manual back on the shelf and headed out the door. It was getting dark, and the mosquitoes were flying out from their daytime hideouts, looking for prey. He mounted his motorcycle, fired it up, and rode back to his quarters to think things over.

As he cruised along, questions kept popping into his mind. *Why is life so complicated for me? I have witnessed the American dream come true at home. My friends' fathers worked in unions or owned small businesses. Their jobs allowed them to finance well-maintained homes and late-model cars, and their kids attended good public schools. They didn't need college diplomas. Success came from hard work and quick wits.*

Crowley mused, "First I discovered that Air Force officers must have a four-year degree to apply for OCS. The more I investigated, the more I found out government organizations and large companies required degrees for leadership positions. The opportunities that remained included store owners, contractors, and union jobs. Even the self-employed needed credibility for financing, where an applicable diploma and a profitable plan were part of the approval process."

He considered his own experiences. "My mentors at the bike shop got bankrolled by their father, who owned a dry-cleaning service, and one brother had a degree. Am I just fooling myself about being able to make it as a business owner?"

As he pulled up to his dormitory, Crowley decided he would wait to call Anna Maria until he knew more about this NSA assignment.

9

A Change in Command

0730 Hours, 20 January 1969

Crowley listened to news about today's presidential inaugural ceremonies on his transistor radio as he walked into the headquarters building of the 1st Special Operations Wing at Hurlburt Field, Florida. He noticed conservative comments coming from the newscaster and wondered if the pendulum was swinging away from the liberalism of the sixties. At his desk, he found another note from the commander. He knocked on the door. The officer looked up from writing a report and waved him into his office.

He saluted, and the major returned the salute as he said, "Good morning, Airman Crowley. I got a message from the OSI. Colonel Franklin requested your presence again. Is there anything I should know about?"

"No, sir. They have just been asking for additional information for my clearance."

Young stared at Crowley with a skeptical look on his face. "The appointment is at 1400 hours today. Do you need any coverage on your duty roster to make that meeting?"

"No, sir. My schedule is clear. Is that all, sir?"

"That will be all."

As Crowley walked through the administration building, he noticed the administration clerks were all looking at him and making comments to each other. Suddenly, Stevens popped up in front of him again.

The first sergeant smiled, "OSI and FBI agents have been crawling all over headquarters asking about you. They said that you are being considered for work on national security matters at the highest level. Of course, we gave you your dues, and they seemed satisfied. So, Airman Crowley, are you volunteering to be a secret agent for the CIA?"

"Sarge, I swore off being a volunteer during combat controller school. The Office of Special Investigation said I will be told nothing until I receive my higher clearance. The meeting this afternoon might shed further light on the subject."

Stevens nodded in agreement and replied, "Keep me informed."

At 1330 hours, he headed over to the OSI building again. The weather was cool for a change, and he had time to note the Quonset hut as it came into view. Painted with a shade of gray that hid dust and dirt while reflecting the hot Florida sun, the hut looked neat and temporary all at the same time. The off-white roof added to the utilitarian appearance of the building. It could have posed as a farm shed out in the country and nobody would have been the wiser.

He was wearing his class B winter blues, composed of a long-sleeved shirt, matching slacks, dark blue tie, and web belt. The epaulets on his shoulders, the creases down the center of the pockets, and the form-fitting tailoring gave a professional impression. The red beret caused heads to nod in recognition whenever he passed by a group of fellow soldiers. When he walked into the building, the secretary took him directly into Franklin's office. Crowley noticed the room was not dimly lit this time. He hoped the light would shine on what was happening. Crowley saluted, and the colonel pointed to a chair. The officer appeared pleased with himself. He took out a pack of Marlboro cigarettes and offered the airman one. He declined, and the colonel lit one for himself.

"Well, soldier, you passed your background check. You are heading to Goodfellow AFB in five days for a cram course in cryptology at the 6940th Air Force Security Wing. Orders are being cut for you to fly to the base at Lackland and from there you will take a Greyhound bus to the City of San Angelo, Texas. Once you have completed the training program, an assignment to a unit in Europe is waiting for you.

"Signals Intelligence? Why do they need me? Isn't this a waste of my combat controller skills?"

The colonel sat back in his chair and took a drag on his cigarette.

"Do you remember as a kid how you could reverse engineer anything and figure out how it worked? People we interviewed for your clearance brought this up."

"I was a small-engine mechanic and would often refer to the manual. How does this relate to codebreaking?"

"That's an example of the aptitude required for a successful cryptologist. Your Air Force entrance exams all point to the fact that you have a unique set of skills needed for this special project."

Crowley wanted to request permission to speak freely, but he stifled that idea, having learned such a stunt only worked in the movies. The military didn't condone free speech.

"Sir, with all due respect, I was hoping to hear about my first permanent assignment as a combat controller, and I am planning to get married. Colonel Franklin, can you throw me a bone? Is there any good news?"

"You will deploy to a unit in West Germany when you successfully complete your training."

A foreboding feeling came over Crowley, making him cringe. Franklin noticed Crowley's change in demeanor.

"One reason for your selection was your background, having lived there before and being fluent in the language."

"I don't have wonderful memories of living there."

"Well, a lot has changed by now. They're even calling it the *Wunder Economy* or some such thing. And you mentioned having a fiancé. What woman wouldn't jump at the chance to live in Europe?"

"She has strong family ties to New York. This will be a complete surprise. Is there anything else you can tell me?"

"The NSA plans to divulge details of your mission during your training. The Security Service is an elite organization and only the top five percent of U. S. Air Force personnel are qualified for this duty. You should consider your selection an honor."

Crowley was dreaming about being stationed in Florida with Anna Maria, but he knew initial assignments for first-term airmen often involved a remote tour with no dependents allowed. He considered how his fiancé would react to the prospect of traveling overseas. At least Germany meant they could be together, and the alternative might be a war zone. He wondered if Major Young would recommend taking this offer.

"Well, sir, I hope the NSA knows what they are doing. I must speak to my commander before I decide. Is there anything else you can tell me about the mission?"

"Goodfellow AFB is a full-scale operation with all the facilities you need to keep in shape and progress in your combat controller independent study courses. I think you are up to the task. Because of this assignment's priority, I issued orders to ship all your belongings and vehicles to Goodfellow at government expense. Since you have passed skill level five requirements, you are eligible for sergeant's rank. I will approve your promotion without you having to wait for the usual time-in-grade required and performance review. Of course, this is all contingent on your cooperation."

He nodded in resignation and responded, "Do you have anything else for me, sir?"

The colonel handed him some papers. "Report to Major Young and give him a copy of these orders. If you decide to volunteer, then take the signed paperwork to the administration building for transfer processing."

He stood up and saluted.

Franklin returned the salute and said, "Good luck, Airman Crowley."

"Thank you, sir."

He about-faced and exited the office. As he walked back to 1st Special Operations Headquarters, Crowley reconsidered the signals intelligence analyst job description and decided he needed to take another look at the government manuals in the Panama City library before he left for Texas. Maybe he could find out more about the No Such Agency.

When he reached headquarters, he presented the paperwork and requested a meeting. Later in the afternoon, a charge-of-quarters runner came to him with a message to report.

"Major Young, I feel like I'm making a mistake. I was counting on a posting to this base as a combat controller and this special duty comes along and ruins all my plans!"

The major replied, "First off, let me remind you as a combat controller, your assignment means that is where your mail goes. You will travel on missions for the rest of your enlistment."

"Sir, I need permission to have my wife accompany me. That means having a permanent assignment."

"Airman Crowley, I got married many years before I cross-trained to Special Operations and am glad I did. Being newlyweds and separated all the time does not mix.

"Well, sir, I wasn't thinking of that, but I see your point."

"I questioned your new orders because volunteers are not lining up at the door to take your place. Our unit has assignments to fill, and you will be hard to replace."

"Yes, sir. That is why I did not commit to this until I spoke to you."

"If you decline the offer, you may still receive orders for this special assignment even though you did not volunteer. Secret agencies have a trump card that gives them priority in what they ask for. They are already clamoring for your arrival date."

"Sir, if you don't mind me asking, what is that trump card?"

"All they must do is wave their hand and call it 'a matter of national security.'"

"Colonel Franklin used that term and told me everything about this was hush-hush."

"See what I mean?"

"Sir, are you recommending I volunteer?"

"If you decline, they can order you to take it anyway and drop the perks because of your lack of cooperation. As President Theodore Roosevelt once said, 'When you got them by the balls, their hearts and minds will follow.' Whether or not you like it, they have you for the rest of your enlistment. No doubts about that."

"Airman Crowley, I heard you're a surfer and motorcycle racer. Is that right?"

"Street racing. Nothing organized."

"I see. My sport is whitewater kayaking. I often find myself at the edge of a river with a strong current. I have no choice but to head downstream and try to stay upright."

"Sir, that sounds like the advice my boss at the bike shop gave me. He said, 'Jake, everyone who walks through the front door thinks they are my employer.' Any sense of freedom in business is illusionary."

Major Young replied, "If you are successful on this assignment, it could mean a lot for your military career, should you decide to reenlist. You will show flexibility, wide-ranging aptitude, and a willingness to get the job done. Why, you've already been fast-tracked to the first rung of the NCO ladder—if you volunteer. Non-Commissioned-Officer rank comes with some perks."

"Then I guess it is time to sign the paperwork, sir."

Crowley later pondered, *It all happened so quickly, and decisions were being forced on me. I have to admit this TOP-SECRET cloak and dagger stuff has an exciting allure. At last, I will be up against the Russians instead of their surrogates. I was hoping to live in Europe someday and playing hard-to-get got me my third stripe.*

After the meeting, Crowley looked for his buddy Tom and found him in the dayroom.

Newman said, "What is the hubbub about? I heard the FBI was questioning everybody about you. They even interviewed me. Sounds important. Stevens says they want to turn you into a James Bond."

"It involves more schooling in Texas and an assignment to Germany for at least a year."

"Just do me a favor, Jake. If you don't take it, then recommend me."

"I thought you loved combat controller duties."

"Jake, the training is exciting, but being wounded on my first mission was not fun. The gunshot wound made my girlfriend realize how dangerous the job is. She is also not happy about my being away all the time on missions. She wants me home more."

"Major Young said I should consider that too, since I am getting married."

"I can't transfer out because combat controllers are in high demand in times of war. Jake, you have a reprieve. Your first year of marriage in Europe. You lucky dog—take it or I will!"

Crowley promised his fiancé a call to update her on his status. He waited for his orders to Goodfellow Air Base to arrive before looking for a phone booth.

"Anna Maria, I am glad I got you at home. How are you?"

"I was waiting for your call. What can you tell me?"

"There is bad news and good news. The bad news is I have another training program for six months."

"You said there is good news too?"

"Yes. After the school, there is a tour of duty in West Germany. It may last until the end of my enlistment. We can get married while I am on leave and travel to Germany to live. What do you think?"

"Jake, who else has an opportunity to travel like that? Nobody I know!"

"You know somebody who traveled to Germany?"

"Who?"

"Me."

"I celebrated my first birthday on a ship off the coast of Ireland and lived with my parents in Wiesbaden until the Berlin Crisis forced all dependents to evacuate the country. I recall a gray and foreboding time there. We had to leave my father behind to help deal with the Berlin Crisis."

"Your mother showed me your baby pictures now that I think of it. The snapshots were all black and white, with bombed-out buildings in the background. Your recollection must come from those depressing scenes."

"I'm not so sure. I was so young."

Anna Maria said, "They rebuilt West Germany like new. I saw color pictures in *Look Magazine* in an article about how the Marshall Plan helped Europe rebuild."

"So, does this sound good to you?"

"One long honeymoon in Europe and the opportunity to sightsee and absorb the culture? Yes! Now we can start planning our wedding!"

At 1400 hours on 22 January 1969, KGB General Gurkin sat down at his desk in Moscow First Directorate building. He noticed the pile of papers in his inbox had grown. Among the stack was an envelope with a red ink SECRET stamped on it.

"I wonder what this message is about. Seems like all my trouble comes in plain manila envelopes."

He fished it out of the tray and opened the end with a gold letter opener. When he blew open the cut side, a single sheet printed by a Teletype on light brown roll paper appeared.

"Must be important. The headers at the top of the page showed a very limited group of recipients."

Since Gurkin was the commanding general of the KGB First Directorate, he held responsibility for foreign intelligence-gathering activities. His organization's identifier was on the addressee list.

The report read, "A very reliable source reported the assignment of a combat controller to the Air Force Signals Intelligence School in Texas. Processing of the orders was being given top priority and required high-level authorization because of the money spent on his prior training. Therefore, the agent believes this special deployment requires serious attention."

Gurkin concluded, "Sergeant Crowley's assignment appears to be related to General Petrenko's Air Defense PVO security concerns. The American's air traffic controller skills are required. We must prevent him from aiding NATO signals intelligence efforts."

10

Goodfellow AFB

1700 Hours, 21 July 1969. Secure Training Room

Senior Master Sergeant Samuelson stood at attention beside his lectern.

"I would like to start this history lesson by explaining the job of the U.S. Air Force Security Service.

With his pointer, he directed the class to a pennant hung on the wall behind him.

"The insignia of our service comprises four sections, which represent the USAFSS mission. Moving in a clockwise direction, the quadrants symbolize a lightning bolt for the unit's electronic warfare role, a sword and shield are emblematic of our part in the national defense, a wing reveals our airborne component, and finally, a globe shows our worldwide presence. Below the crest is a banner with our motto, 'Freedom Through Vigilance.'"

He turned back to face the class for further emphasis.

"I am bringing this symbolic mission statement to your attention because I do not want you to forget that we support three modes of operation: ground, mobile, and airborne. The flying component includes reconnaissance, also known as ferret missions. The USAFSS personnel on these flights volunteered to serve in the Air Force and volunteered a second time for this hazardous flight duty. Their job is to capture our adversaries' air defense signals and radar station emissions, which we cannot intercept with our ground and mobile stations because of their signal characteristics. They accomplish this task by flying unarmed close to our foe's borders."

Samuelson came out from behind the lectern and pointed to his class,

"I want you boys to understand that what I say here stays here. I could go back and review our involvement with the Cuban Missile Crisis and follow that with the attacks on the Navy intelligence ships Liberty and Pueblo. These incidents all involved the Air Force Security Service and our brothers in the Naval Security Group. I should also bring up that the first American soldier to die in combat in Vietnam was an Army Security Agency radio intercept analyst. Instead, I am going to focus on events that have affected the ferret flights of both USAFSS and the NSG. We will review these events because this activity is a major part of our mission. Your job will either be on the ferret mission analyzing intercepts or monitoring the flight from ground or mobile stations for any hostile actions by the enemy."

Samuelson scratched his head and said, "I bet you think I am about to tell you some ancient history I dug up to scare you, or maybe you believe we are living in an age of detente. Well, just this past April, two MiG-21 fighters shot down a Navy Lockheed EC-121 recon aircraft in the Sea of Japan. They were 90 nautical miles off the coast of North Korea, flying an electronic surveillance mission while serving as an early warning platform. You may ask yourself, why would North Korea do that? Folks don't realize we are in a state of war with North Korea. The Korean War never ended. We are still operating under a ceasefire. So, any time they get a burr up their arse, watch out!"

Samuelson walked over to the blackboard and listed the attacks.

"Besides the EC-121 attack by the North Koreans, there have been thirty-one incidents, of which thirteen were shoot-downs of the USAFSS and NSG mission aircraft since the Cold War started."

When he finished writing the list, it covered two blackboards in date order. Samuelson turned to face the class.

"I will not rehash each incident today. Your assignment is to research them all in the classified library room. The unit test will include questions concerning these recon missions, so make sure you take down the complete list and study the material."

Samuelson added, "I am focusing on a shoot down that occurred on 2nd September 1958. The following information is not for discussion outside of this secure area. I have in front of me the TOP SECRET codeword EIDER analysis of this incident, which was issued on 10th September 1958 and titled Shooting Down of U.S. C-130 Transport Aircraft in The Trans Caucasus. Parts of the report contain paraphrased statements for security reasons. It starts off with a summary."

Samuelson read the introduction aloud. "So far, you may think that this wording is rather cold and matter of fact in describing the death of 17 unarmed soldiers. You will see from the following description that the reporter kept his objectivity, but clarified this was an attack carried out without regard for the standards of civilized international practice."

Next, the technical instructor read the account and paused for emphasis between the statements of intercepted voice traffic from the Soviet pilots and ground control.

Samuelson returned to his lectern. "It finishes with a brief paragraph promising to include a flight map as an additional appendix. Appendix A contains the map."

He laid his hands on the lectern and looked up at the class.

"So, what have we learned? At first, the communists denied any knowledge of the flight. When pressed further, they issued propaganda stating the C-130 crashed of its own accord. The story confirmed they had located the wreckage and recovered the remains of six crew members, which they returned to U.S. custody on September 24th, 1958. The Russians would not acknowledge the survival of the eleven other airmen who were USAFSS personnel. Then HUMINT or Human Intelligence Sources, if you haven't heard that term yet, uncovered an article in the January 1961 edition of *Ogonyok,* a Soviet magazine, which reported that their border patrol captured eleven Americans in the town of Yerevan after they parachuted from the aircraft. The authorities denied this report as being contrary to the facts. Further analysis has resulted in opinions ranging from the crash being caused by pilot error to the suspicion that the Soviets placed that beacon to snare one of our reconnaissance flights and shoot it down to find out how successful our missions are. If you believe the magazine's account is accurate, then they may have interrogated our security service crew members and want to keep what they learned secret. We know the Soviets were getting pissed off about the overflights by U.S. reconnaissance aircraft like the U2 photo recon jets. It took the Soviet PVO *Strany* Air Defense twenty-one months to muster the firepower to shoot down the CIA U-2 operation flown by Francis Gary Powers in 1960."

He paused before asking, "Do you boys have questions?"

Hands shot up. The instructor pointed to the first row.

"Why didn't we just show the Soviets were lying by exposing the intercept traffic?"

"That would have compromised our sources, forcing the USSR to change their air defense systems, resulting in us losing access to that intelligence in the future," replied the sergeant.

As the instructor answered further questions about the mission and if its parameters included venturing into Soviet airspace, Crowley considered what he had just heard.

Colonel Franklin, back at Hurlburt Field, had been right. The USAFSS performed white knuckle operations as he had been told, and the codebreakers flew in harm's way unarmed, thought Crowley.

He had misjudged the importance of the unit's mission. This realization came while learning how to analyze intercepted signals and decide if the intelligence warranted a 'CRITIC' message to the situation room in the White House. The intelligence could go all the way to the top and had to be correct.

Samuelson entertained another question.

"How did the Soviet pilots respond to their orders on the voice traffic?"

"You can all read it for yourselves," he replied. "I will post it on the bulletin board after this class. I would just characterize their words as reflecting excitement and enthusiasm for the opportunity to shoot down an unarmed cargo plane."

11

Get Me To The Church On Time

The relief showed on Crowley's face as he neared the end of his cryptologic training. The wedding plans depended on his completion of the course on schedule. He placed a pay phone call to his fiancé, and she gave him an update on how things were going. With him being away, Anna Maria and her parents made all the arrangements for a Long Island Italian American affair, with church nuptials, followed by a lavish reception. Her father was successful in what he called "the rag business." He managed an exclusive men's clothing store on Fifth Avenue in New York City. She was his only daughter, and he would spare no expense to give her a "proper sendoff."

"Hi darling. How are the plans going?"

"The invitations are all in the mail, and we picked up your tuxedo today. I booked the honeymoon in Barbados. Now it's your turn to report. Did you get your leave approved and your airplane reservations for your trip home?"

"Everything is waiting for my successful completion of the course. Personnel says they can cut my travel orders the day I pass the last exam. I booked my flight for the wedding."

After the honeymoon, Crowley knows he must rent an apartment in Germany before requesting permission to bring his bride overseas. As the time passed, and his training program ended, the assignment became a major issue.

He ran to the nearest phone booth after passing his final exam. "Honey, I report to the 6910th Security Group in Darmstadt, West Germany, APO 09175. I have it in writing."

Anna Maria said, "Finally, I can tell everyone we are going to Germany!"

Because he was a sergeant with less than four years of service, they did not receive any command sponsorship for family travel and living expenses.

"You have the paperwork for my Mustang. Put our vehicles in the classified section of *Newsday* as soon as possible."

Anna Maria and Jake planned to sell their autos and ship Crowley's Norton Commando motorcycle to Germany. They agreed to pool their money from used car sales to buy a new German sedan in Darmstadt. She had to book a charter flight from JFK to Frankfurt once he rented an apartment and bought a car. They would be on their own, living in a German apartment building paid for by his ration and housing allowance, which meant a tight budget. Air Force base department stores called base exchanges and food commissaries would help ease some of the culture shock and the expense of living overseas.

By the time 15 October 1969 rolled around, Crowley had met three airmen who joined him in his workout sessions while attending the communications intelligence school at San Angelo. After six months of physical and mental training at the school, he and his buddies had bonded and were always together talking about their judo throws, marksmanship scores and motorcycle adventures. Their classmates kidded them about riding on their iron horses in Crowley's posse.

Darryl Jackson was a handsome young track star who graduated from Howard University with an engineering diploma. Chad Frazer was a surfer from California who got a physics degree from USC before he joined up. And finally, Sam Rothman was a weightlifter from Brooklyn,

New York, where he had majored in mathematics at Queens College. They all learned self-defense and sidearms marksmanship from Crowley, who bartered for help with his math and science problems in school.

Crowley's friends approached him about going to a church social in town to hear a folk-rock band before he shipped out. He missed spending time at nightclubs on Long Island, and this social club administered by the local Baptist church looked harmless enough. His buddies agreed to meet around 2000 hours.

As he pulled up and parked his Norton, he heard music emanating from the coffee house. "That sounds like the Crosby, Stills and Nash hit *Judy Blue Eyes.*"

The building was near the center of town, which used to be where the well-heeled citizens of San Angelo lived. A large Victorian with an open floor plan, the local church staff decided it would be a perfect outreach center for young people to meet, listen to folk-rock music, and discuss the meaning of life.

Crowley walked into the living room wearing his stovepipe jeans, black wellington boots, turtleneck gray shirt and a tan bush jacket. As he surveyed the room, Crowley noticed the room contained worn out donated furniture, and the girls appeared too young to be out this late. The cowboys, however, looked like they were all drinking age. He spotted one guy in a dark corner periodically sipping a drink from a flask in his vest pocket.

Crowley recalled the comment one of the technical instructors made about some of the locals, *Pregnant at fourteen, married at fifteen and divorced by seventeen.*

Couples dressed in western clothes sat in the far corner, listening to the phonograph. The girls noticed him walk in and made comments about how attractive he looked in front of their dates. Crowley found his buddies hanging out by the refreshment stand and headed over to greet them.

"Hey, man! Where is my brewski?"

Frazer cringed and put his finger up to his lips. "Keep it down, Jake! The church ladies will be after us if we talk about drinking."

"Yeah, I would think so with all these fifteen-year-old girls running around with their lemonades. What do you expect to be doing here with this young crowd?" said Crowley.

"This is the best we can do in this town, unless you want to hang out in a bar with a bunch of forty-year-old drunk divorces. I know it's not the 'Action House' on Long Island, but we are trying to make the best of it," said Chad.

The music became more upbeat, and couples got up to dance. Crowley grabbed a coke at the refreshment counter and returned to his posse.

"Well, I'm only two more days in the wake-up cycle before I head back to the Big Apple," said Crowley.

"Yeah, where you will get married, end of story," kidded Frazer.

"No, not the end of the story, just the beginning. Next, my bride and I are off to Germany for one long honeymoon," replied Crowley.

"Well, don't rub it in. Most airman must re-up to get an assignment in Europe. How did you swing that?" asked Frazer.

Crowley smiled. "Like everything else around here, it's classified."

A blond-haired girl walked up to Crowley and asked if he wanted to dance. The invitation took him aback. In New York, the guys made the first move. To be polite, he accepted and joined her on the dance floor. She was a fair young thing with a slim figure, which she showed off in her tight western outfit.

As they swayed to the music, another girl with black hair pulled up in a bouffant style, worked her way through the crowd and called out over the music, "Mind if I join you?"

They both nodded and continued dancing. Two more women joined the group. Crowley kept circling as he danced to be polite and not turn his back on any of them. While dancing around, he noticed the girls' dates were still sitting in the corner, fuming. He wondered if the women were trying to make their boyfriends jealous. One guy yelled, "Cool it! You don't want it to get out that we started trouble in the church coffee house!"

The DJ took a break, and he used this opportunity to introduce the girls to his posse. As Crowley had guessed, the girls were all in high school. It surprised him how comfortable they seemed around older men. Before he knew it, he heard Frazer arranging a date with the blond girl who invited him to dance.

He pulled Frazer aside, "Hey man. How many times do you have to visit this place before they put you on a pedophile list?"

"Relax Jake. She is seventeen. Almost legal. Anyway, I am a short timer too. I won't be here long enough to get into any trouble," said Frazer.

"That's what they all say. The instructors who live here say the jailbait around here play it fast and loose, cowboy. You better watch yourself," cautioned Crowley.

Frazer smiled. "Yeah, I know. No bareback riding for me."

At 2300 hours, the place dimmed the lights, and he said his goodbyes and walked outside to his motorcycle. Standing in front of his bike were three locals from the corner crowd in the coffee house. The biggest one stood in the middle and had over a hundred pounds and eight inches in height on him. The guys on the air base called them "goat ropers."

He thought, *If this guy ropes goats for a living, they must be mighty big ones to build him up like that.*

The man held an ax handle in his right hand. His cohort stood on either side of him and each of them was around six feet tall and well built. It was hard for him to tell their exact height with their cowboy hats on. They grasped baseball bats.

The man in the center stepped forward. "Hippy, what are y'all doing messing with our women?"

Crowley could not help laughing over being called a hippy, given his short hair and military status. This made the leader angrier.

"Look, I don't want any trouble. I'm leaving the coffee house alone and impressed by the southern hospitality of the ladies who attended the dance," said Crowley.

"What are you saying, hippy? You think our women are easy?" shouted the big one.

Crowley thought, *I know they are easy. I don't have to imagine it.*

"No, man, you got it all wrong. I was just impressed by how friendly you all are until now," said Crowley as he raised his palms, hoping to deescalate the situation.

"Until now? You think you can make fun of me to my face and get away with it? We're going to have to teach you a lesson, hippy!"

Crowley saw this guy wasn't taking no for an answer. He turned so that his left side faced his opponent, offering as small a target as possible, planted his feet and raised his arms.

The big one swung his ax handle down at Crowley as he lunged forward. The combat controller side-stepped to the right, making the cowboy fall forward as the wooden shaft missed a solid target. As the cowboy fell, the airman kicked up his left leg and caught his opponent square in the nuts with his steel-toed boot. The man groaned as his weapon hit the pavement and bounced away from his body. Crowley scooped the stick off the ground and clobbered the big guy in the back of the head, knocking him out. The two remaining cowboys looked at each other in amazement.

The smaller one said, "Let's get him together."

They attacked him from opposite sides, like wild dogs after prey. He fended off their bats with his captured ax handle. They kept circling while darting in and out to take swings at him.

The posse emerged from the coffee house to see their buddy struggling with the two cowboys. A police siren blared as a sand-colored cruiser pulled up to the curb. The attackers saw the deputy pulling up, dropped their bats, and ran off down an adjacent street. Crowley put down the axe handle and stood his ground. The peace officer got out of his patrol car, stuck his baton in its holster, and strode up to where the big cowboy lay spread out on the sidewalk. He bent down, felt for a pulse, and noticed the blood dripping out of the unconscious man's ears. He returned to his patrol car and called for an ambulance. After the call, he walked back with a citation pad and approached Crowley.

"Well, boy, is that your ax handle on the ground?"

Crowley frowned. "Watch it, deputy. I am Sergeant Crowley to you."

"Is that your axe handle, soldier?" said the patrolman.

"The axe handle belongs to the cowboy laying on the ground. I disarmed him when he attacked me with two of his buddies. The other two men fled when you arrived. Their weapons are on the ground over there. Crowley pointed at the bats and then turned to see a crowd gathering on the sidewalk.

The posse approached the deputy and told him they were eyewitnesses. They described the two men with bats who got away. Locals said they also witnessed the fight. They claimed Crowley had an unfair advantage.

One local pointed at Crowley and said, "I saw that man assault the cowboy like a cold-blooded, professional killer." Frazer heard enough. He ran over to a phone booth to call base security.

The ambulance arrived with two EMTs. They scraped the injured man off the sidewalk with a stretcher and took him away. An Air Force patrol car pulled up, and an argument ensued between the deputy and military police over jurisdiction. What mattered to Crowley was getting back to Long Island on time. Another headache came over him.

It was 1000 hours the next day and Colonel Chambers, commander of the 6940th Security Training Wing, sat at his desk with a cigar in his mouth as he talked to Mayor Carson on the telephone.

"Colonel, what were you thinking sending a trained killer into my town?" said Carson.

Chambers recalled how many times reports came to him about airmen getting beaten up at bars with no intervention from the sheriff.

"The way I heard it from our security police, three locals with bats jumped my unarmed airman while he was leaving a church social. And then your people had the nerve to say my soldier did not fight fairly! If your law enforcement can't prevent further attacks on my men, we might also decide to take matters into our own hands!"

Mayor Carson said, "Are you threatening me, Chambers?"

"We don't make threats, only promises," he replied before hanging up.

Next to him sat Captain Alan Davenport, upset over the mayor's call. He was in the habit of not making waves. A lawyer by training, he was trying to complete his required wartime service as painlessly as possible.

He said, "Keeping up excellent relations with San Angelo is a key part of protecting the interests of this base."

"Oh, come off it, captain," growled Chambers. "The town needs our patronage to keep their economy going. It is about time they started respecting our soldiers by helping them stay out of harm's way. Sergeant Crowley did us a favor when he rope-a-doped those men. The locals will now think twice before they try to beat up on our guys. I wish I had a service medal I could give him. Let's get this over with."

"Colonel Chambers, you cannot just sweep this under the rug. We must investigate or face charges of dereliction of duty. The mayor will insist on it."

The commander nodded as he buzzed his aide and ordered Sergeant Crowley to report.

Crowley entered the office, stood at attention, and saluted. "Sir, Sergeant Crowley reporting as directed."

Colonel Chambers replied, "At ease, sergeant."

He stared forward at the officers while standing in parade rest.

Chambers said, "I hear you had some trouble in town last night, sergeant. They say you put one guy in the hospital and chased off two others. Where did you learn to fight?"

Crowley replied, "Sir, my father taught me after a bully in high school beat me up. After my second fight with the bully, the word got around, and nobody bothered me after that."

"You mean until yesterday," said Chambers.

Crowley replied, "Well, sir, I guess the news hadn't spread this far."

Chambers laughed and looked at Captain Davenport, who did not look amused.

Davenport said, "An investigation could lead to assault charges requiring a court martial."

Crowley replied, "Sir, this fight was in self-defense and there were plenty of witnesses."

Davenport countered, "Sergeant, that will have to be verified by an official inquiry."

Chambers added, "I see no grounds for a trial. We just want you to lie low while the Security Police investigate the incident. I am asking you to do me a favor in this matter and stay on the base while we address the problem. Can you do that for me?"

"Sir, I have leave scheduled to start in a few days. I am going home to get married."

Davenport said, "You should have thought of that first. A civilian is in the hospital."

"I tried, but my combat training kicked in when I found myself outnumbered."

Davenport replied, "This case may take time to sort out in town. You're restricted to the base until we conclude the investigation."

"Then this might affect my mission deployment to Germany as well."

The colonel cut in. "I am aware of the priority of your assignment, and I can use that to help move things along on our end. The sheriff may be the problem. You have already given your testimony to the Security Police. Stay close to your dormitory for now in case we need you."

"Yes, sir."

They dismissed Crowley and then waited for him to leave before speaking.

"Davenport, I see from Crowley's insignia that he is a combat controller. I have served with them on many air operations. They are a credit to the Air Force. I want the full court press on resolving this issue."

"Sir, there will be no problem in executing the military review quickly. It is the civilian side I'm worried about."

"Then call in the FBI if you must, captain. With all the security clearance investigations we do, don't you have any connections? The NSA is already hounding me to get him over to the 6010th ASAP!"

"Yes, I have contacts, but what do I tell them?"

"Inform them of our need for a further background check on the airman, given this incident occurred just before his assignment to this high-level mission in West Germany. Then refer the FBI agent to the sheriff for their side of the story. I think having the feds show up at their door will get things moving."

At 0900 hours the next day, Special Agent Dan Fortier arrived in San Angelo and parked his unmarked black Ford sedan in a parking space in front of the sheriff's office. He stepped out of the car dressed in a dark gray suit, white button-down shirt and conservative tie. His hair cut was a short flat top, and he wore mirror-coated aviators.

A deputy stuck his head out the door and yelled. "Move your vehicle or you will get a ticket! Can't you read the 'no parking' sign?"

He flashed his badge and said, "I am Special Agent Fortier on official business. Where is Sheriff Clark?"

The G-man stared through his mirror-coated sunglasses and waited for his reply.

Deputy Sikes held open the door and pointed inside. "He just arrived. The staff inside can help you locate him."

Fortier entered the lobby and walked up to the desk sergeant. "Special Agent Fortier, FBI. I am here to see Sheriff Clark regarding an investigation involving Jacob Cowley, Jr."

The desk sergeant rang an extension and spoke in a low tone with his back to the agent. He hung up the phone and turned to face Fortier.

"He is available. Deputy Sikes, please escort Agent Fortier to Sheriff Clark's office."

Clark was waiting at his door and shook hands as they met. The sheriff looked like he had just come from a rodeo. A silver star hung from his leather vest.

"What do I owe this honor? We've not had a bank robbery for a while," said Clark.

The FBI man walked into the office and took a seat. As he sat down, he pulled a notebook from inside his suit jacket, a pen from his shirt pocket, and aimed his mirror sunglasses at the sheriff.

"I am investigating an incident involving Sergeant Jacob Cowley, Jr. I understand an altercation occurred."

"Well, Special Agent Fortier, isn't a brawl outside your jurisdiction?"

Fortier replied, "Sergeant Crowley has an appointment with a matter of national security. I am here to see that he gets to that appointment on time, if you catch my drift."

Clark nodded. "I thought something was suspicious when we first interviewed the injured cowboy, and he would not press charges. He did not want to stay in town. He even waived any further treatment he needed for his head wound."

Fortier said, "Why were the Air Force Security Police not advised of this recent development? I called them yesterday evening before I headed up from our office in Austin and they were not aware of this change of status in the case."

The sheriff replied, "This is a strange incident. The cowboy's Midwest accent surprised us when we interviewed him, and we did some tracing on his name and ID. He was not the local boy he made himself out to be. His identity papers were from Illinois."

"So, what did you find out?"

"His driver's license came up bogus and when we returned to the hospital to talk to him, he had already released himself and disappeared."

The sheriff added, "Like I said, this is a strange case. Why wouldn't the injured cowboy press charges? Is that airman the assassin our town folk think he is?"

"Sergeant Crowley is a Special Forces operative expert in hand-to-hand combat. I am surprised he used restraint when three armed men attacked him at the same time. His service record shows he already has a few notches on his gun. What is the status of your investigation?"

"It's still open. We are trying to find the other assailants."

"Well, I advise you to close it or the FBI and OSI will crawl all over this town, making it appear that you can't do your job. From the priority placed on this situation, it appears Crowley works for the top of the food chain. I am pissed over the fact you did not keep the Air Force informed. I drove all night because of this communication failure. If you do not settle this, I will turn this nothing into a big old something."

"No reason to get all upset. This was just a jurisdictional dispute between our office and the military police. I'll see what I can do."

"Well, I am stuck here until you do your job, and my patience with your territorial issues is running thin. I'll be back in an hour and expect to receive the proper documents closing the case on Crowley. Oh, and another thing. I want all the information you have on that fake cowboy and his friends. It sounds to me like you may have tripped over illegal foreign agents. Trust me. You do not want to be tagged as the reason for his escape."

Special Agent Fortier put his pen back in his shirt pocket and stormed out of the room to find a decent breakfast while he waited.

At 0900 hours the next day, Crowley sat reading at his desk in the dorms when a runner walked through the open door to his room and handed him a note to report to 6940th Headquarters. Crowley took the note and got up to follow the charge of quarters runner back to the headquarters building, where he was directed to the unit commander's office.

Crowley entered and came to attention as he saluted.

Chambers smiled and returned the salute as he said, "Son, you are free to go. The sheriff got the charges dismissed based on additional evidence."

He sighed and remembered he was overdue back home. Crowley knew he would-be dead-on-arrival if he did not make the next plane out of San Angelo.

"Sir, would it be okay if I left now? I have my orders and my duffle bag with me, and my buddies are waiting outside to take me to the airport."

"It looks like you came prepared, and I will not stand in your way. There is a matter concerning the cowboy you put into the hospital. The FBI has reasons to believe he is a Soviet agent. I can send you more on that later if anything develops. Very curious why he would start a fight with you. Anyway, give my congratulations to your family and your bride-to-be."

"I will, sir, and thank you for all your help in getting this trouble cleared up. I did not know how I could explain this to my fiancé."

They saluted, and Crowley hurried out with his duffle bag over his shoulder to a car parked with the engine running. Frazer, Jackson, and Newman were there, eager to hear the results of the meeting in the colonel's office. His thoughts returned to getting to the church on time. His headache eased as they pulled away in the car.

12

New York, New York!
It's a Hell of a Town

21 October 1969. Levittown, Long Island

Crowley woke up to find himself in the attic bedroom with his little brother standing by his bed, staring at him.

"Jake, where are your uniforms? Are you still in the Air Force?"

"My travel orders require me to not wear my uniform."

Tim persisted, "You told me soldiers are allowed to wear civvies on duty in third-world countries, where people are mad at the U.S. Is America now a third world country?"

Out of the mouths of babes, come words of wisdom, Crowley thought.

His orders prevented him from inciting anti-war demonstrations while traveling in his dress uniform.

"Tim, I did such a good job during training that they rewarded me by allowing me to travel home in comfortable causal clothes."

"My friends think your red beret is cool."

"We can have your friends over to the house so they can see me in my combat fatigues and red beret."

Tim's eyes brightened, and he turned and ran out of the room.

Crowley sat up in bed and stretched. "Only five more days and I will share a bedroom with Anna Maria!"

Crowley got up early and showered and shaved. The military routine had adjusted his biological clock, and he could no longer sleep late. His father was having breakfast before he left for work. He joined him at the kitchen table after performing the ritual of preparing a bowl of cereal with milk and sugar. The senior Crowley looked up from his newspaper and smiled.

"Good morning, Dad."

"Morning, Son. What do you have planned for today?"

"Oh, I am seeing a few of my buddies and then over to Anna Maria's house in the evening. Did you have anything in mind?"

"No, but your high school buddy Frank Bishop called a few weeks ago asking when you would be home on leave. He told me he was attending Columbia University and had joined the Air Force ROTC. He wanted to talk to you about it and invite you to a meeting."

"Did he leave a current phone number?"

His father pointed to the kitchen bulletin board and said, "It's on that blue piece of paper pinned up at the top."

He stood up, pulled the pin to release the note, and read it. His high school buddy was not on his list of people to visit while on leave. He thought Bishop was rooming at school and wouldn't be in the neighborhood. Crowley put the message in his shirt pocket and decided to give Frank a call after 0900 hours. He turned to see his father get up and refill his coffee cup from the pot on the counter before turning to face his son.

"Jake, your mother, and I could not be happier knowing you will serve in West Germany with Anna Maria at your side. We hoped for a tour in the states for you and your bride. You know we all love her, and we only want the best for you both."

"Thanks, Dad. We would rather be close to home too, but we're making do. It may be a once-in-a-lifetime opportunity to live in Europe.

Crowley's father hugged his son and returned to the kitchen table to finish his coffee.

At 0900 hours, he called Bishop before heading out to visit his friends at the motorcycle and bike shops, where he had worked before joining the Air Force. Frank picked up on the second ring and it was like they had just talked yesterday. He sang "Surfer Girl" into the phone in his best falsetto, since he was always ragging on Crowley about surfing and Crowley returned the favor with his rendition of the greaser doo-wop hit "Tears on my Pillow."

They both laughed, and then Crowley asked, "So, how's college going?"

"Well, it's been kind of rough. The cost of attending Columbia is quite high and my parents are having a hard time making ends meet. I joined Air Force ROTC in my junior year to help with the expenses. The reserve training pays for tuition plus an allowance, which helps with the other fees."

"That's great! My dad said you had left a message that you had some questions for me concerning the Air Force."

"Well, more of a favor than a question, Jake. With all the war protesters on campus, ROTC cadets are having a hard time, especially when we wear our cadet uniforms to meetings."

"Yeah, I know what you mean. They ordered me to fly home in civilian clothes so as not to cause a riot."

"At Columbia, it's more difficult because they hold Air Force ROTC at Manhattan College. This means we are targets when traveling between the campuses. The SDS protestors read the bulletin boards and then line up at meetings or parade drills. I have already gotten one uniform ruined from eggs thrown at me."

"Who are the SDS?

"The Students for a Democratic Society. They're the agitators who lead the demonstrations. Columbia is full of them."

"So, what can I do about that?"

"A lot of the cadets are getting discouraged and believe they made a mistake in joining ROTC. I was hoping you might have some time to speak at our regular meeting about your experience as a combat controller. I think it will be a real morale booster for me and my fellow reserve officer candidates. There is a meeting this week."

"How do I get there? Anna Maria and I sold our cars to pool the money to buy a new one in Europe."

Frank thought a minute and said, "I can go to my parents in Levittown, change into my uniform at home, and then borrow my father's car to pick you up before heading into Manhattan. This way, I do not have to run the gauntlet between campuses!"

Jake chuckled and replied, "I will do it if you make it this week. As you know, I'm getting married on the twenty-sixth and then we're off to Barbados for our honeymoon."

"Lucky you!" Frank said. "No problem. The cadets and officers want to hear about your experiences."

"Call me back with the details today. I want to check with Anna Maria on her plans. One more thing. Hand-to-hand combat always gets an audience's attention. Can you have gym mats on the stage and volunteers wearing fatigues? The other armed forces tend to stereotype our service as a bunch of desk jockeys and mechanics. I want to show we are a fighting force."

Frank agreed, and they ended the call.

A crisp fall day in New York's Central Park found Herb scuffling through the leaves to an appointment with a particular park bench. He wore a tie-dyed tee shirt, jeans, and high-top black sneakers. His light brown hair hid the bows of his glasses.

He turned his back to Selma and said, "Help me with my backpack. It's cutting into my shoulders."

She sighed, "Why stop here? You will have to sit on the ground to take the weight off that backpack so that I can adjust it. What are you up to, anyway? You look nervous."

Herb spotted the green bench he had been looking for. "Quick, over here!" as he hurried head-first to sit down and claim it.

She raised her voice. "I said, what's going on? You're not doing something for the SDS, are you? My parents warned me about you!"

Herb ignored her questions and took his time to find what he wanted. He pulled out a book, sat back down, and repeated his survey of the park grounds. Herb did not see anyone in his line of sight. In one fluid motion, he reached under the bench seat and pulled off a packet taped to the bottom of the seat.

Selma asked, "What's that?" as he deposited it in his book, which he closed and stuffed into his backpack.

Herb said, "I'm going to my dorm room. Are you coming, or are you afraid of what your parents might think?"

He did not wait for an answer as he slipped on the straps and bent over to support the weight of the books. Still looking around, he trudged off toward the Columbia campus. Selma followed close behind with her head down.

She muttered to herself, "Look at him stooped over with that ridiculous sack on his back! People will think I'm with Quasimodo."

When they reached his dorm room, he sat on his cot and slid the straps off, allowing the sack to drop onto the bedspread.

She said, "Let me rub your shoulders. You know you like it."

He gave a little sigh and Selma dropped on Herb, forcing him back. His head hit the wall behind his bed.

"Ouch, stop that! I have something important to do?"

"What could be more important than this?"

"You'll see!"

He undid the two straps fastening the cover flap of the pack and pulled out the book with the packet inside. He got up, walked over to his desk, used his penknife to open it, and slid out the crumpled typewritten paper. The typing comprised random patterns of five-character groups down the page double-spaced. He grabbed a codebook from his backpack and translated the encoded sheet. She stared with rapt attention.

Herb concentrated on the decryption process and waited until he finished the last group before he rose to look at the decoded version of the text.

She grabbed the paper and began reading it out loud. "The ROTC scheduled a meeting at Manhattan College. It is important that you organize a war protest in front of the Smith Auditorium, where it's taking place."

He snatched the sheet from her and held his left hand over her mouth as he whispered. "I told you the walls have ears! Read in silence."

She did as he said and handed it back. He paced the room, reading his instructions. His controller tasked him with inciting a riot, focusing harm on the target named Crowley. It was important to injure the target severely during the riot to prevent him from carrying out his next assignment. Herb sat at his desk, thinking about the mission, memorizing the names, locations, and description of the target. He tore up the message into small pieces and burned the paper in a large ashtray.

Selma asked, "What is this all about? Don't you just do protests like the other SDS members?"

"I am a member of the Weatherman Underground now. We organize action to bring down the government.," said Herb.

Selma stared at him as she sat down on his lap and kissed.

He returned the kiss and thought, *Wow, she digs it! This sure was a lot more fun than getting my skull split open trying to help the garment workers at my parents' sweat shop at Chelsea Piers. This time I will be the one splitting skulls.*

The car ride with Frank Bishop to Manhattan College gave Crowley a chance to see the fall foliage along the Hudson River. There was nothing like it in Texas and he made a mental note to take Anna Maria up this way to see the fall colors. Bishop arranged the meeting just three days before Crowley's wedding. They arrived early, which gave Bishop time to introduce Crowley to some of his classmates and the ROTC commander. When it came time for Crowley to step onto the stage,

Frank Bishop introduced him to the audience and described the role of a combat controller.

Crowley turned to face the cadet volunteers standing along the back wall of the stage. "Any volunteers for my first demonstration?"

A blond cadet six foot two in green fatigues raised his hand and walked out to the center of the mats on stage.

Crowley faced him. "Okay… attack!"

The student volunteer ran over the mats like he was going to make a football tackle. The combat controller waited until the last moment, lowered his torso, and used the cadet's momentum to propel him up over his back.

The classic judo move made the audience cringe as their friend landed with a big thud on the gym mats. The volunteer stood up slowly and checked for injuries.

Crowley walked over to him. "Let me explain the move to you."

Crowley broke down the steps in a loud voice as the cadet followed along. Once his volunteer understood how it worked, he told the cadet they would switch roles. They took their starting positions on opposite sides of the stage.

The volunteer yelled, "Attack!"

Crowley started running toward him with outstretched arms. As he reached for the man's shoulders, the tall blond crouched low at the right moment. Crowley made contact, and the cadet raised his body and used Crowley's momentum to roll him over his left shoulder. The combat controller fell to the mat, rolled onto his back, and then pumped his arms down to propel him up into a fighting stance.

The crowd clapped and cheered for their classmates.

Crowley said, "Now that we have your attention, I will conduct a hand-to-hand combat class."

He signaled for another volunteer, and the man who stepped forward made Crowley do a double take. A very large black cadet with the name CROWLEY stitched on his fatigue shirt approached him on the stage.

Sergeant Crowley figured this was a practical joke Frank was playing on him, so he went along with it and asked, "Cadet, are we related?"

The man stiffened. "Crowley is my slave-name! I am going to change it to Mohammad Sharif once I graduate."

Crowley thought, *Slave name. I wonder if I am related to any Crowleys down the south. Mohammad and I might be blood brothers.*

"Mohammad sounds like a warrior's name. Let's see you show your fighting ability!" said Crowley.

This comment drew applause from the crowd. His peers liked the cadet, and Crowley showed the future Mohammed how to duck a punch. The class was going well. He asked for ten volunteers on stage to pair up into five groups. Crowley led the cadets for an hour of hand-to-hand combat training. The attendees looked on and cheered when their classmates made successful moves.

At the end of the session, Crowley ordered the men to return to their positions at the back of the mats, facing the audience at parade-rest. Then he signaled Frank, who came up on stage, followed by an Air Force major. As the officer stepped onto the stage from the side stairs, Crowley turned to him and saluted as the officer walked toward him and returned the salute. Bishop introduced Major Phillips to Crowley, who shook hands and smiled as the officer thanked him for his excellent judo class. Bishop brought over a microphone on a stand, and the major walked up to the mike and asked the audience to show their appreciation for Sergeant Crowley's training program. The cadets stood as they clapped and cheered until he asked them to please take their seats.

Phillips said, "You all know from my uniform insignia that I am a pilot. What you don't know is that I flew with TAC on Special Operations. I have experienced how vital the combat controller role is to the success of these missions."

The major described the extensive training required and the respect these airmen earned for leading the way into battle. He turned to Crowley, shook his hand, and the audience again rose to their feet and applauded.

Bishop, who arrived with a stack of certificates in hand, joined Crowley and Phillips and they gave out the awards to the participants on stage.

The cadets gathered around Crowley after the award presentation as he walked to the exit at the front of the building. They asked about his missions as a combat controller. He replied he could not get into specifics because of operational security. This response made the cadets even more curious, so they changed subjects and began peppering him with questions about his weapons and parachute experiences. Everyone was so deep in conversation they did not hear the chants outside until they reached the exit doors in the lobby.

Outside, all hell had broken loose. The signs raised by the crowd showed it was an anti-war protest, and they were present because of the ROTC meeting. As the cadets streamed out of the building, they got pelted with rotten food and eggs while the protestors cursed at them with the usual epithets like "baby killers" and "murderers." The judo students Crowley trained gathered around him in a wedge formation and looked his way for orders. He noticed the ring leaders appeared to all be using bull horns to incite the anti-war demonstrators, and they made the tactical mistake of grouping together in the center near the front line.

Crowley knew how to deal with a situation like this by mounting a concentrated attack to cut off the leadership of the opposition. As more cadets emerged from the auditorium, demonstrators threw more eggs and rotten food at them. It was now turning into a riot. A raw egg hit Crowley's uniform.

He looked down at the mess. "Goddam it, I wore my best fatigues for this meeting. Who do these sons of bitches think they are?"

He moved to the tip of the formation and shouted to follow his lead. As Crowley turned to face the crowd, a rioter swiped at him with a sign pole. He deflected the blow, pulled the stick away, and poked the previous owner in the gut with it. Ripping the placard off the end of the pole, he began using it like a character in a Bruce Lee movie. Bodies started flying in front of him as he dispatched rioters while navigating toward the ring leaders ahead. The cadets behind him snatched makeshift weapons from Crowley's wake and began fighting the mob to cover his flanks.

Crowley thought, *So, this is what it is like to be at the receiving end of a demonstration these days. No wonder they ordered me into civilian clothes for the trip home. At all the demonstrations at my school, the protestors were peaceful. It was the cops who got belligerent when we wouldn't quit. It was all peace and love back then.*

Herb chanted on his bull horn at the crowd of demonstrators he had gathered with the help of the Columbia chapter of the SDS. His fellow Weathermen gathered around him to lead the demonstration and help cheer on the demonstrators to throw the eggs and rotten tomatoes. Panicked by the cadets charging them instead of running away, the demonstrators ran to Herb, begging for more eggs.

Herb replied, "We're running out of eggs. I have some nice bottles and rocks to use against those war mongers!"

Herb called over to his fellow Weathermen, "Remember, first give out eggs and rotten food. After they get excited, then hand out the hard stuff."

Herb used his bull horn. "Baby killers! Murderers!" to goad the rioters on with his chants and name calling until he noticed something strange. He could see a path clearing in the middle, and it was heading straight for him. The crowd was parting with screams and yells as blue and green uniforms headed toward him.

At first, he reacted to the cadets by yelling on his bull horn more frequently to goad the riot on, and then he began pushing demonstrators into the breaches as he looked to his fellow weathermen for help. Things started unraveling fast, and the Weathermen panicked as the guy in the red beret headed straight for them.

Herb called to another Weatherman, "That soldier with the red cap is our primary target. Get him before he gets us! And what's with all these cadets? I thought they were pussies."

The crowd thinned out as word spread about the mayhem in the middle. Demonstrators dropped their signs and started running for the exits of the school commons. This retreat allowed Crowley to gain momentum as his cadets fought their way to the leaders. As Crowley reached the Weathermen, he saw them circle around some boxes and reach back to pull bottles and rocks as he approached. Crowley knocked bottles from the air with his stick as he waded into the group.

They are throwing rocks and bottles. Looks like the leaders are out to injure us. I need to capture one and find out what this is all about, thought Crowley.

When he reached within striking distance, the instigators ran. He was ready for this and used his pole to trip two of them up, forcing them to fall hard on the sidewalk. He exerted a blow to the head of the closest ringleader, knocking him out, followed by a kick in the kidneys to the second man, causing him to drop his bull horn and cry out as he rolled over. Crowley squatted on the man's chest and slapped him a few times to get his attention.

Herb looked up and groaned when he saw the red beret and uniform.

"I'm your worst nightmare, asshole. You failed, and I will have you by the balls if I don't get some answers," threated Crowley.

A couple of harder slaps with the back of his hand and he began asking him who was behind this riot. Herb just shook his head and did not speak. Crowley looked around to see if the police had arrived. Seeing no cops, he grabbed the man's arm, and hyper extended his wrist until Herb screamed in pain. The remaining Weathermen moved toward Herb to free him, but the other Crowley surprised them with a menacing look on his face. The sight of a large Black man protecting the white soldier shocked the Weathermen, and they shouted "Uncle Tom" at him. He growled as he grabbed them and flung their bodies up into the air when they came close.

Crowley thought, *Mohammad is defending me like a brother. I gotta ask my father if there is a southern branch of the family. It has never come up. I know my father would never advertise any former slave owner relations.*

Colonel Chambers' comments about Soviet agents came to his mind, and Crowley twisted Herb's wrist even harder.

"Who's behind this bullshit?"

With tears of pain running down his face, Herb said, "We are the Weather Underground, and you are an enemy to our cause to end the war in Vietnam. Our instructions were to prevent you from reaching your next assignment."

Crowley stood up to see campus police led by Major Phillips, heading his way.

He called out, "Cadets, the cavalry is on the way. Detain the riot leaders and guard the cartons of rocks and bottles until they arrive."

The peace officers cuffed the four Weathermen and led them away. Phillips ordered the cadets to carry the boxes of rocks and bottles to the police station as evidence. The Air Force officer then walked up to Crowley, who stood at attention and saluted.

Phillips returned the salute and said, "I apologize for the treatment you received while on leave in your own hometown. If I had known this was going to happen, I would have given the police a heads up."

He nodded and asked the major, "Who is the Weather Underground?"

He looked surprised and replied, "They are a radical leftist group formed by members of the SDS, whose official name is the Students for a Democratic Society. They believe in the violent overthrow of our government and have claimed responsibility for bombings in Washington. Why do you ask?" said Phillips.

"The riot leader I just questioned told me he is a member, and that I am their enemy."

"I will inform the police about this admission. In the meantime, I need to take you over to the campus infirmary. You have a nasty cut on your head."

He reached up, rubbed his forehead, and looked at the blood on his hand and thought, *What will Anna Maria say about my scar ruining our wedding photos?*

Phillips led him away through the remaining crowd of students.

13

An Affair to Remember

26 October 1969. Long Island

It was a grand occasion. Anna Maria's parents had gone all out and spent the equivalent of a new Cadillac to make sure everything was perfect. The guests enjoyed the four-course meal, drinks, and live music. As the wedding reception progressed, folks wandered outside for some fresh air and a look at the beautiful views of the Great South Bay while they sipped a cocktail in the formal garden.

The couple said their goodbyes, got into a rented car, and headed for their hotel near the JFK Airport. On the way, Anna Maria turned to face her husband as she spoke.

"Jake, I am so excited about getting married, flying to the Caribbean, and on to Europe to live. I could not be happier."

They checked in and a valet escorted them to the bridal suite on the 11th floor. She cuddled in Crowley's arms. "Look, you can see the lights from the airliners taking off in the distance. Soon we will be on one of those flights!"

Crowley kissed her. "Anna Maria, something just came up with my assignment and I have to discuss it with you."

"Your assignment? You told me it is all set!"

"Soviet agents have attacked me twice since I received my orders to West Germany."

"Why haven't you brought this up before? This is all last minute!"

"I thought the incident in Texas was just locals trying to show off. The second attack appeared to be caused by a violent student demonstration. The events seemed unrelated but resulted in calls from Air Force brass warning me that Soviet agents were involved."

"It seems like you handled the situations with your combat training. You hardly received a scratch, right?"

"I'm more worried about you."

"What makes you think it is dangerous for me in Europe?

"Two world wars have started there with Americans getting sucked in."

"Oh please! We have the U.N. now to keep the peace.

"Yeah, and after the First World War, they formed the League of Nations."

"Quit acting like you're my father. It does not become you."

"I am trying-"

"It appears you are trying to delay me from going to Germany, so you have time to practice your German on the *Frauleins*."

"That's not fair. I just want to keep you safe. How could I ever face your parents if something happened to you?"

He heard an odd click. Anna Maria turned, and her arm became a blur as she let loose a knife, which slammed into the door of the suite with a thud and a twang.

Anna Maria stuck up her chin as she spoke. "My family didn't always have it so good. I grew up on the mean streets of New York and learned how to take care of myself, and I don't need you to protect me from every little thing. Nothing is going to prevent me from living in Europe with you."

"I'm not saying you're not going to Europe, just not right away. I need time to check out the situation over there before you fly over," replied Crowley.

"Well, I don't get it. We are going to Barbados for our honeymoon, and they warned us about staying inside the resort compound because of the crime on that island and you don't say boo. Europe is like a big Disneyland. People travel there on vacation all the time," said Anna Maria.

"I will live on a guarded military base before you come over. Once you arrive, we will live with the Germans in an apartment. I must make sure it will be safe and there is no more threat," replied Crowley.

"My father had to take a business trip to Italy to attend fashion shows. When he returned, they asked him if he was concerned about the crime in Italy with the mafia. He told them he was not more concerned than he was traveling to Manhattan, and neither am I," said Anna Maria.

Crowley knew she was high-strung before he married her. Proud of her family heritage and lifestyle, he knew she didn't take shit from anyone. It was one of those things that attracted him to her. He walked over to the door and pulled out the switchblade. Crowley noticed the balance of the weapon as he folded the blade back into the handle.

He smiled. "Where did this throwing knife come from?"

She returned the smile, and those large green eyes flashed in the moonlight from a picture window behind them as she took it back.

"Wouldn't you like to know!"

"Well then, I'll just have to search you!"

"You're welcome to come over here and try."

She put the weapon on the nightstand and beckoned him over with her index finger. He kissed her hard, and she kissed him hard back. They embraced in front of the bridal suite window and the light from a full moon streamed in to form their silhouettes. Still in their wedding clothes, they could have posed for the cover of a romance novel. Fate, however, had a thriller in store for the couple.

14

Arrival at Cambrai Fritsch Kaserne

0800 Hours, 21 November 1969 Frankfurt, Germany

Crowley stood in front of a large gray stone building in the air freight section of the Rhein-Main Airport.

A stevedore towing a crate approached Crowley and said, "*Herr Crowley?*"

Crowley replied, "*Ja, ich bin Herr Crowley.*"

"May I see your shipping papers?"

Crowley pulled out his receipt, and the man reached into his toolbox and opened the container with a crowbar. The worker unpacked the bike and then handled Crowley tools as he assembled it. The German anticipated Crowley's needs by handing him the right tool each time.

As Crowley fastened the green military license plates with a screwdriver, he started a conversion.

"Your English is good. Where did you learn it?"

The stevedore replied, "At the *gymnasium*, as a second language. It helped me get this job at the airport. English is required for international air travel jobs."

"I see. It seems like you know a lot about mechanics too. Does this bike interest you, or do you provide this service with every delivery?"

The Stevedore smiled. “I read the bill of lading and became curious. I have only seen this motorcycle on the racetrack. My friends and I can barely afford mopeds. What made it even more interesting was that you sent it as air cargo. Extremely expensive!”

“Yes, it was important that I prepare for my wife’s arrival, so we shipped it via air freight to avoid delay and potential damage from a long sea voyage.”

“I see you fitted a Grand Prix-style fairing and clip-on handlebars to streamline the motorcycle. You must be in a hurry.”

“Yes, and I also added the upswept exhaust pipes to provide more clearance during high-speed turns. I spared nothing in getting my bride over here as soon as possible.”

The stevedore chuckled. “Did you have it custom painted? I noticed that instead of the standard yellow paint on the GP-style seat, fairing and gas tank, you have midnight blue.”

“I sprayed the colors myself because commandos dress for stealth and come back all black and blue after their missions.”

The German laughed and said, “Good one! I cannot wait to tell my friends that explanation!”

The sky was as gray as the warehouse building and seemed to merge into a giant wall. The weather report on the armed forces radio broadcast this morning forecasted full cloud cover because of a shift in the Gulf Stream.

“I read in a book about Germany once that talked about how many people believed European medical scientists invented psychiatry to counteract the depression caused by the climate.”

The stevedore replied, “Another funny story. I will have to tell my friends that one, too!”

Crowley was wearing black waterproofed full leathers, which shielded him from the cold, damp climate. Elbow and knee armor added protection in case of a fall and made him look like an armored knight ready for combat. As a last service, the German handed him a rag with some hand cleaner on it and Crowley wiped the grease off his hands before donning his helmet and gloves. He pushed the motorcycle forward to bump start the engine as the stevedore waved him goodbye. When he leaped on the saddle, he let out the clutch and the motorcycle roared into life as he rode to the autobahn entrance. He leaned over until a metal skid plate on his knee sparked against the pavement as he steered around the clover leaf while banging through the gears to accelerate down the ramp.

The German watched in amazement and exclaimed, "*Wunderbar!* He rides like a true professional racer. I should have guessed from his serious demeanor that he was not another rich American poser."

Crowley shot up the entrance ramp and passed two trucks before entering the right lane. Using the rear-view mirrors was very important. European sports cars approached at high speed in the passing lane. This expressway linking Frankfurt and Darmstadt was so straight and flat they used it for automotive top-speed record attempts in 1938. The situation made him realize the strange dichotomy that existed in West Germany.

Democratic socialism was the order of the day providing economic protection for its citizens through a pervasive tax system that provided universal health care, free tuition at state colleges and a safety net of welfare programs. The Napoleonic Code served as the basis for the laws in continental Europe. This codification specified a maximum penalty for every conceivable violation, reducing lawsuits and insurance costs.

A comprehensive legal system and social programs created an ordered society. Germans needed some way to let off steam. Their roads became an outlet for automotive enthusiasts. With no speed limits on large sections of the autobahn, a driver could take out his car or motorcycle any day of the week and blast down the passing lane until a faster driver pulls up behind him with his high beams flashing and his engine screaming.

Crowley's Norton was fast, but its top speed was just over 115 miles an hour and the ride was twitchy going that fast. He bought the bike after seeing an ad depicting a beautiful British model straddling a Norton Commando wearing a black leather miniskirt and go-go boots with the caption "Put something exciting between your legs." The advertisement was no lie, but he now realized he needed a motorcycle with a higher top end for the autobahn. He had one of the new four-cylinder Honda CB750 models in mind. That was like riding a two-wheeled Ferrari.

The aerodynamics of the fairing and clip-on handlebars gave Crowley another five MPH top end. Not enough to keep ahead of sports cars. The quick acceleration of the Norton allowed him to thread his way around the diesel trucks, but it was hard work. He used his mirrors to check for approaching vehicles and steer back into the relative safety of the right lane while he set up for his next pass. Traveling fast on these roads required survival instincts. As the third sports car forced him over, he cursed and raised his fist at the Porsche and shouted, "Kill or be killed? Is that the philosophy in Germany?"

He wondered if the low-cost insurance and legal liability limits created a "life is cheap" attitude in Europe. As he rode on, he thought about checking out the BMW 2002ti coupe. Anna Maria had wanted an RV to travel with, but he talked her out of it. Parking, gas mileage and handling were his arguments against a van. They would have to stay in the right lane most of the time, which made for slow going behind the slow trucks.

Crowley took the Darmstadt exit and cut his speed as he drove through the city and pulled into the Cambrai Fritsch Kaserne. This former *Wehrmacht* military base was where the 6910th Security Group administration offices and dormitories were located. He was rooming in the Verdun Dormitory with a staff sergeant whose enlistment was ending, while he worked on getting an apartment and a car. German nationals staffed the chow hall, and the food was good.

He received orders to report on the Dog Flight shift and begin On-the-Job-Training, also known by its initials, OJT. The surveillance and warning center was manned 7X24, with coverage provided by flights of one hundred men, each designated Able, Baker, Charlie, and Dog. The rotating shifts comprised four evening shifts, 24 hours off, four midnight shifts, twenty-four hours off, four-day shifts, and then four days off. This schedule gave him more time to apartment hunt and car shop during daytime hours.

Because he knew how to speak German, Crowley booked appointments to see rentals himself instead of having to go through a bilingual agent. Even with his command of the language, a furnished apartment was difficult to find. With help from the listings in the base housing office, he located one in Arheilgen, a suburb of Darmstadt.

Crowley met with the landlord, a man around his father's age. He wore his class B blues with his red beret and right away, the landlord, Herr Bergholz, had questions about his service.

"I have not seen that hat on an American soldier before. What does it signify?"

"I am an Air Force combat controller. I direct air operations from forward areas,"

"Do you mean behind enemy lines?"

"Sometimes. I work with Special Forces to prepare and direct landing operations."

"Oh, so you are a commando! I thought so from your demeanor. I was one also during the war. We rescued Mussolini. A complete waste of time. The Italian ended up being shot and hanged later by partisans. What are you doing here in Germany? Airplane mechanics and clerks come to rent my apartments. You are the first American commando."

Crowley's face became stern.

He whispered, "They want me to see if anything needs invading."

"Oh, that was a good one! Good to know, *Ami, that you* have a sense of humor. We have a very nice one-bedroom apartment we just redecorated. It is on the fourth floor. Let me show it to you."

Herr Bergholz led him upstairs.

"You can see the apartment has fresh wallpaper, new flooring, and appliances. The furniture is old, but in good condition. It has airy windows with curtains."

"How much is the rent?"

"For you, I give the special commando discount of 360 marks a month, including heat and electricity. What do you think?"

"I'll take it, Herr Bergholz, but first I want to read the lease."

"No problem, your housing office has to approve it, or we don't get on their listing."

"Yeah, I know. I just want to see it for myself."

"A careful man. I like that. That means you will be careful with the appliances in this apartment. Let us walk to my home and we can review the paperwork."

When they reached the landlord's house, he ushered Crowley into the dining room, and Frau Bergholz came in with a tray of coffee and slices of chocolate cake.

Herr Bergholz introduced him to his wife, and she said, "Welcome to Germany, Herr Crowley. When do I get to meet your bride?"

"Now that I can confirm we have rented your apartment, she will fly from New York."

"Oh, so she is a city girl. I cannot wait to talk to her. Does she speak German as well as you?"

"English and Italian."

"A cultured young lady, I am sure. Men like you attract that type of woman. I should know. Herr Bergholz was quite dashing in his uniform. Does Frau Crowley work?"

"Anna Maria worked in a bank in New York. She wants a different job where she can get out and explore the country."

"I wish her luck!"

Frau Bergholz served the coffee and cake and left them to go over the paperwork.

Now it was Crowley's turn to ask the questions.

"Herr Bergholz, tell me about the building's security."

"Sergeant Crowley, a sliding door secures access at the street level to the apartment building and parking area. We made it of oak with steel cladding and it has a regular door embedded in it for easy pedestrian access. I will issue you keys for access to both doors."

"What about the apartment building access?"

"Because the street access doors are key locked, you must come down and let in guests. We have a buzzer for each apartment on the wall outside of the entryway. This prevents a tenant from just buzzing anybody in without seeing who it is."

Herr Bergholz added, "Each residence door is solid wood with a triple hinge and steel frame. A peep hole and heavy-duty lock provide security. This is standard in Germany."

"My wife believes she can take care of herself, but I still have concerns for her safety while I work at night."

"An understandable concern. I believe you will find this apartment to be quiet and secure."

The BMW purchase from the proceeds of their American cars came next. A Dog Flight buddy gave him an address for a dealer on Marburger Strasse in Darmstadt. They sold both motorcycles and automobiles. When Crowley rode up to the dealer's lot and parked his Norton Commando near the front entrance, several of the staff ran up to the large showroom windows and studied him and his bike as he got off and walked toward the building. He was wearing class B winter blues and his red combat controller beret. As he reached for the door, a salesman in a neat three-piece suit greeted him.

"Good day, I am Kurt Schumacher. How may I be of service?"

Crowley replied, "Herr Schumacher, I am interested in buying a car."

"Are you planning on trading in the motorcycle you rode in on?"

"My wife will use the car. My main transportation will be the bike."

"That is too bad. Our salespeople were hoping to buy it as a trade-in. Norton has a great reputation on the racing circuits in Europe."

He nodded and said, "May I see a BMW 2002ti?"

"Ah yes, so you know about the best *autos* too!"

The salesman brought him over to a white coupe on the showroom floor, which he examined as the salesman described the model. It was obvious the German was a car guy, unlike most of his American wheeler dealer counterparts. Schumacher took great pride in describing all the features and capabilities of the 2002ti, which was its due since the car was saving the company from bankruptcy.

"Herr Schumacher, what are the performance figures for the 2002ti?"

"It cruises all day at 176 KMPH and has a top speed of about 185 KMPH. The two-liter four-cylinder SOHC engine makes 130 horsepower.

Crowley thought, *Kilometers per hour. I will have to write up a conversion chart and tape it on the dashboard.*

"And what are the body configurations?" asked Crowley.

"This model comes in only one body style with a classic BMW two kidney grill, four seats, two doors and a large trunk with spare tire."

The sales agent answered all of Crowley's technical questions and waited for his customer's reply.

"The car is simple, yet elegant. I like the black wall tires and alloy wheels instead of white walls and hubcaps popular back in the states," commented Crowley.

He asked for a test drive and Schumacher ushered him to the dealer's lot, where a used blue model stood all clean and polished. He sat in the driver's seat with the sales agent next to him, explaining the controls and the four-speed shift pattern. Crowley started it up and eased out toward the autobahn.

Once they were on the road, he got on the throttle and assessed the car's passing and handling capabilities. It handled like it was riding on rails. He drove the test vehicle back to the BMW dealership and parked it. The sales agent brought him to his desk and reviewed the costs and options. After some negotiating, he purchased the white model off the showroom floor so he would have it when Anna Maria arrived the following week. The problem was it came with a standard transmission. He would have to teach her how to operate a stick-shift.

Herr Schumacher called the service manager to prepare the automobile while he finished the paperwork. Crowley took some forms from the salesman and rode over to an insurance agency that worked with U.S. GIs in Darmstadt. Once he purchased the accident coverage, he returned to the BMW dealership. When he walked into the dealership, the salesman met him and directed him back to the service area. The white 2002ti was up on a lift being prepped for delivery.

As he approached, someone called "*Achtung!*"

Four mechanics moved to the corners of the lift and snapped to attention as the shop steward led him around to inspect the vehicle. Once he completed the inspection, a worker lowered the shiny white coupe and handed the keys to Crowley as he saluted. This show of respect surprised him, but he did not let on.

Crowley returned the salute and in German said, "My wife and I will remember your excellent service and look forward to you taking care of the auto in the future."

He got in the car and drove out to the dealer lot. Crowley was getting used to the deference Germans showed to men in uniform and tried to return the courtesy they gave.

He pulled up to the sales agent and rolled down his window to say, "Herr Schumacher, I will return in an hour with a friend to pick up the Norton Commando."

Herr Schumacher replied, "That will not be necessary. I can drive the BMW to the Cambrai Fritsch Kaserne if you return me to the dealership on your Norton."

He laughed, knowing this was no time saved for him but a joy ride for the sales agent.

"Sure, why not?"

Crowley thought about how well the German people treated him. "If only the weather would improve. I have not seen the sun since I arrived."

He recalled his gray, foreboding memories of Germany as a kid.

He thought, *The weather can be depressing, but not dreadful. The threats of the Berlin crisis gave everyone around me angst back then.*

15

Freedom Through Vigilance

0800 Hours, 18 November 1969 S&W Center

The Senior Master Sergeant appeared at the Surveillance and Warning Center entrance and waited while the guards took Crowley's picture and laminated his green security badge. When they handed Crowley his badge, SMSGT Mathews used that as his cue. He walked up to Crowley as he put the badge chain over his head and clipped the ID card to his shirt pocket.

"Good morning, Sergeant. I am senior NCO on Dog Flight. My job includes giving you a tour of the site before you start your assignment."

He turned and led Crowley through the main entrance of the S&W center.

"The first thing you will notice is the buildings have no windows, just like your tech-school facilities at Goodfellow Air Force Base. A high fence topped with razor-wire and patrolmen walking the perimeter with leashed guard dogs protect the compound. Guard towers provide additional protection against the possibility of attacks by domestic terrorists."

Mathews brought him inside the building to each operational unit and explained their mission, objectives, and job responsibilities.

"You may not know this, but we are in quite a predicament, being located right in the middle of the expected Soviet Union invasion route to Europe."

At the end of the tour, Mathews introduced him to his technical instructor, Staff Sergeant Gibson. Gibson escorted him over to a shrouded area in a corner of the digital transmissions intercept wing of the building.

As his new supervisor pulled back the shroud, Crowley thought, *A mystery wrapped in an enigma.*

Gibson saw his protégé looking at the curtains and explained the shrouds cut the glare from the building's fluorescent ceiling lighting, as he pointed to a console with a large round display.

"Sergeant, if you read the *Art of War* by Sun Tzu, then you know one of his chief strategies postulated that a successful warlord seizes his enemy's weapons and redeploys them against their previous possessor. RUBICON is an example of that strategy."

Gibson moved to center himself between the two display consoles.

"The NSA custom-built this interactive system to intercept Soviet PVO *Strany* semi-automated morse code signals and present the radar tracking they carry from multiple intercepted stations simultaneously on a superimposed graphic map of Europe. The analyst manning the console, which is based on the air traffic controller workstation you know so well, receives the digitized display of air traffic from a Honeywell DDP-124 computer interfaced to removable multi-platter disk drives. A demultiplexer digitizes analog tracking signals and R390 HF Radio operators find the broadcasts, fix their location with DF, and then patch them to one of the demultiplexer ports for identification by the analyst. The analyst decides which signals to keep on-line, which to record for later analysis, and which one's get ditched because of redundancy of area coverage, signal quality, and so on."

Gibson picked up a light pen and interrogated a plot on the screen.

"The dual-overlay graphics consoles can each process plots from up to eight radar stations live and the same number off-line for later playback and review. The controls on the console allow the analyst to monitor flights on a graphic map of Europe and then zoom in and magnify a chosen area so that a single aircraft's flight path fills the screen."

Crowley replied, "Sergeant Gibson, from what I studied about Soviet air defense, this means that we have better coverage of their air traffic than they do!"

"That is correct, and we do more with their tracking than they can do. A console operator can interrogate a plot from any of the eight radar broadcast stations on the display with this light pen for amplification data, like altitude, air speed, and transponder identification. The back-lit function keys are used to capture the plots of interest and compose a report, which is output onto the paper tape punch, ready for Teletype transmission."

Crowley sat down at a console and Gibson taught him how to operate the machine. After a few hours, he left his protégé to work on his own.

Gibson returned in an hour and said, "I will check in periodically to see if you have questions."

Since Crowley was a certified air traffic controller, the operations were familiar to him, and he picked it up fast even though there was a lot more activity to cover than he was used to. At the end of the shift, Gibson stopped by his console.

"Someone is waiting for you over at the coffee bar," Gibson said.

Crowley followed his supervisor, and as they rounded a corner flanked by racks of radio equipment, he caught sight of his posse standing around stainless steel coffee urns. He called out to them over the din of the electronic gear, and they all waved him over. Crowley introduced Frazer, Jackson, and Rothman to his supervisor. They all shook hands and laughed at how surprised he looked to see them. Gibson told him his buddies were going to be S&W analysts, so he should expect to be working with them soon. They exchanged contact information and promised to catch up that evening for drinks at the unit bar on base. Then it was back to their posts to continue their On-the-Job-Training.

At 2330 hours, Crowley arrived for his second shift since starting OJT and Gibson wasted no time in getting in more training on the operation of the codeword RUBICON System. It was already December 12th and Crowley had Anna Maria's arrival constantly on his mind. He forced himself to focus on the training problem at hand.

"So how did this code name RUBICON come to be? Doesn't that name have to do with Roman history?" Crowley asked?

Gibson replied, "It's an interesting story. The designer, Mr. Sedgwick, if you can believe it, wanted to call it SNATCH because it could steal the tracking data from the Soviet Air Defense Network."

Gibson chuckled, then added, "Yeah, the higher-ups told Sedgwick, 'You're right, it will be easy to remember but look up its slang definition and get back to us.'"

Crowley laughed. "Then what happened?"

"The computer engineer told them the problem was their minds were in the gutter. He created another code word, anyway."

"I guess the NSA would have taken a lot of kidding every time they used that codeword."

"He came up with RUBICON, which means 'red river' in Latin. I guess he figured RUBICON was appropriate because we were intercepting a river of data from the reds."

"That analogy makes it easier to remember, but 'SNATCH' would have been more fun. Too bad the higher-ups nixed it."

Gibson replied, "Someone would have objected to its use. They have rooms full of people at the pentagon obsessing over this stuff."

The Soviet radar network (codeword SWAMP) stood down from 2300 to 0600 hours every night, so this was a perfect opportunity to train Crowley using recorded intercept traffic from the previous shift.

Gibson instructed his pupil, "Start displaying plots from the Charlie shift recordings and generate top priority alert reports on the five-channel Teletype punch."

A nearby Teletype printed out the reports and they compared them to the display data for accuracy. Gibson cautioned him to deposit the practice information into a burn bag after they checked them to avoid confusing them with real reporting.

When he arrived back at his apartment, Crowley ate some cereal and fell asleep. As he slept, he dreamed of standing at attention on the roof of the OPS building, holding an M16 as he stared off to the east. A series of mushroom clouds appeared to be traveling toward him, getting larger and louder. He realized they must be from nukes exploding as the Russians tried to advance through the Fulda Gap. Senior Master Sergeant Mathews materialized in front of the clouds and pointed toward the explosions.

"I was not kidding in my briefing about how we deployed tactical nukes in the Fulda Gap. If the Soviets breach that nuclear hell on earth, you might as well crouch down in a fetal position and kiss your ass goodbye!"

The clouds appeared to be marching closer, and the sound grew more intense. Suddenly, Mathews vaporized in a puff of smoke.

Crowley woke up in a sweat with light from the setting sun streaming through the bedroom window onto his face. It was 1600 hours, so he took a shower and dressed in his civilian clothes. He kept thinking about the nightmare and Anna Maria traveling to be in this mess! This assignment was supposed to be like living in Disneyland. Instead, it appeared to be a tour of Dante's *Inferno*.

His bride had said, "Even Disney movies have scary villains!"

That gave him little consolation for what he had learned about the situation in Europe. He headed out for a trip to the shops down the street. The apartment was on *Frankfurter-Landstrasse*, which was the main road from Frankfurt to Darmstadt before they built the autobahn. Crowley found he preferred living in a German apartment. The Air Force did him a favor by not offering base housing. He already met some of his neighbors and shopping was fun because he got to practice his German with the German people.

After walking several blocks past homes in the village, he heard the squeal of pigs.

He wondered, "I guess some of the attached buildings must be barns!"

The sidewalk was spotless, and the houses appeared well maintained, with stucco walls and red-tile roofs in perfect order. There was not a "stick-built" home to be seen. Most of the homes included tenant apartments, which Crowley discovered while looking for their apartment. The staff at base housing told him that rentals were easy to find, because Germans could not get mortgages unless they built or bought a multi-family dwelling. Only the rich captains of industry could afford to build their own private residence, which required a down payment of seventy-five percent of the purchase price. For this reason, even the farmers lived in multi-family dwellings with barns attached.

After shopping at the butcher, he headed over to the bakery for some bread. On the way, he passed a news stand and there, on the cover of the local daily called the *Darmstädter Echo Zeitung,* was a picture of an East German soldier escaping over a barbed wire fence. He grabbed the newspaper and read how U.S. fighter aircraft and West German border guards aided the escape at 0700 hours yesterday morning.

He mused, "Only two days on the job. This is exciting stuff."

Crowley remembered surprising Gibson early on the previous shift, by locating the tracking of helicopters on his console and reporting a border violation when they overflew into West Germany. They appeared to be chasing something because they hovered near the border in a search pattern. After confirmation of the flight from radar, the S&W center issued an alert and Ramstein AFB scrambled fighters to scare off the interlopers. The escapee got away. He thought how alike the security service and Special Operations were. Many times, a good job receives no public recognition to protect intelligence sources, and the lives of personnel involved. It came with the territory.

Crowley wondered aloud, "Let's see if I can scare up some more excitement at work tonight."

16

No Good Deed Goes Unpunished

0800 Hours, 15 December 1969. USAFSS S&W Center

Crowley rode up to the OPS site and parked his motorcycle in the dirt parking lot close to the security gate.

He thought, *The weather is getting colder. I will soon need to use the tram to commute to work.*

He swung his right leg over the seat, turned, and started walking as he pulled his green security badge out of his shirt pocket to let it hang from the chain. As he got closer to the entrance, he took off his helmet, tucked it under his left arm, and slipped on his beret.

The Air Force guards looked at him and then gave him a salute.

Crowley nodded and pointed to the sergeant stripes on his sleeves.

"Why the salute? You know I am not an officer."

The guard smiled and said, "You'll find out."

Crowley ignored the comment, continued to the entrance, and made his way to his workstation to relieve the earlier shift. As he walked down the hallway, everyone he encountered nodded to him, and some even shook his hand as he walked by and patted him on the back. When he reached his desk, the Charlie flight analyst, Sergeant James Conner, was sitting at the display station they shared with his coat on, waiting to be relieved.

Conner, too, stood up, nodded, and shook his hand.

Then he said, "Crowley, you made us all proud yesterday, saving the East German guard who escaped over the border. All the newspapers covered it, and the NSA sent a congratulatory message to 6910th Command Headquarters."

Conner picked up a message from the desk and handed it to him.

"An aide left this for you. It seems important because you must see the flight commander ASAP."

Crowley replied, "You're relieved of duty and thanks for the heads up about the note."

He quickly found Gibson. "Can you cover for me while I report to Captain Hodges?"

Gibson said, "His cubicle is down the hall on the left."

Crowley saluted the flight commander as he entered his office. "Sir, Sergeant Crowley reporting as ordered."

The captain was a former master sergeant who attended OCS when he was thirty-eight. Officers like him were called mustangs.

"Take a seat." Crowley obliged and sat at attention.

"I reviewed your record and believe you can assist me with a special logistical problem. The higher-ups tasked us with using the flight's existing personnel to provide additional security during our assigned shift rotations. Have you heard of the Red Army Faction, better known in the news as the Baader-Meinhof Gang?"

Crowley said, "Yes, sir. I read articles in the local newspapers."

Hodges replied, "Then you know they are a domestic communist terrorist group bent on attacking U.S. government installations and personnel to protest our involvement in Vietnam. Because of the bombing that just happened at an army installation in Frankfurt, the top brass has ordered increased protection for our operational and housing facilities. The training our men received in firearms during basic was minimal. I want to leverage your Special Operations experience and foreign language skills to lead our flight's auxiliary security team and prepare them for the possibility of an assault or hijacking. This may benefit you as well by helping you maintain your marksmanship and fitness to prepare for your return to your primary specialty. As an acting security police officer, you and your men will wear a badge and always carry a sidearm. You must conceal the automatic pistols in public or we will upset the civilian population. The armorer will issue you a shoulder holster, and you must wear a jacket to cover the weapon. Should you volunteer, your duty is to assemble and train the men from this flight. They will be a twelve-man unit of acting security police once you complete the training. You will also train the team leaders for the other three flights."

Crowley demurred by saying, "Doesn't my special assignment take priority? I just got here."

"I received a performance review on you because of the project's importance. You exceeded all expectations and mastered the intercept method. Your supervisors think it is because of your prior training as a combat controller."

"What is the mission once I train them?"

"You will deploy at OPS if we encounter a security alert with sidearms and M16s to augment the guards on duty and serve as a security detail for the flight trick bus to and from the compound. Besides marksmanship and self-defense training, you and your men will take part in anti-terrorism exercises with the Hessische *Polizei*. Do you have any questions?"

In Crowley's mind, the comment about carrying guns and a badge registered.

"When did you say I was allowed to be armed?"

Hodges smiled. "At all times. The only time it is to leave your physical body is when you place it on the nightstand before going to bed."

An MP in Germany, just like my father in WWII. This would help solve my personal security issues.

He wondered if the commander knew that. He tried not to let his excitement show.

"Well, sir, this additional duty should keep my marksmanship and conditioning up. May I have a list of the Dog Flight airmen with marksmen ratings as a starting point for the selection process?"

Hodges nodded and called his aide to get the information.

"I heard you trained a group at school in hand-to-hand combat. Consider asking them to volunteer. They will be required to demonstrate skill with small arms."

He agreed and said, "Is there anything else I should know about?"

"Listen closely to the German *Polizei*. They are great at gathering intelligence on this terrorist group." Hodges stood up. "That's all for now."

Crowley saluted and returned to his intercept position.

The extra assignment and responsibility were a relief. It would authorize him to carry a concealed weapon and have the advantages of German police cooperation and an official badge of authority. The next day, he received the list and started running down the names. Twenty-five airmen on the flight had the top marksmen scores. He arranged a special late bus for the candidates who did not have cars and called a meeting after the shift ended. To his surprise, all 25 men volunteered for the team. The marksmanship and fitness tests would weed out about half of the volunteers based on his experience with combat controller qualification for marksmanship. He set up a class at the target range to start the weeding-out process. Now he was back to being armed and dangerous. Crowley might have to face urban guerillas who were also communist terrorists. Distinguishing friends from foes would again be a problem. That was something his father could relate to when they swap war stories in the future.

17

Let the Games Begin

0900 Hours, 18 December 1969. Target Range

Crowley said, "We will start the qualification process with a numbers game, the standard marksmen test given to all new recruits using the M16. The maximum score for this test is 50 hits performed with ten bullet clips in five positions—prone supported, prone supported with gas mask, prone unsupported, kneeling and standing."

An airman raised his hand and said, "What is the score to qualify?"

Crowley responded, "The cut is at 43, which is the marksman ribbon qualification score."

He added, "Captain Hodges requested the Army weapons training commander at the Cambrai Fritsch Kaserne provide personnel to supervise the target shooting. This means the scores will be official and qualify for marksmanship ribbons."

The staff brought ten M16 assault rifles out and did a one-hour weapon safety session. Next, the candidates took their turns firing the weapons in the prescribed positions. To Crowley's surprise, twenty of the men qualified for ribbons. The twenty marksmen were told to break for lunch and then return for sidearms qualification at 1300 hours. He thanked the five remaining volunteers for their effort and dismissed them. At 1245, the marksmen returned from lunch.

Crowley stood in front of the group and said, "I congratulate you on passing the first phase. The next phase will be a session with Colt 0.45 semi-automatic pistols. I know most of you have not fired a sidearm because they do not include it in Air Force basic training. The weapon has a strong recoil and can be a challenge to shoot on target. The reason I prefer the weapon in combat is the stopping power it provides at close range."

After going over safety procedures, he walked over to a stall on the firing range, put on a pair of noise suppression headsets, and assumed a modified isosceles firing position leaning forward on the balls of his feet with both hands holding the sidearm centered in front of his body. He sighted the automatic, emptied a clip, removed it, checked to make sure the chamber was clear. Then he flipped on the safety catch and set down the pistol. A range staffer cranked the target back and removed it to find all seven rounds in the kill zone.

As the staff member raised the target to show the group, he thought to himself, "Who is this guy?"

Then he turned to look at Crowley more closely and noticed the combat controller badge and jump wings on the man's fatigues.

Crowley looked at the target for a moment and turned to the group, "You must always keep in mind when training that combatants don't stand still. Do not get cocky if you make some good shots. Keep trying to get better. Your life may depend on how hard you train."

The army range staff brought out ten Colt automatic pistols and placed them in the firing range booths with full clips.

Crowley said, "After the range personnel train you how to load, safety, and fire the weapons, you will buddy up two men to a booth. One man will fire his qualification round while the second man spots the target. After the first man completes his round, you will rotate positions. There are enough clips provided for two qualification rounds per booth. Questions?" The pistol qualification brought the list down to 15 remaining candidates.

Crowley made some mental calculations. *The posse made the cut. The obstacle course tomorrow will get the group down to a twelve-man team plus the three flight team leaders. With all the training we did together, the posse should qualify for the Dog Flight Team.*

After the obstacle course, Crowley stopped at the armory and presented his security police shield and ID.

Crowley said, "Captain Hodges told me you have sidearms waiting for me."

"I have two Colt .045 pistols, ammo, and shoulder holsters with your name on them," the armorer replied. "Why two guns? Are you Hopalong Cassidy?"

Crowley replied, "In Special Operations we use overwhelming force. That means two of everything."

The armorer smiled. "Here is your paperwork with two of everything to sign for as well."

The first day at the gym arrived, and Crowley greeted his new team for their morning exercises. The gymnasium was of cinder-block construction with yellow stucco covering the exterior. Large arched windows set high to let in daylight. The inside walls were plastered white and had brown mats hung up to help prevent injuries.

Crowley said, "Men, I intended to congratulate you as the winners of the security team selection process. Because of what is in store for you now, I instead offer my condolences."

The group turned to each other and gave an uneasy laugh.

He addressed the men wearing his red combat controller's beret and camouflage fatigues. He wanted to preclude any questions about why he led the inter-flight training program.

"The next month will encompass hand-to-hand combat training, small-arms practice, and a lot of physical conditioning."

Crowley called out, "Airman Frazer! Please join me on the mat."

Frazer stepped out of the group and assumed a fighting stance. Crowley joined him and they gave quite a show of throws and chops with bare hands. Frazer picked up a stick and returned to the mat.

Crowley yelled, "Attack!" and in the next set of moves, they demonstrated how judo was used to disarm an opponent.

The combat controller noticed the team liked what they saw, and they looked eager to try it themselves. He thanked Frazer and asked for a volunteer for the first exercise. Everybody raised their hand, so Crowley chose Bill Christensen, a six-foot-two blond Russian language specialist. Crowley walked through the moves of a throw with Christensen and then they started repeating the move, alternating who was being thrown. This impressed the men with how easily the combat controller used judo to throw his six-foot-two opponent.

Crowley turned to the group and said, "Alright, your turn. Pair up and I will show you how to break down and try what Christensen just demonstrated."

After an hour of judo, Crowley ordered the airmen to get their coats and line up outside the Gym on the track.

Crowley led them to set an example.

"Just five miles today to get started."

He led the way and noticed Jackson, the runner and Frazer the surfer, keeping pace on each side of him. Rothman, the wrestler, was bringing up the rear behind them.

Crowley called to Jackson, "Darryl! Let's see what they can do."

Jackson took the lead and kept up a torrid pace all the way to the finish line, where he waited for all fourteen men to pass by.

After some men ran past and puked on the grass, Crowley said, "Alright, hit the showers and report back tomorrow for more conditioning and practice."

18

Their First Christmas

24 December 1969. Frankfurt Rhein-Main Airport

After leaving the BMW in a parking garage, Crowley entered the Rhein-Main Airport terminal to find her flight listed as "delayed" on the status board.

He walked over to the information booth. "Any word yet on flight 714?"

The lady in the booth said, "Charter flights do not get their status updated until they land. They do not have a liaison in this airport to service inquiries."

I can't even take a break or eat for fear of missing her arrival.

Crowley waited for Anna Maria's plane to arrive, a special flight out of JFK for military dependents.

He stood behind a cordon marking the end of immigration control, where passengers exited customs with their luggage. The plane landed an hour late and the status board changed from delayed to arrival. He held a bouquet for his bride and when Anna Maria appeared, dragging her suitcase, he waved it to get her attention. When she reached her husband, they hugged, and he leaped over the barrier to grab her bag.

"Jake, it was a long trip, but I made it! There was an hour delay at JFK before we could board the plane."

"Well, darling, it's time to drive to our new home."

"I can't wait to begin our European adventure!"

Crowley escorted his bride to their BMW in the parking garage.

"Oh, I just love the car! It's so cute, and you got it in the same color as my Malibu."

He opened the passenger door, and she stepped in while he put her luggage in the trunk and slid behind the wheel. Crowley had written to her about the manual transmission in a letter before she left New York. Her eyes followed his actions as he worked the clutch and shifted to drive out of the parking garage to the airport exit. She looked determined to learn stick shift and gain her freedom. Tied down in an apartment in Europe was not part of her plan. Crowley drove to the entrance ramp for the Darmstadt autobahn and gunned the engine to give her the experience of life in the fast lane. She liked how it handled and sounded.

He noticed her attention to his driving and said, "I found a quiet country road with plowed fields on both sides. It is a safe place to teach you how to operate the manual transmission."

They exited the autobahn for Darmstadt and headed north to Arheilgen. It was 1200 hours and there was not much traffic. She observed her new surroundings through the passenger window as he drove.

"Jake, all the signs point to *Ausfahrt*. It must be a big city, but I never heard of it," said Anna Maria.

"*Ausfahrt* means exit in German. The road signs are something else you are going to have to learn besides stick shift," replied Crowley.

They reached the apartment building, and he pulled into a driveway between two furniture store display windows and stopped. With the engine still running, he got out and approached a massive sliding door, which he unlocked with a large key and slid to the left. Crowley slipped back in the BMW, released the hand brake, and drove through the doorway to a courtyard. He parked in a gravel area and took the suitcase from the trunk. Anna Maria exited the car and stood to admire a terrace behind the parking area.

"Jake, this view is beautiful, even in winter. The evergreens and statuary frame the entire area. The landlord included a large section for vegetables and fruit trees. They put wire fences up to keep out rabbits and squirrels."

Crowley nodded and followed Anna Maria up the stairs to the fourth-floor landing. He put the suitcase down, unlocked the door, and carried her over the threshold as they kissed. She looked around with approval at his choice for their first home. The simple furnishings included a burgundy-colored sofa, armchairs, and a dining table with four chairs in the large living room. A small breakfast table and chairs filled the tiny kitchen, and a huge German oak bed and clothes cabinet completed the bedroom. A muted floral wallpaper covered all the walls of the apartment.

"Oh, Jake, it's perfect. It's so nice and cozy."

Crowley led her into the bedroom. Anna Maria sat on the bed, and he joined her. Their eyes met.

Anna Maria whispered, "We have only been apart for a month, and it seems like a year!"

"I know. You were constantly on my mind as I prepared for your arrival. Together for two weeks and then separated for a month. It made me think how important you are to me. I don't want to be separated from you ever again."

They kissed, slipped off their clothes, and fell into bed in a passionate embrace.

Crowley awoke to the faint chime of a church bell, jumped up, and glanced at his watch.

"Darling, wake up. We must do some local food shopping and pick up a Christmas tree. Having a tiny refrigerator means shopping daily. The stores close early in Germany on Christmas Eve."

They dressed for the cold and hurried out the door. Since the *Christkindlmarkt* would remain open later, they walked to a local grocery. He translated the package labels as Anna Maria pulled items off the shelves and placed them in a small shopping cart. She chose some fresh meat, rolls, and slices of *Sachertorte* cake as they made their way to the checkout.

Anna Maria said, "Jake, I love the idea of buying fresh cake by the slice. I wish they did this back home."

The couple returned to their apartment and put away the food. Anna Maria squeezed the cake, meat, butter, and eggs into the tiny refrigerator while Crowley put the packaged goods in the cabinets. They hurried back down the four flights of stairs, got into their car, and made a right turn onto *Frankfurter-Landstrasse*. It was about a twenty-minute drive south to Darmstadt. Cars had to share the roadway with trams. As he drove around one, he told her about his experiences riding the tram to various points of interest in the city.

Crowley pointed at the road ahead and said, "They recessed the tracks into the cobblestone streets, making the surface slippery when driving over the steel rails and cobbles in cold, wet weather."

He maneuvered around another tram and continued toward Darmstadt. Once in the city, he found an underground parking entrance, drove down the ramp, and found a spot to park. It was a short walk to the *Schlossplatz*, a plaza situated in the center of the city, bordered by a palace, department stores, and the city hall.

Anna Maria said, "Look how charming this place looks! I will have fun exploring the cobblestone streets lined with department stores and boutiques."

During the Christmas season, the market square bustled with vendor booths and tents selling food, gifts, and decorations. They were hungry after the long day, and the smell of grilled meat drew them to a food stand.

"Jake, the bratwursts smell delicious cooking on the charcoal fire. It reminds me of my father grilling Italian sausages on the backyard barbeque."

They took turns adding spicy mustard and then carried plates away with two double proof Christmas beers made by the local *Rummel* Brewery. They found a table and sat down and watched the shoppers pass by as they ate.

"Jake, why are all the people carrying cloth sacks?"

"The Germans call them a *Tasche*. I forgot to tell you about that at the grocery store. The clerk asked me in German where my *Tasche* was and when I told her I didn't have one, she charged me for the paper bags," replied Crowley.

"I must remember to get one," said Anna Maria.

"Men also use them. Get one for me, too, please."

When they finished eating, they looked for a Christmas tree. Crowley spotted a small tree lot. They purchased a five-foot tall tree with a stand and a strand of lights. An ornament display caught Anna Maria's eye, and she strolled over to the booth.

"Help me pick out some decorations. There is such a variety, I am having a hard time deciding."

The newlyweds finished their shopping before the closing hour and drove back to their apartment just as it began to snow.

"Oh, perfect!" Anna Maria said.

Crowley set up the stand, put up the tree, and strung the lights. His wife unwrapped the new ornaments, unpacked some she brought from New York, and hung them on the tree. They stood back to admire their handiwork. The couple opened a bottle of wine, toasted their first Christmas together, and snuggled on the sofa.

Anna Maria rose suddenly and said, "I almost forgot. When am I going to learn how to drive a stick shift?"

"We were apart for almost a month. I thought we would take it slow and spend some time together through the holidays."

"I want to do that too. But I need to know I can go out on my own when you return to work."

"We will start the driving lessons tomorrow. As I mentioned earlier, I found the perfect spot to practice. You also need to study for the written test. The road signs are much different here."

Anna Maria's alarmed facial expression turned into a smile, and she settled down next to him. He put his arm around her and held her close. He realized he had his work cut out for him, keeping her safe while she wanted to be out "experiencing" Europe. She was high-spirited, and he knew that when he married her. Protecting her was going to be a challenge.

19

Spies Like Us

0900 Hours, 25 January 1970 Controller and Controlled

Eva met her control at the border and traveled with him to a safe house in Darmstadt. Once in the apartment, he briefed her about the mission. Her control, Fritz Lange, fretted over how beautiful the woman appeared with her dark hair, large hazel eyes, and fashionable clothes she had purchased in Darmstadt. He wanted someone less conspicuous, but his Stasi boss told him to take her in case an opportunity to seduce a soldier presented itself.

Eva found the post-war lifestyle in West Germany exhilarating. Ruin from the war no longer existed in the West. She was hard pressed to locate even cannon shell repairs in the walls of older historic buildings and the shopping was fabulous.

"So, Herr Lange, are all the Germans on this side of the border now capitalists?"

"The economic miracle claimed by the West has papered over all the destruction. There is so much building going on, they must recruit construction laborers from the middle east to fill the loss of men from World War Two. However, contrary to West German BRD propaganda, communism is back in vogue with student groups who have protested what they call 'fascist government policies', like the BRD's invitation for an official visit by the Shah of Persia, Reza Pahlavi, in June 1967."

"Why protest against a Persian King?"

"The students objected to his absolute rule and human rights violations. Protests got out of hand while law enforcement stood by and watched brutal beatings of demonstrators by the Shah's supporters. When the *Polizei* finally intervened, they made things worse by shooting one student. Since then, the protestors call the *Polizei* and BRD government 'fascists.'"

"And what about now?"

"From the martyrdom of one demonstrator, the communist movement gained strength because of the journalistic effort of Ulrike Meinhof and the protest leadership of Andreas Baader," Lange explained. "The duo formed what they called the Red Army Faction and began posting manifestos emblazoned with a red star superimposed with a machine gun and the initials 'RAF.' The press sensationalized the urban guerilla group into a cult of personality by referring to them as the Baader-Meinhof Gang."

So, Eva Schmidt, a Stasi illegal agent operating in West Germany, did not feel out of place when Lange helped her infiltrate the RAF movement using her assumed identity. Brought up in an orphanage in the East German DDR, she could walk the walk and talk the talk of a young communist "revolutionary." She also had good survival instincts. In East Germany, families believed it acceptable to dump off their children with behavior problems at the orphanages for rehabilitation. In a short while, she had a progress report for her handler.

Lange inquired, "How goes it with your urban guerilla friends?"

"At first, it was impromptu meetings with a lot of talk and no action. I grew to have nothing but disdain for the group. They appeared to be spoiled rich kids with time on their hands."

"Well, Fraulein Schmidt, the BRD wonder economy has made their parents into rich bourgeoisie and their socialist government has taken care of their every need, including a free college education."

"Herr Lange, it seems the capitalist American victors provided all this opportunity, and the current generation pays them back by becoming communist urban guerillas. The Viet Cong are carrying on a thousand-year struggle for independence and freedom fighters worldwide battle for equality and fair distribution of wealth. The RAF is trying to destroy accomplishments other revolutionaries are fighting to attain."

Lange replied, "As the saying goes, 'Idle hands are the devil's workshop.'"

Eva remarked, "I believe the RAF like to dabble in communism because it is in fashion and helps them get laid. They use it as an excuse for destructive behavior."

"Speaking of which, tell me about your encounters with the leaders Baader and Meinhof."

"*Ja*, they are two very dissimilar characters. Meinhof, a journalist working for her husband's liberal magazine *Konkret*, has strong opinions about workers and women's rights. She is the mouthpiece for the group."

"And what about Baader?"

"He was a troubled youth who now needs a gang around him to carry out his fantasies."

"Well, the RAF must suit the bill in that regard."

"*Ja*, he has become the leader and the second symbol of the movement. It is also surprising that most of the members are women."

Lange chuckled, "Maybe because communism is the new 'fashion statement,' as you said."

"*Ja*, well, Gudrun Ensslin is a good example. She told me she was no stranger to protest movements. Her clergyman father brought her up to take part in parish work and consider the plight of the downtrodden. An excellent student of social activism, she got Baader to change his anarchist tendencies into a political focus on perceived authoritarian government policies. In return, Baader influenced Ensslin to leave her partner and son Felix for him."

"So, are you telling me that besides being a revolutionary, Baader is a sex symbol too?"

"Herr Lange, I believe the role of an insurgency leader has its advantages."

"Yes, power can be the ultimate aphrodisiac."

"*Ja*, Gudrun made Baader focus on their objectives, and things happened. This change in momentum was my opportunity. I brought up the idea of traveling to Palestine to learn the tactics of the PLO. I told them I have a Palestinian friend I met at college who might help us contact them."

"That ploy must have gotten Baader's attention," Lange said.

"He liked the idea of aligning their cause with other freedom fighter groups. I made my request to you and got the invitation from the PLO with travel vouchers."

"And you were off and running?"

"No. As you know, the tickets were for flights from East Germany. Baader balked at the source. He wanted their movement to be a grass roots West German organization with no ties to other European communist countries.

"So, what happened?"

"I explained this away by saying, 'We are being trained by the Palestine Liberation Army. They just receive financial support from the DDR.' Now that I am thinking of the trip, I hope I will not have any trouble with my passport."

Lange laughed. "I'm sure your Stasi friends at passport control will get you through. I hope you do not get homesick from your brief stay in East Germany. The *Deutsche Demokratische Republik* has so many attractions."

His sarcasm made Eva think about how good she had it on this assignment in West Germany.

At 0900 hours, 28 January 1970, General Gurkin sat down in a barren temporary office inside a drab KGB outpost on *Angellikastrasse*,

Dresden. The bone chilling January weather gave the area a stark, gray, and foreboding appearance. As he stared out the window, Stasi Headquarters, situated across the street, brought back memories.

There is the original four-story stucco building I remember visiting when I was a captain. Back then, we had to harass the Stasi to do our bidding, and this office served as a convenient location for monitoring them. As the Stasi adopted our ways, they had to grow larger and that modern building with high ceilings on the second and third floors rose in the '60's next to the original building.

Gurkin was here to meet Colonel Otto Steiger, who oversaw a spy network in West Germany. The colonel arrived at 0930 hours wearing his full-dress uniform, complete with riding britches and boots. As he marched into the room, he snapped to attention, clicked his heels, and saluted Gurkin. The Russian rose from his desk chair and returned the salute. Gurkin noted his ally showed a lack of sensitivity concerning the Great Patriotic war only 25 years earlier. His Prussian-style uniform differed very little from the SS uniforms of World War II.

The general observed, "The more things change, the more they remain the same."

During the war, the general picked up the German language and used it to interrogate prisoners. He offered Steiger the single thread-bare guest chair and asked if he would join him for tea. Steiger accepted the invitation, and he ordered his aide to bring them refreshments as he got down to business.

"We have a high value target in Darmstadt, West Germany. The United States Air Force has a radio intercept facility in the suburb of *Linsedorf.* We desire to find out how effective the Americans are in intercepting our air defense communications."

Steiger replied, "I presently have no assets working on that target."

"We want information from their troops, not from within the operations site."

"Herr General, you mean kidnapping?"

"There is no time for the usual methods of turning soldiers into double agents. We wish to use your contacts in the Red Army Faction to pull this off. Since you have been supplying this group of urban guerillas with weapons and training via the PLO, you are in a perfect position to talk them into abducting U.S. Air Force personnel from this unit."

"This is a risk to our current operation!"

Gurkin ignored the comment. "We need to organize it to look like a terrorist plot by West German dissidents. The Americans must not suspect your organization or ours. The RAF will make the usual ransom demands and then turn them over to us for interrogation. After we are done with the interrogation, the kidnap victims disappear with no one the wiser."

The Stasi colonel had already infiltrated the Red Army Faction as part of the DDR's effort to disrupt the West German BRD government. He did not want the request to appear too easy.

"My sources indicate the group contains dissident students who believe they are in the struggle for worker's rights. They focus on their own government's politics."

He added, "How do I get them to justify this attack on U.S. soldiers considering their domestic agenda?"

General Gurkin leaned forward from his desk chair to make his point. "Convince the RAF that they need to justify their cause by aligning with other freedom fighters. To do this, they must show solidarity with the North Vietnamese communist freedom fighters. Tell them the best way to demonstrate their support is to kidnap American Air Force soldiers and reference the bombing of Vietnam civilians in their ransom demands."

Gurkin's preparedness surprised Steiger. He shook his head in affirmation and said, "*Ja*, the agent we have planted in the organization, could suggest such an operation."

The general nodded and then ordered his Stasi liaison to come up with a plan.

Two weeks later, General Gurkin sat down in General Petrenko's office, opened a folder, and spoke, "I believe the best course of action would be to work with the Stasi to coordinate a kidnapping by the Red Army Faction, a dissident group supported by the Stasi with weapons and other resources."

"How workable is this indirect approach? I need this information right away!" Petrenko replied.

"The East German Stasi have already planted an agent in the revolutionary group who arranged for guerilla training by the PLO in Palestine. Using this group for the kidnapping will make it look like a domestic dissident plot, not a move by us to gain information on U.S. communications intelligence."

Petrenko said, "I know Cold War strategy dictates the use of surrogates to avoid direct confrontation with the West. However, I have reservations. How do we ensure this group captures Americans with the intel we need when we do not control the operation directly?"

Gurkin replied, "The Stasi agents will shadow the Americans who travel to the Security Service operations site. Once the agents identify enough targets, they will work with the RAF to plan coordinated kidnappings at multiple locations. The Stasi trained their agents to make kidnappings appear to be foul play from drug buys or dealings with prostitutes. If kidnapping is too difficult to pull off, they will identify a group of American airmen to hijack as they travel together on a bus or what the American's call 'a carpool' to the site. Once the agents can determine the best approach, the RAF can monitor groups that arrive at the operational site and then backtrack their routes to plan a hijack of the vehicles they use. A hijack will be consistent with other terrorist attacks they are planning against West German politicians. On the downside, they will only get one shot at a car hijack, whereas the kidnappings have multiple chances of success."

General Petrenko considered the two approaches.

"Is it possible to perform abductions and hijacks at the same time?"

Gurkin replied, "It will require additional support to accomplish both a hijack and the abductions because of their limited membership. They need automatic weapons and explosives to be effective in this dual approach. Both efforts must occur simultaneously, because a failed attempt may cause our targets moving to an undercover operation in civilian clothes like they operate in Berlin."

Petrenko repeated his concern. "I am worried about abducting the Americans who know the status of their interception of our flight tracking broadcasts. If the RAF mount both operations, we have a better chance of getting the counterintelligence we need, and they get to claim credit for all the mayhem as actions to support the North Vietnamese freedom fighters."

Gurkin replied, "With automatic weapons, they will require fewer people to perform a hijack. That should leave enough RAF personnel to abduct three or four airmen as well."

Petrenko looked pleased as he asked his KGB liaison to implement this operation as soon as possible.

It was 0700 hours, February 1970, when Colonel Vladimir Rudolfsky stepped out onto the tarmac of Vasylkiv Air Base wearing his gravity flight suit. The cold chill of a typical February day in Kiev stiffened his posture. Rudolfsky had ordered new flight procedures at the beginning of the new year, and he planned to test the results himself. He walked up to a large twin tailed fighter as it was being serviced and handed his helmet to the crew-chief, Sergeant Nicolas Rasmussen.

"I will place it in the cockpit as part of alert readiness procedures," Rasmussen said.

The aircraft mechanics snapped to attention as Rudolfsky inspected the jet while being escorted by his crew chief. The jet's armament included four AA-6 Acrid air-to-air missiles. Rudolfsky grabbed one and shook it to check its mountings as Rasmussen jumped away from the front of the rockets.

Rasmussen thought, *Doesn't the commander understand the danger he just put me in? I was standing right in front of the projectiles when he shook the rack. Hasn't he heard the gruesome stories of ordnance going off during inspections?*

Rudolfsky ignored Rasmussen's sudden movements as he walked over to the landing gear and eyeballed the condition of the tires. Maintenance was a problem, given the short supply of parts, and Rudolfsky made a point of inspecting his plane before every mission. He chastised the mechanics for the wear on the tires and ordered them to go forage new ones from other aircraft being repaired.

Rasmussen mused, "The Comrade Colonel must have shaken that missile while I was standing in its path to distract me. He knows it is against regulations to steal parts from other aircraft."

Rasmussen acknowledged the illegal order with the reply, "Comrade Colonel, I will look into acquiring tires for your fighter aircraft."

Rudolfsky replied, "This MiG-25 must be prepared to fly a high-speed intercept mission. I want those tires replaced with new ones. Am I clear?"

Colonel Rudolfsky commanded a regiment of sixty-three MiG-25P interceptors assigned to the 146th Guards Fighter Aviation Regiment. Their job was to keep the Soviet sky free of spy planes and other potential intruders like the future XB-70 bomber should the Americans deploy it.

Rasmussen nodded and accompanied Rudolfsky as he completed his inspection. When the inspection ended, he stood at attention as the commander saluted the ground crew and returned to the ready room.

At 0935 hours, the claxon sounded and Rudolfsky ran out to his MiG-25P on the flight line, where his crew was waiting.

The pilot stopped at the bottom of the ladder and turned to Rasmussen. "Today, I will fly alone to intercept the U-2 intruder. I want to confirm an intercept is feasible from this base."

He climbed into the cockpit and the crew chief helped him with his helmet and safety harness, while he scanned the blue control panel, examining all the analog gauges.

Rudolfsky called out. "I'll take it from here."

He hit a button to light up the two massive Tumansky R-15D-300 single shaft turbojets.

The crew-chief had to jump down the ladder and pull it back to avoid being dragged along by Rudolfsky as he taxied the plane to the runway.

He shouted over the din, "Again, this officer puts my life in danger with his carelessness! What is he trying to prove?"

The control tower cleared the colonel, and he rocketed down the runway to perform a short take-off. All Soviet aircraft design included provisions for short takeoff and landing on rough runways. That was why he kept a sharp eye on the condition of the tires. Rudolfsky pulled back the stick, and the plane climbed straight up into the stratosphere, where he leveled off and accelerated to his intercept speed of Mach 2.5. The radio crackled and ground control called in vectors to the interceptor. As he closed within fifty miles, the pilot switched on his powerful *Smerch* target acquisition radar. The radar signals set off warning bells in the U-2 and the American pilot started flying a retreat course out of Soviet Air space toward the Black Sea.

Rudolfsky cursed when he realized he would not close with the spy plane in time, so he broke off his intercept after confirmation with his ground controller. As he flew back to base, Rudolfsky wondered when PVO *Strany* was going to deploy his regiment to airfields closer to the borders so that he could catch the Americans in their act of espionage.

20

A Vacation on Their Own

The Crowley's sat at their tiny kitchen table in their cozy Arheilgen apartment eating breakfast.

"Jake, I booked the trip to Garmisch-Partenkirchen we talked about. We can decide what to see among all the castles, mountains, and lakes. The pictures of Bavaria in the snow are beautiful. Like a fairytale land!"

Anna Maria loved the Bavarian Alps bus tour so much she talked her husband into another winter vacation to the same region on their own.

Crowley replied, "That sounds great, but make sure you include a trip to the Zugspitze Mountain by cable car in our travel plans. Oh, I will have to buy snow tires before we drive to Bavaria. They have more snow than we do here."

Anna Maria said, "I found out that Garmisch-Partenkirchen are two distinct villages dating back to the Roman era when a trading route between Augsburg and Venice passed through what was now the main road of Ludwigsstrasse in Partenkirchen. They grew into each other and became united in 1935. Just a brief history lesson with your oatmeal."

Anna Maria found a job in the comptroller's office at *Stars and Stripes*, a newspaper for armed forces personnel. Her new office friends sparked her interest in travel by describing their assignments in Europe.

Franz Schweinsteiger trudged through the snow. "I wonder what they want now?"

Yesterday morning he saw the chalk mark on the hotel wall signifying a message drop.

He muttered, "Wouldn't you know they send their instructions during a snowstorm?"

Up ahead, he could barely make out the railroad station, where he would pick up his packet from the usual location.

He sat down on a bench in front of the ticket office and shivered from the cold. "*Gott im Himmel!* What I go through for the party."

Schweinsteiger reached down and tore an envelope off the bottom of the seat and stuck it in his pocket. He got up quickly and shuffled back to the hotel through the deep snow.

The German worked on building maintenance at the General Patton Hotel. When he reached the building, he retired to his little repair shop in the hotel's basement and rummaged around for scissors to cut the packet open. He found a pair and opened it along an edge, pulled the sheet of paper out and unfolded it to decrypt it.

After a lengthy decryption process, he read the message to himself. It contained detailed instructions about sabotaging a guest's car the evening before their check out.

He wondered, *How did his control know so much about the guest and his departure date? Was a second agent working here? I* must be careful about what I say to the rest of the staff! This must be *another test of my loyalty. After all, no one important would drive a small BMW. They would ride around in a big Mercedes.*

He made a mental note of the car's brand and its green plate license number. Based on the description, he surmised the car belonged to a member of the U.S. military.

Franz wondered, *How did his spymaster get these plates for this loyalty test? Stolen maybe?*

Back in Arheilgen, the Crowleys packed up the BMW using the back seat for their suitcases and the trunk to store the two five-gallon cans of rationed gas. They started out early on their seven-hour drive to the Bavarian Alps and reached the General Patton Hotel before nightfall. Crowley stopped the car at the entrance to the resort to enjoy the scenery.

Anna Maria remarked, "This lodge is a fine example of the quaint Tyrol cinder block architecture with stucco walls and carved wood framed roof. And look at that view! It looks like a picture postcard."

Crowley replied, "Those manicured fields and well-placed thickets of woods set into pristine mountains just didn't happen on their own. We are looking at thousands of years of agriculture. You don't see that in a rustic setting like the Adirondacks back home. I think it is an example of Old World versus New World."

Anna Maria said, "Still, it's so beautiful it looks like my grandfather's Christmas *presepio* brought to life!"

Once inside, she stopped to admire an oil painting in the lobby.

She turned to Jake and said, "Honey, they even have General Patton's portrait on the wall."

The painting depicted Patton standing in the foreground facing the viewer with tanks engaged in a battle off in the background.

Crowley remarked, "The scene shows a lot of detail in his uniform, including those ivory handled pistols he wore. I want to buy some ivory pistol grips in Michelstadt for my sidearms. We can do your knives in ivory, too!"

"Very funny! Ivory is for movie stars like Hopalong Cassidy. Your commander ordered you to conceal your weapons. You can't show them off, so no bang for the buck with that purchase. No pun intended."

"Yeah right! What about your throwing knives? Ivory handles will go wonderfully with your white go-go boots."

"I have kept my knives with their black ebony grips hidden long before concealment became a requirement for your job. Stealth is the name of the game, as is anonymity."

"You got me there."

Anna Maria changed the subject by pointing to the windows. "Jake, the beautiful stained-glass in the lobby depicts scenes of Germanic nobility. They must have survived from when this was a civilian hotel before the American armed forces requisitioned it. Let's check out the dining room. The brochure shows a dramatic picture of the entrance featuring stone archways sealed by massive wooden doors with transoms fitted into each arch."

She caught sight of an archway with a wooden door and walked toward it. Crowley put down their bags and followed her over.

"Jake, tapestry woven with folk scenes of the Bavarian countryside are hanging on the walls and the cherry furnishings are very warm and inviting."

Anna Maria recognized a candelabra made from a large wooden wagon wheel. So far, everything has been turning out as she expected. They took the elevator to inspect their room.

She looked around and said, "No bathroom down the hall this time! Let's eat."

They found the restaurant and Jake ordered. "We will each have the *Jaegerschnitzel* platter and share one bottle of Rhein wine."

After dinner, they walked outside and talked about their plans for the next few days. When they returned to their room, Anna Maria pulled out a tour guide booklet.

Anna Maria said, "Darling, tomorrow we will travel to Fussen where the Neuschwanstein and Hohenschwangau castles are located. We'll drive to the monastery at Ettal after lunch. The following morning, we have lift tickets and ski rentals reserved at the recreation center, capped off with your request to take the cable car up to the observation deck of the Zugspitze in the afternoon."

She looked at the picture in the brochure, depicting the gondola ascending on cables that disappeared into a cloud.

Anna Maria thought, *It figures he would want a scary ride to the top of the highest mountain in Germany. Well, I can pray for our safety in the monastery at Ettal.*

Crowley scooped her up in his arms and said, "Let's start our exciting adventure right now!" as he carried her to the large, hand-carved oak bed.

After a continental breakfast at the hotel, the couple walked out to the parking lot, cleaned the snow off the BMW, and headed for Fussen.

King Ludwig lived as a child in Hohenschwangau, so the Crowleys toured that residence first. The décor of the massive gothic revival palace featured artwork influenced by Nordic myths of knights and fair maidens.

As they prepared to leave, Anna Maria turned to Jake and said, "This appears to be an authentic castle with a rustic beauty. Little King Ludwig must have lived a rugged lifestyle with only fireplaces for heating and large drafty rooms. At least they had indoor plumbing in the royal apartments."

The Crowleys first caught sight of Neuschwanstein Castle as they crossed the *Marienbrücke*, a pedestrian bridge connecting two cliffs.

"Oh, Look Jake. The castle is stunning sitting on top of that mountain with the lake and valley stretching out behind it."

"Disney was able to copy this castle, but not this setting. It is spectacular," declared Crowley.

Anna Maria raised her tour book and read aloud, "King Ludwig designed this palace in honor of Richard Wagner's operas. It is medieval in appearance and the murals and wood carving depict the fairy tales Wagner used. Yet, the architecture reflects up-to-date technology, including central forced air heating and a modern kitchen for its time."

"I think I want to see that for myself. Let's hike up to the entrance and buy tickets," said Crowley.

Anna Maria pored over her guidebook at each stop on the tour. "King Ludwig wanted to have his cake and eat it too in this castle. No more roughing it, like in Hohenschwangau."

After a late lunch, they drove to the Abbey and Monastery at Ettal. They left a donation and then started their sightseeing of the vast Benedictine enclave.

She searched her guide and said, “Let’s go into the Basilica. I read the monks decorated the interior in gold, and it has a beautiful domed ceiling.”

They were not disappointed. When they reached the altar, Anna Maria stopped to light a candle and say a prayer. They emerged from the building into bright sunlight reflecting off the snow-covered fields. Crowley turned to look back.

He said, “The monastery looks a bit out of place. I would expect to find this impressive structure in a city.”

The next day it snowed, giving the Crowleys an opportunity to ski on fresh powder.

“I am glad we took lessons on the first trip to the Alps. I really enjoyed skiing this time,” Anna Maria exclaimed.

They arrived at Zugspitze in the early afternoon. The pair stepped into the gondola, and the door closed behind them. As they glided away from the platform, Anna Maria looked up.

“Jake—the cables vanish into the whiteout above, just like in the brochure!”

The cable car hummed as it continued upward, piercing the clouds along the way. The sky cleared as the gondola reached the end of the ride and arrived at the summit. Low buildings stood on the massive platform and nearby sat the top of the mountain, capped with a gold cross.

Anna Maria put on her sunglasses and said, “The view is spectacular in every direction!”

They looked around and found coin-operated binoculars, which they used to admire the Alps of Germany, Austria, and Switzerland.

23 March 1970. Garmisch-Partenkirchen, West Germany.

Schweinsteiger mulled over his decision to go ahead with his mission until 0100 Sunday morning. He extinguished his cigarette and dressed for the cold walk from his apartment to the lodge. When he arrived, he found the BMW parked near the lodge entrance.

"*Scheisse!* The portico night light is shining on the car."

This made him concerned about being spotted. He was glad he wore his old army off-white alpine coat and ski pants, which kept him dry and invisible in a heavy snowstorm. The patches and rips in the uniform caused by the removal of the military insignia made a tattered appearance.

"What do I do now? *Ja*, I must duck down under the light and crawl behind the car."

The snow packed around his body as he slid under the BMW. He dug his way to his coveralls pocket for a pen light. By the time he got it out, he was shivering from the snow packed up his sleeve.

"Where is the blade? Did I forget it?"

He fumbled around and pulled a hacksaw blade taped to a wood handle out of a coat pocket with his right hand, packing that sleeve with snow as well.

"*Scheisse!*" he shouted as both his arms shook from the cold.

Now Schweinsteiger dropped the pen light. "*Zu kalt! Wo ist es?*"

He fished in the dark on his back, making him feel even colder.

"*Da ist es!*"

He spotted the light and grabbed the pen.

"I must find the brake line for each wheel."

The cuts with the hacksaw blade weakened the rubber lines by letting a small amount of fluid leak out. Franz dragged himself from beneath the auto and brushed off his clothes. He remained crouched down to avoid being seen. Still shaking, he stood up and hurried back to his apartment, leaving Crowley and his wife to their fate.

21

Back to Work

It was 23 March 1970 when the travel alarm sounded at 0500 hours in their room at the Hotel Patton. Crowley shook Anna Maria's shoulder to wake her.

"Sorry darling. My first swing shift starts at 1700 today."

They both rose, got dressed, grabbed their bags, and headed to the front desk.

Crowley rang the bell and startled the clerk. "Excuse us! The clerk would not complete our early departure checkout last night because we must turn in the room key. Well, here it is. We paid already."

Once outside, a surprise awaited them. Overnight, a blizzard dumped a foot of the white stuff on their BMW. The winter wonderland did not seem so wonderful anymore.

"Anna Maria, you get in while I brush off the BMW. I will have to take it slow until the storm lets up. I hope this weather does not delay us from making it to Darmstadt on time for work."

He struggled out of the parking lot, spinning the wheels as the car pushed the fresh snow aside to clear the way. The engine slowly warmed up as Crowley kept wiping the inside of the windshield until the defroster kicked in.

"The plows have not been by yet and I see high snowdrifts," commented Crowley.

“Be careful Jake. Remember, there are no guardrails on these winding mountain roads.”

They exited the parking lot and turned down a descent, which increased their momentum.

He remarked, “This BMW design forms a ship’s prow out of the grill, which pushes aside the drifts. I wonder if that was a practical or aesthetic consideration. They manufacture the cars here in Bavaria,”

The mountain road became steeper, and they started sliding when he put on the brakes. The car transformed into a toboggan with the wheels acting as rudders in the front and runners in the back. When he tried to slow down, the car accelerated as the wheels skidded on the packed snow. A sudden slide sideways forced the car to slow down. He recalled the snowplow maneuver he learned during his skiing lessons. He tried another sideways slide, and it worked better than the brakes.

Crowley thought, “The danger in this maneuver lies in catching on something during the slide and rolling the car into the abyss on the side of the road.”

As they came to another downward slope, he tried using brakes and felt the pedal sink to the floor.

Anna Maria shouted, “Jake, watch out!” as they just missed going over the side of the mountain with the right rear wheel thumping on the edge. He executed another snowplow, and the BMW slid to a stop in the middle of the road. Crowley got out to find a puddle of red fluid on the snow. He sat back in the driver’s seat with an ashen look on his face.

“Fasten your safety belt, my love. We are in for one hell of a ride! The brakes have failed.”

“I thought you said German automobiles are reliable. This is our first trip, and we already have a serious problem. We should have stuck with our American cars!”

“They are hard to get repaired in Europe.”

“I do not remember my Malibu needing any repairs. Just oil changes and tires. It looks like the BMW is going to cost us a fortune!”

He buckled his seat belt and said, "If ever we should live so long."

His comment made Anna Maria's eyes widen as she focused on the steep drop off at the edge of the road. He drove on as fast as the descent would allow, using his snowplow maneuver and the emergency brake lever to control their descent. As he wrestled with the car down around a switchback, he remembered what Anna Maria said about no guard rails. A whiteout from the ongoing blizzard obscured the right cliff side shoulder. He steered the vehicle over to the left, not expecting oncoming traffic. That allowed him enough room to swing sideways whenever they needed to slow down.

Once they reached the autobahn, the snow changed to chilly rain. The automobile limped along to the first gas station exit they could find. Lucky for them, the attendant was a mechanic and had the parts to perform the repair. While the car was up on a lift, the mechanic showed him cuts on the brake hoses. He pointed one out with his wrench.

"Someone doesn't like you very much. It appears to be sabotage."

Crowley replied, "I thought road debris hidden in the heavy snow we drove through might have caused it."

"They are in a protected location for that very reason and the cuts on the hoses are in the same place on both sides. It cannot be an accident or coincidence."

He wondered to himself. "I must increase my vigilance somehow, or we are going to die. Carrying a weapon is not enough."

5 May 1970 found Crowley on duty during day watch at the S&W Operations Site, going through another training session. Under Staff Sergeant Gibson's tutelage, Crowley had become a very proficient signals intelligence analyst.

Gibson commented, "I hear you have been working with the Surveillance and Warning Center analysts to correlate your data with the Morse code and voice broadcast intercept. This is a big step in the right direction. The analysts said you have been performing coordination meetings over the intercom with the S&W team. Very efficient way to go about it."

He added, "I also like how you circulate on the operations floor with the men assigned to the other signal intercept sources to discuss their activity when our mission is down."

Crowley found out that with voice intercept, the radio operator was also the analyst, interpreting messages in real-time. They intercepted air-to-ground nets in Russian and the languages of the Soviet satellite countries.

"Well, I get antsy during training sessions, so when I have a break, I walk around discussing intelligence gathering techniques and areas of coverage with the other analysts and intercept operators."

With the information Crowley gained on the OPS floor, he worked to integrate RUBICON into the real time surveillance and warning effort. Crowley's efforts resulted in him meeting other airmen with common interests of travel and music. Friendships formed, leading to dinner party invitations. One thing led to another, and before they knew it, the Crowleys were also attending rock concerts with their new friends. These events took place in smaller venues than in the United States, allowing them to sit or stand up close and take splendid pictures as bands like Grand Funk Railroad, Jethro Tull and James Taylor performed.

20 June 1970, Captain Hodges called Crowley into his office at 0800. "It is time for you to get acquainted with your West German anti-terrorist counterpart in Darmstadt."

Crowley executed his orders, and his team stood in their dress uniforms, ready to train with a Hessian state police unit. Crowley looked around for the Hessian commander and spotted him wearing a green tailored uniform and coordinating light green shirt with a dark tie. His tunic had a shield shaped patch on the shoulder with the word "*Polizei*" embroidered over a gold crown above a Griffin.

Crowley mused, "With his neatly pressed riding britches tucked into high black boots, he could pass for a state trooper back in New York."

Captain Bauer stood in front of the group and gave them a briefing in perfect English. "Men, the Red Army Faction as they call themselves, began as a student movement protesting alleged police brutality during a demonstration at an official visit of the Shah of Iran on June 2nd, 1967. Their first reprisal was the arson attack of a department store."

The captain added, "On May 14th of this year, the leader, Andreas Baader, escaped from prison with the aid of a small group of the RAF led by the journalist Frau Ulrike Meinhof. Meinhof had him moved out of jail to a minimum-security facility under the pretext of an interview for a special article she was writing concerning young outcasts of society. During the escape, which was aided by Meinhof, a gang member shot and wounded one of the staff at the institute."

He concluded, "The RAF has shown they will use violence to accomplish their aims, and we are now trying to track them down in Palestine. For all we know, the PLO is training them as we speak in urban guerilla tactics."

A meet and greet started as both teams took turns introducing themselves. Bauer recommended they pair up and get in the German police cruisers to "As you Americans say, 'ride shotgun' with us to understand how we patrol the streets of Darmstadt."

He asked Crowley to accompany him, and the captain led the way to a hunter green Porsche 911 Carrera sports car with a white top parked in a space with the captain's name painted on the wall facing the parking space. The vehicle had "*POLIZEI*" stenciled on the sides of the car and emergency lights affixed to the top. He picked up on Crowley's look of surprise.

"We must fight fire with fire. The bad guys steal sports cars and use them in their criminal pursuits, so we need fast interceptors to catch them."

Crowley nodded and grabbed onto a padded roll cage as he slid into a Recaro seat configured with full four-point racing harnesses. The captain performed a Le Mans start by working the ignition switch with his left hand and the shifter with his right while his feet operated the foot pedals. He noted Bauer's quick take off and reminded himself that American cars all have the starter switch on the right, preventing him from accessing the shifter and the starter key at the same time. He would have to make up for this shortcoming with brute horsepower. They roared through the parking lot to the exit, where Bauer steered left onto *Wilhelm Leuschner Strasse* to start his patrol. They drove around Darmstadt, where he showed Crowley locations known to be RAF hangouts.

As he drove, Bauer pointed to Crowley's combat controller badge. "I know that insignia. I serve with the *Bundeswehr Spezielle Operationen*, a reserve airborne outfit headquartered in Stadtallendorf, north of Frankfurt. We perform NATO exercises with your forces."

The captain added, "My military experience led to my appointment to the state police anti-terrorist department. They needed men with training in urban warfare tactics."

As they continued the patrol, the two commandos swapped stories about their experiences.

At a stop light, he turned to face Crowley. "I can arrange for you to jump with us the next time we train. What about it?"

He nodded in agreement but said, "On condition I get permission from my commander."

"Of course, I wouldn't have it any other way."

After their drive, he decided Bauer was the real deal and would be helpful in getting his men briefed on the domestic terrorism situation.

12 June 1970, Crowley sat in Captain Hodges's office discussing the *Polizei* kick off meeting two days prior. His commander told him that the teams from all four flights were going to do some training runs with the German police to practice radio and pursuit procedures. He mentioned the invitation from Bauer to jump with his paratrooper unit.

Hodges replied with an annoyed guise, "I ordered you to get to know the *Polizei*, not become one of them!"

Then he smiled. "Good work on building a close relationship with the German police. That will help in getting cooperation in the future."

"Was the captain answering yes, or no?" Crowley decided to wait for a jump date before asking again for permission.

Hodges sat back in his chair and said, "I almost forgot to tell you, I had a long phone call with Mr. Sedgwick at the NSA concerning the status of the RUBICON Project. He was glad to hear you were armed and dangerous. What did he mean by that?"

Crowley replied, "KGB agents attacked me in San Angelo and then again in New York."

"Why wasn't this brought up before?"

"I thought that was why you picked me for this assignment. I get to protect myself as well."

"No, I did not know. Do not mention this to anyone."

"Yes sir!"

Hodges changed the subject. "The squad is being issued police interceptors from the motor pool. You need to organize them into three four-man teams. Two teams will man the cars to escort each Dog Flight shuttle and the third team rides in the bus from Kaserne to the operations center."

The captain added, "The escorts must coordinate using their radios to make sure they stay close but out of sight, while accompanying the shuttle to OPS. We do not want to form a parade and draw attention. These automobiles are not your usual motor pool ghetto cruisers. They are unmarked security police 1968 Ford Galaxie interceptors with large block engines and heavy-duty suspensions."

Crowley replied, "That should put us on par with the *Polizei*."

The commander continued, "Under the back seats are racks with M16 assault rifles and shotguns. Since you already have Special Operations driver training, I want you to pick the best drivers in your group and assign them to the vehicles, including you. You can decide which four airmen will ride the bus. There is a cabinet behind the shuttle bus driver's seat with long guns for that team. Here are the car keys for your teams."

Crowley said, "I plan to rotate the men on the shuttle bus to keep up morale and communication."

Hodges added, "I found out that the motor pool at Wiesbaden Air Base has a driver's training course laid out in front of an unused hangar. Get some high-speed practice in before you work with the *Polizei*."

Crowley acknowledged with a "Yes, sir!" and left to schedule the driving exercise.

The combat controller had impressed Hodges with his supervision of the security team and his mastery of the radio intercept mission. He made a note to discuss the airman's performance review with the Dog Flight Senior Master Sergeant.

22

Autobahn Cruiser

On 24 June 1970, Dog Flight was on the evening swing shift schedule and Crowley arrived at the motor pool after the shift change at 0800 hours. He spotted mechanics prepping the two Ford Galaxie police interceptors and walked over.

As he got near, a mechanic called out, "Are you Crowley?"

"Yes—is there a problem?"

The soldier moved aside as he approached, revealing the engine as he yelled. "Only if you are the guy crazy enough to run against a machine like this!"

Crowley peered inside the engine bay and smiled. Under the hood sat a 427 SOHC racing motor with twin Holly four-barrel carburetors.

The mechanic had to yell over the engine noise to be heard. "They banned them at NASCAR for having an unfair advantage. In the military, we take any advantage we can get and call it overwhelming force."

Crowley replied, "NASCAR claimed they were not a production engine. They called them crate motors because Ford only sold them in boxes for special racing applications."

The army mechanic replied. "Somehow, a purchasing agent in the Air Force had some fun and specified them on the build sheets for these police interceptors. Since they were special order military vehicles, it did not raise a flag at the factory."

Crowley said, "I scheduled a handling and pursuit course at Wiesbaden Air Base for this morning, to not interfere with our shift schedule. Are you finished with the tuning?"

The mechanic reached through the driver's window and turned off the engine. "Yes, they are ready. Let me give you the nickel tour. The cars are Air Force blue four-door sedans with heavy-duty black wall high-speed tires on steel wheels with the requisite 'dog dish' chrome hub caps. They told us you need a low profile, so we did not stencil any police insignia on the bodies."

After getting accustomed to smaller automobiles in Europe, the vehicles looked gigantic to Crowley and the V8 engines, with their dual exhaust, sounded like they belonged on a racetrack. An autobahn would have to do for now.

The mechanic continued his tour by moving to the rear of the car. "You can see the cruisers have additional brake lights and exhaust pipes large enough for an oil pipeline. Back in the states, those lights on the package shelf are a dead giveaway for an unmarked patrol car. Here in Europe, the lights will not carry the same significance."

Crowley thought, *The vehicle is big and American. That will draw some attention.*

After studying the cruiser, he decided the Germans would see the green license plates and the plain blue paint and think it was just another Air Force staff car. At 1000 hours, the team arrived, and he briefed them on the equipment in the interceptors.

"Men, the military normally requisitions these 427ci engines for special applications like Navy SEAL special ops landing craft. These motors, known in racing circles as 'Cammers', rev to 7500 RPM and produce 658 horsepower because of their displacement and overhead camshaft design. It is unusual to find them in a patrol car."

An airman raised his hand. "Does that mean they are quick? The patrol cars look like my dad's grocery-getter."

Crowley replied, "Bolt this engine into a bus and it would go fast. The navy landing craft I trained on used this engine for rapid land insertions. We had to hold on for dear life. Ford bolted these engines to heavy duty four-speed manual transmissions. There is a chrome stick shift with a white 'cue ball' handle rising from the tunnel next to the steering wheel. Do any of you have a problem driving a standard?"

Two airmen raised their hands and Crowley said, "Remind me at the road course to give you a sidebar explanation of how the shifter works. You may have noticed that the car is slung low for handling and is equipped with heavy duty everything, including the suspension. It does not ride like your father's grocery-getter, but it can carry a family of six in each car. Get in and we will drive to the training course."

Before Crowley got behind the wheel, he noticed how the dog dish hub caps the mechanic commented on completed the stealth image and shook his head as he laughed. They arrived at the designated hanger at Wiesbaden, and he parked the Ford he was driving and reconnoitered the building.

He emerged from the hangar and called Frazer, waiting in the other patrol car. "Bring them inside for some bench racing."

They found Crowley standing in front of a blackboard facing two rows of chairs.

He said, "Men, grab a seat so we can start a lesson in basic pursuit tactics. I will begin by instructing you on how to perform turns using the apex."

He drew a diagram and used it to explain what an apex is and how to use it in high-speed turns. Next, he diagrammed how to reverse direction quickly.

Pointing to the diagram, he said, "To get away from a dangerous situation, accelerate in reverse and then use the emergency brake to lock the rear brakes as you spin around with a hard left or right turn. In my BMW, I steer with my left hand and operate the brake lever with my right. American cars are a whole different story. You speed up in reverse and then activate the brake pedal with your left foot. Then you pop the brake release with your left hand as you swing the car around with your right hand on the steering. The timing and emergency brake pedal pressure are tricky. I found it takes more practice because of the awkwardness of the brake pedal. With a European car, the only foot coordination is the throttle pedal."

After completing the bench racing session, he formed them up into teams.

He pointed. "You two, follow me around the course. Everyone else, pay attention."

The first team drove in pursuit as Crowley accelerated faster and faster until they were using the entire roadway to make turns and keep inside the cones.

He pulled over and stuck his head out of the driver's window. "Now you take the point, and the next pair of drivers mount up in my cruiser as the chase vehicle. The rotation will continue until all twelve of us have performed lead and pursuit driving."

Later, Frazer came over to Crowley. "The cars impress the men with how they handle and keep cool even during closely repeated runs. The heavy-duty radiators and tires on the interceptors are holding up well."

He nodded. "Next, we practice the escape maneuver. Then we will do a timed drill which comprises stopping the cruiser, retrieving weapons from the gun racks, and deploying to defensive positions around the vehicle."

After observing the exercise, Frazer commented, "I'm glad the cruisers have four doors to allow fast exits in case of an emergency."

Crowley replied, "Chad, it is getting late. Mount up for the trip back to Darmstadt."

On the way, Frazer reflected at length as he drove. "The Ford interceptors are imposing in traffic. The large chrome bumpers and split front grill, which angles forward as it wraps around the headlights, makes the car appear to have the shape of a manta ray ready to eat anything in its path."

Crowley replied, "It figures you would come up with some kind of fish analogy—surfer dude!"

Frazer laughed and got into the left lane on the autobahn and hit the gas.

"Jake, the rapping sound of the V8 racing engine's dual exhaust is awe-inspiring. The noise acts like a siren, causing the smaller European cars to scurry over to the right and hide between trucks until the menace passes."

Crowley said, "As they say, size matters and the interceptors are longer and wider than some trucks we passed."

Cruising back to Darmstadt, both cars had the armed forces radio station on. A rock and roll program came on the air playing the current hit "Jumpin' Jack Flash" by the Stones. Chad Frazer heard the song and could not resist the blues beat. He steered his cruiser out onto the passing lane with the second cruiser close behind and let out a yell as they disappeared at the vanishing point, burning rubber all the way. After listening to the *Polizei* brag about European automobiles, the Fords made them feel proud to be Americans. After all, Ford won Le Mans again last year.

23

A Star Is Born

It was early in the morning on 10 July 1970, and Anna Maria stood on the ramparts of Frankenstein's Castle as the director, Jack Murray, came over to greet her and discuss her TV show debut.

He said, "So, how did you get into the travel business?"

"The bug bit me on my first trip to the Alps with my husband. After that experience, I took every opportunity to explore the countryside."

"Is that how you found this location?"

"When Jake worked a weekend day shift, I would head here to the Odenwald, a scenic area with rolling hills dotted with farmland and small towns. I often discovered hidden treasures overlooked by tourists. This is one of them."

"Are you saying you have more locations already to go?"

"Michelstadt is a center of unique jewelry makers who carve their artwork with dental drills. I talked to the shopkeepers about their craft and took pictures of the village with its half-timbered architecture. In Erbach, I found a castle surrounded by a town of wood carvers who fashioned steins, bowls, barrels, and serving dishes from the local oak trees."

Murray said, "Terrific. How did this lead to writing about it?"

“I had acquired the habit of keeping a journal when I worked for a bank on Long Island. This helped me keep straight the details of business transactions. I bought a new logbook in the base exchange and began documenting historical facts, tips, and personal opinions about my experiences. I shared what became my travel diary with friends at *Stars and Stripes*.”

“And just like that, they made you a journalist?”

“The diary circulated and became a popular reference for weekend excursions. It found its way to Helen Scanlon, assistant to the travel section editor. She told me my descriptions brought the locations to life in vivid detail and recommended it to her boss, Frank Barnes. Barnes picked it up on a slow day and asked Helen how he could meet me. She mentioned a dinner party she was hosting and invited him to attend.”

“What did Barnes have to say?”

“After introductions, we engaged in a lively conversation. Frank told me I could be an important contributor to the newspaper, and would I like to write articles for the travel section? Not much for me to decide. I love to sightsee and now I would get paid for it.”

“And next you received a call from my assistant at the Armed Forces Europe TV station in Frankfurt. Frank Barnes reviewed some of your fan mail and decided your reporting would appeal to a wider audience. He arranged your interview with me.”

“Yes, and then you had me audition.”

“What a screen test it was, too! With your striking good looks and fascinating Italian American accent, I thought you would give us the international flare the program needed.”

“Thank you. This TV program, along with my radio show and newspaper column, will keep me very busy. I am going to have to find time to write my travel articles. What if I create in-depth stories about the sites we visit on the shows?”

Murray said, “That is a great idea. It will expose the TV program to a wider audience!”

She recalled how happy Jake was about her promotion and how much he appreciated the extra money the new job came with. No more pinching pennies.

A film crew member announced, “Mrs. Crowley, please step to your mark. We are ready for you now.”

Murray walked behind the camera to direct the filming. Her focus returned to this hilltop south of Darmstadt, named Frankenstein’s Castle, or *Burg Frankenstein* as the locals called it. The structure’s history began in 1252, and it showed its age. A perfect ruin for children to run around in and imagine being knights or damsels in distress or celebrate Halloween. She stood at the corner of a waist-high wall with a stone tower in the background. Beyond the ramparts stretched the hills and dales of the Odenwald. The film crew was doing last-minute lighting and sound tests. When they felt they were ready, Murray shouted, “Roll ‘em!” and she began speaking into a microphone she held. She was wearing a summer jacket and matching miniskirt with white go-go boots. Her short hairstyle accentuated her almond-shaped green eyes and youthful appearance. She reminded the director of Sophia Loren whenever he framed a closeup of her. As she spoke, Anna Maria used her hands to help express herself and point out the various points of interest. She began explaining her surroundings, with one of the two remaining towers in view behind her.

“Viewers may not be aware that a legend of an alchemist, who had lived here, inspired Shelley’s horror novel, *Frankenstein.*”

As she moved through the ruins from scene to scene, the video photographers did not miss a beat. The cues Anna Maria gave with her hands pointed out what was next. The crew followed her lead as if she was conducting and they were the orchestra. Toward the end of the show, she brought attention to the views of the Odenwald from the castle ramparts by turning to her side and extending her left arm toward the hills behind her. She looked straight into the lens as she raised the microphone in her right hand.

"The beauty of the region is visible in every direction, combining nature with history."

As she described the views, the film crew panned in unison. Anna Maria completed narrating the visual tour, and the cameras focused on her. She revealed the next location the viewers would visit on her program and thanked them for spending this time with her in beautiful Germany.

Anna Maria waved goodbye and said, "Ciao!"

The director yelled, "Cut!"

Murray turned to the film crew and huddled with them while periodically looking in her direction.

"Well man! Tell me how it looked on camera!" said Murray.

The videographer replied, "Perfect. She is a natural."

Murray asked, "I have never done a show like this in one take before. Are you sure we got it all?"

He nodded. "It could not have gone any better. Wait till the soldiers get to see her on TV. I can imagine the fan mail pouring in now! With those gorgeous looks and dressed to kill, she belongs in a movie with Gregory Peck."

Murray responded, "I take it you are talking about *Arabesque* with Sophia Loren?"

"Yeah, come to think of it, she does look like Sophia Loren. I can't take my eyes off her," said the videographer.

"Well, cool it, man! She is married to a commando with notches on his gun. I heard he is a one-man killing machine," cautioned Murray.

The smile disappeared from the handsome videographer's face, and he started concentrating on packing up his gear and getting out of Dodge.

Anna Maria stood waiting with the microphone still in her hand. They were taking their time, and she observed the conversation got very animated! She could not help but think something must have gone very wrong.

Murray's discussion with the crew ended, and he yelled, "It's a wrap!"

He trotted over toward her, smiling, with his hands reaching for the sky.

"Congratulations on a wonderful presentation of the castle ruins! I have never done a show in one take, and it amazed me how well you led the camera men through the scenes," said Murray.

Anna Maria felt relieved as she handed the microphone over to one of the film crew, who also congratulated her.

She asked, "Have you approved Prinz-Georgs-Garten in Darmstadt center?"

"I must scout it out myself first. I will let you know as soon as I can."

Anna Maria had driven her BMW to the shoot and offered Jack Murray a ride back to the office.

As she drove, Anna Maria said, "What about Erbach and Michelstadt? They are also located close to headquarters in the Odenwald. We can cover each town in an episode."

Beauty and brains. She could become the star of this season's Armed Forces TV Programming, Murray thought.

He replied, "Yes, I will research those towns as well. You have given me a lot to think about."

Before long, they arrived at the Stars and Stripes headquarters in Griesheim.

He said, "Goodbye for now. I'll call you as I decide on those filming locations so that you can start preparing your scripts from your journal."

He stepped out of the car and raced for a coordination meeting with the editorial staff before heading back to his office in Frankfurt-Main, where the Armed Forces radio and TV stations were located.

Anna Maria made her way to her desk in the newsroom. Her friends were waiting for her with bated breath.

They met her with a chorus of questions. "How did it go? What was Jack Murray like in person? When will the show broadcast?"

Anna Maria wondered, "What else could be in store for me? Europe has become so exciting!"

24

Life in the Fast Lane

At 0745 hours on 3 July 1970, Crowley arrived at the Linsedorf police station fifteen minutes early for the joint exercise planning meeting with Bauer.

The desk sergeant called the *Polizei* captain. "I have Herr Crowley in the waiting area. Should I send him to you?"

The German nodded, hung up the phone, and directed the airman to Bauer's office. When he arrived, the captain was waiting at his door.

Bauer spoke first. "My intelligence service found out the Baader-Meinhof gang is shopping for sub-machine guns and planning bank robberies and kidnappings to raise money for their cause. The PLO made a big impression on them."

"How confident are you about this information?"

"The RAF contacted one of our agents who poses as an arms dealer. They were looking for automatic weapons and grenades. Rumors indicate they are focusing on military targets and high-ranking German officials and businessmen, who may have bodyguards."

Crowley wondered, *Why haven't I heard this from my security service?*

He replied, "So, what has changed? The RAF already bombed a U.S. Army post in Frankfurt."

"The gang is especially interested in attacking American soldiers now because of the Vietnam War. They want to show solidarity with the Viet Cong."

"Well, Captain, this gives our cooperation a whole other level of importance. Are we ready for today's exercise?"

They discussed the strength and readiness of their teams and the day's schedule. After finalizing the plan, they left the building, and Bauer drove off to check on a stakeout.

Crowley returned to the base and met up with his posse.

Frazer said, "The Air Force issued a third interceptor to the team as a back-up."

"We will use all three today for the exercise. Load them up four men to a car," replied Crowley.

They pulled into the Hessische police headquarters and parked in the visitor parking spaces. The *Polizei* observed the Americans rumbling in and left their interceptors to look over their cruisers.

Crowley did the honors of popping open a hood and giving the specs on the engines and transmissions to the Germans.

One of the *Polizei* pointed at the carburetors. "They appear as large as the engine in my family car."

They all laughed and started discussing the radio frequencies they would use for today. Once the coordination ended, the *Polizei*, except for Bauer, stepped into their patrol cars and headed out to stage themselves at points along the training course. Hauptmann Bauer pulled out a road map and spread it on the hood of a Ford interceptor.

He pointed out, "Here is the area of the autobahn we use. There is no speed limit in this section. It has banking and new pavement."

"Use your radios to vector the vehicle in the chase. My car, Griffin 1, is the fox and you, Talon, lead the hounds. Give me a ten-minute head start."

After reviewing the plan, the captain asked if there were any questions. Frazer brought up the operation of their emergency bells and whistles.

He answered, "Use your flashers. Your sirens might confuse the German drivers and cause an accident."

He concluded the meeting and walked over to his green and white Porsche interceptor. As Bauer drove out of the parking lot to begin the exercise, Crowley told his men to mount up and checked his watch to start the ten-minute count-down.

Sitting at the steering wheel of his Ford, He picked up his mike and said, "While we are waiting, let's test communicating on the agreed upon frequency bands."

Once his timepiece ticked off ten minutes, Crowley gunned the engine and took off out of the parking lot, followed by the other two interceptors. They kept their speed down through the town until they reached the south entrance ramp to the autobahn. Crowley got on the gas and steered for the passing lane with his emergency lights flashing and his team following close behind.

After three miles of driving at speeds up to 160 MPH, they got a call from a police helicopter. "Talon, this is Ariel 1. Do you copy?"

Crowley picked up his mike. "This is Talon. Copy that Ariel 1."

Ariel 1 replied, "Griffin 1 is approaching Pfungstadt. Over and out."

Crowley radioed the Pfungstadt interceptor. "Griffin 2, this is Talon. Copy?"

"Griffin 2. Copy."

"Griffin 2, Griffin 1 is approaching your position. Please assist. Copy?"

"Griffin 2. Talon, copy that. On our way."

Griffin 2 took off burning rubber as the BMW sedan slid around the entrance ramp and merged into south bound traffic. Bauer in Griffin 1 passed in the fast lane and the Griffin 2 driver switched on his siren and accelerated in pursuit.

"Talon. This is Griffin 2. Griffin 1 is in sight. Please advise."

"Griffin 2, this is Talon. Hold on to him. We are converging on your location."

"Talon, copy that. Hurry! Griffin 1 is going faster. He must have seen us."

Crowley started red lining his engine at 7500 RPM as he moved up and down the gears and flashed his lights to increase his momentum in the passing lane. The other two Fords followed him, keeping their distance because of the rapid changes in speed.

Crowley yelled, "Damn it! The civilians do not know who we are and what to do. It is like pulling teeth to get them to move over."

They drove on for about five minutes, and then he caught sight of the Pfungstadt patrol car's flashing lights up ahead.

"Griffin 2, this is Talon. We are behind you. Copy?"

"Copy Talon. We are losing Griffin 1. That Porsche is too fast for us."

"Copy that Griffin 2."

The right lane was clear, so he took the opening. The high-speed lane change caused him to slide sideways. He reacted by straightening out and trying again, but less aggressively. The Ford followed his steering input and made it to the right lane.

Suddenly, a car up ahead switched lanes and cut in front of him, doing 120 mph.

Crowley said, "Oh, shit!" as his interceptor struggled over onto the shoulder to avoid the slower car. He spotted chunks of turf in his rear-view mirror flying out from under the rear end of the Ford as it fishtailed on the slippery grass. With all four wheels back on the road, he hammered the throttle again. The front end lifted as he rocketed up the highway and drove around Griffin 2. Talon cut off Griffin 1 and then he got off the gas to slow the Porsche down. Moments later, the other two Fords swung into position in front of Crowley.

Bauer radioed them, "*Ausgezeichnet* Talon! Great job driving. Get your next team ready."

They performed two more chases to give everyone a shot at leading the pursuit. The second session traveled further south and then the third one headed back up north on the autobahn. After the exercise, they all converged at an abandoned farm in Linsedorf close to the *Polizei* station.

Hauptmann Bauer pulled up at the entrance, unlocked the gate, and pointed to a gravel parking area as they arrived. He again used a Ford hood to spread out a blueprint of the barn.

He said, "This will be a live fire exercise. We need to plan a rescue mission. A kidnaped American serviceman is being held by the RAF in this building."

Crowley noticed the bullet holes in the walls and the windows with broken panes of glass. The *Hessische Polizei* used this location for hostage situation training.

Hauptmann Bauer pointed to the road. "The U.S. security police appear first at the scene and deploy their patrol cars as they call for backup from us."

He pointed his finger at the barnyard. "My men arrive and park their vehicles to reinforce the perimeter."

Bauer pointed out a window in the diagram. "The hostage is in the loft."

He added, "The plan calls for stun grenades thrown through the windows by the assault force to take out the terrorists on the ground floor."

Bauer was careful to use "ground floor" instead of the first-floor designation used by the Americans so that his men understood him. Germans called the first floor. "*Erdgeschoss*," which translated to ground floor and the second story, "*Erst Stock*," meaning the first floor.

Bauer turned back to the blueprint and pointed out positions inside the building.

"Once the flash bangs have stunned the kidnappers, we attack and secure the hostage in the loft. To avoid any crossfire, the entire assault team attacks through the main entrance after we set off the explosives."

Crowley added, "The assault force will consist of four men from the *Polizei* and four from the security police. The rest of you provide covering fire directed at the ground-floor windows while the assault force makes its way to the main entrance. Once we break through the door, the cover fire will cease. The two teams will advance and attack the ground floor. Captain Bauer gave out special ear plugs and goggles to protect the attack force from the effects of the flash bangs. Do you have questions?"

He recalled Bauer talking about the explosives at a prior meeting. As part of his reserve duty, Bauer's army reserve unit performed a joint NATO exercise with the British SAS. At that exercise, the SAS demonstrated their 'new toy' for the first time.

Crowley recalled Bauer's later story about being a test subject.

"I volunteered to be subjected to a stun grenade. I had experienced nothing like it before. You cannot see, hear, or walk for up to a minute. I found myself completely disoriented by the explosive, which fires off a pyrotechnic combination of chemicals in a blinding flash with up to 300,000 candlepower of light and 160 decibels of sound. This invention was a genuine breakthrough for anti-terrorist organizations because it allows us to subdue the hostiles without killing the hostages. The key to making it work is to have a highly trained unit storm the enemy before they recover from the shock. After that SAS exercise, I received permission to purchase them from the vendor for our use."

Crowley picked his squad. "Frazer, Rothman, and Jackson. Form up behind me."

He knew they were the best on his team and very steady under pressure. Bauer and he would throw the flash bangs.

As per the plan, the three American patrol cars drove through the gate and pulled up about twenty yards away from the barn. Crowley and Frazer parked tangentially to the front corners of the building. Jackson drove his Ford around the barn and parked parallel to the back wall. They all exited their vehicles with their M16s, using the vehicle's doors for cover. Crowley slid out on the bench seat and ran the radio mike cord through the open-door window as he squatted down and spoke.

"Talon calling Griffin 1. Do you read me?"

"This is Griffin 1. We read you, Talon. What is your status and position?"

"We are in place around a barn five miles south of Darmstadt, where we believe a soldier is being held hostage. We request your assistance."

Bauer replied, "Give me your location."

Crowley said, "We are two clicks outside of Linsedorf on Kaiser Strasse."

In a few minutes, the *Hessische Polizei* arrived, filling in the gaps between the American cars to complete the perimeter. They sprinted out of their cars with their Heckler and Koch G3 machine pistols in hand and ran behind their vehicles for cover. Bauer used a bullhorn to address the mock terrorists. With no response, he signaled to commence fire, and short bursts erupted, knocking out the glass in the windows of the building. This tactic cleared the way for the stun grenades and kept any shooters inside from being able to return fire. The assault force put on their ear plugs and special gas masks with dark tinted infrared goggles. While the shots rang out, Bauer gave a signal, and the assault force stormed the barn entrance and deployed on both sides of the sliding door.

Bauer and Crowley signaled for the cover fire to stop, and each lobbed a stun grenade into a window. A roar from the flash bangs penetrated Crowley's special ear plugs, serving as the signal to slide open the barn door and advance. The building's interior was still smoky from the explosion. A silhouette target of a terrorist holding a gun popped up from the floor, and Crowley put two shots in the target's chest with his M16.

He thought, "So, the *Polizei* rigged targets activated by infrared sensors. Just like U.S. Special Forces live-fire training."

He moved in with Frazer until a second silhouette swung out from a stall.

Crowley raised his left arm, indicating "hold fire." The target had a woman and child painted on it.

They walked around the target and fanned out with their weapons ready as the *Polizei* advanced on the opposite side. Crowley reached the loft stairway and leaned over the railing with his M16 aimed at the landing.

A terrorist picture with an AK-47 popped up, and he fired two shots to the chest. As he climbed the stairs, another bad guy popped out on Crowley's left side and Frazer fired a quick burst, knocking it over.

Once they made it to the upper level, he saw a silhouette with a hostage figure painted on it and a rope tied around it.

He scanned the room and then flipped on the safety switch on his M16 as he called out.

"Clear!"

Crowley waited for "*Klar*" from Bauer below, signaling that the ground floor was secured. Bauer came walking up the stairs with his G3 slung over his shoulder and surveyed the scene in the loft.

He carefully looked over targets and then he turned to Crowley. "The hits on your targets are perfect. It looks like you have kept up your marksmanship training while on this assignment and you told me at our first meeting you are a combat controller?"

"Yes, so?"

"I wondered why your commander had not put an officer in charge of your unit, and now I understand. Why assign a junior security police officer when the U.S. Air Force has a combat controller available, who is capable of the command and control of an entire airborne operation? I checked your background. So, what brings you to Darmstadt? Are you planning an invasion?"

Crowley smiled, and then his face turned serious.

"I would tell you, but then I would have to shoot you!"

Bauer jumped back and stared at Crowley's M16. Then he laughed out loud and slapped him on the shoulder, saying, "*Du bist ein guter Mensch!*" which he understood as, "You are a splendid fellow!"

He returned the compliment with "*Gleichfalls!*" meaning "likewise."

The captain descended the stairs to review the targets on the ground level. Then he stepped out to the patrol cars to speak to his men. When the posse emerged from the barn, the *Polizei* were standing in a line in front of their cars. As Crowley approached, a Feldwebel Meier called "*Achtung!*" and they all clicked their boot heels, snapped to attention, and saluted Crowley as he walked by. He returned the salute and joined his team. Frazer came over and gave him a shit-eating grin.

Crowley said, "What? What!"

Frazer turned away, saying nothing.

25

A Stasi Social

It was a nice day on 25 August 1970 in the center of Darmstadt. Fritz Lange sat down outside a beer hall at a round cast metal table with a beat-up wooden top. He wore a tweed suit with a yellow shirt and floral tie. One could mistake him for a college professor or an accountant.

He looked around and thought, *This place is in an excellent location for meeting agents. The constant flow of pedestrian traffic from the department stores and shops diverts attention, and I can hide in the crowd if I must evade the police.*

Behind Lange's table stood the Ducal Palace, built around 1900. It now houses the town hall known as the *Ratskeller* and a *Bier Stube*. Across the plaza sat the former residence of the Landgraves of Hesse, today a technical institute. The center served as a marketplace for festivals, including the traditional Christmas Market.

A waiter appeared, and he ordered. "Ein *Tasse Kaffee bitte*."

A server returned with the coffee.

A breeze stirred. He buttoned his jacket and thanked the server. "*Danke*."

The server replied, "*Bitte*."

Lange was an East German Stasi illegal agent on assignment in the West. The advantage of his status was that West German counterintelligence did not constantly tail him unless he blew his cover. The Soviet and East German "legals" had diplomatic immunity, which came with the penalty of having to evade their tails when they ventured outside their embassy. This cat-and-mouse game was fraught with risk. The downside for Lange and his associates was no diplomatic immunity. If caught spying, he was subject to the espionage laws of the country he was operating in.

At 1300 hours, Eva Schmidt emerged from the Henschel Ropertz Department Store and strode across the *Schlossplatz* toward the beer hall. She wore a light pink sweater set, a black miniskirt, and dark ankle-high boots with spike heels. The young *Fraulein*, wearing her dark hair in a pageboy style, carried a large shopping bag in one hand and a purse slung over her opposite shoulder. She walked erect with a trim figure that did justice to her outfit as she headed over to Lange's table. When Eva reached him, she said, "*Guten Tag,*" as Fritz stood and offered her the chair next to his. As soon as Eva sat down, the waiter came running over and handed her a menu.

Lange observed, "Beautiful girls always seem to attract this kind of service. Our training dictates being as inconspicuous as possible. She obviously hates to be ignored."

Eva scanned the placard, looked over her large sunglasses and said, "*Ein tasse Kaffee, bitte.*"

He pondered, "I must warn her to dress down more. The men and women at the other tables cannot take their eyes off her!"

The waiter replied, "*Bitte schoen,*" and walked off to fill the request in the beer hall. Eva took out a cigarillo, and he leaned over to light it.

Fritz observed, "It seemed like the women's liberation preached by the female members of the Red Army Faction is rubbing off on her. Or maybe it is vice versa. They did not tell me how extroverted she was when I became her control."

When he saw the attention in the square was no longer focused on them, he spoke.

"You look fit, Eva. Life in a Palestinian camp training with the PLO appears to agree with you."

"The weather was better than here. That is for sure!"

It was a cool overcast day for August, even by Central European standards. A shift in the Gulf Stream had caused cloudy skies for over six months straight.

Lange replied, "I meant to say, how did the Arabs treat you?"

Eva blew smoke from the cigarillo in his face and smiled. "I got the impression the PLO trainers felt like they had been martyred and gone to heaven when they saw us 'virgins' trying to sunbathe nude on the roofs of their encampment. After that, they could not keep their eyes off me and the rest of the Frauleins."

Lange realized, "No wonder the PLO threw them out of their camp. The RAF had shown no sensitivity to the PLO's Islamic culture."

Eva continued, "The trip was disappointing. The RAF learned a few tricks from the PLO and shot off automatic weapons and grenades. It was more fun than New Year's Eve for them. I got to work on my marksmanship. The Palestine Liberation Army impressed me with one thing. Their ability to fund their organization with kidnappings and bank robberies."

Lange changed the subject.

"So, how would you describe the members of the Red Army Faction you met so far? Are they really the urban guerillas the press makes them out to be?"

"Meinhof is the spiritual leader of the faction. She writes the tomes, leads the philosophical discussions, and focuses on strategic matters. Ensslin is more pragmatic and tactical. Her writing and speaking are more of a call to action. Baader is a male sexist pig whom Ensslin adores for whatever reason. It must be her need for self-flagellation from her religious upbringing. I lack an opinion of the rest of them. With the short deadline you dictated, I concentrated on the leaders."

"So, does that mean you are in with the leadership of the organization?"

"I helped the women learn how to fire their weapons and perform hand to hand combat moves during the PLO training. Since we came back from Palestine, Meinhof has been asking for my opinion on operations they are planning, including bank robberies and kidnappings. They talk about kidnapping some right-wing judges and other officials."

She flicked an ash on a tray and waited for a response.

He asked, "Any discussions about the U.S. military and Vietnam?"

"Ensslin brings that up all the time in her call-to-action rants. She has raised an urgent appeal to show solidarity with the North Vietnamese 'freedom fighters' to give legitimacy to their own cause."

"Eva, you are to inform them you have contacts who sell Czech assault weapons and can arrange for them to get the weapons. In return, they will be told to kidnap some U.S. military personnel and turn them over to your Czech friends."

She replied, "The source of the guns must be from West Germany. The leadership will reject any offer from the Czech, Stasi, or KGB."

"Why? They are communists, aren't they?"

"The RAF is a group of left-wing urban guerrillas. They believe Fascists run West and East Germany. They consider the rest of the Warsaw Pact in the same way."

"Is this their opinion or yours?"

"I'm not kidding! They will not knowingly turn over hostages to the East German Stasi. They do not want to be associated with East Germany or the Soviet Union because they think they are home-grown domestic communists focused on the overthrow of their own government."

"I must get back to you on the weapons trade. In the meantime, you talk up a U.S. military kidnapping for ransom in Darmstadt," said Lange.

They stood up, shook hands like business associates, and took off in opposite directions.

As he walked at a brisk pace, Lange turned to watch Eva leave.

He pondered, "I hope Schmidt will be a help and not a hindrance. She is beautiful, opinionated, and believes she can get away with anything. Well, she knew enough to bring up needing a West German source for the weapons. I'll give her that."

26

The Drop

30 August 1970. Prinz-Georgs-Garten

Eva walked along, following the gravel paths bordering the park in the center of Darmstadt.

She thought, *The sky has remained overcast since winter, yet the foliage appeared vibrant, even with the lack of direct sunlight, or maybe because of it.*

As she reached the middle of the landscaped garden, Eva discovered a round pool with a single fountain spraying a narrow stream up into the air.

The Stasi agent turned in surprise. *Oh, now I can see the pristine palace hiding behind its iron gates and high hedges with no sign of damage from the war!*

Built in the 1700s, a three-story building featured windowed gables embedded in the red-tiled roofing forming the facade. A wrought-iron balcony extended out from a full-length window on the second floor, which afforded the former princes a perfect location to sit and view his garden. A promenade with bench seats strategically placed framed the garden. She headed for the palace entrance, turned left, and continued down a crushed stone path.

Sashaying to the first park bench, Eva looked around and sat down. Confirming she was alone; she reached under the seat and tore off a thin packet taped underneath. The envelope came encased in plastic tape to keep out any moisture. Eva put it in her pocketbook and looked around, feeling disappointed. Her dress was to die for, and no one was there to admire her. She got up and walked to Luisenplatz. The ride back to her apartment would give her an opportunity to be seen in her new outfit. After all, a fashionista needs an audience!

Eva arrived at the central streetcar exchange in Luisenplatz just as the tram to Arheilgen pulled in. She hopped on and gave her fare to the conductor, who counted it and dropped the coins in a box as they rolled away.

Eva sat down and pondered, "I must get to my flat as soon as possible. The message decryption takes a lot of time, and I have a meeting with the RAF tonight!"

She arrived at the Arheilgen roundabout, where the tram made its U-turn to Darmstadt. Eva gazed at the shops lining the west side of Frankfurter-Landstrasse. Her inexpensive furnished flat afforded her perfect access to shopping and transportation. The building was a four-family dwelling, and her residence was on the ground floor. She entered and closed the door. Curiosity overtook her. She threw her keys on the kitchen table and opened her purse. Eva withdrew the packet and pulled a sharp knife out of a cabinet drawer to cut it open.

She fished out two typed sheets of paper from the envelope containing her directions. Next, she took out the book she used to decipher her messages and decrypted it. The first sheet contained the details about getting the firearms the RAF would need. The message detailed the contact's name and address in Eberstadt, where Heinrich Todtfeld lived. She would inquire about some World War II mementos left by his father when he died. The inheritance comprised twenty Ceska Zbrojovka model ZK-383 Czech submachine guns with wood stocks using pistol rounds. In addition, the collection included boxes of 9mm ammunition, magazines and six crates of German *Eihandgranate.* The grenades were egg-shaped; hence, their name. Detailed notes on the weapons included how to handle the grenades and the method of activation followed. Eva knew the arms were coming from the Stasi. A cover story concerning Heinrich's father's death followed, describing how they wanted to get rid of the deceased grandfather's war 'souvenirs,' because the family members discovered the weapons work and were therefore illegal.

The second sheet contained instructions for the turn-over of the U.S. airmen to the Stasi. An agent posing as CIA, would meet her in a bar with a letter promising payment of a ransom of one hundred thousand dollars by the American State Department, on condition the RAF keep the deal secret and not communicate with any other parties until after the swap occurred. Eva's task was to bring the deal to the guerilla leadership and convince them to do it. Lange's solution surprised Eva.

She thought, *He created a believable plan and with one hundred thousand dollars at stake, it should not be hard for me to get the RAF to play along. The group is out of money and needs funds and guns to carry out their terrorist plots. Between the weapons and the ransom, this is a win-win proposition for them.*

Eva committed the name and address in Eberstadt to memory, placed the two sheets in an ashtray and lit them with a match.

General Petrenko sat in PVO *Strany* Headquarters at the head of a long conference table in his Moscow office. It was 5 September 1970. Colonel Rudolfsky stood at the side of a projection screen, explaining his presentation with a pointer, as his assistant operated the projector.

"As you can see from this picture, tire wear is a big concern in our training operations. The short takeoff and landing capability of our fighters on rough runways take their toll."

His photographs documented takeoffs on arctic airfields, formation flights, photos of U-2 spy planes over the Black Sea and crews performing aircraft maintenance in all kinds of weather.

Rudolfsky stood and waited while his assistant distributed a hard copy report to the officers attending the meeting.

He said, "I will guide you through the statistics gathered from the performance trials for the MiG-25. I must stress the need to keep the speed of the aircraft below Mach 2.83 to avoid damaging the fighter jets. The manufacturer should add an engine-governor to prevent overheating."

He pointed to the screen image of a spreadsheet listing engine replacement totals to drive home his point.

Rudolfsky continued, "The weight of armaments dramatically affects the aircraft's performance envelope. I tested this by flying sorties against U-2 spy planes. Even carrying just two missiles limited the chances for a successful intercept, both from an operational ceiling and effectiveness standpoint."

Colonel Rudolfsky recommended either a lighter fuselage or more powerful engines in future models to overcome this limitation.

Colonel Bronovich, a MiG-21 regimental commander, got up and started a presentation on a planned exercise involving the recall of older fighters from East Germany and replacement with newer aircraft.

"This flight is a rehearsal for the actual deployment of the MiG-25s to East Germany. Rudolfsky's pilots will learn the routes and practice flight coordination with ground control as they pass through the multiple military districts, ferrying my MiG-21 upgrades. The plan calls for flying three squadrons from Eberswalde-Finow, Dresden, and Magdeburg-Cochstedt to Minsk, where they receive their new equipment and then return to their bases of origin."

Petrenko asked, "Which airfields are the planned destination for the MiG-25s?"

Bronovich answered, "The same airfields used on the practice run will each receive a squadron of MiG-25s. They have completed building bunkered hangers large enough to conceal the deployment."

Discussions began with logistics—refueling, ground control hand off points, pilots who would take part, transport of service crews and billeting. Once they resolved all the details, General Petrenko stood up, causing the entire staff to rise.

General Petrenko's adjutant called, "Attention!" and snapped a salute, followed by the rest of the attendees. The general returned the salute and dismissed the meeting.

Colonel Rudolfsky walked out of the conference room with Colonel Bronovich into a lobby, where they turned to one another as they lit cigarettes.

"So, comrade colonel, are you happy with how the presentation went?"

Rudolfsky replied, "I am proud of the fact that my regiment will be the first production deployment of the secret MiG-25 fighters."

Bronovich replied, "Then why the concerned look? You got what you wanted!"

Rudolfsky nodded and said, "The general must believe that the West is not on to our plan to move my regiment to the forward area."

Bronovich nodded. "The cold war is a shell game. Petrenko wants to distract his opponents while he makes his move."

"I have another concern. We struggled to keep the jets in readiness because of the lack of spares for this new model aircraft. At last, we will find ourselves where we can intercept U.S. spy airplanes, but I will still have to deal with the shortages to maintain operational effectiveness."

27

Chance Encounter

1600 Hours, 15 September 1970. The Commute

Crowley left his apartment and walked down Frankfurter-Landstrasse toward the Arheilgen streetcar round-about.

He looked up at the cloudy sky and recalled his telephone call with Anna Maria before she arrived in Germany. "Darling, the climate makes the city appear to be gray and foreboding, just like my family's photos. I hope you do not become depressed by it."

"Jake, you are basing your memories on old black and white pictures. I cannot wait to be there!"

"Don't believe I am the only one who thinks this way. I read they invented psychiatry in Europe to combat the depression brought on by the climate."

She laughed. "I will just take an umbrella everywhere I go, like the British."

The rain meant no motorcycle ride to work today. His foul-weather gear wrinkled his dress uniform so much that when he used it, his uniform appeared as if he slept in it. He waited for some traffic to pass before crossing Frankfurter Landstrasse and quickened his pace to catch the tram. Once inside, he handed a conductor the fare and found his favorite seat. The tram was almost empty. Commuters were all heading in the opposite direction. He pulled out a journal from inside his jacket and unfolded it to read. The streetcar made its stop at the Merck factory and all, but one other passenger exited. A woman sat with her head buried in the *Darmstadter Echo*. She looked familiar, but he could not quite place her. Crowley decided he must have seen her around town and returned his attention to his reading material.

His uniform of the day comprised wool blend blue trousers, a long sleeve shirt of matching color with U.S. insignia on the collar and a dark tie. A peaked campaign cap and windbreaker with epaulets served as his outer clothing. He left the red beret at home to not look conspicuous. The jacket was bad enough. It hid his weapon but made him warm and looked ridiculous when there was no rain in the forecast. His brown hair and light eyes would have allowed him to pass for a local if not for the attire.

In Darmstadt, he exited the tram at the entrance to the Cambrai Fritsch Kaserne and entered through the gate. As he walked to the motor pool, he sensed he was being followed. He turned suddenly and caught sight of a female figure in the shadows by the gatehouse. Crowley trotted back toward the gate to see who it was. The woman disappeared before he arrived. He called out to the sentry and asked him if he saw anybody. The windows, it seems, were too high for the guard to see pedestrians. A guard house you can't see out of made Crowley laugh at the irony of the situation. He thanked the soldier and hurried back the way he came.

Crowley waved to Sam Rothman and his team as he got on the bus and headed over to an empty seat next to them. The security team greeted him.

Rothman asked, "What are you doing 'slumming it' to OPS instead of driving in your private police interceptor?"

"The cruiser is at the motor pool for service, so I thought I would join you for an update on any concerns you have."

They all rolled their eyes and Rothman said, "All's quiet on the western front."

Crowley laughed. "Then let's talk about the next training exercise with the Hessians."

Rothman nodded his head and smiled. "Yeah, we enjoy working with the *Hessische Polizei*. They are all very informative and serious about what they are doing."

He added, "They can have fun too, as we experienced running the Fords against their police cars. Oh, they make good drinking buddies too! I have learned a lot about European culture. Jake, did you know that most of the Germans live in apartments?"

"Anna Maria and I have one owned by Germans. Here, federally controlled housing rents make them affordable for the working class and single-family homes are a status symbol for the rich. It is the American dream turned upside down. My landlord told me German workers have more leisure time and disposable income than Americans because of the low housing costs and other social benefits. They use their extra money and time off for extended travel vacations."

Rothman replied, "Meanwhile, we chase the carrot for a house in the burbs and spend our brief vacations at the backyard barbeque to afford the mortgage. Which way is the best?"

"Sam, the rat race is not so obvious here. But it exists."

They arrived at the OPS parking lot and Crowley pulled his green ID badge out of a shirt pocket and filed past the security police booth to the main entrance. At 2300 hours, Frazer came by and asked him how he was doing.

Crowley replied, "I had a slow night reviewing recorded intercept traffic from the previous day shift."

At midnight, the Able Flight analyst arrived and relieved him of duty. He found Rothman and walked out to the OPS bus for the trip back to Cambrai Fritsch Kaserne. After being dropped off, he said good night and strolled to the main gate and waited for his tram. As it screeched to a stop, he stepped on and rode to Luisenplatz, where he changed to the streetcar line to Arheilgen.

Because of his Special Operations training, he found the ride on public transport to be disquieting. Hauptmann Bauer's warnings about domestic terrorists planning to kidnap American servicemen stuck in his mind. His combat experience taught him to be aware of his surroundings and look for cover and exits. The interior lights and windows of the tram made him an easy target at night, and the only exits were at the front and back to control the fare collection. For this reason, he tried to sit near the rear exit with his head next to the narrow band of metal which separated each window. This position provided him with some protection and concealment. At midnight, the trams were empty because most retail stores closed at 1830 hours, so finding the right seat was not a problem.

As his commute home progressed, Crowley realized he was being followed.

At first, I thought I was becoming paranoid from all this security team training for terrorist pursuit and hostage rescue. Maybe, but earlier I observed a woman following me on to the streetcar at Luisenplatz. She is now sitting in the middle of the tram reading a local paper.

He had watched her boarding and commented to himself. "She is a knockout and hard to miss with her smart pageboy haircut, fashionable well-tailored European clothes, and a dark raincoat and umbrella. Mysterious and sexy! What a combination."

More locals had boarded as the tram made stops along Frankfurter-Landstrasse. The streetcar reached the Arheilgen roundabout, and Crowley got off.

As he crossed the busy street, he looked back. *That woman exited too and is walking behind me. Well, it is the last stop. Everybody gets off here.*

He reached the sidewalk and started heading north to his apartment. A block up, he noticed her reflection in a storefront window as she disappeared from his view up a side street. Crowley reached his building and unlocked the pedestrian street door. As he pushed it open, he looked south to make sure no one was following him. The sidewalk was empty, so he entered, locking it behind him, and thought.

Was she the figure he saw by the gate house tonight? Was this a coincidence?

28

Sudden Impact

Marcel laid prone on a rise in the ground among the weeds overlooking the highway as rocks and sticks from the brush beneath him dug into his body, making the wait torture. The hedgerow afforded him excellent cover. Wearing a camouflage poncho, he peered under the shade of his short brimmed brown hat to the sight of a Mauser rifle.

The long gun brought up memories. *I recall the day I took the weapon from a dead Wehrmacht soldier. We had to kill Germans to get our firearms. Our OSS allies did not provide enough in their air drops to make up for our losses.*

He surveyed his field of vision and thought about his current predicament. *This vantage point allows me to read the license plates, however, the angle of approach leaves little time to fire.*

Marcel worried, *I memorized the vehicle plate number and description of the bus. Now I must concentrate on the scope and try not to blink. I will only get one shot. This challenge reminds me of how difficult my life has been, born of German descent while living in Alsace-Lorraine.*

He recalled, "I was told Krupp was a name to be proud of in Germany, where the family had an aristocratic history. In France, I found it to be a liability, causing me to be viewed with suspicion and asked embarrassing questions. People wanted to know if I descended from the German arms makers and women came up to me and spit in my face."

He pictured them confronting him. "Krupp weapons killed my children."

Krupp had to work extra hard to atone for his name by killing as many Germans as he could. "Even now, I have to volunteer for every risky or dirty detail that comes along to prove my loyalty to the communist movement."

Marcel's concentration faltered as he tried to remember why he was lying in this uncomfortable position on the side of this lonely stretch of road near the Strasbourg border.

"Oh, yes, the call came last Friday evening, as I was sitting in my home reading the *L'Equipe* sports pages. The voice on the phone said, 'Hello. I must have the wrong number.' and hung up. That was a signal for a message waiting at a park bench in town. I got a dog for just such occasions."

He hated pets, but it was a perfect cover for walks at night to the dead drop.

"I remember decoding the letter. I marveled at how precise the instructions were. Right down to the date, time and license plate number of the target, and the bus driver I had to shoot to cause the accident. I felt justified in performing this act because the license plates are German."

A silver Mercedes Benz bus appeared in his crosshairs and Marcel concentrated as he read off the numbers.

He grew tense as he recognized the number. "I must get my sight on the driver. There he is."

He pulled the trigger as he thought, *Why do I always draw these impossible jobs?*

Just as the sniper took his shot, the vehicle bounced over an expansion joint, causing the bullet to miss its mark and deflect off a wiper arm. The windshield shattered into a thousand jagged pieces as shards blew in, cutting the driver on his face, neck, and hands.

The driver screamed, "I can't see!" as blood ran down into his eyes. He swerved and skidded until the bus came to a stop and then he collapsed over the steering wheel.

The Crowleys were in their seats, relaxing after several days of touring Paris. They had enjoyed their stay in the "City of Lights" and were on a charter bus returning to Darmstadt. The sound of the impact and shattering glass caused Jake Crowley to react by covering Anna Maria with his body, protecting her from flying debris. The bus jerked to a stop.

He looked over at her. "Are you okay?"

She replied, "Yes, I'm fine. What happened?"

He stood up to see the other passengers standing in stunned silence. His eyes fixed on the man slumped over the steering wheel.

"Stay in your seat. I am going to help the injured driver."

Anna Maria nodded. Crowley moved into the aisle, shook the glass shards off his clothes and made his way to the front of the bus. He shouted over the din to his posse, also on the tour, to look after the passengers. Crowley pulled out a first aid kit strapped to the console under the windshield and used his training to help the driver. He picked the glass out of the man's hair and bandaged his wounds.

"What happened? Could a stone do this?"

The driver pointed toward the hedgerow on the side of the road.

"I saw a flash and heard a shot just before the window shattered."

Crowley said, "Get on your radio and call the police."

He called out for a first aid volunteer. One airman raised his hand and Crowley put him to work on the injured passengers. He searched for Anna Maria and spotted her in an animated conversation with another woman. He bounded out the door and ran over to a hedgerow for cover. The posse saw him leave and followed.

As Crowley headed to the edge of the hedgerow, he drew his Colt 0.45 from its holster as he crouched low and listened for any activity. Frazer, Rothman, and Jackson joined him in the thicket.

Frazer reached Crowley first. "What's up, Jake?"

"The driver saw a mussel flash and heard a shot near the side of the road."

The posse took Crowley's lead and drew their sidearms.

Crowley said, "All I can hear is the low rumble of the diesel engine as our bus idles nearby. That might cover the sound of our movements. Follow me!"

He began working his way in the direction the driver had given him, staying in the hedgerow for cover. The posse kept a crouched position in the brush, looking for the gunman over the barrel of their pistols. As luck would have it, Crowley was wearing dark blue pants and a matching windbreaker, which helped hide his figure in the hedgerow's shade. He recalled his wife's comment this morning.

"Jake, I cannot tell whether you are on duty or off. Your outfits all look the same."

Crowley smiled, "I'm not on official business, so this is civilian garb."

She replied, "I have to be the fashion icon for both of us."

His mind focused on the problem at hand. "We must work our way back down the highway, using the hedgerow for cover, and assume the shooter has a rifle and, therefore, a shooting range advantage."

Crowley edged his way toward the clearing on the side of the hedgerow opposite the road to see if anyone had used it to escape through the tall grass. With no sign of tracks, he resumed leading his men further away from the bus.

He could no longer hear the engine idling. The hedgerow was thick enough at this point to suppress road noise. Now, only the sound of birds and insects accompanied their movement. Crowley kept in the shade for concealment and looked for trampled grass or footprints as he went. There were no signs of fresh tracks showing someone escaped from the area.

As Crowley worked his way around a clump of oak trees, he caught some movement at the edge of the woods near the highway.

He whispered, "There is a camouflaged prone figure with a rifle. Looks like he is wearing brown work pants, a camouflage poncho and tweed cap which blends into the brush."

Crowley pointed his pistol at the shooter. The sniper turned to swat a fly, and the movement caught their eyes.

The sniper's appearance registered in Crowley's mind. "A long, thin face, light complexion and he sports a salt and pepper goatee."

As Crowley crept closer, he pointed down and signaled. His men knew he was warning them to avoid stepping on noisy branches. It was slow going because of the thick ground cover.

Crowley decided they needed a diversion to offset the shooter's range advantage. He waved to Rothman and Frazer to come close.

"You two sneak around him using the far side of the hedgerow for cover. When you get into position on the edge, opposite the sniper's location, lie prone and start shaking bushes to get the man's attention."

Crowley turned to Jackson. "You stay with me and keep light on your feet."

Once Rothman and Frazer trailed off, Crowley started working his way closer to the gunman, with Jackson following in his footsteps. The need to keep quiet made it slow going. They worked together, holding branches and pushing aside the tall grass as they approached the shooter. Crowley peeked over a bush and determined the target was in pistol range. He signaled Jackson to hold up, and they both took up firing positions behind two thick bushes.

Now it turned into a waiting game. Crowley monitored the sniper for any change in behavior until he spotted the shooter's head popping up. The sniper's attention focused on a bush in the opposite direction.

Crowley thought, *Rothman and Frazer must be in position.*

They moved closer while the shooter appeared distracted.

Crowley stepped on a dead branch lying under some thick leaves and it made a loud crack. The noise caused the shooter to rise and turn in Crowley's direction, bringing his weapon to bear.

Crowley yelled, "Halt or I'll shoot!" but the man kept turning, so he fired, shooting him in the right arm.

The sniper dropped his long gun in pain, spat, and yelled "Bosche!" at Crowley.

Crowley and Jackson moved in, and Crowley covered the shooter with his pistol while Jackson walked over and picked up the rifle.

Crowley shouted, "I am an American military police officer!" as he pointed at a badge pinned inside his jacket.

"Turn around and lay face down! Spread out your arms and legs. Do it now!"

The gunman got down and said, "American? No Bosche?"

"Yes, you idiot! You tried to kill a busload of American soldiers and their families. I should have shot you in the head!"

The gunman raised his hands to cover his head and cringed. Crowley asked the man why he was shooting at an unarmed passenger bus as he frisked him.

The Frenchman said, "I am with the resistance fighting the Bosche. I just shot at a Bosche transport."

His face was haggard, and he appeared to be in his fifties. Given his aged appearance, Crowley surmised he was old enough to be in the resistance during the war. Jackson pulled him up from the ground with his wounded arm. The man screamed in pain.

Crowley said, "World War Two is over, Jack. Your actions are terrorism, not resistance fighting."

The Frenchman bowed his head as Crowley took the bandana from the man's neck and tied it around the gunshot wound on his right arm.

Crowley said, "Give the all-clear signal."

Jackson pursed his lips and whistled a bird call.

Rothman and Frazer worked their way over to the shooter's position with their guns drawn. When they saw the shooter standing next to Crowley, they lowered their weapons.

Rothman said, "That was easy. Too easy. Did he say anything?"

Jackson replied, "He thought he was killing Germans, not Americans. Some excuse!"

With Jackson holding the rifle, Crowley's posse led the gunman out of the hedgerow and along the edge of the field back the way they came.

As they reached the highway, Crowley caught sight of the bus and said to Frazer, "West German license plates on a bus full of Americans. The American Express used a German Bus Company to charter the tour."

Frazer replied, "Who could have guessed that would be a problem?"

Three French Citroën police cars idled behind the bus with their emergency lights flashing and gendarmes stood by the side of the road, talking to the bus driver, and taking notes. As Crowley led their prisoner to the front of the bus, he told Jackson to point the rifle down and flashed his security police shield at the nearest gendarme. The officer in charge put away his pad as he ran over to the posse. As the gendarme got close, he made out the shield and drew his gun, pointing it at Crowley.

"Put down your weapons. You have no police authority in France, and it appears you have shot a French citizen. You are under arrest."

Crowley thought, "What did the man say about authority? I recall getting sworn in as an acting security police officer. Captain Hodges told me I had police powers in NATO countries."

The head gendarme, Inspector Ricard, picked up on Crowley's quizzical look. "France pulled out of NATO and is no longer a full member. Your law enforcement powers are not valid here."

Marcel smirked. Pain from a headache was putting Crowley over the edge, and he needed to channel the pain to focus. While keeping his gun on the sniper, he glared at the gendarme in charge.

Crowley growled, "The prisoner has delusions of serving in the resistance and fighting the Germans. He confessed when we arrested him."

Ricard replied, "I just informed you of your lack of authority to make arrests in France."

Crowley ignored his comment and continued. "The gunman confessed to us he has been shooting at the Germans for some time now, but they keep coming."

Inspector Ricard replied, "We have no reports of shootings in the area."

Bus passengers walked over and listened to the argument between Crowley and the French police. Two passengers pulled out cameras and started taking pictures of the gendarmes with their guns drawn and Jackson holding the Mauser rifle.

Crowley continued, "The riders on this bus are American soldiers and newspaper reporters. My men have a sworn duty to protect them. If you do not arrest this man right now, how do you think it is going to look in tomorrow's newspapers, when these reporters publish their eyewitness accounts detailing how the French police harbored a terrorist shooting at American soldiers and their families as they vacationed in France."

One reporter took out a pad and started taking notes as he listened to Crowley speak.

"Oh, the terrorist confessed he was only trying to kill Germans. The eyewitness news stories should give your neighbors pause for concern."

Ricard holstered his pistol and waved to his men to stand down. He grabbed the prisoner by his wounded arm and handcuffed him while he continued to stare at the posse.

"Well, cowboys, you are not in Tombstone Territory. You better holster your pistols, or I will arrest you on an illegal weapons charge."

Crowley turned and waved his left hand in a downward motion to signal his posse to stand down as he holstered his Colt automatic in his right holster. He wondered how this shooter got away with taking pot shots in the past. There must have been other complaints. Based on their simple field maneuver, Crowley felt this idiot should have been an easy catch for the gendarmes. A French patrol car pulled up and took the prisoner away. Crowley turned to find Anna Maria running into his arms. They kissed and then she pulled away and gave him a tongue lashing for taking off after a gunman.

A loud "Pardon!" interrupted their discussion. They looked to see the police inspector facing them.

"Are you the famous Anna Maria on the Armed Forces TV station?"

"Yes, I host the show *Travel on Tour*. Do you know it?"

"I am Inspector Ricard. My men pointed you out when you emerged from the bus. They could not believe it! And you are this soldier's wife?"

"Yes, Jake is my husband. Why is there a problem?"

"Madam, if we had known this case involved you, we would have made it our highest priority! We are all big fans of your TV show. When are you going to tour France for your show?"

"I am working on it. Everyone was so helpful in Paris. I hope the same goes for this part of the country."

With that remark, the inspector called over to a police sergeant and whispered in his ear.

Then he turned to Anna Maria and said, "In concern for the safety of you and your fellow travelers, we will escort the bus to the border."

The change in attitude shocked Crowley.

He recalled, "Oh yeah! The attention she had received in Paris and the way the hotel staff catered to her every need. I thought it was just excellent service."

Frazer came over to console him. "Jake, you have always proved yourself as first among equals. Your wife is a TV star now. Get used to it."

The Crowleys spent the rest of the trip huddling together in their seats, fighting off the insects and a cold draft blowing in through the shot-out windshield. Crowley's headache subsided as they approached the border into West Germany, and the noise from the police escort sirens subsided.

That French detective found a way to annoy me all the way to the border, thought Crowley as he watched the Citroëns take the last exit before the border crossing.

He considered the thin veneer called civilization and how it masks the dangers of everyday life. His thoughts turned to Anna Maria and how much she meant to him.

For now, she is safe! How do I keep her that way?

29

They Meet in The Street

28 September 1970. Arheilgen

Crowley stepped from the tram wearing his class B dress blues and strolled across Frankfurter-Landstrasse toward the sidewalk on the other side.

As he walked, he remembered to zip up his jacket and thought. *What a pain in the ass it is to have to hide my Colt.*

He carried the pistol in the shoulder holster under his left arm. His dark blue windbreaker hid the weapon, along with the police badge pinned to the pocket of his long sleeve class B shirt.

A young woman emerged from the grocery store laden with heavy bags. She was pretty, with dark hair cut in a pageboy style and dressed in fashionable European-style clothes. Her face jarred his memory, and he recalled seeing her on the tram to and from Darmstadt. Her figure and height matched the mystery woman at the Kaserne security gate. The style of her outfit and the way she carried herself gave her away as a *Fraulein*. Married German women dressed more conservatively. She was struggling, and that was his opening to introduce himself.

"*Entschuldigen Sie mir! Darf ich ihnen helfen?*"

"You are American?" she replied.

"*Ja, ich bin Amerikaner,*" replied Crowley.

She smiled and shook her head yes as she replied in German, "*Danke schoen.*"

She handed him a package. Then she spoke in English.

"My flat is close, or I would not have bought so much."

He nodded, took another shopping bag from her, and walked beside her as they continued their conversation.

"Judging by your blue uniform, you must be with the American *Luftwaffe.*"

"Yes, my name is Jake Crowley, and I live with my wife in an apartment up the street."

"I am Eva Schmidt, and I relocated to Arheilgen last month."

After saying that, she looked a little sad and her gaze went downward.

He picked up on her mood change and replied. "We just moved here, too. Do you mind if I speak in German? I am trying to get some practice."

"Please continue."

So, as they walked, he told her he served in the U.S. Air Force and his wife worked for the *Stars and Stripes*. Eva had taken a job as a salesclerk in a women's fashion store in Darmstadt. They got to her place, and he held open the main entrance door while she moved the bags into the hallway.

She said, "I have not made friends yet in Arheilgen. I would like to meet your wife. She sounds very interesting. Are you both available to come over for coffee tomorrow evening at 2000 hours?

Crowley replied, "If we can make it, I will leave a note in your mailbox."

They shook hands and exchanged wishes of "*Auf Wiedersehen,*" to each other.

He turned and headed back to Frankfurter-Landstrasse for the short walk to his flat.

He entered the street door and noticed the car was gone. "Oh, how she loves to drive that BMW around town. She left early to do some shopping before work. I will have to tell her about Eva tonight."

Crowley was feeling tired after his midnight shift. He planned to go straight to bed and awake when his wife returned from her office.

He thought about his new acquaintance. "Eva seems a little strange. She acts normal enough, but there is something about her I can't quite put my finger on. How will my wife react to Eva's invite for coffee? Maybe Anna Maria can give me some of her feminine vibes on her."

Crowley thought Eva might be the one stalking him and he did not think it was because she was lonely. "A girl that is good-looking has no trouble making friends."

He decided, "I am probably just paranoid. If Anna Maria likes her, she will have a neighbor to talk to. They are about the same age. Short tours in the military gave no time to be standoffish. We have already thrown several dinner parties at our apartment and have been guests at other Air Force couple's apartments. She may want to add a local acquaintance to her social calendar."

First, he had to confirm if Eva was a friend or foe. Crowley recalled what his wife's Uncle Benny had said before they left for Germany, "Keep your friends close and your enemies closer."

30

Working Out the Details

29 September 1970. 6910th S&W Center

Chad Frazer stood with his headsets on, taking plots from Crowley along the Baltic coast. Grease pencil marks tracked the flight path on the plexiglass map wall.

"Okay, Jake. Keep them coming. There is a C-141 flying a ferret flight in that area, and right now, your intercept is the only asset tracking the mission."

On the aircraft itself, analysts were intercepting ground control voice broadcasts vectoring MIG-21 fighter interceptors toward them.

Frazer added, "The first line of defense for the ferret mission is their own intercept. They are the closest to the targeted radio stations and have the best reception for voice traffic. I just know that we cannot assume they are intercepting relevant signals."

Crowley said, "Roger that. I'm on it."

So, they played this cat-and-mouse game. If the Soviet fighters vectored closer to the Security Service aircraft, they changed course and flew further out to sea. When PVO *Strany* ground control called the fighters back home, the ferret mission flew back toward the border. This pattern of activity went on for the entire daytime shift. In between plots,

Frazer and Crowley were talking about the progress of their work with the *Polizei.*

Crowley thought, *I'm glad I decided to make Frazer my second in command. He is smart and cool under pressure. No wonder they assigned him to the S&W plot board. Reporting situations got hectic, with multiple activities going on.*

Frazer gave him competition on police exercises too. He tied him on several target practices, and he ran obstacle courses without the slightest hint of exertion.

Crowley announced his decision over the intercom. "I am making you my back-up and putting you in charge of the second patrol car, while Rothman runs the bus squad. Jackson will float between squads to cover in the lead position when one of us is on leave or pulls other duties."

Frazer replied, "Thanks man! Does this mean I can do something about weapons access in the cars? It takes too much time to pull up the floor seat cushion and unclip the long guns from their racks. Besides, we are perfect targets having to stand up in back to get out of the way. If they attack us, we will be dead before getting a shot off. The only option is just using our sidearms."

"So, what's your solution? You know better than to bring me just the problem."

"Dude, I was coming to that. It makes more sense to rack the assault weapons behind the rear backrest with a hinge at the bottom and clip at the top to access the racks."

"How does that help?"

"We just turn around, crouch low in the footwell, unclip the backrest, pull it down on the seat, pull the rifles from the racks in the trunk opening, and pass them along."

He considered Frazer's idea for a minute as he gave Frazer another plot for the C-141 ferret mission. The current configuration had probably been easier to install.

"So how do you know the rifles fit?"

"I took measurements of the racks and the hard points in the trunk. The mechanics can weld the gun racks into an opening behind the backrest."

"That sounds good, Chad. We can talk to the sergeant at the motor pool when we return the cars today. If he gives us any flack, I'll ask Captain Hodges to intervene."

"Jake, this will invalidate the timing of our emergency response drill tests.

"Yeah, let's take it one step at a time, knowing how hard it is to make changes around here."

They continued tracking the recon mission for the rest of the shift. When their relief came in from Able Flight, they did their handoff and headed out to their patrol cars, which were parked in a reserved area for security police vehicles. As they drove away from OPS, Crowley took the lead. Frazer waited and then pulled behind the bus to cover the rear. The convoy made its way down the dirt path through fields of Brussels sprouts. After bouncing over the ruts, they turned onto a paved road leading through the town of Linsedorf. The convoy spread out to avoid looking conspicuous and used their radios to coordinate their positions.

In twenty minutes, they drove in one by one to the Cambrai Fritsch Kaserne security gate. Once they arrived at the motor pool, Crowley got the usual runaround from the mechanics about authorizations needed to change the gun racks. He will take up the weapons storage issue with Captain Hodges tomorrow. The posse waved to him and headed to the Air Force billets. Crowley then strolled around to the side of a garage, where he kept his motorcycle parked. He took off a rain cover and stored it in his locker and retrieved his helmet. After he mounted the bike, he put on his helmet and goggles. It was a nice fall day, and he looked forward to the ride home. Once out of the main gate, he gunned it and headed for Arheilgen. That evening, the Crowleys saw *Easy Rider* at the Cambrai Fritsch Kaserne theater.

During the drive back to their place, Crowley asked, "What do you think about our neighbor, Eva Schmidt?"

They met for coffee at Eva's apartment and stayed until 2300 hours the previous day. The conversation was lively, and Eva could hold her own in English with Anna Maria.

Anna Maria replied, "She is very interesting, especially when she talks about what is going on in Arheilgen and Darmstadt from a local point of view, but I need to keep an eye on her. Boy, does she have the hots for you!"

"Oh, you noticed the way she stares at me right in front of you?"

"Yeah, she has a lot of nerve."

"What about the kiss on each cheek? Then she took a little nip out of my ear!"

"I saw that! You would believe we are describing a feline."

Jake laughed and said, "Can we fix her up with Frazer? I think he would like to absorb some of the local culture."

Anna Maria smirked. "Do you really mean sleep with the local culture? Chad is all about California and the West Coast. He does not seem to be interested in Europe. The only time he spends off base is with you and the German Polizei, shooting up the countryside."

"He is single and does not have the opportunity to socialize outside of work except at bars."

"Are you sure you want to do that? Didn't you meet her under suspicious circumstances, or are you just getting paranoid? Has Bauer got you believing there is a terrorist hiding in every wood pile?"

"Chad can work 'undercover' on a double date. It might resolve what Eva has on her mind. I'll warn him to watch his back. He knows how to take care of himself."

Anna Maria said, "Isn't the greeting a European thing? Don't they all kiss cheeks like in Italy? Anyway, the sooner you get your trust issues resolved, the better. She knows her way around town, and I would enjoy her company."

31

The Cold War Gets Hot

5 October 1970. Vasylkiv Air Base, Kiev

Colonel Rudolfsky conducted himself with a serious military bearing as he moved down the flight line, inspecting the flight crews. His regiment would fly this evening's exercise as a rehearsal for their deployment to the East German DDR. Aircraft inspections passed muster, and he climbed into his MiG-21.

Rasmussen said, "Good luck, comrade colonel!" as he handed him his flight helmet and helped him buckle up.

The commander fired up the turbojet engine as his crew chief descended the ladder and pulled it away. He taxied out to lead the rest of his squadron to the runway.

Details raced through the colonel's mind. "Redeployments of upgraded MiG-21 aircraft are a routine process going on all over the Soviet Union, so we do not expect this flight to raise any flags with the NATO allies. What could go wrong? All my men flew this model jet as part of their qualifications for my regiment."

Rudolfsky worked his controls and took off. Once at cruising altitude, he continued thinking about his mission. "The jets have similar characteristics. The MiG-21 cruises at Mach 2 and my regiment enjoys flying this aircraft, which is a good dog fighter. On the downside, it becomes unstable when low on fuel. These upgraded versions have a new long-range capability, covering distances of over 250 km before refueling. This means fewer stops before we touch down in the Deutsche Demokratische Republik."

Rudolfsky's transport itinerary ended at the Eberswalde-Finow airfield, while the other regiments would land at the Dresden and Magdeburg airfields. They would use the same flight plan on the MiG-25 deployment. His regiment would have to fly within the older plane's performance envelope during the upcoming stationing to masquerade as MiG-21s.

1700 Hours, 7 October 1970. 6910th Surveillance and Warning Center

It was 1700 hours when Crowley reported for another swing shift on 17 October. He later found Frazer at the coffee bar.

"Chad, I met Hauptmann Bauer earlier today to brief him about the terrorist attack on the bus returning from Paris. It surprised Bauer that the gendarmes had not been more cooperative given the situation."

"Yeah, tell me about it. I thought I was going to jail. Was he any help?"

Crowley smirked, "He laughed and said, 'If you really want to be mistreated by the French, try visiting Paris during August. The only Frenchmen left are in tourism. They are not happy working in the sweltering city while their families are off on vacation enjoying cool mountain breezes.'"

Frazer replied, "The Parisians treated Anna Maria like a rock star. It was on the road back that we wore out our welcome."

"Yes, I know. Bauer received a report via INTERPOL, which said the attacker was a communist agent, and they were rolling up his network, thanks to us."

"Having your famous wife involved got their attention."

"What do you mean by that? Her travel show only appears on armed forces TV."

Frazer replied, "Jake, the Germans and French are very interested in American culture. They all watch the programs on that station. Anna Maria has become very popular in Germany and now France too. You need to wake up and smell the roses."

"Yes, but her fame did not help find out why Marcel was trying to kill me and my fellow travelers. Like I said earlier, this incident tells me there is a pattern forming, and it has my name on it. The Soviets want to kill me. I must figure out the reason and make the problem disappear."

Back at his workstation, Crowley recalled the rest of his conversation with Bauer.

"Anna Maria and I are having a dinner party next Saturday evening. Would you and your wife do us the honor of attending?"

"That sounds like fun. I will ask my *Frau* and get back to you."

"And since you mentioned INTERPOL, I have a favor to request from you."

"Ask."

"I believe a young German *Fraulein* I met may have been following me prior to the encounter. With my history of attacks by communist agents, I would appreciate your help to figure her out. Her name is Eva Schmidt, and she lives in Arheilgen. I can give you the address."

"Okay, I'll do a background check and see where it leads."

"Thanks, I owe you one."

"With all the discussion over terrorists, I forgot to tell you I met up with some of your Special Operations buddies from Florida last week. I was doing my reserve weekend warrior service by participating in a NATO joint exercise.

Crowley replied, "And you didn't call me?"

"I spoke to your commander for permission to invite you, and he responded you were busy."

"Yeah, they have been keeping my nose to the grindstone at OPS."

"Your guys flew out of Ramstein and met up with us for a HALO insertion over the Fulda Gap. After the jump, I met some special ops guys from Eglin Air Base, and they said hello. It was strange though, one of your buddies kept on referring to you as 'the bat.' When I asked the SEAL why he called you that, he claimed you beat everyone in nighttime parachute competitions, so your rivals started calling you the bat as a left-handed compliment for your jumping prowess at night."

"Yeah, I never liked that name."

The police captain laughed. "An understatement if I ever heard one! An airman, Sergeant Newman, told me the SEALs don't call you that to your face."

"Newman, was on that training mission? I will have to send him a letter and see how he is doing. I'm glad to hear that he made sergeant's rank."

On 8 October, Crowley was taking advantage of the mild weather by putting a few miles on his Norton, instead of riding the tram. He hummed '*Born under a bad sign*!' as he rode to work and realized the lyrics were trying to tell him something. Crowley recalled having nothing but good luck as a combat controller, even with all the operational hazards involved. Now he was serving in the safety of an intelligence analyst job and bad luck and trouble seem to follow him. Crowley's troubles started with a fight in Texas with a Soviet spy. Then the riot in New York organized by American communists followed by the attempted sabotage of his BMW in Bavaria. Next comes the episode in France, where a communist and former partisan shot at the tour bus he was riding back to Germany with Anna Maria on board. When he told Captain Hodges about it, he got no sympathy. He needed to sort this out because his wife's life was at stake. He could never forgive himself if something happened to her.

Crowley arrived at OPS and had all the input channels on his display locked and loaded in an hour.

He reported to Gibson. "I am monitoring three flights originating in Kiev and traveling through Poland. Voice and Morse confirmed the activity intercept as well. There are indications they are MIG-21's based on their tail and transponder numbers."

Gibson replied, "Sounds like one of their upgrade fights. They ferry upgrades back and forth to Kiev. Make sure we keep monitoring them."

The ferry operation made two stops. They took off from the second airfield at Kolobrzeg in northern Poland. The destination was next. At the border, the formation split up and landed at Magdeburg, Dresden, and Eberswalde-Finow. If this was an upgrade deployment, they should see a return flight of three squadrons of replaced planes back to Kiev tomorrow.

Crowley called his supervisor over. "I'm going to cut a paper punch tape of the tracking data and walk it over to OPS COMM for transmission to the NSA at Fort Meade."

Gibson agreed. On the return to his workstation, Crowley tapped Chad Frazer on the shoulder. As Frazer spun around, the cord from his headset wrapped around his arms.

Crowley said, "Hey, dude, surfs up!"

"Jake! You know you cannot talk to me while I am taking plots. What do you mean by 'surfs up?'"

"Are you dating anyone right now?"

"Are you kidding? I tried to 'surf' the bars in Frankfurt and got wiped out."

"Were you alone?"

"Yeah, so what?"

"The *Frauleins* assumed you were a werewolf with no friends.

"I never thought of that."

"Well, we can fix you up."

"How's that?"

"Anna Maria and I know a German *Fraulein* who is dying to meet you. Anna Maria brought up double dating with us to the Jethro Tull concert at the *Festhalle* in Frankfurt this weekend. Ian Anderson puts on quite a show with his flute playing and his music is unique."

"So, dude, what does she look like?"

"I thought you can't talk while you work."

"I am plotting—my next move."

Crowley laughed and said, "When I see her, I feel mesmerized—as if I am looking into the eyes of a serpent. She does not blink, and I see her tongue dance out of her mouth to catch my scent. Am I her prey, or is she mine? After all, I am the one with eyes in front of my head."

"Jake, are you shitting with me?"

Crowley's smile disappears. "Eva is beautiful, with an aura of danger. She speaks perfect English and does not suffer fools gladly. Appearances can deceive, so you better watch your back. I met her under suspicious circumstances. Oh, I almost forgot. She smokes cigarillos. Just your type."

Frazer, conjuring up images of a femme fatale, replied, "Okay, you are describing Mata Hari with a Mona Lisa smile. She sounds exciting — count me in!"

It was the morning of 9 October 1970 as General Petrenko looked out of his window at the gray sky and considered the plan. He walked back to his desk and stood next to his adjutant.

Major Abramovich said, "We have reviewed the MiG-25 status reports, including the crew deployments, bunker construction in East Germany and the dry run MIG-21 ferry operation."

"What about the Air Defense Network, which is part of my PVO Strany command-and-control responsibilities?"

"As you know, for the past ten years, your command has been investing military resources to provide extensive surveillance capability and redundancy. We concentrated on radars west of the Ural Mountains, around Moscow and in the eastern European Warsaw Pact countries. During that ten-year period, we developed a semi-automated radar network using HF broadcast frequencies and more secure microwave communication links where available for added security."

Abramovich saw the growing concern on Petrenko's face as he spoke. The size and complexity he described did not allay the general's concerns about the operation.

"What makes this system so important in your mind?" queried Petrenko.

"The term semi-automated signifies that a radar operator selects which plots to broadcast up the chain of command using machine generated frequency shift keying. This selective manual control allows the operators to pick flights of interest and not clog the higher echelon display systems with useless or redundant information."

"If I understand what you are saying, the system facilitates consolidation of aircraft tracking over our far-flung flight routes and strategic border activity," replied Petrenko.

"*Da*, it is a massive network comprising over 4000 radars positioned in our air defense zones (ADZ) along the borders. Over 1000 additional radars are at three hundred Warsaw Pact sites in Eastern Europe."

Petrenko asked, "How resilient is this system?"

Abramovich replied, "The network maintains a high degree of overlapping coverage, which is required to support surface-to-air missiles and intercept fighters during a time of war.

Petrenko frowned. "In time of war, a nuclear electromagnetic pulse could knock out this entire network. What then?"

"To increase reliability through redundancy, we still broadcast using older technology manually keyed Morse code and voice broadcasts as a backup to the semi-automated transmissions," replied Abramovich.

"How does using older technology help? Won't just slow down reporting?"

Abramovich saw the general's eyes grow larger and his neck turned red as he waited for a reply.

"The various frequencies used by these different network technologies provide some protection against the use of electronic countermeasures. If NATO destroys the semi-automated sites in combat, the Morse and voice networks will assume primary tracking responsibility."

"Which networks track the fighter deployments to the DDR?" demanded Petrenko.

"The plan is to use the newer semi-automatic network to monitor the MiG-25 regiment deployment to East Germany. It has the best coverage in the forward area," answered Abramovich.

Petrenko thought, *It is vital for the mission to know if the American Air Force Security Service can intercept and decrypt this new transmission technology. I must call Gurkin and get his ass in gear!*

When Gurkin got on the phone, Petrenko screamed into the receiver. "Where is the counterintelligence you promised me?"

"Comrade General, we have made that problem our highest priority."

"Gurkin, if this operation does not deploy on time, it will be on your head!"

"I have been making some personnel changes to get the assessment back on track. We relied on the Stasi who put the emphasis on process instead of product."

It was 10 October as the KGB general sat in his temporary office in Dresden, holding his head in his hands in disgust while waiting for the Stasi officer to report.

He turned to his aide. "I read a report that agents under my control are trying to kill an American soldier assigned to the American Air Force Security Service. Countermand those orders at once. This Crowley fellow is in the very unit we have targeted. We must kidnap him, not kill him! He knows too much now to be expendable. Since the Stasi has been useless so far, maybe this American can tell us the information we need."

Before the aide could reply, Steiger entered wearing a full-dress uniform, clicked his heels, and saluted. The general did not offer a chair. The lack of progress on Steiger's assignment incensed him. He did not return the salute either.

Gurkin got up and looked Steiger in the eye. "We started this operation at the end of January, and you do not have one U.S. soldier for us to interrogate."

Steiger spoke, and the general cut him off.

"You have moved at a glacial speed which is holding up critical operations. I have assigned KGB Colonel Vladimir Soukeroff to take over this operation, including your agents. He will be in contact with you to get your files on the mission. That is all!"

Steiger knew better than to argue with the general. He saluted, about faced, and marched out the door. He prayed that his office would still be there when he returned to the Stasi Police headquarters across the street.

32

Fall Festivities

12 October 1970. The Festhalle

Crowley drove the BMW down a cobblestone street with high-rise buildings everywhere he looked. He was searching for an open parking garage and not having much luck. Anna Maria was sitting next to him and in the back, Chad Frazer was talking to Eva Schmidt, describing the surfing lifestyle in California. Frankfurt was one of the cities in Europe Crowley believed could compare to New York. Still, no place intimidates drivers like Manhattan.

He recalled checking his seat belt before entering the midtown tunnel to Manhattan as the paranoia set in. This city, with its skyscrapers and limited parking, gave him the same feeling.

He spotted a big Park-Haus sign and pulled in.

Crowley climbed out, looked around, and opened the passenger door for Anna Maria.

Frazer took the hint and exited from the back seat and offered his hand to Eva as she stepped out of the car, revealing her long legs and short black miniskirt. She was wearing dark stockings and high black boots with a white blouse under a black velvet jacket.

Frazer pointed and said, “I see an exit sign in that corner.”

Crowley watched Frazer follow Eva and thought. "He looks like he died and went to heaven."

He took his wife's hand as she followed Eva and Chad to an elevator. Anna Maria wore a pink miniskirt with a matching blouse, a white motorcycle jacket, and go-go boots. Topping off her colorful mod attire was a short brimmed white leather cap. Frazer was keeping close to Eva. They were not at the hand holding stage yet, so he used his hands to help describe California to her. Jake thought having to explain one's home was a sign of an inferiority complex.

He pondered, *Did I ever hear anyone from New York City explain where they come from? No, they just say, 'I am a New Yorker' and assume everybody knows what they are talking about. End of story.*

Two blocks down they ran into the Festhalle, a sixty-year-old building built in 1907. Designed with an elegant facade and super high doors and windows for that grand effect popular back in the day, it served as the centerpiece of the Frankfurt exhibition grounds. Crowley found it to be a bit too old-fashioned for a rock concert. He was used to attending concerts in sports venues. This building seemed better suited for operas. At the entrance, Crowley gave the usher their tickets.

The usher looked over the tickets and then stared. "Are you the famous Anna Maria on Armed Forces TV?"

She smiled. "Yes, I am the host of *Travel on Tour*."

He blushed. "I thought I recognized you. I am a big fan. You make Germany appear so beautiful and inviting. My friends all watch your program. They want to become folk dancers so they can appear with you on TV!"

"Oh, well, the folk dancing episode was at a location in Bavaria. We do not dance on every show."

The usher replied, "Please wait one moment. I will be right back."

He returned with a larger man in tow, dressed in a dark suit and tie.

"This is our director, Herr Mueller. He wishes to speak to you."

Mueller bowed and handed her his card as he said, "I want you to know that I and my staff here at the Festhalle enjoy your travel show very much. We would appreciate it, if you would allow us to seat your party in the VIP section."

Anna Maria replied, "Well, we do not wish to be any bother to you and your staff. We have already purchased our tickets."

"Please, we do this for all our honored patrons. It is a security measure. Keep my card and call ahead in the future to arrange secure accommodations for you and your friends."

He bowed and kissed her hand as he waved over the usher to escort them. Anna Maria thanked Herr Mueller, and the usher led them to a roped-off section of front row seating.

The concert was a blast with Ian Anderson doing his thing, playing the flute while standing on one leg and singing songs like "Nothing Is Easy" and "Aqualung."

Frazer turned to Eva and said, "This is like attending a private concert. Ian Anderson is looking right at us."

Eva thought, *Yes, the musician seems embarrassed seeing us watch him carry his keyboard man away after he passed out on the piano. Drugs are affecting the audience as well.*

Smoking from hash and marijuana billowed in the stage lights and made its way to their section.

Eva looked around. "This area we are in is the only one with seats. All the fans are standing. The promoter removed the seating to maximize attendance and profits. What makes Jake's wife so important? I must watch the TV show Herr Mueller spoke about in such glowing terms."

She glanced over at Jake. "I am developing a thing for that man. Control ordered me to meet him and see what he was up to. It surprised me to find his good looks, athletic body, and modest personality so attractive."

Eva thought, *My upbringing in that East German orphanage taught me to keep my emotions in check. However, I can't block out the thought of seducing him to gain the information I need. What a pleasure that would be! Accepting the invitation for a double date might help me get closer to Jake. Chad is just along for the ride.*

Eva considered Frazer. "Chad is young and handsome, but not the alpha male Jake is. I can tell by the way he tries to emulate his friend and gives deference to his opinion, even though they are at the same military level. How did Lange know this man was a person of interest? Well, I do not believe for a minute he works in material control."

With her sharp hearing, Eva overheard Jake whispering to Chad about an upcoming exercise and target practice, as if that were an everyday occurrence.

Eva realized, "This would not be a supply sergeant's concern. Besides, I have seen him ride to the Linsedorf U.S. Air Force site on the shuttle bus. Frazer is also a potential opportunity for my efforts, but I think the controller is right. Crowley should be my primary aim."

She thought, *This will be the first time I enjoy seducing my victim.*

As they exited the concert, she imagined Jake's image on an East German propaganda poster. His likeness depicted the ideal worker: slim and strong from hard work with an axe over his shoulder. She pictured him coming alive and walking right into her arms. Eva's mind focused back on her thoughts about her chief roadblock to his seduction—*seine Frau.*

33

A Change is Coming

15 October 1970. Darmstadt, BRD

Fritz Lange looked over the park. "Three brick walls are all that remains of the bombed-out church. I will wait for Schmidt outside the structure."

Yesterday, he left a signal to meet at the Kapellplatz in the central part of the city. He stood next to torch basins, which sat on high wrought iron stands in front of the ruins, guarding the entrance. A large crucifix stood before the back wall. Surrounding the cross were flowers and cards left by mourners. Children played on the grounds surrounding the monument while women with strollers walked the many shaded paths through the park.

Lange observed, "Although this is in the central part of the city, I don't see any tourists with cameras and fanny packs. They must stay away out of respect."

Fritz strolled the remains, inspecting the walls and arched window openings from outside the structure. He stopped and admired the modern apartment buildings surrounding the area.

He thought, *I recall a picture in the city library of the area taken in 1944. The photograph showed the allies had bombed the entire neighborhood, leaving not one building intact.*

Eva Schmidt emerged from the main entrance of the Henschel Ropertz, heading for the Kapellplatz. She was moving at a brisk pace, because it was a long walk, and she was on her lunch break. Yesterday, she saw the meeting signal chalk marks on the corner of the department store on her way home.

As she walked, thoughts of Crowley came to her again. "I must not let my feelings affect the mission. Still, I cannot get him out of my mind."

Raised a staunch communist in East Germany, she supported equal rights for women as an important part of that struggle. Her belief system taught her to distrust, but she felt Jake was different. He was a gentleman who put his wife on a pedestal.

Eva recalled seeing him for the first time. "Those blue eyes, handsome lean face, and the body of an athlete. He speaks German well and is interested in the culture and history of Germany. His lack of arrogance is so unusual for such an attractive man."

She wondered who his ancestors were. "He looks like the Nordic prince in the Germanic fairy tales I read as a child."

As she approached the rendezvous, her mind focused on the obstacle to Herr Crowley—Frau Crowley. He praised his wife and the work she was doing for the military establishment newspaper *Stars and Stripes*. She also hosted a show on Armed Forces Radio and TV, where she extolled the "good life" of military men and their families in Europe while they occupied West Germany under the guise of being a NATO ally. To lure him to her trap, she needed a plan. She smiled as the church ruins came into view.

Eva strolled the sidewalk past the park entrance and caught sight of her control.

She observed, "There is Fritz! The structure has only one way out and he is staying outside the walls. It is comforting to see he practices good spy craft by positioning himself to observe anyone approaching instead of wandering into a trap in a church with only one exit."

As she reached him, she said, "*Guten Nachmittag*" and gave him a kiss on the cheek. Then he took her arm, and they started walking the paths around the park like a typical German couple out for a stroll.

"So, Herr Lange, a lot has happened since we last met. I have introduced the Red Army Faction to the family in Eberstadt to do the Czech weapons deal."

"Any feedback from the arms sale?"

Eva smiled and said, "The leadership of the RAF has been singing my praises. This accomplishment allowed me opportunities to talk with Baader and encourage him to show solidarity with the North Vietnamese against the Americans. He has agreed to plan a kidnapping of American troops to raise money from ransoms for their cause."

"Eva, what are you up to now?"

"Once the abduction order came down, I started surveillance of U.S. Air Force personnel in Darmstadt around the Cambrai Fritsch Kaserne and the roads to the Operations site in Linsedorf."

"Any results?"

"So far, I have made friends with a sergeant and his wife. They have introduced me to another single male friend who is also in the same military unit. I went on a date with him and the couple to a concert in Frankfurt. Both soldiers have told me they are supply sergeants, but I followed them both to the operations site where they reported on a changing shift schedule."

Lange whispered, "They have given our operation to a KGB agent. He is your control for the remainder of the operation. The Soviets were behind this effort to abduct these soldiers. They are now in a big hurry."

He gave Eva the German cover name of her new boss and date and time of their first rendezvous. There would be no hand off. No sense risking two handlers from different nets in one encounter.

34

Experiencing the Impact of His Work

18 October 1970. 6910th S&W Center

Chad Frazer stood in front of the map board of the Baltic area, taking plots on a C-141 reconnaissance flight heading northeast along the Latvian coast.

He thought, *I'm getting spotty tracking from the voice and Morse positions, but not from RUBICON. Jake has become so good at his job that he produces relevant data faster than we can plot and report on it.*

This issue led to a decision to bypass the process and have Crowley punch paper tape reports from his computer and forward them back to the states via encrypted Teletype. In tandem, he called in a summary of the plots over the intercom to the surveillance and warning center.

Frazer recalled, "Several letters of commendation have come back from the program director, Bart Sedgwick at NSA, praising the timeliness of Jake's reporting. Sedgwick also announced that based on the efficiency improvement, they had taken it out of prototype status and approved the system for operational deployment."

While calling plots on the intercom, Crowley talked to Frazer about RUBICON.

"Last week, I arrived to find my section was down for routine maintenance."

"Oh yeah, I remember that. What had to be fixed?"

"The disk drives had to be aligned, the air filters changed, and the display stations cleaned."

"So, what was your back-up?"

Crowley interrupted, "First here is another plot—57.8657 North, 23.4731 East, the recon is midway past the Gulf of Riga."

"Anyway, I had to go to the backup manual intercept procedures for the night, which required me to maintain a plastic transparency imprinted with the Soviet tracking grid for each radar station being intercepted."

"That must have really cramped your style. When you are operating RUBICON, the data from you flows like a fire hose aimed at the S&W center. We can hardly keep up," said Frazer.

"Yeah, When I switched the input cable on my analog CRT to display tracking for a different radar station, I had to center the corresponding transparency for that station on the display. I used my grease pencil to mark the plots on the transparency as I interrogated the plots with my light pen for altitude and tail number data, which I also noted on the transparency. All very slow and time consuming," said Crowley.

"How did you figure out where the plots were located so that you could call them into us?" asked Frazer.

"Periodically, I walked the transparency over to my map board to center it on the location of the Soviet radar station being intercepted. Finally, I translated the Soviet coordinates to latitude and longitude while calling them off to you. Then it was wash, rinse and repeat."

Frazer laughed. "You earned your rations that night."

"Not really. The backup process turned my real-time analysis of events into a playback of history and limited my effective coverage to one radar station at a time. It was a wake-up call for me. I realized what a game-changer RUBICON is."

"What do you mean by that?"

"Chad, I had to perform all that manual work for one aircraft's flight tracking data on the old method, while I can monitor eight stations at the same time on RUBICON and report on multiple activities simultaneously."

"Oh, I get it Jake. We now have better coverage of your targets."

"Being forced to use the previous analog system, I found I operated in reactive mode, relying on traffic from other sources to direct me to the specific Soviet broadcast of interest. Using RUBICON, my coverage is real-time and proactive. Because I have so much real-time data in front of me from multiple sources, the other intel sources are playing catch-up to my lead. That is how I can turn on what you call the fire hose."

Frazer continued to take plots as their conversation turned to the Dog Flight security police team.

"Our ride to work in your BMW was a gas."

"When was that?"

"Come on! The night I rode with you to a mid-shift, and we were running late after watching TV coverage of a bicycle race in Italy."

"Oh, that was no big deal. I drove a little fast because there was no traffic."

"The next thing we know, you get pulled over by a Hessian Police cruiser."

"Well, he just gave me a warning and let us go."

"That's not what I saw. The *Polizei* clicked his heels and saluted when he recognized you. Suddenly, we are speeding behind an escort to OPS with sirens and lights flashing."

"I told him we were late for work."

"Oh yeah, they do that for all the Americans! That's why the guards at work started kidding you about your special status with the Germans. They asked me, 'What's with Crowley and the Germans? The group commander doesn't get an escort like that.'"

Crowley laughed. "The guards at the gate asked me if I had dual citizenship."

"See what I mean? And then Captain Hodges heard about it and kidded you by standing up and clicking his heels as you passed by on one of the swing shifts."

Crowley pondered, "Politics made for strange bedfellows. My German friends had been my father's enemy, and my father's former Russian allies are now my enemy."

"Chad, why don't you take another tracking plot and change the subject?"

Frazer recalled, "The kidding was the flight commander's way of letting Jake know how well he had associated his team with the local police."

Later in the evening Crowley was on his way to the comm center and he passed by Frazer in the S&W center. He waved and Frazer nodded as he listened for plots on his headset.

Crowley called over in German, "Guten Abend, Herr Frazer."

Frazer was too busy, so he ignored him.

Later, when he recalled Jake's greeting, it reminded him of Eva. "I took her to Crowley's dinner party last week at their apartment. Captain Bauer and his wife were among the guests, and it surprised me how Eva avoided them after being introduced. Bauer's wife, Frieda, a statuesque blond and born extrovert, adored Anna Maria and praised her TV show. I recall how they tried to include us in the conversation, but Eva shied away from it."

That was not what Frazer expected. He thought she would compete for Anna Maria's attention, given how she brought up Jake's wife all the time in their discussions.

"Eva's behavior could be cold and calculating. When I went bar hopping, the German girls I met did not act that way. She seems to let her guard down by appearing to be annoyed when speaking to me in English. She tries to portray a normal lifestyle, yet she is out alone at night and offers no explanation." thought Frazer.

"She asks me all kinds of questions about work, and I must repeat my cover story over and over! Is she just curious, or does she have an ulterior motive? Why was she dating me when our relationship was going nowhere? Was she using me to get to Jake? That look she gives him and how she speaks to him with that soft, purring voice. I don't get it!" mused Frazer.

He recalled Crowley saying, "I think she stalked me until our meeting in the street. Something about her is not right. Keep an eye on her."

Frazer pondered, "I agree. Now, what to do about it? I have no proof!"

35

A New Spy Master in Town

18 October 1970

Colonel Vladimir Soukeroff stood in front of St. Mary Magdalene Chapel. He cast a shadowy figure dressed in a black trench coat with the brim of a gray fedora shading deep-set eyes and a dark mustache. The Russian gazed at the three bright gold onion-shaped domes forming the spires of the ornate facade. He rubbed his hands to warm them in the cool night air and started walking along the promenade that encircled the grounds. White domed lights on tall poles projected light on the walls of the building and the walkways. He recalled from the tour book he used to pick a meeting place, that in the late 1890s, Tzar Nicholas II built this edifice for his use during visits to Tsarina Alexandra's family in Darmstadt.

As he rounded a bend in the walkway, he noticed a train station platform. It reminded him of an amazing story about how the Tzar had all the stone and dirt needed to build the church shipped from St Petersburg, so that he could worship on Russian soil during his bi-annual visits.

He looked up and marveled. "The decoration and artwork adorning the façade is outstanding! Gilt covering gingerbread trim accentuates the roof lines and beautiful frescos decorate the front and the back exterior walls. In Mother Russia, the orthodox churches are in ruins. I picked the perfect spot to take over this mission."

He cleared his throat and continued walking, reminding himself that his cover name was Hans Becker, and he should begin thinking in German before the Stasi agent arrived. As the intelligence officer rounded another turn in the walkway, he noticed a figure standing under a light pole twenty meters away. Without appearing to be too obvious, he wandered in her direction. He approached a woman matching Schmidt's description, studying a fresco at the front of the church.

He called out, "*Fraulein Schmidt, nicht wahr?*"

Eva looked surprised and waved. When they were near enough, he bowed, took her hand in his, placed it under his arm, and led her down the walkway. As they walked, she started briefing "Herr Becker" on her mission status. He pulled her closer to listen to the report.

"So, to summarize, I positioned myself as a tactical advisor to the leadership of the RAF on matters of obtaining weapons and explosives while teaching the women members on hand-to-hand fighting techniques."

"The Stasi liked the progress you made on their objectives. I want to know about the plan to abduct the American Security Service personnel!"

"I was coming to that. First, I convinced the RAF leadership into planning the kidnaping of Americans to show solidarity with other communist guerrilla organizations like the Viet Cong and to protest the continued occupation of Germany."

Becker prodded, "Yes, go on."

"Second, I followed airmen to the spy site to verify they worked for the target organization. I confirmed this by monitoring their travel and schedules. With this knowledge, I befriended a security service airman and his wife. They introduced me to a bachelor friend, Chad Frazer, whom the husband works with at the spying operation."

"Are you telling me you have already seduced the bachelor and have the information we need?"

"He is closed-mouthed and suspicious. I am working on the married man as my primary target."

"Why is that? It seems the unmarried soldier is perfect!"

"The married soldier appears to be in charge, and I believe knows more about their operation. The bachelor defers questions to his friend and asks his opinion. I befriended the man's wife and now believe I will get to him through her."

"I see. What else?"

"I reconnoitered the three hijack targets myself, which include a shuttle bus and two staff cars. We will attack this convoy en route to the Linsedorf operations site."

Becker liked what he heard. It appeared the Stasi had handed him the operation on a silver platter, but he still needed it reviewed by his assistants.

"*Fraulein* Schmidt, meet me at the Frankfurt safe house address I gave to you in my contact information. I need to review the Red Army Faction plans to confirm the proper coordination of the abductions."

"I am going over the notes with the RAF members selected for the hijack teams tomorrow afternoon. If that meeting is successful, I can give you everything you require."

"Excellent! You must get this abduction done as soon as possible. This is the highest priority."

"I supplied them with Czech assault rifles and hand grenades. They employed a friend's farm in the countryside to practice with the new weapons.

"*Fraulein* Schmidt, please summarize the overall plan."

"*Herr* Becker, five stolen fast sedans will be used to hijack the soldiers from the bus and staff cars. The leadership armed the RAF guerillas with machine guns and grenades. The sedans will scatter and rendezvous at their safe house in Frankfurt. They will then move the prisoners to a secluded farm in the countryside. You will arrive posing as a CIA agent and pay the ransom in dollars for the airmen.

Eva described the rest of her plan and got approval from Becker. When she arrived back at the RAF hideout that evening, Baader was there holding court.

She listened and thought. "The KGB operative was very polite. What a relief it will be to finish this mission and be able to enjoy some of the good life in the West. Working with Baader and Meinhoff is monopolizing all my time!"

It was now 28 October. Although he put up a good front, Colonel Rudolfsky grew restless, waiting for the orders to deploy his unit from Vasylkiv to the West. His four squadrons of fifteen aircraft were each being maintained at a high level of readiness and he was conducting exercises to maintain the pilot's skills. They struggled with supply problems to keep the jets in the air. Central planning could not react fast enough to the demands for material used up in the training. The crews resorted to stealing parts from sidelined fighters to meet the demand. This tripled the workload. First, find the part. Steal the part. Mount the part. Put back the stolen part when the replacement arrives. Not knowing where they were being deployed added pressure on the troops and their families. Increasing the frustration were the U-2 over-flights. His MiG-25s could not intercept them, because of the distance from their airfield to the spy plane flight routes, which allowed them to get away when the regiment scrambled a jet. They were banking on solving this problem in the close quarters of Western Europe.

The regimental commander drilled his men and made his calls up the chain of command to obtain some definitive date for the deployment. On each call his superior, General Polzin tried to deflect the issue by questioning him again about their readiness and then needling him about the U-2 situation. He would answer the questions calmly and then return to the stationing timetable question. Polzin relented at last and admitted the holdup was by the generals at PVO *Strany* headquarters. Polzin told him that once they solved this dilemma, the colonel would receive his orders to fly his organization to East Germany. He was relieved to know the obstacle was being discussed at the highest levels. This gave him a sense of how important his operation was. He redoubled his efforts to make sure his regiment was up to the task.

36

Circle the Wagons

1600 Hours, 5 November 1970

Five sedans pulled up at a junction in Linsedorf. The four-way stop comprised three paved town roads and a dirt pathway leading into the farm fields. Two cars parked on opposite sides of the intersection on the edge of the field and the others drove a short distance away and stopped. Hans Schell called everyone over for last-minute instructions.

"Let's go over the plan. Ingrid and Elise, you set up your positions at the corner house across the street and wait for the caravan. You will allow the first car and the bus to pass through and turn down the farm road."

Ingrid interrupted. "How do we know when to attack?"

"When the trailing staff car pulls up to the stop sign, you jump out of the bushes and order the soldiers out of the car at gunpoint."

"What if they don't obey us?"

"You shoot one of them to set an example. Once they surrender, Ingrid will march two prisoners to Fritz to be searched, tied up, and put in the trunk of his Mercedes. Elise does the same for Heinrich. There are no bodyguards, and the Americans do not carry weapons. The sedans must leave in opposite directions to the safe house. Is that clear?"

The women nodded.

Schell replied, "Okay, take your positions."

They ran across the street with their heads covered by hooded sweatshirts, looking like students carrying heavy musical instruments to school. The pair lugged black satchels with the barrels of their assault rifles protruding and deployed behind ornamental evergreen bushes in the front of the vacant corner house. Hans watched them get into position and then turned to the remaining RAF members.

"Okay, Karl and Horst. You transport your groups down the farm lane midway to the American military facility. There will be an intersecting path you can turn down and conceal your vehicles from view. Your assignment is to hide along the route, commandeer the bus, and take hostages. My group's task is to intercept the first staff car. We plan to travel up the road past the junction, hole up in the crops, and wait to waylay the lead staff car. Questions?"

Fifteen minutes later, Crowley pulled up to the stop sign and put on his brakes. He checked the cross street for traffic and looked up. The Air Force shuttle bus appeared in his mirror off in the distance, so he slipped the stick shift into first gear, let out the clutch, and gave it some gas. His team peered out their windows, looking for anything unusual. They advanced into the crossroad and then turned a hard left onto the dirt road as the big Galaxie squeezed between the tall grass and stand of farm crops. The heavy-duty suspension bounced and rocked as it made its way.

Five minutes later, Chad Frazer pulled up to the Linsedorf stop sign in the second blue escort vehicle. His right eye caught a figure with a ski mask pushing through bushes in front of the corner house. Then another flash of movement as someone ran carrying an assault rifle. He stomped on the gas pedal and the big Ford engine erupted, sending tire smoke out of wheel wells as his car leaped forward. Charging through the intersection, he made a hard left, causing the still spinning rear wheels to slide the car counterclockwise so that his door faced the attackers as he jammed on the brakes.

He drew his Colt from his shoulder holster as he rolled down the window and took aim.

"Draw your guns. We are under attack!"

Frazer fired at the assailants and then ducked as a hail of bullets raked the Ford. The ZK-383 assault rifles sounded to him like the German Police weapons only slower. The 9mm rounds punched dents in the Ford's body as it idled in the middle of the intersection. Some shots penetrated the sheet metal and tore into the bench seats and interior trim. Two of Frazer's men kicked open the doors and jumped out to return fire from behind the doors and fenders. That left Frazer and one squad member still caught inside. The airman in the rear kneeled in the footwell and pulled down the backrest to grab the M16s and ammo. While he was getting the long guns out of their racks, bullets kept drilling through the windows and ricocheted off the interior overhead. Frazer waited for his team's cover fire before dropping below his window and crawling down the bench seat, using his elbows and feet for propulsion. Before he reached the passenger door, he raised the microphone he was dragging along and called the *Polizei* for assistance.

He exited, squatted down, brushed glass off his uniform from the shattered windows, and one of his men handed him an M16. He wondered why the assailants fired at the body of the car. It was not until he returned fire that they started shooting to kill.

Frazer frog-marched over to the hood of the automobile to support his assault rifle just in front of the windshield.

He took aim and thought, *Are they kidnappers or assassins? I see two shooters gesticulating at each other as they lie prone behind low bushes. It appears they are arguing about what to do next.*

He pulled on the microphone cord to get some slack and hailed the *Hessische Polizei* again for back-up and added his suspicions about the attackers being the RAF. He hoped Crowley was monitoring his police band transmission.

Frazer turned to his men. "Fire your M16s in short bursts to keep the terrorists pinned down!"

As the squad volleyed at the gunmen, Frazer took a bead on a target beneath a bush. He lined up, using the hood for support, and squeezed off a round, hitting the terrorist in the head. The attacker rolled over and dropped his assault rifle. His partner shook the wounded man with no response. Panicked, the figure rose and made for a tree, followed by a hail of bullets. Frazer could not get a clear shot from his current position, so he crouched low, using the police cruiser for protection, and moved over to where his team members shielded themselves behind the trunk of the car. Once in position, his squad pointed to where the terrorist concealed himself behind a large oak tree on the front lawn. He placed his M16 on the trunk lid and lined up on the tree as he ordered the squad to continue their cover fire. They fired with brief pauses to draw the attacker into shooting back. As the terrorist stuck his torso out on the fourth pause, Frazer triggered two shots. The gunman spun and fell to the ground. A third assailant appeared, wearing a ski mask and gray coat to join the fight from a car parked nearby. He saw his pal get snuffed and ran off behind the house with a pistol in his right hand. The entire squad fired at him to smoke him out. The shooter returned fire, but Frazer could not get him in his sights. They stopped firing after hearing no return fire. Then a single shot rang out. They waited with their rifles ready for another onslaught. Frazer spotted a small green flag with the Hessian Police insignia waving from the corner of the house.

Frazer yelled, "State your identity!"

"This is Hauptmann Bauer. Are you clear?"

"If you got the gunman who went behind the house, we are clear."

"Then all clear. We have also arrested another man in a parked car we came across when we approached the area. He carried illegal automatic weapons."

Frazer walked over to Bauer with his M16 over his shoulder and shook his hand.

Bauer said, "Do you have any casualties?"

Frazer looked back and waved. The three airmen rose from their positions behind the shot-up Ford and signaled they were okay. More *Polizei* arrived at the scene and checked on the two dead RAF guerrillas.

Suddenly Frazer realized this might not be over. "What happened to the rest of the convoy?"

He ran to his vehicle to call Crowley. When he picked up the mike, he heard gunfire coming from the speaker.

Frazer called out, "Captain Bauer, over here!"

When he arrived, Frazer pointed to the radio and Bauer stuck his head in to hear the gunfire and static.

Bauer turned to his men. "Mount up, the attack is not over!"

He joined Frazer and his guys in the security police cruiser. The Ford pulled out with a roar and the *Polizei* followed, making for the farm lane.

A short distance up the trail, they stopped the cars and proceeded on foot to avoid being ambushed.

As they reached a crossroads, Frazer heard gunfire off in the distance.

He signaled to Bauer, and the *Polizei* provided cover as Frazer's men crossed the roadway to join them.

"Herr Frazer, the gun fire is close by. It is coming from either the bus or Jake's police cruiser. Too loud to be from the operations site. Another contingent of the RAF must be attacking the convoy," said Bauer.

Frazer replied, "I think you are right. The Red Army Faction would not attack a guarded facility. It is not their style."

They split up again and approached the source of the noise from both sides of the lane, using space between the rows of crops for cover.

Meanwhile, Crowley could hear automatic weapons erupt behind him as his vehicle bounced over the dirt road.

"Men, the sound of those guns is unfamiliar to me. It sure isn't M16 or AK-47 fire. I might have mistaken it for *Polizei* MP5 submachine pistols, except the volleys are slower."

The roadway was too narrow to pull a U-turn, so he switched off his engine.

"Weapons ready, I believe the bus is under attack!"

As he went to open his door, two RAF guerrillas in ski masks popped up from behind the Brussels sprout stalks on both sides of the road, brandishing assault rifles. They looked like vintage World War II guns with wooden stocks. Crowley signaled, and his men raised their sidearms and positioned their left hands on the inside door handles. The attackers, assuming they were approaching unarmed soldiers, came right up and pointed their weapons at the windows.

Crowley said, "Go!" and the airmen pushed on their doors so hard the windows knocked the muzzles of the assault rifles aside and slammed into the gunmen. They jumped out and aimed their Colts down at the would-be 'urban guerillas' and kicked their weapons away. Airmen Baker and Cruise opened the rear doors of the patrol car and jumped out to pull down the backrest and withdraw the long guns from the racks, along with the ammo belts. The pair covered Crowley and French as they cuffed the prisoners face down in the dirt.

The squad buckled on the ammo belts and checked their M16s. Baker kneeled next to one prisoner and pulled off the ski mask. To his surprise, the captured RAF member was a woman! He pulled the mask up on the other captive and found another female.

Crowley looked them over and thought about what Captain Bauer stated. "There were more women than men in the gang, and Frau Meinhof freed Herr Baader from jail at gunpoint."

Crowley ordered, "Cuff the prisoner's legs and roll them back over face down."

He returned to his Ford and keyed the radio mike. "This is Talon calling. Shots fired! Please advise me on your status."

A grenade exploded with such force that it drove the door behind Crowley into his back and propelled him on to the car seat. His head banged into the armrest on the opposite side, knocking him unconscious.

Back on the trick shift bus, Sam Rothman and his team were lying in the aisle with the other passengers as bullets rained in on them. Glass windows shattered and holes appeared in the thin aluminum body. The steel seat frames, and chassis rails of the bus were the only protection from the gun fire. They stayed down on their stomachs with their sidearms pointed at the door in case the gunmen tried to enter. The firing ceased, and someone called in English with a German accent.

"Come out with your hands up."

Rothman clenched his teeth. "Come and get us!"

His team could not get a shot off from the floor of the aisle.

Rothman whispered, "They must think we are unarmed. Let's give them a surprise greeting."

Someone outside started shouting and pulling on the door and when that did not work, machine-gun fire riddled the doorway as the dead bus driver's body jumped around in his seat from the impact of the bullets. Rothman held his Colt with both hands as he trained the sight. Squeaking sounds came from the folding door being wrenched open. He spotted a figure and fired two shots, propelling the intruder out the way he came. This led to another barrage of bullets racking the bus as the terrorists cursed about the "*Ami*" having pistols.

While the RAF discussed what to do next, Rothman dragged the M16s out of the locker behind the driver's seat and passed them with the ammo belts down the aisle.

"On my command, stand up with your rifles on automatic, fire a clip out the windows, and duck back down. Maybe we can scare them off."

They followed Rothman's orders and heard the Germans shouting and cursing outside. Machine guns racked the bus again and Rothman caught a bullet in his side. One of his men crawled over and used a tee-shirt to staunch the bleeding. They reclined on the rubber flooring of the aisle and waited. M16 and MP-5 assault rifles started firing and voices shouted in English and German. More gunfire erupted and then it grew quiet, and Sam recognized Captain Bauer's voice call over his bull horn.

"This is Hauptmann Bauer. We have subdued the gunmen. You can come out now."

Rothman came out first, holding his side, and a teammate called out for a medic. *Polizei* officers cuffed two RAF members lying face down in the mud field while others searched the bodies of the dead. The attackers wore typical college student garb, right down to the gum soled shoes, tie-dyed shirts, blue jeans, and army surplus drab green fatigue jackets.

Rothman's squad lowered him down to the ground in a sitting position, so that a *Polizei* medic could work on him. He saw Hauptmann Bauer and called him over.

"Captain Bauer, there was an explosion further up the trail where Crowley's squad should be. Can you check it out?"

"Yes, Sam. When did it happen?"

"I was lying on the floor of the aisle after being shot. It was a short time ago."

Bauer waved Frazer over and filled him in. They hailed over their teams and headed up the dirt road, keeping behind the rows of Brussels sprouts to screen their movements.

Meanwhile, Rothman asked the medic to attend to the driver. He hurried over, checked for a pulse, closed the soldier's eyes, and asked men to help take the body out and cover it with a blanket from a patrol car. One by one, the passengers gave their eyewitness account to the *Hessische Polizei* before making their way by foot to the operations compound. An ambulance arrived and rushed Rothman to the hospital.

Hauptmann Bauer observed, "I don't see Sergeant Crowley or his car. He should have reached the bus before us."

Bauer walked down the dirt road and spotted a Ford police cruiser with the engine running. He signaled to Frazer and moved closer. It was a scene of carnage. Three of Crowley's men and a terrorist lay sprawled out on the ground. A second terrorist's body sat plastered up against the Ford from an explosion.

Frazer yelled, "Jake's squad is down, and I don't see him anywhere."

Bauer said, "Men, it looks like a fragment grenade exploded. See if you can help the wounded airmen and stay clear of the RAF bodies. I'll call the bomb squad."

They spread out and found all three Americans dead from shrapnel wounds. So were the terrorists.

Frazer made his way to the Ford police interceptor. Guts and holes from the explosion covered the patrol car's body. He poked his head over the edge of the vehicle's window and saw his buddy face down on the front seat. He pulled on the car door and found Crowley bleeding under a pile of glass shards. Frazer sent a squad member around to the passenger door. They prodded Crowley for signs of life.

Frazer called out, "He's alive! Help me get him out."

Some men came over to pull him out. They carefully picked the glass off his body and then sat him up to dress the wounds. After a few minutes, he spoke.

"What happened? I was grabbing for the radio mike, and I must have blacked out."

Bauer replied, "Looks like that big American car door saved your life. A grenade exploded in the pocket of what remains of a RAF terrorist. They were carrying old egg-shaped grenades in terrible shape, and one went off. We are staying away from their bodies until the bomb disposal crew arrives."

Crowley's head throbbed from being thrown against the car door handle. He wondered if he would have to see the physician at Wiesbaden Medical Center again. He recalled his last visit, where they diagnosed him with migraine headaches without aura and gave him medication. The doctor told him there was no going back to Special Forces, but he could keep his Security Service job. He had not mentioned his extra police duties.

Crowley said, "Communist terrorists in the heart of Germany. Never thought I would see the day! Extremism is still alive and kicking in Europe, itching to cause another world war."

Bauer nodded. "*Ja*, I'm glad we performed those field exercises. I feel bad for your squad members. They never saw it coming."

"Yeah, I regret we weren't more cautious. There was no warning of grenades."

Bauer added, "Something more to train and plan for."

More emergency vehicles converged on the site, followed by the USAF Security Police. The German medic pulled up and gave first aid to Crowley. After getting patched up, he drove to OPS and briefed Captain Hodges.

"Captain, it was a botched abduction based on how the attack transpired and the reputation the RAF has made for themselves by kidnapping for ransom."

"I relieve you and your men of duty for tonight. Take care of those cuts and bruises at the infirmary. The guards for this shift will escort the flight back to the Kaserne when relieved."

Crowley gathered the survivors and headed out of the operations compound to their patrol cars. They drove to the hospital to check on Rothman. He was sitting in his bed reading a newspaper when they arrived.

Crowley walked into the room first. "Sam, I thought you would be sleeping by now from painkillers. How are you feeling?"

"The medic patched me up to stop the bleeding. I am waiting for a surgeon to look at my x-rays and tell me if I need an operation. I feel pretty good knowing we did our duty to protect and defend."

"It appears the RAF wanted to kidnap, not kill us. Hauptmann Bauer is questioning the terrorists."

Rothman replied, "Still, we did our job protecting the troops."

Crowley said, "Except for me. Everyone on my team is KIA."

Frazer chimed in, "We thought you were dead too. It was a horrific scene. I don't know if I can handle a grenade again."

Rothman piped in, "Jake, I was told they found you sleeping on the job."

"Yeah, the explosion knocked me out while everyone else got killed."

"It wasn't your fault! That Ford saved your life."

They wished Rothman good luck with the surgeon and headed out to the patrol cars to return them to the Kaserne. Eager to get home and rest, they decided during the car ride back to skip the infirmary and lick their wounds instead. Frazer drove the married men to their apartments, including Jake. Crowley's consolation was how well the security team performed in their first military engagement. He also knew he could count on his posse when push came to shove.

37

What Is a Lady to Wear?

1300 Hours, 5 November 1970. Arheilgen, Germany

Anna Maria sat on the side of her bed and pulled up her stockings as she listened to the radio. She liked this local station because the program called '*Music in der Luft*' featured romantic American music. She was enjoying a piece by Mantovani's Orchestra, as she thought back to the dinner party the Crowleys hosted last week. It was a tremendous success, and Jake was the life of the party, introducing his police friends and discussing European culture.

She recalled their conversation. "You were so animated tonight! My work colleagues commented on how interesting it was and how informed you are about the situation in Europe. Our *Polizei* guests enthralled everybody with their stories and friendliness."

"Darling, it seems I just had to interject topics I am interested in, and everyone responded appropriately."

"Yes, and you surprised them with your command of German and how you got on with the local police."

"It helps to have friends in high places. Captain Bauer and his wife were very sociable and knowledgeable. Eva, however, seemed to be shy, especially with the other Germans."

"I noticed her come out of her shell whenever you were around, which means I must keep an eye on her. She has been a great help to me at the fashion salons."

"Anna Maria, I don't understand what game she is playing, if any. Chad said she is strange."

"Well, it takes one to know one. You are both trained to be suspicious."

"Still, you must be cautious. She gives me bad vibes."

"Eva has been such a darling, taking me out clothes shopping and introducing me to the owners of the best boutiques and restaurants in town. I don't understand why you do not trust her."

Anna Maria's thoughts turned to her current plans.

Besides, I enjoy her company when you work odd hours. Eva invited me this afternoon for tea at her apartment and I accepted. I should be home before Jake, and I will leave him a note, just in case I am late. A girl from Brooklyn knows how to take care of herself. He shouldn't be such a worrywart.

Anna Maria smoothed out her stockings and then stood up in front of the mirror to check her make-up and fasten her earrings. Her large green eyes and short chestnut brown hair gave her a catlike appearance. Her favorite animal was the Bengal tiger. No surprise there. She walked over to the clothes cabinet her landlord called a "*schrank*."

"What should I wear? Oh yes, that beige top and green miniskirt.

As she carried her choices over to the bureau, she looked in the mirror and held them in front of her.

"The colors are great together!"

She slipped on the outfit and decided it needed a belt to break it up. A wide brown one with a big buckle and studs hung in the closet. She bought it in a market in Spain and it still smelled like new Moroccan leather. After fastening it around her waist, she returned to the cabinet and reached down to pull out a pair of high brown boots she had stored with other shoes on the bottom shelf.

She thought, *An Italian bootmaker crafted these in Brooklyn. He had a lot of questions.*

Anna Maria felt a chill as she pulled two stiletto knives out of a drawer and slid them into the leather sheaths inside her boots. She couldn't help recalling that cold fall night as she made her way home from band practice.

I was late for dinner, so I took a shortcut through a housing project I had been told to avoid. I spotted the punk on his bike as she turned a corner. He looked like a Hollywood cliché, with his dark hair slicked back in a pompadour, white tee-shirt, black leather jacket, jeans, and high-top black sneakers. I avoided eye contact, yet he still rode right up to me and dropped his bike.

"What's with you? Too good to say hello?"

I turned to look at him. The face was pimply and dirty around the mouth, like he just ate a candy bar and wiped it with his hand.

"A gentleman would have waited to introduce yourself at school, not in this dark back alley."

"What are trying to do? Insult me in my neighborhood?"

He pushed me back, and I dropped my schoolbooks as I reached down to cushion my fall. The punk bent over and grabbed me by the hair and pulled me towards him. I palmed a stiletto from my boot as I rubbed my leg in mock pain. The click as I pushed the release gave him pause. He knew that sound, but it was too late. As he loosened his grip on my hair, I used my free hands to balance myself as I reached up and carved a gash on the left side of his face from his ear to his mouth. That face became a walking billboard for my prowess with a knife, but fame had its price. I had to take my cousin from New Jersey to the prom.

Anna Maria forced the recollection from her mind and finished her ensemble with a leather jacket and a brimmed cap. She checked her lipstick and picked up her purse and shopping bag while heading out. The heavy door closed behind her with a thud, and she descended three flights of stairs, illuminated by the light streaming in through the translucent glass block stairwell windows facing the garden. When Anna Maria reached the ground floor, she pushed down the handle for the foyer door and walked outside into a rush of cold air. She used the big old-fashioned key to unlock the street door and passed through the entrance to the wide sidewalk in front of the building. Though she felt she could take care of herself, she regretted not telling Jake about Eva's invitation to tea.

It was 1330 hours in the early afternoon as Anna Maria strolled down Frankfurter-Landstrasse toward Eva Schmidt's apartment, window shopping, as she made her way past the stores lined up opposite the tram roundabout. When she reached the side street Eva lived on, she felt a chill.

"I guess I better get inside!" she murmured as she pulled her coat tight and crossed the cobblestone street. She entered the apartment hallway to find Eva waiting to greet her. They kissed cheeks and Eva led her to the living room, where she already had a tea service and finger sandwiches set up.

She sat down and looked around. "I love what you have done with the place. Thank you for inviting me. With Jake working crazy hours, it is nice to visit with a neighbor while he is at work."

Eva sat down next to her and reached for a box on the floor and held it out. "Please accept this gift as a token of our friendship."

Anna Maria unwrapped the box to find a beautiful German wooden nutcracker carved and painted like a toy soldier.

Eva smiled. "You can keep this toy soldier to remind you of your real soldier."

Anna Maria gave Eva a hug.

"Have some tea," she said as she poured Anna Maria a cup from the pot. She noticed Eva already had her cup half full. They raised their tea and toasted each other as Anna Maria took a sip.

"How is your work going at 'Stars and Stripes?'"

"I am working on an article about our tour of Paris."

Then the conversation turned to the shopping Anna Maria had just done in Darmstadt. Eva said, "The next time you are in the city center, we should meet for lunch."

After the third sip of her tea, Anna Maria felt lightheaded and sat back on the sofa to rest for a minute. She tried to say something as she passed out.

Eva gave the knockout drops time to take effect, moved to her kitchen and picked up her phone.

"Hello, yes, she is out. Come pick her up."

Five minutes later, a panel truck with no markings pulled up at the building entrance. Two men with long hair and gray smocks stepped out and buzzed her apartment. Eva let them in, and they grabbed Anna Maria by the shoulders and feet as they lifted her into a cedar chest. They closed the lid and carried it out to the waiting transport van. Eva got in and they drove up to the Crowleys apartment, where she slipped a note into their mailbox. Eva climbed back into the truck, and they headed south to a rest stop on Frankfurter-Landstrasse, where she got out to catch a tram back to her apartment to pack up. The men transported Anna Maria to a safe house in Frankfurt, while Eva coordinated the move to a better hideout in the Odenwald provided by the Stasi.

38

Femme Fatale

Frazer mulled over his relationship with Eva Schmidt. "Her questions were not, 'how are you' or 'what do you want to do today?' Instead, the conversations revolved around my work and how we traveled there."

She grilled him constantly. "Why do you travel using a bus and cars? Isn't the bus sufficient?"

Her favorite question was "What is the big secret at OPS?"

He evaded by changing the subject. She claimed curiosity, but Frazer became suspicious when she brought up questions about weapons and if the airmen carried them.

This time, he told her a white lie. "Only Air Force Security Police carry weapons because of NATO regulations."

She accepted that answer without asking if he was one of those policemen. He kept to the supply sergeant cover story when she asked what kind of work he did.

Eva's possible duplicity stuck in his craw.

He recalled, "The RAF carried out the attack against our convoy in their traditional fashion, as if they were attacking the usual civilians to take hostages. The terrorist guerilla marched right up to my car and shot low to the ground, trying to disable the vehicle instead of assuming that the passengers carried arms and shooting to kill. This convinced me that Eva conveyed my white lie to the RAF, inferring we were unarmed."

After Frazer checked on Sam at the infirmary, he grabbed a pay phone in the waiting room and called Eva. She picked up her phone on the third ring and he could tell his call surprised her.

"Chad, I didn't expect to get a call from you at this hour."

"I was hoping to reach you. I have something urgent to discuss."

The alarm bells rang in Eva's mind. She thought, *What happened to the planned attack and why was he calling this late? Did he need someone to confide in after his ordeal? He should have been abducted by now. Why haven't they given me the bad news? I must deal with Frazer before I call for my ride to the safe house where Frau Crowley is being held.*

"I see. Do you wish to come over? I will make some tea, and we can talk."

"I'll be there in a half hour."

"*Auf Wiederhören, Liebchen*!"

He hung up and thought, *Till she hears from me again. My sentiments exactly.*

He ran to his dorm, picked up his badge, pistol, and put on his leathers. Once outside, he donned his helmet and took off on his motorcycle. As he rode across town to her apartment, the situation came into focus.

He thought, *I have no actual evidence against her. All the women I have known asked about my job, but not about weapons I carried or if I had ever shot anyone. Other dates avoided the subject as if it was distasteful. Eva is not shy and the way she acts around me makes me suspicious.*

That certain coldness she displayed put him on edge.

He reckoned, "I must get her off balance with questions about her whereabouts. Then I will try to confront her and force out the truth."

He reached her apartment and parked on the street in front of her building. He could see her looking out the window.

Eva was feeling the pressure. "Frau Crowley's abduction was all planned out. What do I do with Chad?" as she prepared the tea and lit a cigarillo to calm her nerves.

She took a drag and remembered, "Oh, the knock-out-drops!"

Eva squeezed some drops into the teapot.

The bell rang, and it startled her even though she expected it.

Frazer spoke into the intercom, "Hello, it is me, Chad."

She buzzed him in, and he opened the door to find her standing there holding her cigarillo. They kissed cheeks, and she directed him over to the sofa where they sat together as she poured his tea. Her teacup sat on the coffee table, already filled.

Eva said, "I thought you had to work today, darling. What happened?"

"I reported for duty. On the road to operations, German terrorists tried to abduct us."

"What do you mean by terrorists?"

"The Baader-Meinhof Gang. You know—The RAF."

"When did that happen?"

"Like I said, on the way to work. The Air Force security police broadcasted alerts after the army barracks bombing in Frankfurt but gave us nothing definite to prepare for. We did not expect it."

"You are lucky they did not kill you. The press has reported the RAF kill hostages."

"Yes, I know. We killed them before they killed us."

"I thought you told me that only security police carry weapons in public."

Frazer opened his jacket to reveal his badge.

"That's what I said."

"You lied to me."

"No, I didn't. You asked me if the security service carried weapons, and I said only the Air Force Security Police carried weapons. Did you ask me if I was a policeman?"

"But you said you worked as a supply sergeant."

"I also serve in the auxiliary police. I help with transportation security."

This comment floored her. *The operation was a failure and all because Chad lied to me! Now I must worry about the RAF coming to kill me for the botched intelligence. Oh, there is Herr Becker to deal with, too. He won't be happy either. I wonder if I can use Frazer as a peace offering?*

"I am sorry to find out you had such a trying day. Drink your tea before it gets cold and then we can move to the bedroom. I know what will relax you."

Frazer drank his tea and then he posed another question.

"So, how did I catch you home today? What personal business did you have to take care of?"

Eva replied, "I had to run to the post office and straighten out my telephone account. They had not applied a payment I had made."

Frazer nodded and then felt woozy as he put down his cup. He tried to focus on Eva and then sank back unconscious on the sofa. Eva jumped up and opened his jacket. She found his gun and pulled it from the holster. Next, she picked up her phone and called her RAF contact for another furniture pick up.

After the call, she thought, *What if the RAF finds out he lied, and she fell for it? That would be a problem. No, I cannot let that happen. It will jeopardize all I have done to infiltrate the organization.*

She grabbed his pistol, put a throw pillow over his head, and fired through the pillow to deaden the sound.

She mused, "It is Crowley I am after! Frazer is expendable."

Luckily, she had put a blanket on the sofa to hide some stains. It caught the blood from Frazer's head wound. She stuck his gun in the holster and waited for the "moving men" to arrive.

The men arrived in their smocks, carrying the cedar chest up to the apartment. They picked up the body, wrapped it in the blanket, and placed it in the chest.

Eva pointed and said, "Dump the body on a back street late this evening and leave the gun next to the body. Make it appear to be a suicide."

They threw in the bloody pillow and slammed the top shut.

39

Cry Havoc

Crowley maneuvered his motorcycle up near the pedestrian entrance of their apartment. The glass cuts on his arms and bruises on his head made him feel sore all over. He longed to see his wife and take a long, hot shower to soothe his wounds. He dismounted, withdrew the key from his pocket, and walked toward the door. His eyes focused on a white envelope sticking out of their mailbox by the side of the entranceway, and his hair stood on end.

He muttered, "My God, what is this? We never get mail here."

As he grabbed the envelope out of the mailbox, his mind raced over the possibilities. The streetlights were too far away to read anything, so he unlocked the pedestrian door, stepped into the courtyard, and turned to lock the door. The only light available glowed from the portico of the apartment building entrance.

Growing wary, he drew his pistol and scanned the dark space around the garden. With nothing suspicious appearing in his sights, he holstered his Colt and headed for the portico.

He recalled, "Anna Maria told me she planned to go shopping in the morning and return home by noon. We have all our mail delivered to the APO mailbox at the Kaserne, so she should have grabbed the letter when she returned out of curiosity."

He held it up to the light. "It has Herr Crowley typed on it and no postmark, so maybe it is from the landlord!"

He tore it open and withdrew a single sheet of typewritten paper. At the top was a red stamp mark depicting a five-pointed star framing an assault rifle with the letters RAF superimposed. His blood ran cold as he read the message under the portico.

Herr. Crowley–The Red Army Faction wishes to inform you that your actions to support the fascist pigs controlling the *Polizei* have not gone unnoticed. In addition, we find your wife, Anna Maria Crowley, disseminates propaganda on TV concerning American forces in Vietnam and the continued occupation of Europe by the U.S. The RAF has captured her, and she is being held hostage. Only you can free her. If you ever want to see her again, submit to our demands. Our directions begin with a telephone call to this number. Leave a message with your pay phone number and we will respond immediately with further instructions.

Crowley's head was pounding. Fear and rage swept over him as he stuffed the letter in his fatigue jacket and bounded up the four flights of stairs to their floor. He unlocked the door to find a note scotch taped to the China closet. He grabbed the paper.

"Hi, Jake, just wanted to let you know I got an invitation from Eva to join her for tea at her apartment. I should be home soon. There is food in the fridge if you are hungry. Love, Anna Maria."

Crowley shouted in anguish. "I told her I didn't trust Eva, and she visited her on her own, anyway! I should have never introduced Schmidt to her. What am I going to do? The brass will not allow me to take part in the rescue of my wife. They would consider me too emotionally involved to make decisions."

He gathered his thoughts. During the RAF attack earlier today, his posse proved themselves under fire. Crowley knew he could count on them. He also learned he could rely on Captain Bauer. He decided his best course of action would be to ask the *Polizei* for assistance but stay in reserve. His posse would employ their anti-terrorist training to overwhelm the Red Army Faction.

As he removed his fatigue jacket and flung it on the bed, he transferred the RAF letter to a pocket of a denim shirt. Next, he pulled on his civilian clothes and reached for the pistol magazines he kept on top of the cabinet. After stuffing the magazine clips into the pockets of his coat, he then flipped the safety on each of his Colts and stuck them back in the shoulder holsters as he strapped them, crisscrossing his chest.

Crowley looked down at the leather jacket he had tailored in Frankfurt to hide his handguns. He recalled Anna Maria saying, "Your chest looks so wide, you could pose as a superhero on the cover of a Marvel comic."

He would give anything to hear her tease him right now. Crowley sat on the bed and pulled on his wellington boots and ran out of the bedroom, grabbing his helmet and gloves on the way. As he rushed through the living room, he scooped up his motorcycle keys from the *Schrank* and headed to the stairwell, slamming the door behind him.

Flying down the four flights of stairs, Crowley hung on to the railing as he made the turns at the landings to prevent the extra weight of his guns from pulling him toward the outside wall. He reached the ground floor landing and raced out the gate to his motorcycle, parked where he left it in front of the apartment building. He began kicking at the starter and adjusting the choke until the engine coughed and sputtered into life.

Crowley looked around for traffic while he resolved what he should do. "I'll head for the Kaserne and get the posse organized."

He twisted the throttle and merged onto Frankfurter-Landstrasse toward Darmstadt. The roadway shined under the lights.

He thought, *On, shit! I better be careful to avoid the tram tracks, or I will be on my ear in a split second from the slick steel rails lurking between the cobblestones.*

He proceeded, varying his speed to the driving conditions. As he neared the Kaserne, he pulled out his security police badge and waved it at the guard shack as he blasted past the entrance gate.

Crowley screeched his bike to a halt and raced up the stairs and down the hall to the Charge of Quarters office. Staff Sergeant Dobbs manned the CQ desk and was on the phone.

Not having time for introductions, Crowley called out. "I have an emergency," as he grabbed a handset to call Captain Bauer's unit.

Polizei officer Weber answered on the first ring and Crowley started speaking in German. He asked for Hauptmann Bauer. Weber recognized his accent from the joint training exercises and told him to stand by as he pushed the hold button and rolled his desk chair in front of his radio set. He picked up a microphone and called out to Bauer's unit, while still holding the telephone receiver under his chin.

The CQ hung up his phone as he looked at the intruder dressed in leather biker clothes and speaking German like a native. He could tell the guy was growing impatient sitting there on hold. Before Dobbs could speak, the stranger turned his swivel chair and stared back at him.

"Just don't sit there! I am Sergeant Crowley. Send a runner to wake up airmen Frazer and Jackson. Tell them to report here with their weapons and bikes."

The CQ shouted, "What makes you think you can give me orders?"

While still holding the phone to his ear, Crowley unzipped his jacket, revealing his Air Force Security Police badge and the two sidearms. Dobbs sank back down in his seat and called the runner over as he wrote the airmen's names and room numbers on a slip of paper, along with Crowley's instructions. The runner put on his hat and coat as he double timed it out the door to the dormitory buildings.

Bauer was in a seedy part of Frankfurt supervising a stake out of a suspected terrorist cell when he heard Weber's request on his radio and replied to the broadcast. The desk sergeant gave him a call-back telephone number. Bauer walked over to a pay phone booth on the corner and called Weber.

Bauer demanded, "What's going on that is so important? You pulled me away from a surveillance operation."

Weber replied, “The American Sergeant Crowley has an urgent message for you.”

“I will take the call. Conference him in.”

“Hello, Sergeant Crowley. Weber tells me you have an urgent message for me. I thought you would be home recuperating.”

“When I arrived at my apartment, I found a ransom letter from the RAF and Anna Maria was missing. I believe Eva had her kidnaped.”

Bauer replied, “I have her address from the Interpol investigation you requested. I’ll have detectives investigate immediately. How do you want to proceed?”

“Keep this quiet or my commander will take me off the case.”

“I understand. For now, we are making this part of our current surveillance operation. We will dispatch a patrol car to take you to my current location. This way, we coordinate the rescue together. Hang up and I will give instructions to Weber.”

Crowley disconnected and Bauer spoke. “Send detectives to *Fraulein* Schmidt’s apartment and canvas the area. Her file is in my active folder. Also, send Schultz to meet Crowley at the Kaserne and guide him to my current location.”

Bauer hung up the receiver and got back in his Porsche interceptor to monitor his radio. Weber called an extension for one of the on-duty detectives. Detective Wichs answered the call, took notes, and grabbed his coat as he waved at his partner to join him. They raced out of the office, jumped into their unmarked sedan, and headed out of the station toward Arheilgen. Next, Desk Sergeant Weber broadcast to Schultz’s patrol car and gave him instructions on where to meet Crowley. He then radioed the captain to report on the completion of his orders.

Hauptmann Bauer was supervising a surveillance detail, monitoring activity at a bar in Frankfurt. Earlier that evening, he watched a van arrive and park behind the building. Two men in smocks moved a heavy piece of furniture into the building. He waited for evidence to develop, because a magistrate would not allow a search without 'probable cause' and besides, he was waiting for the RAF leaders to show.

Weber grabbed the telephone handset from under his chin and dialed the number Crowley had given him. Crowley picked up on the first ring.

"Sergeant Crowley! Is it you?"

"Yes, what do you have for me?"

"Hauptmann Bauer is investigating a situation which might help locate your wife. He asked you to join him at a surveillance operation."

"What can you tell me about the operation?"

"Because of security protocol, I cannot say on the telephone. I dispatched a patrol car to bring you to the location. Hauptmann Bauer will brief you there and you can observe the situation for yourself."

"Thank you, Sergeant Weber. I'll wait for your man to arrive."

As he turned around to face Dobbs, a rumble outside announced his posse.

Crowley thought, *Sounds like Jackson's BSA.*

The Musketeers

When he spotted the Norton parked at the entrance, Jackson realized Crowley had woken him up.

Jackson mused, "The commando's Commando. Something important must have happened. The runner did not know who requested me to report. Security service personnel only get to know airmen on their own flight because of the crazy rotating shift schedules. It was understandable the messenger did not recognize Crowley by sight."

Jackson pushed his bike next to the Norton Commando, set the kick stand, took off his helmet, and walked up to the headquarters entrance. He was about to open the door when the sound of another motorcycle caught his attention.

"Hey, it's Sam! I could make out his gold metal-flake Triumph Bonneville in a snowstorm."

Rothman rolled up and maneuvered his bike next to the others.

Jackson called out, "Sam, what are you doing here? I thought you would at least spend the night in the hospital."

"It turns out the bullet only grazed me. They gave me a few stitches and marked my chart 'ready for duty.'"

"Man, why don't you take it easy? Crowley and I can handle this."

"It only hurts when I laugh and anyway, the runner woke me up when he came for Chad. By the way, where is he?"

"I don't know. The last time I saw him was when we visited you at the hospital. Maybe he is bar hoping to relieve some stress."

Rothman replied, "With Chad missing, we can't say 'all for one and one for all'! Let's go find out what D'Artagnan wants. His bike is over there, so he must be in the CQ office."

It was 2100 hours as Eva Schmidt walked into the farmhouse and flung down her suitcase as she picked up the phone in the living room. She dialed the number of the bar and asked for Hans. The barkeeper answered the call and handed the receiver to him, saying it was his girlfriend as he laughed.

Hans put down his beer and took the call.

"Darling, I thought we were going to spend time together tonight! I reserved a room for us upstairs."

"In your dreams! Everything is ready. Bring the American hostage to the farm in the Odenwald." Then she hung up.

He gestured to a man at the end of the bar as he finished his beer. They wandered over to a stairwell leading to the apartments above. The body odor and breath of the tall German startled her awake.

It's the brute who lifted me out of the chest and shackled me to this awful bed. What is he going to do to me now? she thought.

He unlocked the handcuff on her left foot and then her right. Anna Maria watched him as he walked around the bed and freed her right hand. Her knife was now within reach. Suddenly, another man appeared in the doorway with a pistol pointed in her direction. The brute grabbed her by the arm.

"Here is a little something to help you sleep."

He jabbed a syringe into her shoulder. Anna Maria passed out, and he unlocked the remaining handcuff and looked over at the gunman.

"Fredrich, get over here and give me a hand!"

The gunman stuck his pistol in his waistband and grasped her legs while Hans took both her arms. They brought her over to a wooden chest and lowered her in.

Hans said, "This piece of furniture has come in handy. I cut holes in the wood to allow air to enter from the bottom."

They closed the lid, adjusted the carry straps, and lifted it down the apartment stairwell. Once they reached the ground floor, they eased it to the floor, and the gunman walked over to open the rear exit.

"Okay, Fredrich, let's slide her into the truck."

They raised the chest again with the straps and hauled it out of the hallway and opened the double doors at the back of the van. Fredrich hoisted his end onto the cargo bed. They pushed the chest into the truck and locked it.

Hans smirked. "Let's go to the Odenwald and have some fun with the American!"

Fredrich smiled and walked to the passenger side. In a few minutes, they were heading south to the farmhouse.

It was 2100 hours when the posse reached the CQ office in Cambrai-Fritsch Kaserne. A grim-faced Crowley hung up the phone and turned to them as they entered. They hurried over, and in a low voice, he told them to huddle up as he guided them outside.

"Where is Chad? And Sam, what are you doing here? I just visited you flat on your back in the hospital."

"Chad must be out on the town. I was on my bunk when the runner came for him. The doctor stitched me up and marked me as fit for duty."

Crowley nodded, "Men, I returned to my apartment to find a letter from the RAF stating they abducted Anna Maria for ransom. I believe Eva Schmidt had a hand in it."

Jackson replied, "Wow, Eva? She seemed so friendly to you and Anna Maria."

"When I got to our place, an envelope was sticking out of our mailbox. That struck me as odd because we have all our mail sent to the Kaserne. I opened the letter to find a Red Army Faction logo on the top and instructions to follow or I would never see my wife again."

Rothman spoke up. "What makes you think Eva is involved?"

"I just got off the phone with the *Polizei.* I told them Anna Maria left a note about having tea with Eva. They sent detectives over to Schmidt's address, and there was no sign of Eva or my wife. I am waiting for an update on the investigation at Eva's apartment."

Rothman said, "Jake, you can count on us, right, Darryl?"

Jackson replied, "I'm all in. What should we do?"

Crowley lowered his voice to a whisper, "We must keep this just between us. Bauer and his men are assisting for now, but if our command gets wind of this, they will bar me from the case because it involves my spouse."

Rothman added, "Because they think your personal emotions might get in the way."

"Exactly, and they will proceed using police procedures and coordinate everything with everybody. We don't have time for that. Military tactics are the only way to get my wife back alive. The *Hessische Polizei* must also use hostage negotiation protocol. Captain Bauer is holding off for now in a support role, so I can control the response. A patrol car is being dispatched to guide us to a suspected RAF hideout."

Sam said, "What made Bauer agree to take a support role?"

"RAF terrorists have killed all their hostages, and he believes no amount of police negotiation will help. The anti-terrorist training we received from the *Hessische Polizei* means we are best equipped to apply overwhelming force to get Anna Maria out alive. But you must volunteer. I won't use our chain of command and lose control."

Jackson and Rothman looked at each other and nodded their heads in agreement. A German police car pulled up, and the driver waved them over to his window. As they all approached, Crowley recognized Karl Schulz from the training exercises.

Schultz said, "We have located a Red Army Faction cell in Frankfurt, which Hauptmann Bauer has tied to the kidnapping of Frau Crowley. Please follow me."

Crowley asked, "Wait a minute! What is the connection with my wife's abduction?"

"The surveillance team observed men behind the bar moving furniture in the building from a van."

"What do moving men have to do with all of this?"

Schultz replied in a calm voice, "The description of the men and the cargo truck matches one seen by a neighbor of *Fraulein* Schmidt at her apartment building. Two men carried items out of Schmidt's place and loaded them into their truck. The witness mentioned a long chest that appeared to be heavy to carry."

Crowley had heard enough. He turned to his posse and said, "Mount up! Schultz will lead the way."

Schultz called to the posse as they got on their bikes. "The stake out is in the red-light district of Frankfurt. Follow me!"

Schultz flipped on the flashing lights and headed toward the main gate of the Kaserne in his patrol car. The three riders formed up behind Schultz as they steered west toward the autobahn. Dobbs heard all the noise and ran out of the building to find out what was going on. As he saw them take off, he scratched his head and went back inside to cover the phones.

40

The Red Lights of Frankfurt

The flashing lights on Shultz's car caused the traffic in front of them to pull over as he raced through the city of Darmstadt and entered the autobahn entrance. Once in the left lane, Shultz put his foot down on the gas pedal of his Mercedes until his speedometer registered 160 kilometers an hour. Being a motorcycle rider himself, he knew the men following him were not capable of much more speed without becoming unstable. Schultz exited the autobahn and headed for the main railroad station. Known as the *Bahnhofsviertel* or railway station quarter, this area was where the red-light district was located. As they turned down Kaiser Strasse, the sex shops and boutique hotels came into view. Women dressed in negligees posed under red backlighting in the windows of the hotels. Schultz turned off his emergency lights and parked on Weser Strasse. Bar crawlers wandered all over the sidewalks in small groups. They were a major source of income for this part of the city.

As Crowley dismounted his bike, he recognized a hunter green Porsche with a white roof parked up the street with two men inside. He hurried to the car, and Captain Bauer told him to get in. Crowley walked around to the passenger side as Bauer's assistant commander opened the door and got out, giving Crowley a nod as they changed places. Crowley sat down and Bauer handed him a police report while telling him how concerned he was about Anna Maria.

Bauer said, "This gives you an idea of what we are up against. The RAF members we have identified so far are all small potatoes. We have been waiting for their leaders to show up before we move in."

Crowley read the list of names and descriptions on the report and then handed it back.

He said, "I can't wait for some people to drop by. My wife's life is in jeopardy! You told us yourself these terrorists don't play by any rules. They get their ransoms and still kill their hostages. I'm going in with my posse and you can clean up after us. We won't show our badges. They will take us for a pissed off husband and his buddies."

"Do what you feel you must! So far, Schmidt is only under suspicion. I can't act before we have proof."

Crowley left Bauer's car and walked over to his men. "We are going to a RAF safe house and check it out. It is above a beer hall down the street."

They all checked their weapons and mounted their bikes. Crowley pulled his motorcycle over to the curb opposite the Lowe Bier Stube.

He turned to his men. "Undercover detectives monitor the comings and goings trying to catch some of the big fish. So far, no luck. Only RAF members and sympathizers frequent the bar. Nobody else is welcome."

The roar of a steam powered freight train pulling into the nearby station gave Crowley an idea. "Now is our chance. We'll just drop in and say hello using the train noise for cover."

He gunned his bike and let out the clutch while turning the front wheel toward the picture window of the bar. Once the bike straightened out, he twisted the throttle grip as the bike crossed the street and hit the curb. As the motorcycle jumped the curb, he pulled up on the handlebars and the front wheel rose level with his helmet. He was at full throttle when the rear wheel hit a ramp formed by steel cellar doors. This caused him to become airborne as the bike hit the picture window.

The crowd inside the bar was making a racket and did not notice the roar outside.

One bartender caught sight of Crowley as he crashed through the window and shouted over the din, "Everyone get down!"

The motorcycle landed in a shower of broken glass and shrieking tires, accompanied by the roar from the freight train. Crowley skidded to a stop on the dance floor in front of the bar. The crowd froze as he got off his bike, put down the kickstand, and drew his two pistols from their shoulder holsters. He surveyed the crowd and backed up to the side of the smashed window to widen his field of fire. Through the window rode Rothman and Jackson, standing on the foot pegs of their bikes, to maneuver in like they were joining Crowley on a trail ride. They all kept their helmets on and their visors down, concealing their faces. The steam locomotive noise coming through the blown-out window seemed to foretell an apocalypse to the crowd.

Crowley shouted in German, "Where is the American woman?" as he scanned the crowd with his pistols.

"Her name is Anna Maria." As he said her name, a barkeeper reached down and drew up a shotgun. Before he could take aim at the posse, Crowley double-tapped him with two shots to the chest and forehead. The shotgun fired, shattering a large mirror on the wall as the barkeeper keeled over and dropped out of sight.

"I won't say this again! Where is she?"

Crowley threatened in German as he scanned the crowd with his pistols.

This group of urban terrorists was not used to confrontation. Their modus operandi comprised sneaking around and doing their dirty deeds incognito while hiding behind their lame logo and press releases. Crowley was making his issue with them up close and personal. A man wearing a beige sweater stuck his index finger upward as he moved his head and nodded toward the door. Crowley waved his pistol at the remaining bartender, ordering him to get out in front of the bar. He barked out "sweater man" in German and pointed to the doorway. As Crowley followed the men to the stairwell entrance, Jackson joined Crowley while Sam covered the crowd.

Crowley looked up and thought, *I hate the vulnerability of climbing in a confined space with no room to duck. I always feel like I am sticking my neck out.*

Crowley asked the sweater man if he knew where they were holding the American woman.

The German replied, "*Dreihunderteins am dritten Stock*."

Crowley asked him how he knew Anna Maria was in this apartment. The German said he overheard a conversation at the bar.

"He claims Anna Maria is in apartment 301 on the fourth floor. Bring him back to the bar and help Sam cover the Germans while I check out the apartment." Said Crowley.

Jackson nodded and left with "sweater man." Crowley holstered his left-hand pistol and began climbing the stairs close to the inside wall with his free hand holding the railing. When he got to the first floor, a fluorescent light flickered like a strobe. He flipped up his helmet visor to get a better view. There were doors on opposite sides of the landing. He checked the closest one, labeled 101, by putting his ear up against it with his gun hand up in the air. No sounds, so he walked across the hall with his pistol pointed up to 102 and listened. That one was also silent. Next, he tried knocking. No answer, only silence.

He started up the fourth-floor flight of stairs, following the same procedure as he used on the second level. There was no noise and no response to his knocks. He removed his helmet and walked up to 302. His head pressed against the door, and he listened. Not a sound. He crossed the landing to 301 and pressed his ear against that door.

"Nothing!" he thought to himself. "Maybe she is alone right now."

Crowley looked the door over. It was solid with three hinges, an industrial strength door handle and lock. In Germany, this was a normal residential configuration. Crowley backed away and shot out the lock and performed a side roll into the apartment. He came to a stop on one knee using his pistol sight to scan the room.

It was a mess and smelled like one giant ashtray. He waited for any movement or sound, but there was none. Crowley got up, still holding his Colt straight-armed with both hands, and walked across the living room, trying to avoid tripping over boxes and wrappers strewn all over the floor. He reached another door and eased it open to reveal another mess. This appeared to be a bedroom with a single bed. Crowley flipped a wall switch by the entrance and cleared the area with his gun. What he saw shocked him.

A single unmade bed with brass head and foot boards sat in front of him with four pairs of chrome handcuffs attached to the thick rails.

"Oh God, they handcuffed her in this mess and then they must have moved her again!"

Captain Bauer's comment earlier today about the furniture movers came to mind. "They must have smuggled her in and out in a hope-chest."

He searched around the bed, looking for clues. A shiny object caught his eye.

"Anna Maria left a bread crumb to confirm I am on the trail."

Crowley scooped up her earring and put it in his pocket. He had it made for her in a shop in Michelstadt.

He surmised, "The instructions on the ransom note are the key to rescuing her. Now is the time to make the RAF believe I am playing their game."

Crowley picked up his helmet in the hallway and put it on as he descended the stairs. The gunfire upstairs increased the pandemonium in the bar. They began talking to each other, asking who the next victim of the American biker hoodlums would be.

"God in heaven! The RAF sure picked the wrong hostage this time," exclaimed a woman in German.

Her boyfriend replied, "This can't be real! I feel like we are in a bar scene from a spaghetti western."

Crowley walked into the room, still holding one of his Colt pistols, and the crowd went silent. He ordered his posse to mount up, and they started up their bikes in the bar and rode them up a makeshift ramp into the night via the picture window, while Crowley stood there and pointed his gun at the crowd. Once the posse was outside, Crowley rode up the ramp with his pistol pointed behind him. There was a roar of engines and they disappeared.

The bar crowd started their own uproar.

"Who was that guy? Did he think he was Peter Fonda?"

"No! No! Captain America had no guns, and that was his undoing. This cowboy with no name rode in on his iron horse with two guns."

"Where do you expect he has gone?"

"To kill some of our friends, I am afraid."

41

The Chase

The posse rode back to Weser Strasse and found Bauer's Porsche parked in an alley with the engine running and the radio crackling out dispatches. Bauer was giving them cover by monitoring alerts concerning activity at the RAF's bar. As Crowley pulled up, the German police captain rolled down his window as he turned down the radio volume.

"So, what happened? Did you go in? I was expecting to hear sirens and radio dispatches."

Crowley replied, "I shot a bartender in self-defense. He drew a shotgun from under the counter and aimed it at me. I'm not sure they are going to report the death, because the crowd looked as guilty as hell when I questioned them about Anna Maria. One patron told me he overheard a conversation about an American woman being held upstairs in apartment 301. He acted like it was common knowledge. I searched the place and found an earring I had given Anna Maria next to a bed they shackled her to. I know she left it as a bread crumb. It still has the clip on the post."

Bauer put a hand on his shoulder. "We have to come up with a plan for the rescue."

Crowley thought about it and pulled the ransom note out of his pocket.

Bauer looked up from reading it and shook his head in sympathy. "We must coordinate with portable radios. I can give you and your men walkie-talkies, but you must conceal your communications from potential observers along the way. You can't do that on a motorcycle."

Crowley nodded and walked over to a phone booth on the corner, dropped a one-mark coin in the slot and dialed the phone on the ransom note.

He spoke into the receiver. "I need a call back as soon as possible. Here is the telephone number."

The operator repeated it and said, "*Danke schoen*!" and disconnected.

While Crowley waited for the callback, Bauer called in on his police radio to get the report from the detectives at Fraulein Schmidt's apartment.

Desk Sergeant Weber reported, "The description of the truck you observed in Frankfurt matched the truck seen this afternoon outside *Fraulein* Schmidt's building loading furniture from her residence. Detective Wichs reported a neighbor observed what appeared to be a large hope chest and a few chairs being packed. I broadcast a dispatch to look for the truck, but not to apprehend it."

Bauer ordered, "Keep me updated on the search," and signed off.

The pay phone rang, and Crowley picked up the receiver.

A man answered with a German accent and asked, "Is this Herr Crowley?"

"Yes."

"Drive to Darmstadt and go to a telephone booth in the marketplace opposite the palace museum. There you will call the answering service again, leave the number and wait for a reply.

Crowley answered, "Okay!" and hung up.

Bauer waited as he hung up the phone. "The *Schlossplatz*. I can pick up an Air Force police cruiser on the way!"

Crowley called out, "Sam, take this walkie talkie and ride your bike over to the motor pool. Tell them to get a Galaxie ready for me."

Bauer waved over Polizei Sergeant Schultz and said, "Escort Rothman to the Kaserne at emergency speed."

The captain grabbed two more walkie-talkies out of the trunk of his Porsche and handed them out to Crowley and Jackson.

Then he took out a satchel from his trunk and gave it to Crowley. "Here are some flash-bangs. If anyone asks you where you got them, tell them they are leftovers from one of our exercises."

Crowley turned to Jackson. "I am going to follow the instructions from the RAF for now. You and Sam are tracking me from a distance, using your walkie-talkies to coordinate with me and the *Hessische Polizei*. Use your call signs BSA and Triumph. The destination is the *Schlossplatz*. I will pick up the patrol car, so we have long guns and cover."

Jackson mounted his BSA and headed out to the autobahn. Crowley waited a few minutes and rode after him. Bauer drove off in his Porsche to follow at a distance while keeping in rapid response range. He decided the dead barkeeper situation would take care of itself, since there was no report of the shooting on the radio.

As Crowley rode on, he thought about how the RAF would lead him on a wild goose chase until they confirmed he was alone. As a countermove, he would take Bauer's advice and switch from his bike to the police interceptor. The car had no markings and provided cover to duck down and coordinate on the walkie-talkies without being seen. He believed they probably posted spotters at every stop to see if anyone followed him. Walkie-talkie communications would help him keep his posse on the trail. Their job was to follow him at a distance, using the next destination point to guide them rather than trying to tail the Ford. Crowley missed Frazer, who always served as his second in command. He would have to rely more on Rothman and Jackson. It was not like Frazer to miss any action.

Crowley flew past the gate house and sped to the motor pool. There he saw Rothman standing in front of one of their patrol cars idling in a garage bay. Crowley pulled his bike over to the side of the building and parked it. He ran over to the interceptor, opened the trunk, and placed the bag of flash bang grenades inside. Next, he grabbed an M16 and extra clips from the back seat rack. Crowley confirmed Rothman and Shultz knew the way to the destination.

They nodded, and he said, "Go! I will be right behind you."

Rothman hopped on his Triumph and bump started it as Schultz stepped into his sedan and they both peeled out. Crowley jumped in his vehicle and nailed it, causing a cloud of smoke to spew out of the garage as he drove out of the service bay. Once on the access road, he did a sharp right turn, heading for the exit. As he blasted out the gate with the Cammer engine at full bore, the guard came running out of the shack. The roar drowned out his shout to halt, so he raised his arm and blew a whistle as tire smoke enveloped him. Crowley made another hard right, creating more wheel noise as the rear wheels fought to gain traction and propel him down the street. As he approached his destination, he backed off the throttle to quiet down the beast of an engine. Searching around, he found a parking space big enough for the Ford.

He got out and started walking. "Okay, there is the *Schlossplatz,* and it looks deserted. Where are the phone booths?"

Crowley scanned the plaza for a cluster of public telephones, as per the RAF's instructions. He located them opposite the Ratskeller and headed in that direction. When he reached the first booth, he picked up the receiver and dropped a one-mark coin in the slot. The mark dropped through to the coin return.

"Oh shit! The phone is dead. It looks like someone smashed the receiver against the booth."

Crowley moved over to the next booth, and someone broke that phone, too.

"What the hell! Is the RAF playing with me?"

He reached for the third phone and got a dial tone. Crowley dialed the answering service and left his contact information. Then he waited.

It was 2300 hours at the farmhouse as Eva Schmidt took the message from the answering service operator and waved over Otto.

"Otto, take these instructions I have written, including Crowley's current contact number. Drive out and use a telephone booth to dial it."

Otto said, "Now it's my turn to face 'the man with no name'?"

Eve replied, "What are you talking about, Otto?"

"That is what our supporters back at the Frankfurt beer hall called him when they phoned in their warnings. They said he rode in on his iron horse and shot the barkeeper as casually as if one would swat a fly. They think we are in over our heads."

"*Ja,* Otto, he is a genuine cowboy! Just like in the movies. I am sure of that now. Not the office clerk he claimed to be. Anyway, we have a nice trap all ready for him and his iron horse."

Otto stuck the note between his teeth as he pulled on his jacket and headed out the door with a smile on his face. He relished the idea of giving this American soldier the run around. He hated American capitalism and the Vietnam War and other acts of aggression against the proletariat. Outside, Otto cursed as he brushed a cigarette ash off his new Levi jeans and slid into his Ford Capri. He started the car, extinguished his Marlboro, and drove off down the street.

Crowley paced back and forth on the brick paving stones in front of the pay phones, trying to take his mind off his throbbing head. As the minutes passed, he used his movement to see if he could spot anyone watching him. The *Schlossplatz* was quiet and deserted. He resumed his pacing until the phone rang and he ran over to pick up the handset.

Raising the receiver to his ear, he heard, "Is this Herr Crowley?"

Crowley forced his mind to focus through the haze of his headache. He replied, "This is Crowley. Who is this?"

"Wouldn't you like to know!" said Otto with his German accent.

"Your instructions are to drive to a pay phone at the town square of Michelstadt. Do you know where Michelstadt is located?"

"Yes, where they carve ivory, right?"

"That is correct. Call the answering service as before for further directions when you arrive."

Knowing he spoke German, Otto added, "*Alles klar?*"

Crowley replied, "Yeah, everything is clear."

Otto smirked, hung up, and got back in his car,

As he drove toward Michelstadt, he recalled his orders. "Schmidt gave me the job of watching him to see if anyone followed the American to Michelstadt. This assignment is a piece of cake. I have my friend Helmut, and his house is right in the town square. I called him to expect a visit."

Crowley dropped the pay phone receiver and jogged out of the *Schlossplatz* and searched for the Ford. The blue color and absence of chrome made it hard to spot at night. Not that he was complaining. It looked like an ordinary base model American sedan. The brass wanted unmarked police cars, so no insignia or graphics. He was glad to have it in case he needed the interceptor's power. He found the cruiser and, after driving a few blocks, checked his rear-view mirror as he pulled over and parked.

Crowley grabbed the walkie-talkie from under the passenger seat and called, "Talon calling Triumph."

"Triumph here. What's next?" replied Rothman.

"Town parking area in Michelstadt. Do you know where that is?"

"Yeah, I went there and bought a necklace for my mother. She won't wear it because of the elephants."

Crowley shuddered as he recalled Anna Maria telling him she did not care for the jewelry when they visited a shop there. His headache became worse.

He recovered and said, "Wait with BSA outside the town. I will radio you when I know the next destination."

Talon signed off and tossed the walkie-talkie back under the seat as he pulled out. He drove south on the autobahn toward Michelstadt.

Otto arrived at the Michelstadt town square. He stopped and looked around.

I don't see anyone standing in front of the pay phones. I better head over to Helmut's place before the American arrives.

He parked his Capri in the back of the house and walked to the main entrance.

Helmut opened the door and greeted him. "Hey, Otto! What's up?"

Otto said, "We have a new hire at the office, and I am testing him on following instructions."

Helmut laughed. "I hope he follows them better than you do!"

Otto looked annoyed and a little hurt. He asked to be brought to the upstairs window.

Helmut said, "I'll show you!" and led Otto up the stairs to a front bedroom overlooking the town square.

Otto thanked him and turned his attention to the square, hoping to break off their conversation. Helmut, however, insisted on staying to catch up on lost time while they waited.

A few minutes later, a blue Ford Galaxie pulled in and drove around until it reached the stand of pay phones.

Helmut said, "We don't get many American cars in this town except during tourist season, and those are all soldiers and their families. What is with this new hire?"

"He seems odd. That is why we are testing him."

"Oh, I see what you mean. What German buys a Ford Galaxie with *Benzin* being so expensive?"

Otto nodded as he watched him park and walk over to the telephones.

The first phone he picked up was in working order this time. He made the call to the answering service and left the new phone number. As Crowley waited for a return call, Otto took out binoculars and looked him over to confirm his identity. Then he scanned the town square for any movement. Otto saw nothing out of the ordinary. The pay phone rang, and Crowley picked it up.

"Hello, this is Crowley."

An unfamiliar voice replied on the line. "Herr Crowley, your directions are to drive to Erbach and park in the visitor parking in front of the castle. There are pay telephones by the entrance. Use one of them to call for further instructions."

Crowley grimaced. "How long is this going to take? I want to see my wife!"

The RAF terrorist replied, "Your wife is safe and if you desire to keep her that way, you will follow our directions to the letter!"

"I have no proof she is alive and well. If I don't get confirmation soon, I will have to assume you are lying and call the *Polizei*."

The contact paused and then said, "You must go to Erbach. From there, I will direct you to your wife's location."

That was the break Crowley wanted. He confirmed he was heading for Erbach and hung up the phone. As he looked up, he noticed a light with two shadows in a second-story window. He made a mental note to have the *Hessische Polizei* check it out. He jumped into the car and headed for Erbach, a short distance away. Driving down the road, he saw a grove of trees, pulled in, and parked. The walkie-talkie had wedged itself under the front passenger seat. He wrestled it out and turned it on.

"Triumph, this is Talon. Erbach is next and then I was told they will direct me to where Anna Maria is being held. I want you guys to meet me outside of Erbach. After I check in with the RAF, we will meet and go together in my car to the last stop. Over."

"Sounds like a plan, Talon. Over." replied Rothman.

Crowley added, "I will pick a meeting point on the way and radio the position to you before I reach the town. Over."

"Roger that, over."

Crowley pulled out of the thicket and got back on the road.

At a sign indicating 5 kilometers to Erbach, Crowley spotted another thicket of trees just past the sign and pulled in. He stretched out on the front bench seat, pulled up the walkie-talkie antenna, and called Sam Rothman.

"Triumph, do you read me?"

"I read you loud and clear, Talon."

"Trees just beyond the five-kilometer sign to Erbach. Stash your bikes and wait for me there." Directed Crowley.

"Roger that."

Rothman realized they were beginning to sound like a TV cop show.

Crowley signed off, stuck the walkie-talkie under the seat, and drove out down the main road to Erbach. As he approached the town, he could see the cone-shaped roofs of the fortress towers and headed in their direction. He spotted the pay phones under a streetlight. The parking area was empty, so he drove up in front of the phones. His hand was shaking a little as he pulled out the ransom note and read the number as he dialed the pay phone.

Crowley muttered, "This had better work! How must Anna Maria feel right now?"

The phone connected, and the operator answered.

He started the same drill for the third time and thought, *This is torture. Every stop has a problem. Now I can't see. The lighting in the phone booth is so dim, I am having trouble reading the callback number to the answering service.*

He craned his neck to get help from the streetlight and hung up. It was late now, close to midnight. The castle was dark and quiet. Crowley recalled the trip here with Anna Maria to scout out a show she was planning on the best spots in the Odenwald. As he continued to think about her and their visit, the phone rang, and he picked it up.

"Hello, this is Crowley."

"Hello, Herr Crowley. You are now on the last leg of your journey. A meeting place is located back the way you came. A driveway entrance on the right side marked 922 in black numbers on a white gate is three kilometers away. Park your car on the roadside and sit there with your hands on the steering wheel. Someone will come out to greet you. Do you understand?"

Crowley said, "*Alles klar*," and hung up the phone. He drove around to make sure nobody followed him. Then he pulled over, laid down, and got on the walkie-talkie.

"Triumph, do you read me?"

"I read you loud and clear, Talon." Sam picked himself up from the brush he was sitting in and held the walkie-talkie to his ear.

"Triumph, ride your bike down the road toward Erbach. Look for 922 on the left side. The number is on a white entrance gate. Drive by in high gear to lug the engine and make it sound like you are having a mechanical problem, as you check out the area. Do not continue to Erbach. Instead, stop a kilometer past the farmhouse and call me from behind the bushes. In case they have spotters, make out like you are trying to fix an engine problem. Have BSA give you a head start for your reconnoiter and then follow you at regular speed to reach the meeting location. I will join you on the way from Erbach. You got that, over?"

"Roger that, Talon. I am taking off, over."

"Talon here. Over and out."

Crowley tossed the walkie-talkie under the seat, put the car in gear and eased out of his hiding spot. A couple of turns and he was heading for the rendezvous.

42

The End Game

Rothman reached the farmhouse and slowed his bike as he passed by.

He mused, "The front of the house has two multi-pane windows and a solid looking large front door. Except for a wooden gate, there appears to be an unobstructed driveway to the farmhouse. Where are their guards?"

Rothman looked for guards and found them on both sides of the entrance, talking.

As he passed by, his headlight shined briefly on their faces. "They are staring at me. I better lug my engine and appear to be looking down for a problem. My next stop is the clump of trees Crowley told us to meet at."

Rothman stopped by the landmark of trees and pulled the walkie-talkie out of his coat.

"BSA, I have the recon info, and I am now in position."

Jackson replied, "Triumph, get on your bike and look busy working to start it. I am on my way."

Rothman put the bulky walkie-talkie back in his saddlebags and looked around. He could see headlights coming from Erbach and started pumping the kick starter with the ignition off to look like he was having engine trouble. The vehicle slowed as it got nearer, and Rothman could see it was the Ford Galaxie. He pushed his Triumph down behind the trees and hustled back up to the road to meet Crowley. Crowley stopped the car and Rothman jumped in the back and pulled down the backrest to access the gun racks, as he filled Crowley in on his recon.

It was 2330 hours when Herr Becker pulled up to the farmhouse gate and encountered two RAF men holding Czech assault rifles across their chests. They approached the car and looked inside. The guards nodded at Becker, opened the gate, and waved him through. They knew Herr Becker well. He was the German arms dealer friend of Eva Schmidt, who helped supply them with machine guns and grenades. Now they believed he was here to assist them in receiving ransom money from the Americans.

Soukeroff was getting used to his "Herr Becker" cover and enjoyed driving his Mercedes around West Germany. He steered the sedan around the farmhouse and parked behind a detached garage, opened his window a crack, lit a cigarette, and waited. Schmidt had left a message earlier to be at this farm at 2330 hours. Her message stated there would be a package ready for pickup surprised him because he knew the attacks this morning had failed. The kidnap plot must have worked!

He recalled their meeting at the Frankfurt safe house.

Schmidt said, "The hijacking failed. The Americans had weapons, and the RAF was not prepared for that. I have a backup plan to abduct the Crowleys. The RAF did not approve of this until after the hijack fiasco. The RAF leaders feared Frau Crowley's celebrity status would bring too much attention from the police. I appeased them by using you as an intermediary for the ransom exchange."

I said, "How did you convince them of my contacts with the Americans?"

Schmidt replied, "I told the RAF you had CIA contacts for many years as an arms dealer and you can negotiate the exchange with the Americans and keep the RAF out of it."

Becker thought, *The package, of course, is the American Sergeant Crowley. Schmidt plans on drugging him like the others and then stashing him in the trunk of my car. We will smuggle him and his wife over the border to Stasi headquarters in East Germany.*

The KGB officer smoked his cigarette and reflected on how hard it had been trying to kill Crowley. "First, we had illegal agents sent to the spy school Crowley attended to see if they could sabotage his training by injuring him in a street fight. Instead, Crowley beat up the lead agent and the American Air Force, requested an FBI investigation to find out why our men suddenly materialized in the middle of a Texas desert, posing as locals. We had to extract the agents from the country to save them from arrest."

Becker took another drag on his cigarette. "When the attack in Texas failed, we ordered our control in New York to arrange for Crowley to be injured in an anti-war demonstration to prevent him from deploying to Europe. The airman turned the tables and got our agent arrested as a domestic terrorist. Then an illegal agent in Germany tried to kill him by sabotaging his car during a trip in the Alps. It resulted in a thrill ride for the couple as they used their car like a toboggan to careen down the mountain roads to safety."

Becker took a final drag and put it out. "The last attempt occurred in France where an agent tried to kill him by shooting the bus driver of a tour he was on. Crowley and his henchmen captured the agent and were so pissed off, they forced a confession out of him by stepping on his wounds. The interrogation by the gendarmes blew the cover off our entire French network. I recall reading the KGB report and thinking someone had stuck a comic book in the file. As luck would have it, the incompetence saved Crowley for my kidnap operation."

Becker concluded, "When Crowley arrived in Germany and began his spying activities, our KGB top echelon revised their strategy from sabotage to abduction. The Stasi sent Schmidt to be the honey trap, and when that failed, they sent me to get things moving. With the Red Army Faction acting as our surrogate, we masterminded a terrorist attack and found out the hard way that Crowley and his friends were armed to the teeth. Not your usual terrorist prey, to be sure, and they naturally failed at it. So now the RAF is doing what they do best, capturing unarmed civilians and holding them for ransom. Schmidt turned Crowley's wife into bait, which became a perfect cover for the abduction. The cover is so deep it is like Matryoshka nesting dolls one inside the other."

At 2345 hours, Jackson rode down the road at a normal pace past the farmhouse and continued until he saw Crowley's car parked at the rendezvous point. The back door to the police cruiser was open and Rothman was inside preparing the M16's and gas masks.

Crowley said, "Stash your bike behind the trees next to Rothman's and make it fast. If I take too long getting to the farmhouse, they will get suspicious."

Jackson did as he was told, and when he returned, Crowley rewarded him with an M16 and ammo belt.

"Okay, here's the plan," said Crowley. "Based on Sam's recon, I want to go in fast and assault the farmhouse from the front, since they are probably holding Anna Maria somewhere in the back for security. We will ram the gate and drive up to the building. Then you guys will lob flash bangs through the windows before we use a battering ram on the door."

Rothman piped in, "What about the guards?"

"Yeah," said Crowley. "I was getting to that. You two need to keep your windows open and take them out with pistols as we pass their positions at the gate. Sam, you ride shotgun in the front and Darryl, you sit in the back seat and take out the guards from the driver's side. I will steer the car, so the driver's side ends up facing the front door of the farmhouse. Because he has cover from the car on the passenger side, Sam will jump out to lob the flash bangs through the farmhouse windows after we stop. We will first fire out of the driver's side to cover you and knock out the windowpanes. Sam, leave the doors on your side of the car open. Darryl and I will exit the car from the passenger side after you lob the flash bangs and bash in the door with the battering ram. Questions?"

Rothman asked, "What about Bauer and his *Hessische Polizei*?"

Crowley replied, "Clip your walkie talkies to your ammo belts. Bauer agreed to hold back and wait for a call. We keep in control of the situation if possible and call him when we are successful or overwhelmed. Anything else?"

They said no, feeling confident the *Hessische Polizei* would back them up like they did in the training exercises. The posse checked their weapons before getting into the car and rolling down their windows. To make up for time lost at the rendezvous, Crowley accelerated gradually toward the farmhouse to keep the engine noise down.

The sound of the Ford Galaxie reached the RAF guards, and their curiosity got the better of them. They moved together in front of the gate at the edge of the road just in time to see headlights veer at them. Crowley improvised and ran the guards over as he drove through the entrance, plowing the gate up and over the car as he went through.

Sam Rothman thought, *Looks like Jake's overwhelming force mode just kicked in.*

As Crowley approached the farmhouse, a shift to a lower gear helped him to spin the rear wheels as he made a right turn to swing the car in front of the door. Gravel flew up from under the car and pelted the facade as they slid to a stop. Rothman jumped out, holding a flash bang in each hand.

Machine-gun fire erupted from the woods by the roadside, strafing the Ford cruiser. Jackson and Rothman dove for cover and Rothman grunted as he landed on his injured side. Crowley closed the car doors as he slid to the ground and drew his pistols.

Crowley called out, "We have no time for this, Darryl! They are trying to kill us. Return the favor and use your fragment grenades."

Jackson crawled around using the car for cover and pulled the pin on a fragment grenade. Rothman crawled over after him and popped up, holding his side while providing cover fire with his Colt as Jackson lobbed the grenade. It exploded, and after a minute, more gunfire emanated from the woods. Jackson responded with another toss and the return fire ceased.

In unison, Jackson and Rothman lobbed a flash bang at the two windows on either side of the main door and then swung their M16s up from their sides and covered the front of the house as Crowley stood next to them with his M16.

It was just before midnight as Anna Maria lay in a dingy dark room on a cot with her legs lashed to the footboard and her hands tied to the metal rails of the headboard. She twisted her right hand to loosen the rope while she listened for any sounds beyond the closed door. She heard steps in the hallway and froze. Two women entered and asked if she wanted to use the bathroom. Her right hand was almost free, so she declined. The women sat in chairs and in German, they started talking about a man called Hans and what an excellent lover he was. Anna Maria understood bits and pieces of the conversation. The girls got up and one said, "Hans has plans for you this evening." They giggled and shut the door behind them.

Anna Maria trembled and listened to be sure they were gone. She resumed her effort to free herself. It was a slow, arduous task, and her wrist got bruised from the twisting and pulling. It seemed like an eternity, but she finally worked her right hand free and reached down to pull a stiletto from her boot. She pushed the switch to release the blade and hid it behind her left shoulder. Then she wrapped her right hand and the headboard with the rope. With her arms and legs back in the position they left her, she waited for what seemed like hours. The door lock unlatched, and her body tensed. A big man with shoulder length light brown hair filled the doorway. He closed the door and locked the latch. He walked toward her and stood at the foot of the bed.

Anna Maria thought, *This must be Hans.*

She stared at him and asked, "Are you Hans? The girls say you are quite the ladies' man."

Hans put his hands on his hips and laughed.

"*Ja, ich bin Hans.*"

A sudden loud explosion distracted Hans. Anna Maria sprang into action and grabbed the stiletto behind her left shoulder as Hans turned back to face her. Forced into a sitting position because of the ropes tied to her legs and left hand, she held the knife overhand, and, in a quick blur, it flew toward Hans and caught him in the throat. He could not utter a sound as he slid down the wall behind him with a blank stare. A red stain on the wall traced his fall.

Anna Maria pulled another stiletto out of her left boot leg and cut the ropes holding her left hand and feet to the bed. Once untied, she jumped up and walked over with her stiletto held out front until she got to where Hans sat. The large pool of blood forming around him told her he was dead, so she placed her right boot on his chest, pulled the knife from his neck, and wiped the blade on his shirt.

Anna Maria crossed herself and said, "God, please forgive me. They don't free their hostages. It was him or me."

Anna Maria stood up and put her ear to the door. She unlocked the latch to find the hallway filled with smoke. She returned to the bedroom and cut a piece off the bedsheet with her knife and tied it over her face to filter the smoke. Back out in the hall, she crept along, hugging the wall, until reaching a flight of stairs. She made her way down to another hallway. A faint stream of light came through the back entrance. The light guided her forward. Midway, she halted as a figure appeared in front of her, heading for the light.

Anna Maria must have alerted the figure with her breathing because it turned toward her to reveal Eva Schmidt's face staring at her in the moonlight. As Schmidt raised her arm to aim her Luger pistol, Anna Maria countered with a left-hand flick of a stiletto underarm which landed right in the middle of Schmidt's chest. The impact of the knife threw Schmidt backward as she fell in the doorway. Anna Maria held her right-hand dagger out and retrieved the stiletto from Schmidt's chest with her left hand. She bent down and picked up the pistol as she stepped over the body. Schmidt grabbed desperately at Anna Maria's leg as she stepped over her.

Anna Maria turned and stuck a stiletto in Schmidt's throat as she hissed, "Don't you know when to quit?"

As Schmidt choked, Anna Maria recalled the Sicilian proverb uttered by her Uncle Sal, "Vendetta is a dish best served up close with a dagger."

She pulled herself together as she unlocked the door, ran across the yard, and hid behind a garage to get her bearings. Bending down to clean the blood off her remaining knife in the grass, she retracted the blade and slid it up her coat sleeve. She raised up the Luger with an unsteady hand, pointed it at the farmhouse, and waited.

At midnight the flash bangs exploded with a roar as Crowley and his posse pulled on their night vision gas masks. Crowley shouldered his M16 and dragged a battering ram out of the trunk as Jackson grabbed the other side. Rothman, now in position behind the car to give covering fire, yelled, "Ready!"

The sound of explosions from inside the house shocked Becker.

He thought to himself, *Those dummkopfs must have blown themselves up making a bomb.*

His knee jerk reaction was to run, but he recalled his general saying, "If you blow this mission, you won't need those new suits and a Mercedes in the gulag."

He drew his pistol and crept to the back of the garage to wait.

Meanwhile, Rothman and Jackson moved around the car and rammed the front door of the farmhouse. It took three tries to break open the solid oak door. It cracked on the third ramming and broke in half. Crowley ran from behind the car to provide covering fire. They threw down the ram, pulled the door pieces away from the frame, and Crowley entered. Not knowing where they held Anna Maria, he did not sweep the room with machine-gun fire. By now, he was operating on instinct and adrenaline.

He shouldered his M16 and scanned the area with the sight of his pistol in a two-handed grip. It appeared to be a sitting room furnished with a sofa, chairs, and a coffee table. A couple of pistols were lying on the table, and Crowley used his arm to sweep them to the floor. One of the RAF men got up to feel his way toward the sound. Seeing him through his infrared goggles, Crowley gave him the butt of his rifle and the terrorist fell face first on the carpet. An infrared figure of another man with a pistol appeared, and Crowley shot him in the chest with his Colt. The terrorist fell back behind the sofa.

The two airmen followed Crowley through the front entrance. A machine pistol opened fire. Crowley shouted, "Suppress that hostile fire!"

Rothman and Jackson spotted mussel flashes coming from a doorway. They provided covering fire while Crowley crawled to the back of the room. Once he got closer, Crowley peered down the hallway through his infrared goggles.

He thought, *I see the heat signature of a warm body on the floor. I also see some faint heat signatures forming handprints on the walls, as if someone used the wall to guide them in the dark down the hall.*

He crawled to the doorway and there in the moonlight he recognized Eva Schmidt staring up at him with a knife sticking out of her neck.

Crowley gasped, *That is one of Anna Maria's throwing knives.*

He made for the door, scanned the outside through the door window and walked outside with his pistol drawn and his rifle slung over his shoulder.

Crowley pulled down his gas mask and shouted, "Anna Maria!"

"Jake—Stay back!"

Her cry came from behind the garage. The backyard offered no cover except for a picnic bench and some chairs visible in the moonlight. Crowley bent down low and used the picnic table for cover as he made his way over toward her voice. A man's voice called out to Crowley.

"Herr Crowley, is that you? I have your wife here at gunpoint. I will shoot her if you don't surrender."

Crowley held his goggle lens like a mirror to look around the corner of the garage. "I see a man behind her holding a pistol."

A flash caught his eye as a stiletto blade slid out of Anna Maria's sleeve into her hand. Crowley thought, *I must do something before she uses her knife!*

He gave up thinking and instinct took over.

Crowley called out, "I am coming out with my hands up."

"Okay, let me see them."

Crowley rounded the corner, holding up a pistol in each hand. Before the KGB agent could tell him to drop them, Anna Maria jabbed her stiletto into his side and dove away as the Soviet agent cried out in pain. Becker adjusted his aim downward in response to Anna Maria's sudden movement and then remembered Crowley's pistols. Anna Maria hit the ground, and Crowley lowered his right pistol and shot Becker in the chest as the KGB agent tried to correct his error and turn his aim back to Crowley. He marched directly to the Russian like a robot on autopilot, emptying his pistol into the man's torso as it shook from the hits. He reached the body, took aim with his second Colt, and waited for any movement.

Anna Maria recoiled from the noise and put her hands over her ears as she rolled up into a ball.

Crowley holstered his pistols, ran over to her, and lifted her off the ground.

He wrapped his arms around her. "Are you hurt?"

"No Jake, I'm not hurt, but why did you have to kill him? I had already stabbed him with my knife. He would have surrendered to avoid bleeding to death."

Still seething, Crowley said, "He pointed his gun at me after you stabbed him, and my instinct kicked in. The man didn't know when to give up."

Anna Maria was aghast. Had she married a killing machine? Then she remembered what she had just done to Hans, Eva, and Becker. She buried her head in Crowley's chest, as he held her close.

"I guess we protected each other. Are we safe now?"

"Yes, I think so. Sam and Darryl are in the house guarding the terrorists until the *Hessische Polizei* arrive."

"Jake, how did you get those cuts on your arms and face? Did you break through the farmhouse window?"

He replied, "This was not our first rodeo today. They attacked us this morning on the way to work. Then they came after you and me."

She shivered in the chilly night air. Crowley slipped his M16 off his shoulder, took off his leather jacket and draped it over her shoulders.

The wail of sirens announced police and emergency vehicles. The couple walked around the farmhouse to meet the *Polizei*.

Crowley borrowed the sheet she used as a mask and waved it from the corner of the house. "Siegfried, this is Talon. All clear?"

Captain Bauer responded, "*Alles klar,* Talon! Where is Anna Maria?"

Crowley replied, "We're both here and okay!"

43

Check Mate

Swing Shift, Linsedorf S&W Center, West Germany

Crowley reached for the phone next to his console. "Hello, Hauptmann Bauer. Do you have any news about Chad? He did not show up for work today and we are all worried."

Bauer replied, "I am sorry to have to tell you this. One of our patrols found Chad Frazer's body lying in a street near the Frankfurt railroad station early this morning with a gunshot wound to the head. The wound was consistent with a pistol shot at very close range. We will perform ballistics and fingerprint tests on the weapon found at the scene. I am so sad to give you the bad news about your good friend."

Crowley replied, "My concern for Chad grew when he did not report for duty today."

"I promise we will get you the results of the tests as soon as possible. So far, all we can say is the death occurred yesterday, not this morning. The coroner will perform an autopsy, which may shed some light on the cause of death," said Bauer.

Crowley was stunned. He was sure Eva and Becker were involved, but they were also dead. He vowed to avenge Chad's death.

"Chad was my closest friend and a brave soldier. He will be missed. I'll tell Captain Hodges. Please keep me informed."

"My condolences to you and your comrades. I will inform you when the coroner releases Chad's body for burial," replied Bauer.

Crowley said, "Thank you, Hauptmann Bauer, for all you have done."

Crowley reached to hang up the telephone and winced from the soreness of the injuries he sustained during the hijack attempt. Ace bandages covered glass cuts. A migraine added to his melancholy as he fixed his eyes on the screen, wondering why he was alive, and Frazer was not. He pulled a prescription bottle from his pocket and swallowed two pills with some water. A doctor examined him at the base infirmary this morning and put him back on duty since he didn't have to be very mobile to operate his display console.

Judge Advocate General's office directed Captain Hodges to reassign the posse's security police duties until further notice. Stories about terrorists and spies were all over the news media, along with accounts of American soldiers taking matters into their own hands. Discussions by the brass ranged from a medal to a court martial. Crowley's personal security problems had been resolved for now, and it gave him time to think. He knew Bauer had their back. Although the posse subdued the terrorists, the West German government credited Bauer's group with the capture to avoid legal repercussions for the Americans. Bauer told the press the airmen followed their training and coordinated the hostage recovery with the *Hessische Polizei*. This got the posse off the hook with the Air Force brass.

Crowley returned to his workstation after informing Captain Hodges and his posse about Chad. Flight members started coming over and offering their condolences over the loss of their comrade.

Crowley thought, "I hope Anna Maria has a good day today. *Stars and Stripes* requested an interview about her role in the capture of the terrorists."

He picked up his phone and rang her at the office.

"Hi Jake, guess what?"

"After yesterday, I gave up guessing what's next. You better tell me."

"Okay, *Life Magazine* called me to do an article about our ordeal. I thought they were kidding when they mentioned the working title, *Venus Spy Trap*."

"Well, I get the Venus part. You have the aura of a mother earth goddess lately. What do they mean about 'spy trap?'"

"Really? That's so sweet. Anyway, I declined the interview and told them it would be a conflict of interest. Oh, the spy part. Haven't you heard? They identified Becker as a KGB colonel. We killed a high-level Russian agent!"

"Anna Maria, I have bad news. They found Chad dead on a street in Frankfurt this morning. I believe Eva and Becker had something to do with it. We may never know for sure. Captain Bauer is looking into it."

"That's terrible, Jake. He was such a good friend to you. We will all mourn his loss."

"Well. Don't forget to give credit to the *Polizei* in your interviews and keep me out of it. I am just a supply clerk."

"Yeah, I know. Just a supply clerk who just happens to wear two Colt 0.45 pistols and keeps an assault rifle in his car. I'll tell them that and see if they laugh."

They hung up, and Crowley checked the status of his console. "Charlie Flight worked a busy prior shift identifying targets because of a broadcast frequency change. The codeword SWAMP target network started at 0600. Employing frequency usage charts, call sign analysis and triangulation from a minimum of three direction finding antennas called DF results, the prior shift identified the major Soviet tracking stations in East Germany, Poland, Ukraine, and Southwestern Russia."

Crowley reduced the display scale until he could view a map covering all Eastern Europe and the Western USSR.

Crowley muttered, "Come on, cursor! This trackball can be a bitch to handle sometimes. I need to position it in this exact area. If I enlarge the scale a little, it should help."

Crowley continued interrogating plots by manipulating the cursor with the tracking ball and examined the amplification data in the intercepted messages for tail numbers, altitude, and number of aircraft. He punched up other function keys to calculate speed and heading of the aircraft.

The combat controller, now an intelligence analyst, mulled over what to do next. "Oh, yeah! I look up the tail numbers in the reference binder lying between the two display consoles. Eyes-on-the-ground had compiled the reference book from attending air shows, interviews with tourists traveling to Soviet Union and East German bases, and other sources."

From the tail numbers, call signs, frequency usage and DF reports, Crowley and the other analysts of his section could reconstruct the PVO *Strany* Air Defense Order of Battle as regiments of aircraft deployed throughout the Soviet Union and their satellite countries.

Crowley pondered, "It seems to me the Soviet Union treats East Germany as their top priority, based on the strength of the Soviet air defense forces and the PVO *Strany* radar network density. The only area with a higher density is around Moscow."

He continued monitoring intercepted traffic at his console and responding when his co-analyst called him over to help with radar station identification. Some stations were harder to identify than others. The PVO *Strany* tracking stations in East Germany were easy to figure out, because the flight patterns of the Berlin Air Corridor gave them away. Other stations in Poland, Ukraine, and Hungary he found tougher. Triangulation of DF results were a must and call sign usage helped. Another aid was matching up overlapping tracking from another known station, broadcasting at a lower echelon.

By 2030 local time, the tracking activity was slowing down. There usually wasn't any aircraft activity in the Soviet Union after midnight Moscow time. Crowley noticed some tracking started up in Western USSR. He manipulated the track ball until it was over the flight path and punched a function key to get the coordinates of the takeoff point.

The coordinates 50.2333324 X 30.2999988 displayed on the screen and he noticed something familiar in the four threes and nines in the coordinates. He jogged over to a map wall and checked the coordinates, which correlated to the city of Vasylkiv in the Kiev Oblast, Ukraine.

"Why did that sound so familiar?" pondered Crowley?

He ran back over to the console and grabbed a current Soviet air order of battle printout to look up Vasylkiv Air Base. The listing was in alphabetical order, so it took Crowley a minute to thumb through the pages until he reached the V's. There it was in black and white, Vasylkiv Air Base, Kiev, an interceptor base with MiG-21 and new MiG-25 aircraft deployed there.

Crowley mused, "Since Kiev is a military fighter base, this must be either a defensive scramble or a deployment. If it is a deployment, the Soviets must be trying to keep it a secret, given the late takeoff time. My first task is to rule out an air defense scramble. Given the flight path is heading west, I doubt this option, but I must rule it out, anyway."

He called out on the intercom, "This is Crowley. Who is available to take some plots?"

Sam Rothman was on duty and standing with the plotters in the S&W central tracking room. "Hi Jake, I am free. What do you have for me?"

"Take these SWAMP plots and check for overlapping voice or Morse code intercept. If this is a Soviet fighter intercept flight, voice intercept should be able to hear a ground controller vectoring the aircraft."

Rothman marked the plots on the map wall to check for a match.

Seeing none, he patched his intercom to the Russian linguists in the voice intercept section.

Rothman called out, "Can any of you guys verify some plot coordinates?"

One analyst responded and Rothman gave him Crowley's SWAMP plots. The traffic analyst took down the location and walked the line of intercept stations, checking the tracking maps above their positions for coordinating activity.

While he was waiting for Rothman, Crowley started interrogating the plots with the cursor for aircraft flight heading, air speed, altitude, and tail number amplification data. He used a function key on the console to capture the air speed for the flight.

"That is surprising. In a short string of plots, I am computing an air speed at 700 knots."

He hit a function key with the cursor over a plot. "Look at that! The altitude is 60,000 feet based on the tracking data, which is close to the maximum performance for a MiG-21, and unless they are on an intercept course, it was unusual for them to fly near their maximum altitude. The MiG-21, NATO codename of FISHBED cruises at 550 knots."

Crowley checked the heading for the flight, and it showed a westerly course with no activity being tracked in front of the flight.

Crowley called on the intercom, "Does voice intercept have anything?"

Rothman replied, "So far, voice intercept reflects only take-off chatter at Vasylkiv Air Base. The chatter includes a flight number 72 and nothing else of significance."

Crowley interrogated more plots with his light pen and found tail numbers.

"Sam, I captured tail numbers. Give me a minute to check them out."

"Roger that Jake. They might tell the story. Since they are MiGs, we should call them fuselage numbers. They are not on the tail."

Crowley pulled the tail number reference from the counter to his right and thumbed through the book.

Crowley exclaimed, "Wow! All three tail numbers are for MiG-25 NATO codename FOXBAT interceptors! FOXBAT fighters explain the speed and altitude which are all within the performance envelope of a MiG-25 when cruising."

He got back on the intercom and said, "Sam, I have confirmed the flight to be MiG-25 FOXBAT aircraft out of Vasylkiv Air Base, heading toward Poland. I identified the MiG-25's based on their tail numbers in the amplification data. I also got flight number 72 out of the data. Can you check it out?"

Rothman called over to the desk analysts. "Sergeant Howell, can you check out Soviet flight 72? Crowley is tracking one on his screen."

Technical Sergeant Craig Howell waved back to him, showing he was on it.

Rothman spoke to Crowley on the intercom. "Jake, S&W wants all the plots from now on. Stay on the intercom or be relieved by Staff Sergeant Gibson."

Tech Sergeant Howell came over to Rothman at the tracking board and said, "I have found several Flight 72 references in voice traffic over the last six months, which referred to MiG-21 ferry flights of upgraded versions between Vasylkiv and air bases in East Germany. PVO *Strany* flew these flights during daylight hours to upgrade equipment on aging MiG-21 planes deployed in East Germany."

Howell added, "It is not normal procedure to be having these ferry flights at night, and this is the first time we are seeing them deploy MiG-25 aircraft to their forward areas. I think they are trying to pull something over on us. The previous flight 72 deployments landed at Kolobrzeg Air Base in Poland for refueling before flying onto bases in East Germany."

"Let Crowley know the failsafe point is Kolobrzeg. If they take off heading west from that air base, we will have to issue a CRITIC Report to Ft Meade and Washington. We will need a detailed tracking report from Crowley with everything from take-off." instructed Howell.

Rothman buzzed Crowley's intercom, "Hey Man! You are on to something. Howell is talking CRITIC if this flight goes beyond Kolobrzeg in Poland. Get your tracking data ready in a backup report. Well done, Jake!"

Crowley started tagging the plots with a light pen to be included in his first report. The plotting continued to Kolobrzeg Air Base and then it stopped at 2150 local as flight 72 landed for refueling.

The flight resumed thirty minutes later with the same heading, and Crowley got on the intercom to call in the plots.

Rothman said, "A CRITIC has to be issued to report deployment of MiG-25 fighters to a forward area."

While the desk analysts in the S&W command center led by Howell prepared the report, Crowley completed flagging flight 72 from take-off at Kolobrzeg Air Base.

He buzzed Sam on the intercom. "Sam, I reviewed the data to make sure the plots include altitude and tail number data. I am ready to generate the tape."

Rothman replied, "Howell is ready with his CRITIC. Cut the tape for transmission."

Crowley keyed in the proper report message header and trailer data and finished the procedure by pressing a function key to punch the paper tape.

Once the report generation ended, Crowley tore off the roll of tape and ran it over to the comm-center to be transmitted over a secure line of sight infrared transmission to intelligence consumers in Europe and by Atlantic cable to the states. The message room clerk took the tape and mounted it on a Teletype to broadcast it as Crowley double-timed back to his display console to update his data capture with his light pen for the follow-up information.

Back in the states, the White House and NSA received the CRITIC message at the same time. Crowley's initial tracking data report arrived after the CRITIC message at the NSA. The CRITIC arrived via a Teletype at the National Security Council Office in the situation room. Manning the NSC office were two officers sitting at gray metal desks with burn bags attached to the desktops and a wall of clocks behind them. The clocks were used to correlate Zulu time on reports with other time zones. Zulu time was Greenwich meantime in a 24-hour military format to correlate worldwide events. All the reporting they received in the situation room reflected Zulu time.

One of the NSC officers tore off the message from the roll of paper on the Teletype, determined its priority, logged information in a register book, and read the message content. Using the subject of the report, the NSC would triage the information to members of the situation room staff based on their areas of expertise.

An NSC duty officer handed Colonel Robinson, who was sitting in the conference area, a copy of the CRITIC report. The staff nicknamed the area 'The Woodshed,' because the dark mahogany paneled walls created acoustic problems, making it difficult to hear speakers. The lowest bidder must have gotten the job.

Robinson picked up his phone and speed dialed the NSA. He was the USAF Intelligence Officer on duty, making him responsible for opening a line to his counterpart at Fort Meade to coordinate situation analysis.

He spoke into the encrypted line. "This is Colonel Robinson. Who do I have on the line?"

"Colonel Robinson, this is GS-15 Bart Sedgwick. I know why you are calling. We are loading the tracking data from Darmstadt as we speak. I have the CRITIC printout in front of me."

The paper punch tape from Crowley loaded into an NSA computer, which processed the data and displayed it on a display console.

Sedgwick added, "Our NSA analysts are seeing exactly what the intercept analyst has on his display in Germany. As you know, we use the Zulu time of reference. Since Germany is in Zulu plus 2 hours, the times in the reporting are two hours earlier than the local time in Germany. The local time is six hours earlier in Washington, so at 1430 local time the situation room was reading a message dated 2025 Zulu reporting intercepted messages reported in Germany at 2225 local. With a Zulu clock on the wall, everyone can determine how current the reporting is without having to convert from local time."

Robinson conferred with Sedgwick on the source and reliability of the data. Once Robinson verified the source, he started going over the details of the tracking information.

Robinson couldn't believe the level-of-detail and timeliness NSA had. "They have every plot from take-off with flight data, including altitude, speed and tail numbers."

The presidential security advisers on duty in the situation room included a representative from the Secretary of State, the two NSC watch officers, an Air Force Colonel from NSA, a CIA watch officer, and senior officers from the other branches of the military. The Department of State duty officer received a carbon copy of the CRITIC, and he picked it up and started reading it.

CRITIC

At 1630 Zulu, a flight of NATO codename FOXBAT fighter intercept aircraft took off from their base at Vasylkiv, Kiev Oblast Ukraine at 50 Degrees 10' 42" N in a westerly heading at an altitude of 60,000 feet and speed of 700 knots. It identified the flight as flight 72, which is a flight to ferry upgraded MiG-21 fighter interceptors as replacements at their bases in the DDR. On this occasion, the flight contained MiG-25 FOXBAT tail numbers based on information we have received from very reliable sources. The flight landed as normal at Kolobrzeg Airbase, Poland, location 54 Degrees 10' N 15 Degrees 34' E time 1750 Zulu for refueling. At 1820 Zulu, Flight 72 resumed course on to the DDR, where it will split up and land at multiple soviet air bases in that country. This is the first confirmed attempt to deploy FOXBAT aircraft in a forward area.

After reading the CRITIC, Simmons walked over to Robinson and waved the hard-copy report at him.

Simmons said, "Why have concern over fighters being ferried to East Germany? Don't the Soviets regularly deploy upgrades to the field?"

Robinson put his phone call to the NSA on hold and turned to the State Department staffer.

"These are not just your run of the mill Soviet fighter planes. They are the new MiG-25 Mach 3 fighter interceptors capable of over 1000 miles cruising range. They are a triple threat, having fighter intercept, reconnaissance and hydrogen bomb delivery capability at top speed and range."

Simmons replied, "Yeah—so we already know about them. What makes this flight so important?"

Robinson bit his lip and came back. "This is the first time the USSR is attempting to deploy them to a forward area. It appears they are doing this stationing at night to conceal the operation."

Simmons asked, "What is the threat assessment of this stationing? We can't go crying wolf every time they move a few airplanes around!"

"We know they will pose a threat to our air surveillance flights if they deploy to bases in East Germany, because of their high-speed intercept capability. Of particular concern are the SR71 blackbird and the U2 photo-reconnaissance missions, which we used to verify weapon reductions resulting from treaty negotiations."

Now Robinson was talking Simmons's language.

Simmons thought, *This could impact the secret ongoing peace negotiations between the Soviet Ambassador to the U.S. and Nixon's Special Security Advisor, Dr. Henry Kissinger. Negotiations had been progressing for over two years. This aggressive act by the USSR could kill the whole deal.*

Robinson handed Simmons a written summary of his verbal assessment and grabbed the telephone for the NSA and took it off hold. With Robinson's analysis in hand, Simmons made his own call to Kissinger's office and got his staff to use their hotline to contact counterparts in the Soviet State Department to head off this deployment before it screwed up the peace talks. They must confront the Soviets.

Robinson pondered, "It is a tricky business. The State Department's objection must be phrased, so the Soviets believe HUMINT was the origin of the leak. Intercept of their own defense system had to be concealed. This is the reason the S&W center in Darmstadt sent the intelligence data and the CRITIC to the NSA, whereas the White House Situation Room received the CRITIC message only. The CRITIC phrased information as received from a known credible source, whereas the data at NSA made it obvious where the flight tracking was coming from. My clearance allows me to review the data and determine the credibility of the source of the intelligence."

At 1645 Zulu time, Crowley was still in the S&W station calling in flight 72 to Rothman on the intercom as tracking reflected a slow turn to a north-west heading.

He buzzed Rothman's intercom. "Sam, can you ask Tech Sergeant Howell the destination of the previous flight 72? I want to note any deviations."

As he keyed a report on the Teletype, Howell chimed in on the intercom. "Sergeant Crowley, I confirm the flight path is identical so far to the previous flight 72. The previous destinations were fighter bases in East Germany. Keep the plots coming, Sergeant Crowley, and I'll let you know when there is a deviation."

At 1715 Zulu, Simmons, still on duty in the Situation Room of the Whitehouse, received a return call from the Security Advisers' Office.

"Simmons, we have communicated with the Soviets through diplomatic channels, and we have confirmation of receipt, but not a reply. As usual, we must sit on our hands and wait."

Simmons walked over to Robinson and gave him an update after he put the NSA on hold again.

"Colonel Robinson, no response yet from Moscow. What can we do to show them we mean business?"

"There is a Wild Weasel outfit at the air base in Bitburg. If we send them up, it will get their attention."

Simmons asked, "What are Wild Weasels?"

"They are supersonic tactical fighter-bombers equipped to take out SAM missile sites and their radar. Their mission is to weasel into enemy territory and pave the way for heavy bombers. If we scramble the wing out of Bitburg, the Soviets will know the squadron's mission."

Simmons replied, "Let's run this up our respective chains of command right now while we wait for a Soviet reply. I don't want to hear the Russians say they thought we were kidding about our objection to the deployment."

At 1730 Zulu, Colonel Rudolfsky reached cruising altitude in the Polish Flight Corridor and heard a crackle on his radio. "This is Kolobrzeg Ground Control to Flight 72. Do you read me?"

Rudolfsky replied, "This is Flight 72. Go ahead."

"Flight 72, your orders are to proceed to Eberswalde-Finow, Magdeburg and Dresden airfields."

Rudolfsky thought, *My radar shows clear sailing ahead to the East German border. I wonder why the deployment went forward without General Polzin letting me know he resolved the issue at PVO Strany headquarters. Well, in a few days, my squadrons will start catching the U2 spy planes in the act.*

At 1745 Zulu, Crowley, still at his post in the Linsedorf S&W center, noticed unusual tracking from a SWAMP site in Dresden.

He called to Sam on the intercom, "Sam, a SWAMP site in Dresden is tracking a flight out of Bitburg, West Germany."

"Yeah, so?"

Crowley replied, "Tracking that far out is unusual. SWAMP concentrates on their own territory and border activity. Start taking these plots and find out what flies out of Bitburg. Dresden appears to be really interested in this flight."

"Jake, these plots are deep inside West Germany. Why is this important?"

Crowley replied, "The Soviets think it is important, so we should too. It is unusual for them to track this far inside West Germany. Their priority is planes trying to get out rather than planes trying to get in. Like a Berlin Wall in the sky."

"Jake! Howell says Bitburg is a tactical fighter base. They have fighter-bombers and Wild Weasels."

"Sam, we have our answer on the unusual tracking. Wild Weasels are used to suppress SAM sites and their radar before a bombing strike. Dresden just started tracking a C-130 tanker which appears to be rendezvousing with the flight out of Bitburg."

"Jake, sounds like they expect to be flying for a while."

"Yeah, Wild Weasels have a motto. First in and last out!"

"Jake, it looks like someone at the Situation Room got a burr up their ass over this deployment of MiG-25s. The flight out of Bitburg is now headed for the East German border!"

"Roger that! The Dresden SWAMP station is tracking the Bitburg flight with a plot every minute and it appears to be headed right for them. I now see plots out of Eberswalde-Finow. It looks like they scrambled MiG-21s from that airfield in response to the Wild Weasels!"

"Jake, give me the MiG-21 plots as well. Howell wants all this activity for the CRITIC. Looks like the Russians are stirring up a hornet's nest! Dresden is now tracking F4 Phantoms out of Ramstein airfield. They are all buzzing around the border and waiting for a kill shot!"

At 1750 Zulu, as Colonel Rudolfsky's formation cruised the Polish Air Corridor, he received a radio call from the ground control at Kolobrzeg Air Base, ordering the squadrons of flight 72 to return to Kolobrzeg Air Base and await further instructions.

He couldn't believe it! His powerful radar showed clear sailing ahead with no possible detection by passing flights.

He replied, "This is flight 72. Confirm your orders to scrub the flight!"

The controller confirmed and Rudolfsky swore under his breath as he took the lead and made a wide turn, heading for Kolobrzeg. With some luck, they would land in fifteen minutes, and he would find out why ground control diverted his flight.

It was now 1800 Zulu when Crowley noted how plots for flight 72 were swinging south in a wide arc, indicating the flight might abort because of equipment problems. He used his light pen to capture the plots for his next report, as he called in the coordinates on the intercom. Rothman was still manning the plot board in the S&W Command Center.

As he ended dictating coordinates to Rothman, he said, "Sam, can you ask Howell to confirm this deviation from the previous flight 72 route? I want to note that in my report data."

Rothman turned from the plot board and called over to Howell, who was deep in concentration, typing his CRITIC addendum on his Teletype.

Howell raised his hand like a traffic cop. "Hold the question, while I confirm with the S&W senior NCO on the wording chosen for the follow-up report."

Then Howell called out to Rothman, "Give me the new plots."

As Rothman called the coordinates out, Howell jotted them down on the printout sheet on his Teletype.

Howell said, "Give me a minute while I compare the coordinates to a Teletype report of a previous Flight 72 on my clipboard."

Howell finished his comparison and looked up to Sam. "These latest plots show deviation from the normal flight 72 flight plan. It looks like they are changing course, because of the threat from our tactical air forces still orbiting near the East German border. I will include this in my current follow up, since the plot is within the reporting timeframe."

Howell finished up his report, tore off the punch paper tape and gave it to his assistant to run it over to the comm-center for transmission. Next, Howell started typing the preamble for another follow up and stared at Rothman as he put more plots on the board. As the tracking continued, Howell realized flight 72 was heading back to Kolobrzeg. The tracking stopped at the air base and Howell changed his follow up

CRITIC to a final. Howell's Teletype chattered as he typed the final and sent off the punch tape.

Rothman buzzed Crowley and said, "Howell wants to wrap up this CRITIC and send out a final. You should prepare to do the same."

Crowley gathered the data for his final detail report and as he sat at his console and waited for the report to punch out to paper tape, he noticed some activity on the CRT in front of him and to his amazement the flight started again out of Kolobrzeg Air Base heading east. When he interrogated the pilots, flight 72 came up on the amplification data. The flight did not have mechanical problems. It was being ordered back to home base!

Crowley called out to Rothman, "Hold the presses! This CRITIC is not over yet!"

Rothman called over to Tech Sergeant Howell, "Jake said to hold the last tape! The CRITIC is not over yet."

Crowley started giving Rothman the new plots for Flight 72 as it maintained a course for Vasylkiv, Kiev. Cruising at 700 knots, the flight made it back in less than an hour and landed. There was no further activity for flight 72. The CRITIC was closed, and Crowley punched out his final report on tape. Something caused flight 72 to return to their home base, and it did not appear to be equipment problems. There were no delays for repairs. Washington must have scrambled the Wild Weasels to convince the Soviets to countermand the deployment.

As Crowley spun his trackball on the console to center his screen on Western Europe, Rothman came over to congratulate him. "Have I just witnessed history in the making?"

Crowley replied, "What do you mean?"

"Was this action we just took part in foretelling the future? Will national military power equate to the country's computer power?"

Crowley replied, "Do you mean no more blood and steel?"

"Yes, that is what I mean."

"Well, not in the short run. My recent foray into Honduras was proof of that."

Rothman said, "Even so, does what happened today predict soldiers will become system analysts armed with computers like yours to fight wars in the future? What will winning mean?"

Crowley said, "Today we intercepted enemy communications using a computer and with that information we interdicted an enemy tactical deployment. Tomorrow we may not be so lucky."

Rothman responded, "Hit and miss today, but what about tomorrow? The Soviets used computers too! Will things develop where our computers fight their computers directly? We break their communication codes now. Tomorrow will we be breaking into their computers? Will a computer attack become more devastating than a nuclear attack?"

Crowley replied, "Sam, I think you are getting ahead of yourself. The RUBICON System did its job today and I know from personal experience this on-line real-time computer is more effective than the old manual methods. We will have to stay vigilant and see how the Russians react. In the meantime, this is for Chad. Bless his memory!"

Rothman said, "You are underestimating what we just did. Howell got a message back from NSA saying it was a good thing we caught the MiG-25 FOXBAT deployment. If they had succeeded, NATO would have no choice but to attack those airfields once they detected the MiG25s because of their nuclear bomb capability. You may have prevented a war."

With that comment off his chest, Rothman returned to his post in the S&W center.

Crowley received a telephone call from Bart Sedgwick at NSA when the CRITIC was over. "Congratulations Sergeant Crowley. That CRITIC you raised made RUBICON famous at the NSA. Your name got mentioned a lot as well because of the great job you have done. There is talk of bringing you back here to work directly on the project."

"How could I contribute there at Fort Meade?"

"There is a programming course offered in Frankfurt by the Control Data Corporation. That is the company that manufactures display consoles and disk drives used on RUBICON. Control Data has just opened their first overseas training institute at their European headquarters, and I can endorse your acceptance. We are their biggest customer."

Epilogue

Crowley drove home after his shift, tired but feeling good about the outcome of the night's events. His thoughts turned to Bart Sedgwick and his recommendation of pursuing a computer programming career. He was interested and would discuss it with Anna Maria. When he arrived at the apartment, she was sound asleep. He undressed and as soon as his head hit the pillow, he was asleep.

The next morning, they enjoyed breakfast together and talked about their future.

"An opportunity came up for me to take a programming course at night in Frankfurt. Control Data Corporation just opened their first technical institute in Europe."

Anna Maria replied, "That sounds like a great opportunity. I read that computer programmers are in demand."

"Sedgwick told me there will be an NSA civilian contract job waiting for me when I complete the programming course. They want me to contribute directly to the project at Fort Meade."

She liked that news, too. Anna Maria planned to continue her travel show and column in *Stars and Stripes* until his enlistment ended.

Anna Maria frowned. "Jake, when I was being interviewed at the police station, I was told the RAF terrorists confessed they were going to make a one hundred-thousand-dollar random demand because of my celebrity status. I'm confused. I thought we eliminated Soviet spies."

Crowley replied, "None of this is your fault. I found a ransom letter in our apartment mailbox, demanding I turn myself over to the Red Army Faction in return for your freedom. Hauptmann Bauer determined Eva Schmidt and the man who captured you behind the farmhouse were illegal agents. Eva was an East German Stasi agent, and that Becker guy was a Soviet agent. Bauer said the RAF were pawns in the game. The Soviets used them to attack us and kidnap you as a cover for a counter-espionage operation."

Anna Maria thought about what Jake said and breathed a sigh of relief. She turned to him with a sparkle in her eyes.

"Jake, I have some news to share. I saw the doctor yesterday, and following a pregnancy test, he announced I am going to have a baby! Our family is growing, Jake."

A big grin spread across his face. He jumped up, put his arms around his wife's waist, lifted her, and spun around.

He hugged and kissed her as he said, "Wow! That's wonderful, darling!"

They were both excited and continued their conversation about the Crowley family's future.

It was 1700 on another Dog Flight swing shift. Things moved fast after Bart Sedgwick spoke to his contacts at the Control Data Corporation. The CDC Institute accepted his application, and Crowley attended his first class in Frankfurt before reporting for duty. He looked forward to completing the nine-month course.

Crowley contemplated, *Computer Technology offers a promising future and Sedgwick's offer will be my first stepping-stone.*

Meanwhile, Anna Maria sat on the sofa in their apartment, sipping her tea while Jake was on the swing shift.

She smiled and thought, *Jake's dream of starting his own business may come true after all... as an independent government contractor!*

U.S. AIR FORCE
69
10th
SECURITY WING

About The Author

In 1969, my wife and I traveled to West Germany courtesy of the U.S. Air Force, where I served as a military operative for the National Security Agency. Rising to a non-commissioned officer rank, I worked as a cryptologist, signal intelligence analyst, and computer programmer. My wife worked for the Stars and Stripes newspaper in its Darmstadt headquarters. When not at work, we traveled extensively in Europe, with Darmstadt's central location as our base. As a Staff Sergeant, my responsibilities included the tasking and supervision of a 7X24 surveillance and warning operation utilizing on-line, real-time computers to gather signal intelligence. This was the dawn of cyber warfare, and my team was in the thick of it.

On completion of my tour of duty, my experience in the Air Force led to my civilian career as a computer system architect, where I designed and led the development of systems for medical, publishing, banking, and marketing database platforms. At night, I went to school on the GI Bill and a New York State Regent's Scholarship to earn my Bachelor of Science Degree in Business Management and Communication from Adelphi University. I still regard my work for the NSA as the hardest and most exciting job in my long career.

Warpath Press is dedicated to publishing the very best in military writing from around the globe.

We believe that writing that is rooted in the human experience of war and conflict, even when written by non-veterans, allows us as a society to examine how human nature responds under extreme pressure. It also gives us a means to ask the big questions about life.

"Military stories" aren't all action-adventure novels. We are committed to finding ways to push the boundaries of "military writing" in new directions, bending it into new shapes that serve society in better ways.

Many of the literary greats of the early to mid-20th century wrote about war and its effects. But Hemingway, Remarque, Dos Passos, Faulkner, Wouk, Greene and Waugh, only had the impact that they did because they were published.

Today, they would likely have been ignored by the major publishers.

And that is why we do what we do.

www.ingramcontent.com/pod-product-compliance
Lightning Source LLC
Chambersburg PA
CBHW030624310726
48979CB00003B/874

* 9 7 8 1 9 9 8 5 0 1 5 9 5 *